Road of No Return

a Sex and Mayhem novel

K.A. Merikan

Acerbi & Villani ltd

Road of No Return
K.A. Merikan

--- Don't talk to strangers. ---

Zak. Tattoo artist. Independent. Doesn't do relationships.
Stitch. Outlaw biker. Deep in the closet. Doesn't share his property.

On the day of Stitch's divorce, lust personified enters the biker bar he's celebrating at. Tattooed all over, pierced, confident, and hot as hellfire, Zak is the bone Stitch has waited for life to throw him. All Stitch want s is a sniff, a taste, a lick. What follows instead is gluttony of the most carnal sort, and nothing will ever be the same. Forced to hide his new love affair from the whole world, Stitch juggles family, club life, and crime, but it's only a matter of time until it becomes too hard.

Zak moves to Lake Valley in search of peace and quiet, but when he puts his hand into the jaws of a Hound of Valhalla, life gets all but simple. In order to be with Stitch, Zak's biker wet dream, he has to crawl right back into the closet. As heated as the relationship is, the secrets, the hiding, the violence, jealousy, and conservative attitudes in the town rub Zak in all the wrong ways. When pretending he doesn't know what his man does becomes impossible, Zak needs to decide if life with an outlaw biker is really what he wants.

As club life and the love affair collide, all that's left in Zak and Stitch's life is mayhem.

WARNING Contains adult content: a gritty storyline, sex, explicit language, violence and torture

POSSIBLE SPOILERS:

Themes: Outlaw Motorcycle Club, organized crime, homophobia, family issues, coming out, first gay relationship, tattoo, piercing

Genre: contemporary homoerotic dark romance

Length: ~ 100,000 words (Standalone novel, no cliffhanger.)

Chapter 1

Stitch downed his third beer of the day and slammed the glass on top of his divorce papers.

"Another?" asked his best friend, Captain, and Stitch squinted at him. He could never be sure whether Captain was winking at him or just blinking. The perils of only having one eye. It didn't stop Captain from driving a bike like a madman or being the VP of the club.

"Go on, I earned it," Stitch rasped and leaned his elbows on the greasy counter. He could feel at home in the Hounds of Valhalla club bar. If worse came to worst, he could always fall asleep in one of the guest rooms in the back and not have to face going home. The Louisiana heat was getting to him today so he wore his cut over naked skin, but in hindsight it hadn't been such a great idea, since now the leather was sticking to his back.

It was a busy Friday night, and the bar was full. Most of the patrons were local so Stitch knew them one way or another, with a few outsiders sprinkled all over the large room. During public parties like this one, Valhalla catered to everyone, from old friends, gathered in comfortable booths, to the crowd that spent their time at the counter, to the drunken dancers by the pool table. It was more crass than class, but to Stitch it felt like home, from the beat-up counter to the small room in the back where Stitch had fucked a girl for the first time. Good times.

Captain poured Stitch some whiskey and grinned, rubbing down his black beard into a more sensible shape. "One down, brother. You'll find yourself a better woman."

"Of course I will. Not a cheating slut like Crystal." Stitch sipped his liquor with a frown.

"You fancy any of the pussy by the pool table?" Captain gestured toward the ever-present crowd of hangarounds in sparse clothing. The pool table was off limits on Fridays, unless you were a member of the Hounds of Valhalla. Or a hot bitch.

Stitch followed his friend's nod (to keep up appearances), but he looked right past the girls. He was not dipping his dick in that lot again. Not to mention that none of the girls were even his type. Most of the ones who were in today were cute blondes, like they got the wrong bar or something. That was what had drawn him to Crystal in the first place, she was all tats and rock 'n' roll.

"Nah, I'll pass." Stitch downed his whiskey and tried to pretend he didn't see any of the direct looks from the pool table. The sudden spike in interest could only mean one thing: they all knew he was back on the market. "Where's the rum, Captain?" he said, but his mouth remained open when someone new walked into the bar and stopped at the door, looking around as if he had lost his way. The dimmed blue light made all the tattoos on the stranger's arms pop out immediately, and while Stitch couldn't see what the patterns were, the ink was dense, mostly black and white.

The man was tall enough to stand out in the crowd, slim but toned. He walked through the bar with a self-assured sway, looking like a character from a futuristic movie. Stitch didn't know where that comparison came from because the guy wore a simple outfit consisting of narrow pants stuck into knee-length combat boots, and a tank top, but he did look like an outsider in the old-school biker bar. His hair was pitch-black, with shaved sides and the long strands at the top of his head gathered into a ponytail. There was a sly smile tugging at the corners of his lips as he approached Stitch of all people.

A silly grin surfaced onto Stitch's face like a dead body floating in the bayou. That would be his choice of 'pussy' if he could have his way. He knew it wasn't gonna happen, yet he still straightened up on the bar stool far too small to properly hold his bulky body and turned to the stranger. The man was first to speak, but he looked past Stitch as if he were made of glass.

"Hi, how are you doing?" he asked in a rich, velvety voice, reaching out to shake the hand of Joe, one of the Hounds of Valhalla's prospects, currently serving at the bar. He had short, blond hair and a small gap between his front teeth. Stitch always saw him as a younger brother he never had.

Joe smiled at the tattooed man and shook his hand. "What can I get you?"

Stitch never took his eyes off the stranger, now even more set on getting his attention. The newcomer had large, expressive eyes the color of a cloudless summer sky and a heavy brow line over a firm, straight nose and pale, wide lips. It was a handsome face, yet it somehow made Stitch think of a malevolent spirit, which could be due to the piercings on his face. There were two balls on either side of his nose between the eyes, a small ring with a purple ball in his septum, and then a piercing in his left brow, and a round metal hoop circling the mid-point of his bottom lip. In contrast to the moderate size of those were thick spirals plugged into the flesh of the man's earlobes, stretching them over their normal capacity.

"A beer would be nice," said the stranger with a grin. "Listen, I'm new in town. Do you think it needs its own tattoo studio?"

A drop of sweat trailed down Stitch's spine and into the back of his pants like an invisible hand.

"Get the man a beer, Prospect." Stitch waved a hand at Joe, never taking his eyes off the hot, tattooed flesh. There were so many designs on the stranger's skin that Stitch wasn't sure which ones to focus on. "You should ask someone who's actually inked, not baby boy Joe."

"Oh yeah?" The stranger's blue eyes were on him immediately, but they soon trailed lower, and Stitch felt heat rise in his chest under the skull and fire tattoos the guy was looking at. "And I suppose that would be you?"

"Yeah, I know a lot of guys who'd like to visit a good ink pusher. And I suppose that would be you?" Stitch smirked and couldn't help but flex his stomach muscles.

The guy gave him a crooked smile, still looking down at Stitch's chest, but then raised his gaze and offered his hand. "I'm Zak."

"Stitch." He shook Zak's hand with a smile, making sure not to hold it too long. Joe put a beer on the counter, and Captain passed Stitch a glass of rum that smelled like catnip for pirates.

"Oh, I know a tattoo Stitch needs to cover up!" Captain chuckled. Stitch frowned, knowing exactly what his friend meant and imagining ways in which he could scalp Captain's black, furry head for mentioning the unmentionable.

Zak raised his brows and gathered the bottle in his hand, tapping it with a whole array of heavy signets. "Confess."

Stitch had some rum and poked Captain's ribs so hard the guy yelped. "Okay, okay. Prospect, out," he ordered Joe, and the guy walked to the other side of the bar to bother other customers. Stitch got up from the stool and stole a second of breaking into Zak's personal space before circling the bar and gesturing for Zak to follow. It was good to have free access, it made him almost feel as if he were the sole owner of the whole place. "I got divorced today, you see. So I need to get rid of a love crime."

"Sounds interesting." Zak marched behind him, and Stitch noticed that the handsome newcomer was even a bit taller than him. As soon as they disappeared behind the counter, the man leaned in, flooding Stitch with the smell of a musky, fresh cologne. "Is it on your dick?"

Stitch snorted and winked at Captain. "Nah, almost." Stitch opened the big skull buckle on his belt and went on to unzip his jeans. He was trying not to get too excited and not being alone with the guy was helping him keep his cool. This was probably as close as his dick would come to Zak anyway.

"So, what do you want to get?" asked Zak, loud enough for Stitch to hear his voice through the noise.

"I haven't thought it through yet." Stitch pulled his pants down low enough to expose the ink on the inner side of his hip, next to his pubes. He took out his cell phone and turned the screen on to illuminate the tat for Zak, who unceremoniously scooted down. It brought him face to face with Stitch's crotch, and made Stitch's heart stop, even if for a brief moment.

"Yeah, that shouldn't be a problem."

Captain started laughing so hard that Stitch reached over the counter to smack the side of his head. "Shut it!"

"Sorry, man. It just looked like--"

"I know what it looked like," Stitch growled and looked down to Zak. "Good. I'll make an appointment then," he tried to talk without slurring and pulled up his pants.

Zak got to his feet, unfazed by the mocking and produced a card, which he passed to Stitch. "Have a look at my portfolio first."

"I will. But anything will be better than that fucking name on there. I'd rather have Captain's face inked." Stitch pointed at his friend with a scowl. A massive one eyed bastard with an eye patch, black beard, and a mess of hair. Yep, he'd still prefer that broken-nosed mug to Crystal's name. Stitch buckled up his belt and walked out from behind the counter.

"A picture of devotion," chuckled Zak, following him. "Are you somehow associated with this bar?"

"Pop quiz. What's this place called?" Stitch plopped his ass back on the stool and took the glass of rum in hand.

Zak blinked. "Valhalla."

Stitch turned around in the seat, to present the back of his cut. He was always proud to show it off. It had their patch with 'Hounds of Valhalla' over a dog's head sticking out of the triangular Valknut symbol. A hound with more teeth than any animal should have in their jaw. "You could say we're all... shareholders." He took another sip of rum and clinked with Captain's glass.

Zak crooked his head. "In that case, I guess my fate is in both of your hands, gentlemen," he said with a widening grin. "Could I leave my leaflets, and a poster? I run the studio in my home."

"Sure." Stitch patted the counter. "Do I get a divorce discount?"

Zak chuckled and bit his lip, watching him with small wrinkles of humor appearing in the corners of his eyes. "If you promise to be my poster boy, I can do you for free."

"Hear that, Stitch?" Captain snorted his rum. "You're such a catch, he'll do you for free."

Heat travelled up Stitch's chest and he avoided those big blue eyes. "Shut it, Cap, unless you wanna lose your teeth. It's my night tonight, remember?" he snarled at Captain. The last thing he wanted was for Zak to get some stupid ideas. "If it's free, I'll come round on Sunday. You better not be shit though." Stitch finally looked back up at Zak, but he found no trace of intimidation in the handsome face.

"I'm not," Zak said, relaxed as ever.

"We'll see about that. Go on, leave the leaflets." Stitch was looking forward to seeing Zak walk out, just so he could ogle his ass in those tight pants.

Zak gave him a firm pat on the arm. "I'll get them from the car." He nodded at Captain and Joe, and turned around, beer in hand. It was a great ass. Round but slim, underneath the black denim it seemed as firm as a newly put on tire.

Stitch licked his lips, suddenly wishing he could do more than just watch that ass. "I wanna see his ride, be right back," he said to Captain and was already the wolf following the black sheep.

Zak jumped off the porch like a gazelle and made his way across the lawn, which served as an impromptu parking lot. Stitch squeezed his hand into a fist, spotting a car he hadn't seen in town before. He couldn't be certain as it was dark, but it looked like a 1970s Chevy, matte black, with purple flames scorching on its sides. If Satan drove a car, this would be it.

The vehicle was so cool it even distracted Stitch from Zak's ass. He strolled over to the car's side and scooted to have a better look at the paintwork.

There was the sound of someone clearing his throat. "Can I help you?" asked Zak, and all of a sudden, his gaze burned Stitch's back. He couldn't help a smirk as he got up and turned around.

"Nice ride."

"Thanks. A friend did it for me. Birthday gift." Zak leaned against the car, his slim body molding to the vehicle. With the streetlight close enough, Stitch could take a better look at the beautiful ink. There were people in goggles and fabric masks on one of Zak's arms. They reminded Stitch of one of those medical horrors, where a character is being experimented on by mad surgeons, and the sight alone was enough to give him a little chill. On the other bicep was a whole array of pills and syringes floating around a man in a straitjacket who seemed to cower in a corner, but what really drew in Stitch's attention was a sentence inked in bold letters over Zak's collarbone.

He walked up closer and had a better look at it. "'Don't talk to strangers'," he read it out loud and poked it. "You don't follow your own advice."

Zak chuckled and looked down to the finger at his neck. "I know. And that's what I get. A big bad biker crouching next to my car."

Stitch pulled back his finger. *Too much touching.* Yet the guy didn't seem scared. "Is there a story behind it? A warning to yourself or to others?"

Zak shrugged, watching Stitch with a sly smile. "It's something I heard a lot as a kid. And incidentally it's also the title of the first chapter in my favorite book. All of my tattoos are inspired by it."

"Oh yeah? What book is that?" Stitch stroked the back of the car in a way he wanted to move his hand over Zak's inked skin.

"You heard of *The Master and Margarita*? It's about demons throwing Stalin's Moscow into chaos, and there is a romantic plot, between the Master and Margarita, obviously." He sighed, moving his hand over the side of the car, toward where Stitch was keeping his.

Goose bumps broke out all over Stitch's skin. He had no idea what book Zak was talking about or why would he be interested in a romance with demons in communist Moscow, but Zak could tell him it was a story about a horse shapeshifter in North Korea and it would be just as interesting. "So what do you like about it? And what happens when you talk to strangers?"

Zak relaxed even further against his car, and the more Stitch was looking at him, the more he liked his handsome, but somehow cocky face. "Well, it was a play on the fact that everyone felt watched and spied on at the time, but in the actual chapter, this guy meets a foreigner, who's actually the devil. They talk, and the foreigner reveals that the Russian guy's gonna die. It's not atheist and rational, so the guy doesn't believe Satan and then dies a page or so later. He slips on some oil, and a streetcar cuts his head off," Zak said with a wide smile.

"And the moral is: don't talk to strangers?" Stitch chuckled. "Nothing happens to the devil though?"

Zak stepped closer and poked his long finger against Stitch's ribcage. "Duh, he's the devil. He saves the Master."

Stitch's cock felt a surge of excitement at the touch so he backed off, pretending he wanted to have a better look at the hood of the car. "You not afraid to talk to a devil?" Stitch looked into Zak's eyes.

"Nah, the devil's fair. It's the people around you who grasp you at the throat and don't want you to overstep some preset boundaries. That's what this book is about for me."

"Sometimes the devil has boundaries as well..." Stitch cocked his head to the side, not sure anymore what this conversation was about and wondering whether maybe he should end it.

"Does he?" Zak's teeth sank into his bottom lip, and he moved back to the trunk. "He's the devil," he said, opening the door.

Stitch played with his signets. "I suppose he should act any way he wants to then..."

Zak pulled out a block of fliers and shut the trunk, making his way to Stitch. "That would be my actual motto."

"Maybe *I* shouldn't talk to strangers then." Stitch held out his hand, and Zak placed the papers on top of his outstretched palm.

"So far so good." Zak smiled at him, and the silence became strangely long.

Stitch swallowed. "So... yeah, be good Zak, don't talk to strangers." He took the leaflets and turned around before the rum in his veins could push him to do something rash. Something was off and he couldn't pinpoint it.

He walked straight into the bar without looking back, in case Zak would hold his gaze again in this chilling yet blood-warming way. Captain hadn't moved a muscle since Stitch last saw him, but took the top leaflet as soon as Stitch placed the pile on the counter.

"So, how's his ride?"

"Cool. It's this repainted old Chevy."

Captain looked at the leaflet, and then suddenly slapped Stitch's arm. "I thought he was gonna go down on you back then." He pointed behind the bar counter.

Stitch groaned. "Come on, the guy seems all right." Yet he couldn't shake the weird vibes he got from Zak.

"A bit of a weirdo though. What's he doing in Lake Valley of all places?" Captain downed his liquor. "It might be different where he comes from, but he should be more careful, you know what I'm saying?" he asked, lowering his heavy eyelids.

Stitch took a deep breath. "Yeah. I can see he's just clueless, but some people might not get his jokes."

Captain emptied the small bottle of whiskey into his glass and tapped it with his thick fingers. He turned his head away, so Stitch found himself facing the eye patch with the club symbol. "You heard what happened to a fag biker over in Edmonton? I have a friend in The Rippers."

Stitch had to use all of his drunken self-control not to sneer. He didn't wanna hear it. "What?"

Captain gave him a wide grin. "The guys wanted to teach him a lesson, and they overdid it a bit. After being dragged behind a bike, naked, any man would lose interest in riding. He's got no skin on his ass now, that must be tough luck for a fag."

"Yeah." Stitch pushed away the empty glass and took the whole bottle of rum. This was not going to be him. He knew to keep it in his pants. He didn't even feel all that gay anyway. "He knew what he was going into. Rippers don't fuck around."

"Yeah, fuck him. Better tell your new friend to behave when you visit him on Sunday. Some people won't get his sense of humor." Captain shrugged and sipped the whiskey with a self-satisfied smile.

Stitch snorted. "I'll tell 'im while he's looking at my dick. He's not from around here. Has to settle in." He kept quiet for a while, just enjoying the jukebox music in the background and drinking his rum. "You know that Rippers guy? How did they find him out?"

Captain put the glass back on the counter. "This guy I know said somebody saw him fucking a guy in a shitter at a gas station. If you ask me, he had it coming."

Stitch nodded and looked to the door when tattooed hunk Zak walked back in.

So off limits.

Chapter 2

Stitch jerked awake when Joe patted him on the shoulder.

"Go on, you're home," he whispered, reaching out across Stitch's lap to open the passenger's door. The nighttime chill immediately bit into Stitch's skin as he raised his head to look at the small house he was still forced to share with his ex-wife. It was old and needed constant renovations, but he always did his best to maintain it in the best possible state: doing all kinds of repairs and even making some of their furniture. Dealing with the house was what first got him into carpentry. And what got him his first few stitches when he was younger and fell through the rotting, century-old balcony. It was then that he had declared he would *make* a new balcony if it killed him.

Right now though, he was drunk, and all he wanted was a good hearty snack before falling face-first into bed. Stitch thanked Joe for the ride and stumbled into the house through the backdoor, straight into the kitchen.

As he pushed the door shut behind himself, he realized something wasn't right. There was bright tape running across the floor, and he frowned, switching on the light. The kitchen was modest, sort of cramped, but tidy. Or at least it had been before something had turned the floor into a board game.

He looked to the fridge and went straight for it once he spotted a note. One he couldn't bother to read. But opening the fridge wasn't a happy experience either. All the food was moved to the left side where the shelves were marked with a glittery 'C', whereas the other side would be completely empty if it weren't for a bottle of ketchup and a yellow note with Stitch's name on it.

"The fuck?" he grumbled and closed the door to read the note on its outer side.

'Stitch,
Now that you're single, you're free to fill your side of the fridge. Since I don't want to see your face, I made a schedule for using the kitchen, so we don't have to see each other.'

Stitch looked at the allocated hours and then to the clock on the wall. His drunk mind wasn't ready for this. He just wanted some food. He'd buy it back for the bitch. Stitch groaned and slid his fingers into his hair. He wasn't even sure when he'd lost his hairband.

There were the eggs, only two, but he could fry them with... lean ham because it had been ages since Crystal bought any bacon. He could have the banana for dessert, covered by canned whipped cream. Crystal was on a permanent diet anyway, she should be thankful for having the temptation removed from her sight.

He put on the gas, fished the pan out of the cupboard. and got the eggs ready. First, he threw the ham into the pan, and followed it with the eggs. He even put some bread in the toaster. He had this. Fucking schedule. How did she come up with these stupid ideas? It had to be her new boyfriend's suggestion. Four-eyed, rat-faced Milton. It was just typical that she met him when he came to fix her computer. Who the fuck called themselves 'Milton' anyway?

Stitch dropped his ass in the chair on Crystal's side of the table (as marked by the same glittery 'C' as in the fridge) and peeled the banana, immediately spraying a generous dollop of whipped cream on top of it.

"There we go." Stitch grinned before putting half of the banana into his mouth at once. He didn't know how the connection came to his mind, but it suddenly got him imagining having Zak's cock in his mouth. He sucked on the banana with a frown. He was both nervous and excited about getting the tattoo done. It wasn't an everyday occurrence for him to speak to a man so much his type, and sucking the sweet juices out of the banana was kind of nice. Good enough for him to take a bite. He groaned with pleasure when the cream and fruit mixed in his mouth, but when smoke filled his nostrils, he jumped to his feet and rushed for the burning pan. It shouldn't have heated up so fast!

Stitch screamed when the handle burnt his hand, and he dropped the scorching food into the flames. "Fuck!" he growled, grabbed the pitcher with filtered water, and poured its contents all over the cooker. The flame died, and he stared at the mess, wide-eyed. The quick footsteps in the corridor were like nails being hammered straight into his head.

"Stitch?" hissed Crystal as she rushed into the kitchen, red hair all rolled up with what looked like pink snails made out of plastic. "What the hell? You'll wake up Holly!"

"I was just making a snack," he growled, not even sure how to start cleaning up this shit. "It wouldn't have happened if you didn't make this crazy schedule and separated the fridge. Did I divorce the kitchen or something? Fuck this!"

Crystal opened her mouth to speak but she sniffed and turned off the gas with a deep frown. "Christ, you can't even cook eggs without burning them? That's pathetic. And you can't just leave it on without the flame. You could kill your own daughter, do you understand that?" She stabbed the middle of his chest with her index finger. It was hard to understand how so much force fit into her tiny body.

"I was gonna turn it off!" Stitch spread his arms to the sides. "Bacon wouldn't burn like that. If you had bacon, this wouldn't have happened!"

"Well, then buy bacon if you want to clog your arteries and die at forty! Go on, it's not my concern anymore," hissed Crystal. "At least Holly won't have to see her sorry excuse for a dad!" Crystal's eyes went to the banana on the floor, and her face tensed more than Stitch had ever thought possible. And he'd seen her in a mud face mask. "That was for her breakfast, you greedy fuck."

"What?" Stitch actually paused, now feeling dirty that he'd compared the banana to Zak's dick. "Oh, come on, it's just a banana. Can't you tell *Milton* to get her some fruit?" He would go himself if he weren't still drunk. Fucking Crystal, always knew where to hit for it to hurt. If there was one thing he wanted to do properly in life it was to be a good dad.

Crystal shook her head. "She's not Milton's kid, she's yours, sadly." She gestured to the water all over the stove and the burned ham. "Clean this before you fall asleep on the floor." And with that, she stormed out. The phoenix tattoo on her back and the flames on her ankles really fit her personality.

For a moment, Stitch considered going up to Holly's room and apologizing, but she was probably still asleep. Then again, the last thing he wanted to do now was cleaning the kitchen. *For fuck's sake.* He groaned, grabbed the chair Crystal had labeled with his name and took it out into the backyard. Their garden was messy, full of weeds and old trees, since they were both shit at gardening, but they did manage to keep a small section tidy. Stitch had used the space to create a playground for Holly, with a little sandbox, and a swing attached to a thick branch.

Stitch took the chair and smashed it against the tree with full force, sending splinters flying. He screamed his anger out into the silent morning, repeatedly hitting the tree with the chair. He'd made it, so he could destroy it if he wanted to.

Fucking Crystal. Fucking lean ham. Fucking cock-banana distractor. Fucking fucked-up marriage. Fucking Milton stealing Crystal away.

Stitch took deep breaths and threw away what was left of the chair. He slid down the tree and sat in the sandbox. It was just his fucking luck that he didn't notice one of the plastic toys and crushed it with his weight.

Stitch hid his face in his hands. Maybe Crystal wouldn't have divorced him if he could get it up for her. She was probably sick of a limp-dicked husband. She'd signed up for a biker stud and got a fag.

Chapter 3

The low buzz of the tattoo machine harmonized with the raw sound of the bootleg record playing in the background. Zak was slowly adding the shading on one of the three skulls he'd tattooed over the name of his customer's ex-wife. It was a pretty shitty name too, but he didn't comment on it. He would never stop being baffled with people who ink their bodies with names of lovers. Even a pet's name would have been more reasonable. He'd just opened his small home-based studio in Lake Valley, and the last thing he wanted was to possibly offend a member of the local motorcycle club. Doing a good job meant a large group of potential customers that he didn't want to lose.

Zak discreetly glanced up the fine piece of meat that was Stitch's bare chest. The first time Zak had locked his eyes with Stitch in that dim bar, chemistry had sizzled like water poured into hot oil. The big bad biker did his best to get some attention, and even followed Zak to the car. With his bright eyes tracing Zak's whole body as if he were made of chocolate, it was hard not to connect the dots. Finding such a hot and eager guy in a small town like Lake Valley wasn't what Zak had expected so soon after moving over here. And now that they were finally alone in Zak's house, it was hard not to look up at the guy's body every now and then. Almost as tall as Zak, but bulky like an overgrown pitbull, with sandy hair and stubble that was bound to feel nice and rough to the touch. The veins on his arms were pronounced and spread out like the roots of an old tree, and Zak would just love to lick them up all over. Especially with the tattoos on Stitch's arms being such a delicious sight. Two ornamental Mjölnir hammers with runes turning into wolves on one side and ravens on the other.

Stitch sat in the chair he was being tattooed in, in just his cut, with jeans and briefs pulled halfway down the thighs so Zak could reach to where the tattoo was, low on the hip. It wasn't easy to focus when that ripped stomach kept moving up and down with each of Stitch's breaths. And as soon as Zak got to see Stitch's abdomen in good light, it became clear where his nickname came from. There were three scars on his stomach, two of them small, one long and too prominent to miss, all tattooed over with flaming skulls and runes, but clearly visible because of how protruding they were.

And while Zak usually wasn't the type to ogle his customer's dicks in an unprofessional manner, Stitch's vibe was ticking all his boxes, and with that thick cut dick in plain sight, below Zak's face as he leaned over Stitch's hips, he caught himself stealing glances. It was a good size, resting between two defined thighs and overseen by trimmed blond pubes. From inches away, Zak could smell the rich musk and fresh sweat mingling with the scent of ink to create the most intoxicating combination.

"Does it have any particular meaning for you?" he asked about the new tattoo. Not the dick.

"Yeah," came a low grunt that had the hairs of Zak's forearms bristle. "I'm burying the memory of that bitch. So, you know, flowers, and death and shit."

"Sounds about right." Zak grinned, moving the tattoo machine in a circle on the inner side of the outline of an empty eye socket. "At least you're free as a bird now, eh?" He glanced up the full chest, over the meaty pecs, all the way to the handsome, rugged face. Stich had a nice, firm jaw, but the longish blond hair gave him a softness that most probably had nothing to do with his personality. A certain confidence oozed out of Stitch's pores, engulfing him like the cologne he was wearing.

"Exactly. I can do whatever. What about you? What brings you here?" Stitch shifted in the chair when Zak pulled away slightly. "And I mean, *here.*" He pointed to the wall with his chin, and this slight movement got his dick to brush against Zak's forearm. It made Zak's skin explode with thousands of sparks, but he raised his head and looked at the coppery brown walls he had painted himself just weeks ago, adding some texture with a sponge. With the additional decoration of some metal skulls, and a painting of a demonic cat taking up one of the walls, he'd managed to achieve a dark, gritty look for his studio room.

"You know Virginia Abbot? She died two months ago," said Zak, trying to ignore the persistent tingling in his forearm, where it was closest to the hellishly hot cock.

"I suppose. The old lady with the fancy poodle?" Stitch's chestnut-colored eyes focused right back on Zak. They seemed to see right through him. Only now Zak noticed Stitch had another scar on his upper lip. This one looked nicely healed and pale, but cut through the stubble in that place.

Zak sighed. The poodle wasn't that fancy anymore because unlike Aunt Virginia, he wouldn't bother grooming him for shows. "That's her. She was my gran's sister, and she left this house to me. So I chose to move here and see how it goes. It's not a good time for selling property," he said, keeping his eyes on the handsome face. It was as if whole armies of ants marched down his back each time their gazes met over Stich's cock. There was this freakishly intense chemistry that made the air throb in the same rhythm as Zak's blood. He could imagine Stitch was a beast in bed, with all that muscle helping him pump his hips like a piston. He was a top dog, one that wouldn't hesitate to grasp his lover's neck to keep them in place.

"Yeah, I guess Lake Valley isn't exactly the Silicone Valley when it comes to property value. It's not all that inviting for guys with tats all over either." Stitch took a deep breath, and it made his chest expand in the most appetizing way. "Some nice redecorating you did here."

Zak let out his breath slowly, not to sound flustered. "Yeah, I'm still thinking whether I'm gonna stay here or not. This house is pretty much... the dream of a cheesy old lady, if you know what I mean." He shook his head, remembering two whole cabinets filled with porcelain poodles in the living room. Those things had to go eventually if he were to stay. But as much as he detested Aunt Virginia's taste, she was the only person in his family who hadn't forgotten about the 'faggy punk' that he apparently was, even though they never met. In fact, until he got the phone call from her lawyer, Zak hadn't even known his gran had one more sister, but he supposed some of the things Aunt Virginia did as a young woman must have made her even more of a black sheep in the family than he was. At least no one pretended he didn't exist, although a brief look through the desk in one of the rooms revealed Gran did have contact with Aunt Virginia until she died three years ago.

Stitch took another heavy breath. "Then again the only *good* artist around is over twenty miles from here so you would have a steady flow of customers."

Zak could swear the guy's dick was getting a bit of a chub, but he didn't want to stare. "Yeah, but I'm not sure yet if I like the small-town atmosphere, you know." He switched off his machine and rolled back on his chair to grab the sanitizer and all the other supplies he needed. "You like how it turned out?"

Stitch looked down at his hip and spread his thighs a bit wider, only triggering a sea of filthy fantasies in Zak's mind. Oh, how he wished Stitch spread his thighs this way for a whole other reason. His mind went blank though when he sat back and got to assess the state of Stitch's cock. It was getting all darker and was stiffening before Zak's very eyes.

"Yeah, good," Stitch muttered without looking up.

"See me in a month to do some touch-ups, yeah?" Zak moved like a sleepwalker, glancing at the cock as he sanitized the tattoo with gauze, and then quickly fastened the dressing with tape. His eyes zeroed on the dark head, but he stopped mid-move as blood drained from his brain, rushing to his crotch when he noticed that the gorgeous, fat prick was slowly arching up like a shy snail peeking out of its shell.

"Sorry, inking gets me horny," Stitch muttered in the most raspy voice Zak had ever heard. It was a throat definitely used to cigarettes and alcohol, but for a short moment, Zak also imagined it could have gotten this way through a lot of deepthroating.

Zak let out a shuddery breath. Yeah, right. The guy was soft throughout the whole process, and now he was getting into the mood? He would not believe that, but he still said, "Yeah, happens to some guys. Myself included," he rasped, surprised at the sound of his own voice. He raised his eyes to look into the deep, dark irises that seemed like twin black holes in the squarish face. The temptation was simply too great, and he started languidly sliding his gloved hand up the meaty thigh, toward its goal. "Have you considered getting it inked?"

There was a tiny twitch on Stitch's face, followed by a deep exhale. "Considered," he said, and Zak felt all that glorious muscle tense up under the golden skin. Stitch's cockhead kept arching up in a never-ending demand for petting. A tiny glint of precome appeared at the dark tip. The smell of Stitch's cologne intensified, as if luring Zak in as well.

One brief move, and he had Stich's dick in his hand. The warm girth left him lightheaded, with a sudden pulsating sensation in his gums and a cock so hard that the confinement of his skinny jeans was getting painful. He couldn't feel the softness of the skin through the latex glove, but the heat was so intense it seemed to burn through. "Hurts like a bitch, but it's worth it," whispered Zak, breathless. So the big bad biker was into guys.

Stitch exhaled so deeply, his breath seemed to ripple through the air. "Holy fuck," he whispered and didn't move a muscle, as if he were glued to the seat. A drop of precome slid down the rock hard shaft and onto Zak's hand, as if in slow motion.

Zak bit his lip, pushed forward by an unstoppable urge, a hunger that seemed to open up his throat and make his mouth salivate. He yanked the glove off his other hand with his teeth and put the now bare palm on Stitch's stomach. Pure muscle. There were some blond hairs below the navel, leading him right back to the stiffening dick. "I'd have lots of space to work with on this one."

"Get the other fucking glove off," Stitch uttered and sat up, watching Zak from above. His chest was heaving like a pair of bellows. "Let's fuck the chit-chat. You want to suck me, don't you? You want to." There was a clear tremble to his voice, but there was nothing nervous about the way Stitch's hand gripped onto Zak's nape, just like Zak had fantasized earlier. It was big, hot, a bit damp.

Zak gave a breathless laugh and let go of the cock, letting it slap against Stich's stomach as he removed the glove, empty-headed. A thick vein went all the way up the underside, and he was overcome by the urge to follow it like Dorothy followed the yellow brick road. "Sure I do, it's a great cock."

Stitch was worked up as if it was the first blow job of his life and judging by the tattoo that had been covered earlier, Zak highly doubted that. "Then get to it," Stitch whispered, while a bead of sweat trailed down his abs and into his navel. He gave Zak's nape a squeeze to emphasize his point.

"Someone's too bossy," murmured Zak, stroking the cock with his hand. He was kneading the vein with his thumb, greedily drinking in every twitch between his fingers. With his left hand he zipped open his jeans and pulled out his own dick, relieved when the pressure was finally gone.

The fact that Stitch actually bowed forward to see it was making the situation painfully obvious. "Come on, I just want that cocksucking mouth... sucking cock." It sounded offensive to say the least, but the desperation in Stitch's eyes and the gentle stroking of his thumb against Zak's neck softened the blow.

Zak pulled closer, leaning over Stich's thighs to get comfortable. He grasped the dick again and followed its slow ascent up the length with his tongue. Even the smell of antiseptics could not kill the mood, and he sucked on the warm skin, pressing his tongue against the vein.

"Oh, fuck..." Stitch uttered, massaging Zak's neck with a hand so hot it burned. He spread his thighs to accommodate Zak better, only making him wish he had gotten a glimpse of Stitch's ass. Not that he couldn't imagine what it looked like minus jeans, but it wouldn't be the same thing. The background soundtrack of Stitch's gasps was making Zak's cock throb. He'd love to hear the guy moan and lose control, and that was precisely what he intended to make him do.

"Yeah," agreed Zak and flicked the tip of his tongue over the underside of the corona before sticking it into the wet slit at the tip. His body shuddered at the bitterness of the precome, but the sensation only made him hotter for the guy. He bobbed his head, sucking in the bulbous head and squeezing his own cock with his other hand.

Stitch slid both of his hands to the sides of Zak's head and gently pushed it down. He was one impatient bastard. The heat his body produced was making Zak dizzy and transported him to a reality where they lay together in bed, all sweaty and satisfied, with Stitch still clinging to Zak's back. Would he stay? Why not? He didn't have a wife to go home to anyway.

Zak took the cock in deeper, inhaling the scent of arousal and male sweat, which was the more intense the closer his face was to the trimmed bush over Stitch's cock. It was one magnificent piece of meat. Heavy, soft on the outside but hard as steel beneath the skin. Zak's tongue was a red carpet, ready to invite that prick deep into his throat.

"Yes," Stitch hissed, holding onto Zak's head with that delicious force. One of the hands slid over the shaved sides and untangled Zak's ponytail, only to get a better grip on Zak's hair. This was so odd. Zak never went for guys so deeply in the closet they chose to marry. Those who did were open enough to write about their preferences on Grindr or go to a gay club. It seemed that Stitch was a different kind of animal, rough, uncultured, demanding, but so hot Zak never once considered pulling away. Stitch's fingers were so rough on his skin, like they had been sprayed with acidic chemicals, but the cockhead was sliding so smoothly over Zak's palate that he was already jerking off under the tattooing chair, with hair bristling all over his skin.

When the cockhead started hitting the back of Zak's throat, he got the most arousing moans out of Stitch, long and guttural, accompanying the pulsing in the dick. Stitch's hips rocked forward to meet Zak's lips, leaving the leather seat with a slapping sound. "Yeah, suck it like that," he whispered, moving his thumb over Zak's jaw.

Zak shivered, trapped between the firmest thighs he'd ever touched, breathing slowly to fight off his gag reflex, but the sensations coming from the assault were making his knees soft as butter. He started jerking his cock at a higher speed, massaging the head at the same pace as Stitch's cock was moving in his mouth. He still tried to suck on the delicious prick, and the slobbering sounds he made seemed to excite them both. Zak was getting so hot, he'd love to just rip off his tank top, but he gave up on the idea since it would mean having to unsuck himself.

The grip on Zak's hair became painful, but he was beyond caring. Stitch held him in place and fucked his mouth with a vengeance, pushing deep into his throat every now and again. Stitch's precome was already covering all of Zak's taste buds when he came with a grunt, holding onto Zak's head as if belonged to him. "Fuck, yes!" he moaned as he made his last thrusts, thighs trembling with strain.

Zak coughed, clearing his abused throat but pressed his face against Stitch's spent member. It was damp with his own spit and clung to his cheek as Zak groaned, squeezing an orgasm out of his painfully hard dick. The comedown was so sudden he was close to falling asleep with his face in Stitch's crotch, possibly to awake to another erection poking his cheek like a greedy pup. His jaw muscles and throat were aching, but it was the kind of pain he associated with a good, rough fuck. He'd had it worse anyway. "You have somewhere to go?" he muttered.

Stitch fell back to the chair, desperately gasping for air, his stomach nicely displayed when he stretched. "Yeah, I— yeah," he uttered between one breath and another. Zak had no idea what his train of thought could be, but he wouldn't let that affect him and got up, with his dick slowly softening where it stuck out of his open zip.

"Remember to call me about your tattoo, or if you happen to need something else," said Zak with a grin.

Stitch pulled up his pants with more urgency than seemed appropriate. "Don't get any stupid ideas, yeah?" he rasped, clinging onto his briefs as if he weren't sure what he wanted to do next.

Zak frowned. "Stupid ideas?"

Stitch pulled his pants all the way up, over the tattoo, and buckled his belt up so quickly as if the demonic trio from *The Master and Margarita* were after him. "You know, gay ideas, how the fuck do I know?" He raised his voice and spread his hands to the sides.

Zak frowned. All of a sudden the rough edges all over Stitch didn't seem all that tempting. He pulled off the band off his messed up hair and put it back into a ponytail. "Said who? It was you who asked me to suck your dick, so what the *fuck* is your problem?"

Stitch's nostrils flared, and Zak assessed the bulky body more for how much damage it could do than how hot it was. "It's you who was all over my dick! No one told you to do shit!" Stitch slid off the chair and took a step closer, suddenly making the room seem smaller.

Zak stepped back, touching the drawer where he kept scalpels and other paraphernalia. His brain was waking up rapidly, as if someone had given him a shot of pure caffeine. "Get out of my house."

"No, you listen to me, and you listen to me good," Stitch hissed and grabbed Zak's arm. The grip was nothing like the exciting force in sexual context, and Zak felt blood draining from his face. With one swing of his wrist, he opened the drawer and grabbed a heavy steel object from a plastic tray inside. He brought it against Stitch's throat and pressed the blade against the Adam's apple. He wasn't able to breathe, completely lost in the moment as his eyes met Stitch's.

As much as Zak didn't want to go there, the scalpel did make Stitch pause and struggle not to swallow against the blade.

"Watcha gonna do with that, huh?" he said quietly, but lessened the grip on Zak's arm.

Zak gritted his teeth. Was that the gratitude he was going to get from this bitter fucker? The soreness in his throat that previously was so satisfying turned into a nauseating sensation. "Depends. Now get lost."

Stitch slowly pulled his hand back, never even blinking. "Okay, okay," he said in a calm voice. He took a step back, but the moment Zak dared to lower his hand, Stitch made a swift move at him. Before Zak could slash him with the blade, he met the wall face-first. It hurt like a motherfucker and for a moment got him so dizzy, he forgot what got him into this position in the first place. Stitch slammed Zak's hand against the wall so hard Zak dropped the scalpel himself, and froze, shocked by the pain spreading through his wrist. A sudden panic overcame his senses at the notion that it could have been damaged and prevent Zak from carrying on with his work. Stitch's big body was right behind him, pushing him into the wall and forcing him to his toes, one hand in Zak's hair, the other on his right wrist.

"You know how I got my nickname?" he whispered into Zak's ear in a low hum.

Zak gasped and glanced at his hand, trapped in the grip of that meaty hand. It was aching all over, and he was afraid to move his fingers. Hell, at this point he didn't dare to move his other hand, which hadn't been restrained in any way whatsoever. He stiffened with the realization that he was defenseless. There was no doubt Stitch knew what he was doing. The frightening ease with which he'd slammed Zak into the wall and had made him lose his only weapon froze Zak in place. Cold shivers were dancing all over his spine but he refused to talk, afraid his voice would tremble.

"It's because I got all those stitches in me after a guy stabbed me in the gut and tried to cut me up." Stitch's breath licked Zak's ear in the most unpleasant of ways. "You know why I got skulls and fire inked up all over those scars? Because I burnt his fucking house down with him inside. So *do not* pull a fucking blade at me. Understood?"

This time, Zak wasn't able to stop himself from shuddering. He'd never been in a situation like this, and his mind went into chaos, as if dozens of different voices were screaming at him from all directions but ultimately left him disoriented and powerless.

Stitch backed off and pulled Zak with him, only to push him right back at the wall. "Some fucking advice? You get lost. Better leave this town before you settle in because you're not gonna like it here."

Zak gritted his teeth, curling the hurting hand against his chest. He looked back with a snarl. He *would* talk to strangers. "Or what?"

Stitch took a step back toward the door and crossed those beefy arms on his chest. "You don't wanna find out, sweetheart. But it will be nothing like blowing me."

Zak was struggling to get his breathing back to normal, raw fury rising in his veins. "Fuck you."

"Do we have an understanding?" Stitch raised his voice again and ripped a poster off the wall in the most random of attacks Zak had ever seen.

"Like what? You're throwing me out of *your* town?"

"Yep. People don't like your kind around here. Go on, stay. Try me." Stitch said and threw the poster to the floor before storming out and presenting the patch on the back of his cut. 'Hounds of Valhalla' over the triangular Nordic sign with the head of a snarling dog sticking out.

"Don't you ever set your foot in here again!" yelled Zak, picking up the scalpel and following him at a safe distance. His temples were pulsing like mad. "No wonder you don't have anyone to suck your junk!"

Outside, Stitch was already approaching his beast of a bike, but he turned around to show Zak the finger. "Shut your cocksucking mouth!"

Zak saw white. "Then get your faggot ass off my property!"

All he got in reply was Stitch spitting on his lawn before putting the helmet on and getting on his bike. A black Harley worthy of one of the Riders of the Apocalypse.

Zak reached into an open bag of charcoal Aunt Virginia kept on the porch and threw one at him as hard as he could. It bounced right off the dog muzzle on Stitch's cut and fell into the dirt. Zak needed a gun. No, a *shotgun* to scare off this closeted bullterrier.

Chapter 4

Zak looked at the white ceiling for what seemed like the hundredth time that night. The moonlight cast a cool, unearthly glow onto the flowery wallpaper, the antique furniture, the framed portrait of Versailles, Aunt Virginia's show poodle, which dozed off in his basket by the wall.

Zak couldn't sleep. Every sound had him clenching his hand on the kitchen knife he'd brought upstairs, just in case. The blade was a pleasant weight on top of Zak's chest, right over the pristine white covers, which belonged to his late aunt. He could only hope that if danger came knocking, the knife wouldn't get entangled in the lace trim Aunt Virginia seemed to have loved.

Despite all the impromptu confidence he'd expressed earlier, the more time passed since Stitch's visit, the more nervous Zak was getting. He couldn't believe the attitude he got from that fucker, but he'd lie to himself if he claimed not to give Stitch's threat some thought. Stitch was a dangerous man, and Zak felt that in the way he had been held against the wall and the ease with which Stitch had disarmed him. Zak could hardly believe what it had brought out in himself. Holding a scalpel to someone's throat? That wasn't him. Or was it?

A creak in the corridor made goose bumps pop up all over Zak's skin. He shot up to his feet and stopped on the flowery rug in the middle of the room, his head empty. His rapid moves must have woken up Versailles out of his slumber. The dog ran past him with a low growl and stared at the closed door. Zak's chest became so tight he could barely breathe. "Who's there?" he yelled, reaching for his cell phone.

No answer came, but Versailles lowered his head, bristling up and uttered a gurgling sound of warning. What if Stitch really did come back to deliver on his promise? Zak was no coward, but the guy was trouble. Who did shit like that? Get a blow job and then go all mental? Weren't blow jobs supposed to make a man gullible? They were in *his* book.

Zak grasped the knife tighter. Slowly, he placed his foot farther toward the door and inched closer step by step, his stomach tightening with nerves. "I'm gonna call the police."

He really did expect this to be a false alarm despite Versailles going crazy, but he heard a voice from behind the door. There was an intruder in his home. An intruder who had threatened him just a few hours before. "Chill! I just came to talk."

Zak froze, his eyes darting to the green numbers on the electronic clock. It was almost 3:00 a.m. He looked between the knife and his cell phone. The situation was so surreal he didn't know what to do. "It's the fucking middle of the night."

There was a slight click when the doorknob turned along with Zak's stomach, but before Stitch could come in for Zak to stab him dead, Versailles rushed at the intruder, all teeth and barking worthy of a rottweiler not a poodle.

"Fuck! Fuck! Get the dog away!" yelled Stitch, backing off. For the first time since Zak came to Lake Valley, he was truly glad he'd kept the dog. Both beasts were struggling in the corridor like two demonic shadows when Zak rushed out of the bedroom and turned on the light.

"Versailles, let go," he yelled at the ball of gray and white fur that used to be a well-groomed show poodle. The scene in front of Zak was a picture so pathetic that he let his hands drop to his sides.

Stitch was propped in the corner with Versailles's teeth holding his calf. He nudged the dog with his other foot, but all it did was agitate the beast further. It took one more twist and turn of the boot to finally push Versailles away. The dog cowered behind Zak with a high-pitched whimper, leaving Stitch panting on the other side of the corridor.

Zak took a deep breath through his teeth and raised his hands in anger. This night couldn't possibly get any worse. What was next? Would his house be set on fire? At least it was still insured. "Fucking hell, you're bleeding!" He opened his cell phone's welcome screen. "I'll end up getting an asshole burglar into the fucking hospital."

"No, no, no! Don't call anyone!" Stitch yelled as if the house really was burning and limped his way, just to have Versailles snarling at him again. "I'm fine."

Zak put the blade against his forehead, in desperate need of cooling down. "Considering you're rabid anyway, maybe."

Stitch stomped his foot in front of the dog all of a sudden and snarled at it with a face so wild Versailles whimpered and ran back to the bedroom. So much for protection. "Whatcha doing with that knife, sweetie?"

Zak frowned at him, taken aback by the nickname. "Amputating your bleeding leg."

Stitch straightened up and took another look at the knife. "Don't be like that." He spread his arms to the sides. "I thought we already had a chat leading to the conclusion that stabbing is not a good fucking option."

Zak shook the knife in front of him, his jaw tightening with barely held-back anger. "Listen, you stupid fuck, I don't want to see you anywhere near this house. What the fuck do you think you're doing breaking in here?"

Stitch rolled his eyes. "I kinda thought about shit and wanted to talk, okay? Didn't want you screaming in the street for all the neighbors to hear," he groaned and took another step closer. Fucker had a death wish.

"Stay where you are", uttered Zak, stepping back toward the bedroom. Stitch took up far too much space in that corridor for him not to feel intimidated. The outrageous fuck was acting as if nothing happened, even with the wounds in his leg. What was wrong with him?

"Where're you going?" Stitch followed, limping slightly as he went along. "Is this an invitation?" he asked as if he had no comprehension of 'stay put'. Freaking Versailles was better at following simple commands.

"Stay and talk," growled Zak, hunching his shoulders, just in case he needed to fight. He could not show this guy any weakness.

"Man, I'm not so good at this talking shit." Stitch took a deep breath and stilled. "I was thinking maybe I overreacted, you know?"

Zak gave him a wide-eyed stare. He was *not* going to make this easier on Stitch. He kept watching the guy's moves, his body ready to act immediately.

"If you can keep your mouth shut, I-I'd wanna get another tattoo appointment."

Zak could hardly believe it, but Stitch actually wiggled his eyebrows.

"Told you, the ink needs a month to settle," said Zak, pretending not to understand the subtext. There you had it. A closeted gay biker who believed he could just come and go as he pleased, leaving dirt on the floor. Or blood for that matter. Zak's frown deepened at the sight of the dark droplets on the carpet.

"Me on the other hand," Stitch started walking toward Zak again, his figure eerily illuminated by the blue moonlight despite the artificial light shining from the back. "I only needed a few hours to 'settle'."

Zak dropped the knife to the floor and leaned against the wall, shaking his head. "Cut the bullshit."

"No bullshit here, sweetheart, it's all true." Stitch gave him a crooked smile as he approached. "I'm just... you know, gotta keep things like this quiet."

"I'm not your 'sweetheart', I'm not your 'sweetie', and I may suck cock, but I'm not a 'cocksucker'," growled Zak, not backing away by an inch, even when his heart skipped a beat at the presence of such a dangerous but alluring man.

Stitch stood inches away from Zak, his body heat already exuding along with an intense smell of wood chips. For a longer while, he kept silent, but then he put his hand on the wall next to Zak's shoulder. "You wanna show me the rest of those tats? You seem to have a lot."

Zak dragged a hand down his face. This was beyond him. "Look, I'm gay, you don't have to use some stupid euphemisms. What do you want?"

Stitch groaned, his hazel eyes trailing over the floor. "I wanna fuck you. I had a rethink, took some time, and I really wanna fuck you, okay? As long as you keep this shit quiet, we could have a, you know, mutually optimal situation here."

Zak frowned, slowly moving his eyes down the massive chest, the package at the front of Stitch's jeans, his firm legs. It was an attractive prospect. "Why do you think I'd want that after what you did earlier? Are you mad?"

For the first time Zak saw real confusion on Stitch's face. "But you're a—you're gay, you said it yourself."

Zak eyed him, startled. This guy had no idea how the world worked, apparently. "You might have noticed that I am also pretty hot. I don't need to settle on whatever someone throws my way. If you want me, you need to convince me why should I want *you*. There, I'm waiting," said Zak, feeling very twisted and cruel.

Before he even knew it, Stitch's lips were on his, tongue forcing its way in, as Stitch's hands gripped the sides of Zak's face, like a physical reminder of how he'd held Zak in place during the blow job. When Stitch's body pushed on Zak's, he actually regretted not sleeping naked. The kiss was just too good. It sent trails of heat wandering all over Zak's skin. They made his lips tingle, and his throat ache again. He hardly even noticed when he melted into the wall behind him, gasping for breath. Stitch's tongue was hot and teasing, never leaving Zak's mouth, not letting him speak.

Stitch pulled one of his hands away, but before Zak knew it, it was on his hip, fingers already sliding under the waistband of his tracksuit bottoms. Zak grasped his wrist, keeping it in place. He opened his eyes, looking straight into Stitch's. The display had been pretty convincing. "You're a good kisser. Way to go, using an asset like that," he uttered breathlessly against the soft lips. His cock was already stiffening from the close contact.

"So, do I get to fuck you now?" Stitch groaned and gave Zak's lips a quick lap. He didn't push his hand farther down Zak's pants, but he curled his fingers and scratched the side of Zak's buttock. Fucking charmer.

"We get to fuck, but only as long as you guarantee me you won't be lashing out or intimidating me again. That kind of shit's not on," growled Zak, trying to ignore the warm shivers racing all over his body. He needed to set boundaries.

"Promise." Stitch licked the side of Zak's face, leaving him speechless. The guy really was a dog.

"And you'll be fucking nice, or else," grunted Zak, leaning into him. It was so hard to resist such warmth, and the smell of freshly chopped wood that enveloped him like a warm cloud.

"I'll be *fucking* very nice." Stitch chuckled and ground into Zak as if he couldn't wait to get a piece of him already.

"I still need to patch you up, you know." Zak sighed, looking between their bodies. He would not wake up next to a dying man tomorrow.

"I'm good, really." Stitch ran his fingertips along Zak's buttock and exhaled with a low grunt.

Zak shook his head, yanked the invading hand out of his pants and pulled Stitch along to the staircase. "Come on."

"You're tattooed all over, aren't you?" Stitch asked in that sexy low voice of his and leaned over closer to... sniff Zak's hair. He was hot like a radiator, and his breath tickled the back of Zak's neck, which almost made him stumble.

"Yeah, why? You into that?" he asked, walking down the stairs without switching on the light. The hand in his was warm and rough, so much so that he wanted to soothe it with his tongue.

"Hell yeah, I'm into that." Stitch watched him intently, as if Zak were a fresh bowl of doggie treats. A fitting meal for a rabid dog like Stitch.

"I only left my hands, neck, and face tattoo-free. Everywhere else is fair game," said Zak and before he could react, Stitch pulled on the back of his waistband to have a look. The cool air brushing over his buttocks made Zak flush.

"Come on, I'm sure a grown man can wait five minutes," he whispered, picking up his pace as they left the stairs and rushed for the studio. He couldn't believe the audacity this man had, he was no different than a dog stealing food from the table.

"I've waited twenty-seven years. I'm kinda done waiting," Stitch said, his footsteps only inches behind Zak. He did leave Zak's pants alone though.

Zak stopped, and then the bigger, heavier body knocked into him. Before he managed to do anything to save himself, thick arms enveloped him in the smell of fresh wood and leather. Cool air trailed through his windpipe with every breath he took. "You've never been with a guy?"

"So? I'm no virgin, you know." For emphasis, Stitch ground his hips into Zak's ass. His dick was already half-hard.

"Yeah, but... do you know what you're doing here?" Zak found himself murmuring the words into the stubble on Stitch's cheek as he turned to face him, never trying to break the embrace.

"Are you kidding me? I'm gonna fuck you so good your knees will still be weak tomorrow." Stitch tightened his arms around Zak and nuzzled the side of his neck with a low groan.

Zak let his head fall back to take a deeper breath. Someone was a little too happy with himself for Zak's own good. In his experience, guys who boasted about their skill usually turned out crap in bed. "We'll take things slow, yeah? But we need to deal with that leg first. You're limping."

Stitch pulled away and went into the studio backwards, giving Zak a crooked smile. His brown eyes glinted in the light. "I'm not a baby, but I'll do it for you."

Zak's lips curved into a smile. "You're crazy." He followed him as if Stitch pulled him along on an invisible leash. He'd never met a guy this bold.

"So, I'm guessing you want my pants off?" Stitch wiggled his eyebrows and unbuckled his belt by the chair he had been tattooed in earlier. He stood tall and never broke eye contact, as if he weren't getting ready to have his injury assessed but stripping for Zak. It filled Zak's stomach with sharp little tingles that made him restless as he looked at the blond Norse god before him.

"You might as well get naked altogether."

"Oh, really? You don't want me to stay in my cut?" Stitch pulled on the sides of his leather vest with a grin. His unbuckled jeans slid lower, barely hanging on his hips and revealing black briefs. "Girls usually love that."

"I'm not a girl," said Zak, opening the cabinet where he kept medical and quasi-medical supplies he used for body mods. From the corner of his eye, he watched Stitch the manvirgin. Who would have thought? The guy was clearly into guys.

Stitch pouted, slightly deflated as he carefully pulled off his jeans. "I have a hunch that I should keep it on anyway."

He winked at Zak, who narrowed his eyes. What was up with that? Did Stitch have scars somewhere, or some malformation? "I think it's hot when a guy's completely naked. Come on, show me your back, and all the rest." He closed the drawer with a nudge of his hip.

Stitch stalled for a moment, but continued to push off his boots. His face lost the smile, but was no less sexy because of it. "Shouldn't I be doing the looking?" Despite his words, he took off his vest and threw it over the leather seat. Stitch stood there in just his tenting briefs, like a biker chick's wet dream, all tall and bulky, with a few tattoos scattered over his body. Several strands of hair slid out of his ponytail and hung over his face.

"Why? I like to look," said Zak with a grin as he approached Stitch in slow, calm steps. He was happy to see that the wounds weren't that bad, even though they'd reopened when Stitch ripped the jeans off. The studio felt small and intimate now that it was filled with the hunky presence of an almost naked Stitch. Zak wondered how hard it would be to educate an adult biker about gay sex.

"Well, I like to look as well, so take that top off." Stitch pulled on the hem of Zak's tank top.

"I will if you lie down and show me your leg, you pest," chuckled Zak, pushing him away. The guy was needier than Versailles on his bad days.

Stitch groaned and lay on the tattooing chair stomach down, since the injury was on the back of his calf. It turned out that Stitch didn't need his vest after all, because he had the symbol of his club tattooed all over his back. Zak's gaze slid lower, to the firm ass, and he could already imagine himself riding it while watching how the tattoo moved on that broad, muscular back.

He sighed and moved the back of his hand all over the dog's head. It was a fitting symbol for such a feral man. "Nice job," he said, pulling off the tank top. He was a man of his word.

Stitch arched his back, eager for petting, but instantly looked back at Zak. "Thanks. Club is for life, has to be good." His gaze ran up and down Zak's torso, but if the wound was to be tended to, Zak couldn't lose his head. He looked at the small puncture marks. Stitch was lucky his pants and boots were so thick because it really didn't look as bad as Zak would have expected. He sanitized the skin and started wrapping it with clean bandage.

"So what do you do in that club? You guys ride together?"

"Yeah. The club owns a bar and a workshop so there's always jobs to do around that as well. Not to mention the moving company." Stitch was going to have his neck aching if he kept looking back over his shoulder.

"What is it?" asked Zak, unable to ignore the hungry stares any longer. He briefly stopped wrapping to pet Stitch's upper calf and smiled at the ticklish hair growing all around it.

"You have pierced nipples," Stitch stated the obvious, pushing himself up to his elbows. His lips were slightly parted, as if they were already inviting a cock.

Zak smirked and fastened the dressing so that it wouldn't drop. It was giving him a strange boost of confidence that a man as hot as Stitch was ogling him like a delicious meal after days of hunger. It made his skin go hot, like it was sizzling on a grill, and as his nipples stiffened under the scrutiny, Zak looked to the steel hoops glinting on his chest. "Yeah, I do." He slid off the glove and patted Stitch's thigh to let him know they were done.

"I like that." Stitch stood up and slid his hand up Zak's stomach. "I like this as well." He took a deep breath and pulled Zak closer by the waistband.

"What?" teased Zak, suddenly breathless. He put his hand on Stitch's thigh and looked him straight in the eye, despite the flush that was slowly creeping to his face.

"The ink. It's hot." Stitch looked down to Zak's torso, but his hands were already sneaking toward the nipple piercings. "And your body. Nice and firm."

Zak sighed, unconsciously pressing his chest forward, his nipples already swelling with heat. He put one hand on Stitch's nape and remembered the kiss as he watched his pale mouth, surrounded by rough stubble that would tease and scratch.

Zak was approaching sensory overload when Stitch's fingers started playing with his nipple, and his other hand slid down his stomach, around his waist and went straight under the waistband to squeeze his buttock. Stitch let out a shallow breath and bowed for a kiss, all while pulling Zak closer by gripping his ass. It was too much, Stitch's touch was all over his body, teasing, caressing, and then exploring Zak's lips again with that hot tongue.

Zak melted into him, sliding his arm around the thick neck. He moved his other hand up Stitch's forearm, cupping the back of the firm hand at his chest. "Harder," he whispered as his eyes closed, which left him to savor the influx of sensations.

Stitch groaned and turned him around. In one swift move, he slid his other hand to Zak's ass as well and picked him up to lift him into the leather chair. The loss of ground was so sudden Zak wanted to say something, but Stitch's lips were on his again, and he didn't want them to part. He opened up completely, coaxing the impatient tongue into his own mouth and spread his legs farther to accommodate Stitch's hips. The sheer closeness of their cocks was now pulling his into action.

"I think these need to go," Stitch said and started pulling down Zak's pants. "You really are inked everywhere." His breath got deeper as he shamelessly ogled the body in front of him. It gave Zak a sense of pride.

"Jealous?" he murmured, pulling the loose pants to the floor with his feet. He didn't wear any underwear, so his hardening cock sprang out eagerly and pointed straight at Stitch's face.

"Kinda. I like it all over like that..." Stitch mumbled, losing focus as he looked at Zak's dick and kneaded the demons inked on Zak's thighs.

Zak let out a sharp breath, gazing down at the serpent circling his own cock and the small steel hoop pulled through the skin right over its base. He was moments away from overheating with excitement. "You can touch it. Go on.'

And for the first time, Stitch actually hesitated, looking down but still only petting Zak's thighs. Zak could only imagine what was going through Stitch's mind, but the flush on the guy's cheeks was telling. "I will," he rasped.

Zak covered Stitch's hand with his and gently pulled it to his crotch, wanting to help him. So much internal conflict at twenty-seven years of age. He did not envy him. "You make me so hard."

Stitch was breathing as hard as if he were in a steam room, and when he did finally enclose Zak's dick in his firm grip, the touch sent sparks of excitement to Zak's balls. Stitch's hand was rough, but all the more arousing.

"Fuck, that's good." Zak kissed Stitch again, pulling him close and kneading the ripe meat on his arms. His cock was radiating little shivers all the way to Zak's chest. "How does it feel?"

"Like... good. Thick." Stitch gently tugged on the cock as if just taking a test drive. His hair tickled Zak's face as they kissed. "You have lube?" he whispered.

Zak chuckled. "Someone was watching gay porn." He gave Stitch a long smooch and gently scratched the back of his head, enjoying the tender moment. "I even have condoms. The bottom drawer of the cabinet."

Stitch grumbled something beneath his breath as he walked off to the cabinet. Watching him was pure guilty pleasure. The firm ass still hidden under thick cotton, the wide back, the beefy arms all combined to create a perfect masculine form. The splashes of ink here and there on his skin only made Zak hotter. Despite Stitch's fit of aggression, Zak was beginning to think he might have actually gotten lucky. He could groom him, teach him everything he knew, make him his own massive, sexy disciple.

"What was that?" he asked, grinning at the dog on Stitch's back.

"I don't watch gay porn," Stitch said as he came back with lube and a whole packet of condoms. He put them next to Zak and pulled off his briefs in one swift move, revealing the cock that was as ready for fucking as ever, and pronounced hip muscles that got Zak salivating.

"No? Never? Maybe we should educate you then." Zak grinned, out of breath as he slid his hands up and down Stitch's pecs, squeezing the meat in his palms. He was relaxing into the touch, every bit of Stitch's warmth seeping into him and fueling his arousal.

Stitch groaned and pulled Zak closer with an abrupt grip at his thighs. "Just shut it with the gay porn already," he raised his voice, never looking into Zak's eyes, too busy ogling his body and touching it all over.

Zak sighed and pulled down Stitch's head while leaning back himself. His nipples were up for the taking, and the mere idea of having Stitch play with them some more made him so unbearably hot that he opened his legs even wider.

"Yeah? You want it?" Stitch ran his hands up and down Zak's chest, teasing his nipples as he brushed over them. "You spreading your legs for me?" he whispered, finally looking up to Zak's eyes with an intimidating intensity. Only then did Zak notice that the scalpel had left a cut on Stitch's throat, and he brushed his fingers over the scab.

"I am," he whispered, gently pulling on one of his nipple piercings without ever looking away from Stitch. He wanted him to go mad with lust.

Stitch took a deep breath and bowed down for another kiss, pushing their cocks together. "Turn around," he whispered into Zak's lips. His weight was getting Zak lightheaded, and even the slight movement of sliding off the bench and turning away from Stitch was lazy, slow. He leaned over the chair, resting half of his weight on his elbows and looked back, stroking Stitch's healthy calf with his foot.

Stitch straightened up behind him, kneading Zak's buttocks as if he couldn't get enough of them. "This is the best ass I've ever seen," he said breathlessly as he rubbed his dick against its side. Stitch ran his hand up Zak's spine, his move confident, even though he couldn't hide the tremble in his fingers. He had to be incredibly excited, maybe a bit scared. Zak could relate to that. The first time he had taken a guy had been a disaster. He'd had no idea what he was doing, his then-boyfriend was in pain, and Zak went soft. It took them a total of five tries to actually get Zak's cock in, but even then the sex only lasted half a minute or so. At least Stitch seemed to have experience with penetration.

A shudder ran through Zak as he arched his back and rubbed his buttocks against the hard cock. His hole was already tingling at the prospect of having it inside. "Finger me," he whispered.

Stitch opened the lube and bowed down to kiss Zak's back. The touch was surprisingly tender and followed by a lot more kisses, as a slippery finger started exploring the skin between Zak's buttocks. He arched beneath Stitch with a low moan and spread his legs farther, letting his head rest in the crook of Stitch's neck. His body was so ready for this man he could hardly believe it. The moment the thick finger flicked over his anus, his cock twitched so violently he uttered a low yelp.

"Oh yeah? You like that?" Stitch panted and pushed his slippery finger in, all the way to the knuckle. "You like to be fucked like a little bitch?" he groaned and laid his weight on top of Zak, grinding his cock into Zak's hip.

Zak's ass accepted the thick digit without question, but his mind rattled in alarm even as he ground back, fucking himself on the finger. He wasn't against dirty talk but he didn't know this guy, and it felt very off. "No, I like to be fucked like a man," he whispered.

Stitch snorted. "Oh yeah? And how does a man get fucked, huh?" He pulled out his thumb just to replace it with two other fingers, screwing in even harder. "Up the ass, yeah?" His hot breath tickled Zak's skin.

"A man isn't a bitch," whispered Zak. "He's choosing to get fucked up the ass, and he's proud of it." His breathing became shallow as he relaxed to the penetration after initial discomfort. He squeezed his muscles around the digits, anticipating Stitch's reactions. He would show him how good it would be to fuck a real man.

"So why don't you stop lecturing me and take it like a man, huh?" Stitch snarled at him and added another finger, fucking Zak with them in quick, harsh jabs. "I don't like being told what to do."

Zak frowned and reached back, grabbing Stitch's wrist hard. He didn't mind the burn but as much as he wanted more, rules needed to be brought up with this tough bastard. "I don't like the idea of being someone's fuck toy. Behave."

Stitch pulled out his fingers, his weight gone, leaving Zak's back to cool down. All Zak could hear were deep, long breaths. He looked back, swallowing when the silence struck him as eerie.

Stitch eyed him, standing just inches away, with his hands on his nape and his frown making him look like the biker god of thunder, yet he wasn't speaking, and he wasn't fucking either. "What?" he snarled when their eyes met.

Zak blinked, confused. "Why did you stop?" he asked and slowly tugged on the stiff cock that would soon be inside of him. It twitched in his hand, the liquid on its tip spreading over Zak's wrist and making it burn.

"I just— I'm not a trained monkey. Don't tell me to 'behave' or I'm gonna fucking snap," Stitch lashed out, though he didn't back away from the touch.

"It was a joke," muttered Zak, slowly circling the cockhead with his thumb. He wasn't all that comfortable in this position, but he could bear with it for a bit longer. He just wanted to fuck so badly. It had been ages since he last hooked up, and it hadn't been all that good either. "Don't offend me, and we're fine, yeah?"

Stitch took another deep breath, looking more bare than ever, with his eyes wide. "I didn't mean to. I'm... so fucking horny, I see your gorgeous inked ass. All I want is to fuck you good. I don't wanna use you or nothing." He sighed, looking into Zak's eyes.

Zak swallowed, surprised by the raw honesty. He nodded, unsure what to say, and patted the condoms before delving his own fingers into his hole to stretch it out. Stitch's jaw dropped, and Zak snorted at his face. "Come on, you said you want it," he urged him on, drilling his hole with three fingers. Warm waves of shivers cascaded all over his body.

"Fuck yes, I want it." Stitch took the condom out of the wrapper and rolled it on his thick dick. "Let me in," he moaned and put his hand on the side of Zak's buttock. The heat between them was becoming unbearable.

"Add more lube?" whispered Zak, slowly pulling his fingers out of his stretched hole. He reached back with his other hand and spread his cheeks to show Stitch what he had been missing all this time. He moaned, curling his toes on the tiles beneath his feet as anticipation reached its peak.

"Oh fuck, you're so sexy, baby. So dirty, so sexy." Stitch poured some lube down Zak's crack before aligning his dick with the welcoming hole. Even feeling the pressure of the cock against his anus was making Zak want to rub himself all over this man. As horrible as it was, his body didn't care whether he was a 'baby' or a 'bitch'.

Zak tilted his hips, laying all of his weight across the chair. He buried his cheek in the leather upholstery and looked back, biting his lip. His cock was so heavy it was hardly bearable. He wanted this rough stud on top of him. "Fuck me, Stitch."

That was all the encouragement Stitch needed to push his cock in halfway in one rough push. "Like that?" he grunted and put his hand on the small of Zak's back. "Tell me how you like it in you."

Zak's ass radiated pain all over his legs and hips, and he raised one foot, hooking it over Stitch's calf. He had overestimated his preparation but wouldn't back down. "Gimme a moment, yeah?" he uttered, turning his face into the upholstery. Stitch's pheromones clouded his mind, and he forgot all about just how much prep he usually needed.

"Yeah, sure." Stitch bowed down and started kissing Zak's back again, holding onto his hips in a firm grip. It made Zak imagine this was the way Stitch held his bike. Steady. There was no more trembling in his fingers. "You feel so good," Stitch whispered and his cock pulsed inside Zak's tight channel like it wanted to communicate just how excited Stitch was.

Zak gasped and just as the pain started receding, he moved his hips back and forth, fucking himself on that stiff, meaty rod. His whole body was alert to the sensation of a prime piece of man touching him. "You're so heavy..."

"You like that?" Stitch whispered into Zak's ear, tickling him with warm air. Stitch's whole body was like a living radiator. One that started moving in the same rhythm as Zak's hips. Maybe Stitch had no experience fucking men, but he was learning fast and sure knew how to ride the wave. His hands kept sliding up and down the sides of Zak's body, but it was when one of them reached down between his legs that Zak saw stars.

"Hold me down," he whispered, moving his hips to get Stitch's cock where he wanted it. He was one big shuddering mess already, and they'd barely started.

Zak didn't have to ask twice. Stitch grabbed onto his arms and held him in place, giving Zak a taste of his strength. Zak's knees turned into goo when Stitch started slamming his cock in, suddenly nailing Zak's prostate every now and again.

"This is what you like? This is how you want it?" Stitch uttered between one gasp and another.

Zak moaned when the pistoning cock hit his sweet spot again, and he struggled against Stitch's grip just to check if he could get free. He was drunk with lust. "Yeah, right there... fuck, so good..."

"I'm gonna come soon," Stitch rasped, never stopping to ride Zak's ass. His hands were occupied, but he let his lips roam all over Zak's nape. It was such an overwhelming experience, with those powerful hips slamming against his ass in sharp jabs, and the meaty hand jerking Zak off. Even the feel of the dressing over the tattoo on Stitch's hip was like an experience in its own.

He groaned, tilting his hips again. "Do, please do."

Stitch slammed into him, his body sweaty from all the heat. "So fucking sweet." He bit onto Zak's nape as he made his last deep thrusts and came in him with a guttural moan.

Zak bit into the upholstery when the cock twitched in him, milked by the muscles of Zak's own ass. Stitch lay on him, panting for air, but never stopped to jerk Zak off. He even made those languid, round moves with his hips, the spent but still hard cock brushing over Zak's prostate.

"Yeah? Come for me. Come all over the fucking floor." He bit on Zak's ear.

Those raspy words did it for Zak. He trembled, and heat pulsed up his dick, knees going softer with each spurt of come. "Fuck, you're so hot," whispered Zak, fervently stroking Stitch's calf with his foot again. He wanted to take this man to his bed, and do it again with him in the morning.

Stitch kissed the side of his neck, running his hands up and down the sides of Zak's body. He didn't say a word and in the end, he put his cheek on Zak's back, scratching Zak with the stubble. It felt like thousands of little needles that seemed to exist for the sole purpose of enticing him. Zak arched into the hard body, trying to mold his back and ass into it as perfectly as possible. The cock was softening within his body, but he still gave it a little squeeze with his ass.

Stitch groaned his appreciation, but slowly pulled away, leaving Zak a panting mess on the studio chair. He gave his ass a pat as if commending him for a job well done.

Zak spun around with a wild grin and grabbed Stitch's neck, pulling him in for another kiss. His body was both pleasantly tired and pumped up. The thick arms were around his waist before he could ask for it, and Stitch's hot tongue once again explored Zak's mouth in the sweetest way. There was no awkwardness to the kiss, no hitting teeth or drooling all over each other. Stitch was the best kisser Zak had ever had, all soft lips and agile tongue that made his knees go weak.

He'd love to just lie with this guy on the tattooing chair and fall asleep, relax, waking up to the sun, not Versailles's whining.

"Intruder," muttered Zak.

"You didn't seem to mind the intrusion," Stitch whispered with a crooked smile.

Zak snorted, delighted by the flirting. "You managed to convince me to its merits."

Stitch looked like he wanted to put his hands into his pockets, but only realized he was naked and put them on Zak's hips. "It was worth getting bitten by a dog."

Zak stared at him, unsure what to say to that, but he eventually chuckled. "Romantic."

Stitch laughed and pulled away, to get the condom off and throw it into the trash. "More like horny as fuck."

Zak watched him with a small smile. What a gorgeous body: bulky, toned in just the right way, with a healthy tan, not too hairy... just as he liked his men. "You have some weed?"

Stitch cocked his head to the side and frowned. "Maybe."

Zak grinned and reached out, touching the blond hair under Stitch's navel. "Wanna get high?"

Stitch had a healthy color to his cheeks. "Hell, why not." He slowly smiled and reached for his pants.

Zak took a good, long look at that firm ass, complete with sexy dimples at the sides. He squeezed his sphincter, enjoying the slight soreness. Stitch could have lasted a bit longer, but it was understandable considering he'd never fucked a guy before. Was he a closeted gay guy? Bi? It was not the time to ask when the big bad biker was in denial even about gay porn.

"At least I'll know where to get it now. Are you the dealer, or do you know someone?"

"You're straightforward." Stitch chuckled and pulled on his briefs. "I know someone, but I can get you some."

Zak leaned his butt on the chair and smiled at him. He could definitely see this being more than one hookup. Fingers crossed. "That would be nice. Alcohol gives me a terrible hangover."

Stitch's gaze kept licking Zak up and down as he pulled out a little tin. "Kitchen?"

Zak wiggled his brows. "Bedroom?"

There was a moment of silence, but then Stitch moved forward and patted the side of Zak's ass with a nod.

Zak grinned and walked out of the studio with acute awareness that there was a pair of eyes glued to his naked buttocks so he kept his shoulders straight and gave a gentle sway to his hips from time to time. When they started moving up the stairs again, the gaze started burning his skin, from his back to his scrotum. "Let's hope the dog can restrain himself from attacking you again."

"Keep *Versay* away. I don't really have the heart to kick dogs." Stitch's fingers trailed Zak's balls from behind. It was unexpected enough to make Zak stop and look back with a raised eyebrow. Did he want to fuck again? That would have been some impressive stamina.

"That dog needs another name."

Stitch grinned at him and instead of shying away, he massaged Zak's scrotum in a lazy manner. "Yeah."

"Feel something you like?" whispered Zak, spreading his feet a bit more. Tiny shivers were dancing all over his skin. He could not predict what this man would do next.

"I like everything about this." Stitch pulled his hand away and gave him a harsher slap on the ass. "Go on."

"Ouch, what if I kicked back?" Zak laughed and walked all the way up to the first floor.

Stitch snorted and passed him on the stairs. "I'd have to pin you down."

"That's right, you already have," whispered Zak and pinched the meaty thigh.

Stitch tensed up for a second, but continued through the dark corridor. "I should think of something else, because you seemed to like getting pinned down."

Zak supposed this was a good moment to bring up some facts. "It feels good," he said simply.

"I sure hope it did. I'm not looking for a charity fuck." Stitch put an arm over Zak's shoulders.

Okay, some things he seemed to know. "You don't have to, do you? Such a hot stud?" Zak slid his arm around Stitch's waist.

"It's... complicated." Stitch sighed, but didn't move away.

"But you do date girls, right?" asked Zak, leading him to the bedroom at the end of the corridor.

Stitch stopped in front of the bedroom door. They could already hear the dog growling. "Yeah, sure... just not now. I'm kinda tired with all the divorce shit."

Zak frowned at Versailles as they entered and pointed his finger at the doggie mattress. "Bed. Now."

The beast whined but hesitantly obeyed and curled up on its tiny bed. Zak then looked back at Stitch and found his hand with his fingers. So was the biker bluffing, or was he really bi? He certainly couldn't have faked the enthusiasm for gay sex. "I imagine that must be tough."

"Not the most pleasant thing, no. What about you?" Stitch walked in and put on the light, giving Zak an amazing view at the muscular ass under a layer of cotton. He looked so out of place in the old lady's room, complete with flowery wallpaper and pink curtains.

"I'm gay," said Zak without a moment's hesitation.

Stitch licked his lips, looked to Versailles, then to the window, and started rolling a joint.

Zak walked around the bed and sat down on the edge of the mattress, with the soft white cotton under his ass. That was one awkward silence.

"You do any other drugs?" Stitch asked all of a sudden. He passed Zak the joint before scooting back on the bed, so close to Zak their thighs touched.

Zak chuckled and accepted his treat. "Oh, come on, weed's *not* a drug. It's a feelgood herb." He nudged Stitch's side with his elbow and rested his head on the muscular shoulder. The stuff smelled real good too.

"Yeah, I just wanna make sure. I can't trust a junkie, and I need to trust you." Stitch lit up Zak's joint.

"I'm healthy, don't worry," said Zak, just to make that clear. He was always making sure to play it safe. Smiling at the joint, he pulled in some smoke and felt it worming through his lungs, spreading a gentle glow all over.

"You're really... hot." Stitch breathed in some smoke and bowed down to kiss Zak. Now that was a good start. Zak fell to the mattress, pulling Stitch down as well and smiled against his mouth. As silly as it was, he was enjoying this new closeness with a stranger who broke into his home an hour ago.

"What do you like the most?"

Stitch took another big drag of smoke, relaxing into the comforter. "What do you mean?"

Zak put one arm under his head for support and smiled, taking another slow drag. He was feeling more relaxed already. "You know, about me being hot."

"I like the ink. I was never— I like all of it." Stitch spoke slowly, as if it was hard for him to chose the words.

"So, I'm your first guy, huh?" murmured Zak, in hope that the drug would loosen Stitch's tongue.

Stitch took another long drag between answering. "Yeah," he said, looking at the ceiling.

"Why?" Zak brushed the back of his hand up and down Stitch's side as they enjoyed the smoke.

"Oh man, I'm not like you. It's not exactly a part of my lifestyle." Stitch closed his eyes.

"I guess you're lucky to have met me," said Zak and moved his head to rest against Stitch's bicep. If this would end up as a recurring thing, he would scrape Stitch out of that shell of his like a juicy oyster.

"It was definitely unexpected. I don't know what's gonna happen now, but if you do stay quiet, we might both get lucky more often." Stitch smiled, even though he didn't open his eyes. He had such a strong, handsome profile with a wide nose and succulent lips.

"I am discreet. I get why you'd prefer to keep a low profile."

"I don't want people to get any stupid ideas, you know?"

"Like what? That you're weak, or something?" Zak rolled his eyes, watching the hunk by his side. This was a small town, and he could imagine many people, especially from a similar background to Stitch's, would have misconceptions about gay men.

Stitch turned his head to Zak and opened his eyes slightly, looking like the most tempting of men with the smoke swirling around his beefy body. "Guys in my club wouldn't appreciate that."

Zak nodded and crossed even more space, breathing in the scent of Stitch's underarm, slightly spicy but still fresh, with a hint of some musky deodorant.

Stitch laughed at the tickle and put the tiny bit he had left off the joint into a cup on the nightstand. Zak pulled on the comforter to protect them from the cold slowly creeping up his skin. He was relaxed, warm, and entertained the thought of waking Stitch at night with a surprise blow job. He was sure they would both enjoy a development like that.

Chapter 5

Stitch opened one eye. The pink curtains made him slowly realize where he was. The day before felt like someone else's life. He looked to the other side of the bed, but Zak wasn't there. Nor was Versay for that matter. Fucking rabid poodle.

This wouldn't be the first time Stitch woke up in someone else's bed, but he already anticipated an unnaturally high level of awkwardness, and all his senses screamed for him to pick up his stuff and run. On the other hand, it wouldn't be enough to just run. As girly as this bedroom was, with its pinks and baby blues, with the dried flowers in a huge vase, the room belonged to a guy, and nothing could erase what Stitch had done the night before. The logical part of his brain kept suggesting that since he already went for it, fucked Zak like a bunny in heat, then he might as well continue because there was no taking it back. If the guy knew how to keep quiet, Stitch could finally have a hot guy to fuck. Not to mention the mind-blowing head Zak had given him. He'd love to have that inked up body under him again.

Stitch got up and sneered when his calf stretched, reminding him of the bite from yesterday. He looked around the room, cursing beneath his breath. All his clothes were downstairs so his chances for a quiet backdoor exit were slim. All he could do was to dress and sneak out before Zak returned from wherever he'd gone. Stitch pushed back the strands of hair that escaped from his ponytail and walked out of the weed-smelling bedroom.

The moment he stepped into the corridor, he heard the sound of old school rock and roll music from downstairs. *Crap.* This meant Zak was home, which amounted to the necessity of some awkward small talk if

Stitch wanted to fuck him again. What was worse, as he descended down the staircase, his nose was immersed in the rich smell of bacon and coffee.

Was this guy actually making him breakfast? A guy. Making him breakfast. It wasn't even about Stitch's comfort zone. It was so out of his experience to have interactions of this sort with a guy that he felt as if he were fifteen again and clueless about how sexual relationships worked. Stitch tiptoed into the studio and pulled on his jeans as quietly as possible. The moment his belt buckle rattled though, he could already hear Versay's claws tapping on the wooden floor in the corridor.

"Rise and shine!" yelled Zak from the kitchen. "I've made us a little something to start the day."

Stitch let out a deep sigh. He needed to have a talk with that dog. He put on the rest of his clothes and headed for the kitchen, feeling painfully sober. When he opened the right door, he couldn't help but bite his lip at the sight before him. Zak was hotter than the bacon sizzling in the pan. A colorful pair of boxer briefs sat low on his hips, uncovering the sharp hipbones and clinging to the cock hidden underneath the cotton. There were some silver chains on his neck, one of which caught on a nipple hoop as Zak turned the bacon in the pan.

He had the most gorgeous tattoos. Vibrantly crisp, black-and-white with just a touch of color, mostly red. On his back was a naked woman mounting a broom over a dark, somewhat grotesque cityscape. Her red hair tangled across the sky, as if it wanted to reach the bright moon tattooed at the back of Zak's shoulder. The buildings were inked all around Zak's midsection at his front overseen by three expressionist figures, one of which was a grinning cat. He had smaller figures, demons and monsters, drawn into what looked like two neverending queues running all the way up his legs, each of the monsters crawling to worship that amazing ass and cock. Zak's arms were like the canvas for an asylum-themed fantasy, with men in straitjackets, creepy medical instruments, and demonic doctors. Stitch had a sudden urge to read the book the ink was inspired by.

He turned to smile at Stitch. "Hi."

A silly smile bloomed on Stitch's lips, and he walked closer. Zak was perfect. If he were a girl, Stitch would marry him. Today. "Hi." He still remembered how that body felt in his hands, all firm and masculine. Nothing like Crystal's soft curves. Stitch took one more step and slid his fingers under the waistband of Zak's briefs at the back. The feel of that hot body forced a low grunt out of him.

Zak chuckled and divided the bacon between two pink plates with poodles at the edges, which already housed two eggs each. Sunny side up. There was also toast, which Zak pulled out of the toaster, and some coleslaw. "How do you like your coffee?"

Seeing no protest, Stitch slid his hand lower and squeezed Zak's ass. "After sex." He watched goose bumps appear on Zak's forearms, and he wanted to lick each one. This was madness. He shouldn't be doing this yet it felt so right.

Zak switched off the cooker and dipped his chin to look Stitch in the eyes, one brow rising even as a smile tugged on the corner of that sweet, kissable, cocksucking mouth. He pushed back into Stitch's hand.

So fucking eager that Stitch could come in his pants just from fingering that tight ass. He leaned closer for a kiss, hoping Zak wouldn't mind his stubble. All he wanted was to have those inked thighs spread for him again.

Zak turned to face him as though he was waiting for it and moved his thumb up and down Stitch's neck. Judging from the broad grin on his face, he didn't mind the prickly hairs in the least.

"No hard feelings for cold bacon then?" he whispered, his succulent lips closing over Stitch's.

"No." Stitch smelled Zak's skin, all fresh and tangy. So unlike Crystal's favorite perfume. He slid his other hand to Zak's ass as well and picked him up, surprised by the weight he had to bear. He sort of expected it after yesterday, but it was still completely new. Like riding a new brand of bike. Almost the same, but slightly different. He stepped forward, just enough to set Zak on the wooden table.

Zak grinned at him and slid his hands to Stitch's hips, pulling him in between the spreading thighs. He kept smiling as he leaned in for another kiss, his breath coming in a shuddery gasp. So fucking inviting it made Stitch's cock twitch.

Stitch sucked on Zak's bottom lip, blood throbbing in his head as if it wanted to explode. He unbuckled his belt, already imagining his cock back in that tight ass. Zak had fucking milked him yesterday. It had felt so hot that Stitch's knees were getting softer by the second when he remembered the sensation. He couldn't imagine any of the guys he knew melt into him like that, want to get fucked up the ass, and smile at him after.

"Oh, baby, you're so hot," he rasped and pulled on Zak's briefs, eager to reveal the penis and the naughty piercing above it. That Offspring song? *Want you bad*? Zak was its epitome, and his charisma made Stitch want to lick each metal stud and hoop in Zak's body. He was the male version of a Suicide Girl.

Zak raised his hips slightly to make it easier to take off his briefs and deepened the kiss, pressing his chest against Stitch's. His body was so hard, as if muscle was compressed over his bones, making his body denser than any other Stitch had ever touched this way.

"Am I getting you hard already?" whispered Zak, suddenly biting into Stitch's chin. The sensation bordered on pain and sent little explosions all the way to Stitch's cock.

"I got hard the moment I walked into the kitchen." Stitch pushed Zak's briefs to the floor and unzipped his jeans. It was hard to focus though when he got to see Zak's cock, all ready to come for him. It had been glorious to feel that gorgeous, warm dick pulse in his hand, almost on command.

"Yeah? I should have blown you when I woke up to your morning wood," whispered Zak with a bright grin. "I would have gotten rid of you sooner, Trouble."

Stitch took a deep breath at the idea. He loved how shameless Zak was, talking about cocksucking like it was licking a lollypop. "You wish. You just wanted all the bacon to yourself, right? Tough luck, I've got a different kind of meat for you." Stitch chuckled and gave Zak a kiss before pushing his own pants lower. Damn, it wasn't like pussy sex. He needed lube. Stitch turned around and got some butter on his fingers.

Zak grabbed his wrist and shook his head. "Condoms and butter don't mix well. Left drawer," he added with a wink. He seemed genuinely happy about the perspective of getting dick up his ass, and he wasn't feminine at all. It was unbelievable. Completely blew Stitch's mind.

"How about we skip them then?" Stitch rasped, wiggling his fingers. He wanted to howl. "I wanna come in you. It's not like I'm gonna put a baby in there."

Zak snorted and nuzzled Stitch's nose, unfazed. "Yeah right. One time I did it without a rubber, and the guy gave me chlamydia. Thank you very much."

Stitch sighed, strangely feeling rejected. It wasn't logical, and he knew it, nor was it enough to soften his dick, but it still stung. He would fuck Zak without one someday. At the moment, he was too horny to argue. "Okay, okay, jeez." He brushed the butter into the sink and started searching for the right drawer. He found it without much trouble. Among some pens and notebooks was a small bottle of lube and several condoms tossed over the stationery like colorful sprinkles.

"Don't you care about that?" asked Zak.

Stitch looked to Zak's spread thighs and concluded he didn't care about much else right now. "Sure I do," he said just for the sake of it, as he got some lube on his fingers.

Zak grinned and leaned back, resting a fraction of his weight on his elbows as he raised his legs and rested the heels on the edge of the tabletop, spreading himself for inspection. His cock was ripe and ready, and the long sack drew closer to Zak's body, shaven so clean it seemed to glisten, as if polished. Then there was the dark swirl between his buttocks, not quite exposed yet.

Stitch had died and went to heaven. Zak was the perfect breakfast in the sunshine, on the kitchen table, if the thought didn't paralyze Stitch, he'd lick that meal all over. Instead, he smiled back and pushed his slippery fingers against Zak's anus. Even touching it sent a shiver up Stitch's cock.

Zak's features went slack as he made a guttural sound and spread his thighs wider, maneuvering his ass closer to the edge of the table.

Stitch slid two fingers in, spreading the muscles as he watched Zak's face. It was the one thing he'd missed yesterday. He wanted to see Zak writhe and moan for more cock. Zak dropped to his back and moved his hands down his body in a snake-like movement. Having sent one lower, to his stomach, he pinched his nipple with the other and grinned at Stitch. "They're so thick and rough..."

"You like that? Tell me." Stitch was mesmerized by how the rings in Zak's nipples glinted in the sunlight. He pushed his fingers farther and moved them in a lazy manner. He needed Zak to get addicted to him. To beg for it. To come round and wait outside the club just to get fucked. This would not be a one-time thing and Stitch already knew it. Those inner walls were so incredibly smooth. He couldn't wait to feel them without the rubber sheath, to feel the full extent of their warmth and creampie Zak's sweet tight ass.

Zak blinked and licked his lips, which seemed to have darkened and become fuller since their first kiss just minutes ago. He started gently massaging his cock, split his balls with his thumb and gasped as his hole twitched around Stitch's fingers. "Yeah, it's very hot, very masculine."

"You never had a guy like me, have you?" Stitch bowed down for a kiss and let his fingertips trail up Zak's thigh.

"No one was as much of a pest as you," murmured Zak with a mad grin only comparable to the vicious smile the cat tattooed on his chest had. He buried one hand in Stitch's shirt and held on, looking him in the eye, as if challenging him.

"Oh, yeah? So you want me to go?" Stitch grinned and pulled his fingers out in a languid move, never looking away from Zak's eyes.

"Not really. You're my favorite intruder after all," whispered Zak as if he were sharing a secret.

"I'm gonna intrude whenever I want then." Stitch grinned and put a condom over his dick. It was already all too eager to push into that hot tightness.

With this masculine body spread over the table, ready to submit to his cock, Stitch could hardly focus on anything else than Zak's handsome face, and the incredibly sexy body covered by demonic creatures. The pulsing in Stitch's head made him oblivious to anything else when Zak opened his mouth.

"Fuck me."

Zak didn't have to ask twice. Stitch aligned his dick with the slippery hole and pushed in without waiting any longer. He put his palms on the table by Zak's sides and kissed him again, ready to explore that hot mouth as he thrust his dick inside. God, he wouldn't last long with a guy like this.

Zak stirred against him, growling into the kiss but didn't try to push him away. Instead, the long, inked legs pulled him closer, settling over his ass. Another pair of strong, patterned limbs curled around his neck, keeping him in place for the deep kiss that made them both tremble and gasp. It was nothing like kissing Crystal. There was a slight stubble to Zak's skin, and as he pushed his tongue deep into Stitch's mouth, stroking his, plundering every sensitive crevice, Stitch's cock became even harder where it was lodged in the sweet hole between Zak's buttocks.

Stitch slid one of his hands to Zak's cock with more courage than the night before. He had to remind himself that he was the conqueror, taking what he wanted, not some deviant who wants to touch guys' dicks. He pushed in farther, thrusting his shaft into the tight heat. It was so unbelievably good. Like having all his troubles melt away like fat off bacon. It was just him, Zak, and a fast rhythm of thrusts and grunts as he jerked Zak off at the same pace.

They were going at it hard and fast in no time, and he couldn't unglue his eyes from Zak's flushed face and glossy eyes. The guy was even pulling in Stitch's hips to make him thrust into him harder, gasping and groaning in the rhythm of the wooden table slamming against the wall. Zak's sweat smelled so good it could be the basis of some pheromone perfume, an aphrodisiac to lure Stitch in.

When Stitch came, it was as if his dick was getting hugged by that tight channel. He groaned into Zak's lips and licked the sweat off his cheek. He never stopped stroking Zak's cock as he was making his last thrusts, imagining there was no rubber barrier between them, that he would cream him, mark him with his own come.

Zak gave a breathless moan and came right after, his spunk spilling all over Stitch's hand, warm and sticky. Its smell tickled something deep in Stitch, but instead of pondering on that, he leaned in and kissed the trembling mouth.

"Ohh, fuck," whispered Zak as his legs slowly relaxed around Stitch's hips. With his eyes half-lidded, he seemed like someone who'd love to just cuddle into the covers and fall asleep after the most mind-blowing fuck of their life.

Stitch grinned at him, ignoring the fact that he wasn't sure what to do with his hand. "I'm not 'trouble' after all, am I?" He kissed Zak's lips once more before straightening up.

Zak dragged his hands down his face, his chest still working hard. "Why did I even bother putting on clothes. I knew this would happen, you pest."

"You didn't, you only had briefs on. Afraid oil would spill over your junk?" Stitch chuckled and pulled off the condom, his gaze drawn to Zak's slippery buttocks.

"My junk's priceless to me," whimpered Zak, not even bothering to get decent. He had this self-satisfied smirk firmly in place.

Stitch looked up at the puppy-shaped clock on the wall as he zipped up his pants. "I don't have time for breakfast anymore, but it was worth it."

Zak nodded and started smearing the string of spunk on his stomach all over the skin. "See? You're trouble. But Versailles will thank you for the cooked breakfast."

"Versay had a chunk of my calf yesterday, so he should be fine." He couldn't take his eyes off Zak. How the fuck was he supposed to get back to reality now?

"I bet he'll like you better than anyone else now that he knows how you taste." Zak lazily slid off the table and reached for the food.

Stitch buckled up his belt and gave Zak's ass a pat. "Just like you."

"I want your number," said Zak, nodding at the stationery drawer.

Stitch smirked. "Not enough that I have yours?"

"No." Zak shrugged. "What if I'm in dire need of protein?"

Stitch chuckled and got himself a piece of paper. "You're so freaking shameless. Come round to our bar sometime. I bet the guys would like to meet a talented tattoo artist," he said as he wrote down the number. It would be nice to see Zak around. Even if he wouldn't be able to touch him.

He didn't know how things would develop with this guy, but he knew that by the end of this week, he would fuck him again.

"And Stitch, I scratch your back, you scratch mine, yeah?" Zak raised his eyebrows and packed his mouth full of egg.

Stitch blinked, unsure what to say. "Huh?" Was this Zak's way of saying he wanted to fuck him as well? He clenched his buttocks reflexively and felt himself going pale.

Zak frowned. "You know, I don't know how this club thing works. Give me tips, and no fag jokes, yeah?"

"Oh. Yeah, yeah, I'll introduce you and stuff. But you're not 'out' are you?" Stitch frowned. That wouldn't go down well at all.

Zak bit off some of the crispy bacon. "I'm not boasting about it."

"Yeah, so just… keep it quiet, and you'll be fine." Stitch hesitated, but leaned over to kiss Zak's cheek and cupped the sides of his face as he smiled. "So fucking pretty."

Zak kept his gaze but smiled in return. "I'm looking forward to it."

"See you around then." Stitch finally pulled away and walked out of the kitchen. He hadn't felt so light in years.

Even Versay growling at him from beneath the living room table couldn't spoil Stitch's mood. He walked out into the sunny yard and went straight for his shiny black bike. He knew he'd think about Zak's sleek body when he mounted his machine.

But just as he was looking to the window to check if his Pollyanna was there, gazing back, his cell phone rang, and it wasn't Crystal.

"What's up?" he asked Gator, their club president.

All he got was, "Get your ass to the clubhouse right now, we have a problem."

Chapter 6

The clubhouse was busier than a swarming ant colony. All the guys rushed around in pairs, carrying large appliances they had obtained from a major company's warehouse a week ago. Obtained for free. Stitch and Captain were dragging a large side-by-side fridge up into the moving truck belonging to the club, which was normally used for their legal business. It had been hard to load those fresh, new babies when Hounds of Valhalla took them under their wings, but knowing there could be police officers knocking at their door any minute now made the process even more frantic.

"How the fuck did the police get a sniff of this?" Stitch grunted as they carried the fridge to the beat-up truck and passed it to Joe, who pushed the equipment to the back so that they had space for the other items being carried their way like cars taken by the flood. Televisions, game consoles, phones, all boxed up and fresh. Stuff that needed to be moved ASAP.

Gator passed them with a stack of boxes, sweat glistening on his bald, tattooed head. "Toby Flaren called me from the station. Rat left fingerprints. We need to move this shit in case Cox shows up, so you know who to thank for all this."

"What a fucking idiot," muttered Captain as they put the fridge on the floor inside the truck. He brushed the dust off his hands and jumped right off the trailer not to block the way for two more pairs of men carrying the remaining stock.

"Hey, Stitch, you drive!" Gator snapped his fingers in the air and stood on top of a few boxes, which made him look like a slave monger, men moving under his gaze as if they were carrying blocks to build a pyramid.

Gator looked like no pharaoh though, all muscular and red on his pasty face. In moments like this Stitch really did believe the guy had wrestled an alligator once and broken its neck.

Stitch nodded but ran his fingers through his hair, watching more boxes pile up in the truck. "Where are we taking this shit? Where the fuck are we supposed to unload all of this?"

"I'll arrange a space in Bayou Cane, I know some guys down there, but you need to be on the road."

"Go!" Captain slapped his thigh and ran around the truck to get into the passenger seat.

"Are you sure we have everything?" Stitch slammed shut the back of the truck as soon as Gator jumped off. Neverending fucking problems. He'd rather be in the workshop, polishing a table.

"If one thing got overlooked, we'll deal with it. Now go!" growled Gator and Stitch wasn't about to argue with the club president. Gator gave the back of the truck a slap, as if it were a girl's ass.

Stitch opened the driver's door and hopped inside, where Captain was already going through a map. In the wing mirror, he could see the other guys rushing around like a swarm of bees preparing their nest for an attack of giant hornets. He bit his lip and started the truck, squeezing his hands on the steering wheel. Gator ran up to the gate and as he pressed the button, the white door started slowly rising. Inch by inch, it made its way up, all too slow for Stitch's liking.

"Go northwest first," said Captain, slipping a pair of shades on his nose.

The moment burning sunshine hit Stitch's eyes, he knew it was time to put on sunglasses as well. It only took a few minutes to get out of town. Stitch made sure to choose a neighborhood where half of the houses stood empty so that as few people as possible would see them. He'd much prefer to be on his bike, not locked in a giant can that couldn't go any faster, or even get off the road like a bike could.

"I'm gonna kill Rat when they let him out," Stitch growled, completely focused on the asphalt road.

Captain shook his head. "With Gator's new plans, the kid needs to get his shit straight or he'll be out," he said, patting his eye patch. "Go right."

Stitch turned without question. "What new plans?" he hissed, but the issue became irrelevant the moment he saw Cox's police car in the wing mirror. "Fuck! Call Gator. We need to lose this motherfucker."

Captain dropped the map and looked into the other wing mirror, his chest expanding. "Sonofabitch!" He patted his thick fingers against the window, and glanced to Stitch, pulling out his cell phone. "Forget what I said, go left, pass by my house, yeah?"

Stitch gritted his teeth, but he had to trust that Captain had a plan. He hated being out of the loop, and his forehead was already so hot he could fry an egg on it. Not that he was good at frying eggs, as proven by the last fiasco. He nodded and took the first turn to the left and off the highway, just as Captain pushed his hand into Stitch's front pocket, fishing out his phone as well. He wouldn't assume Stitch had anything to hide from him.

"Melissa? Take the car now, we'll be there in three minutes," Captain told his old lady, watching Cox in the mirror, all tense. "Don't ask stupid questions, just do it, you need to do something for me, baby."

"I can see his whites! I can see his whites, he's too fucking close!" Stitch was bristling up like a cornered bear. He stepped on the gas. "What are you doing with my phone?" He took a glance at Captain's thick fingers fiddling with his smartphone. It was pretty pathetic. Captain's phone was one of those old-people's phones, with big numbers, but he did manage to open a new message and was now typing something addressed to Gator. Stitch needed to get a new phone for communicating with Zak, in case Zak decided to send him some dirty texts.

"Just drive and don't keep him too far away from us when you turn into my street, yeah?" growled Captain just before returning to the conversation he was having with his woman.

Stitch stopped listening in and just pressed on the gas pedal, eager to expand the space between them and Cox while making sure not to break any traffic regulations. They could not give the fucker any excuses to stop them with a ton of stolen goods in the back of the truck.

This wasn't what the plan was. They were supposed to acquire the electronics and get rid of them quickly. Bam! Profit. Instead, Stitch was sweating like a pig in this can of a vehicle. "What's the fucking plan?" he urged Captain as they approached his house.

"Keep him on your tail and speed up as soon as you pass my yard," growled Captain. He opened his mouth to say more but instead picked up the phone as soon as it buzzed. "Gator, we're at mine, how much time do you need at the gas station?" He was bumping his fist into the dashboard like a living metronome.

Stitch could smell the tension in the air, mixed with the scent of a bonfire at a trailer park they'd passed. He wished *he* was roasting some fucking marshmallows instead of risking his freedom for a bunch of TVs and freezers. The bills weren't gonna pay themselves though. He only wished Cox wouldn't get some stupid ideas like trying to pass them or something. As soon as they reached Captain's house, he stepped on the gas.

"Just don't pass the limit," Captain reminded him, practically glued to the window, and the sudden cackle he gave was the sign Stitch needed to take a glimpse of the wing mirror. His mouth curved into a smile when he saw Melissa's car parked across the street, blocking Cox, who hit the horn before getting out of his car only to be joined by Melissa, who raised her hands in a gesture of helplessness. That was all he could see before they turned right.

"That's my woman!" grinned Captain and hit Stitch's shoulder with a fist. "It's a shame she only has brothers."

Stitch let out a deep breath and banged his hand on Captain's thigh. Right now, Stitch would do any of Melissa's brothers. "Fucking close! I need to buy that woman a drink! Or… a new TV?" He started laughing like a madman.

"Don't tempt her, I'll treat her to something because she sure deserves it. What do you think? Should I go down on her tonight?" Captain grinned and put his boots on the dashboard.

Stitch chuckled, still glancing into the mirror every now and then, but with a heart much lighter. "Go for it." He wanted to add something more, but nothing came to his mind when the image of himself sucking Zak flooded his brain. He wasn't ready for that change of dynamic, but it still got him to take a deeper breath. He could trace that serpent tat with his tongue and flick the piercing over it.

"She'd agree with you." Captain stretched his body, clearly relaxed. "Take the shortest way to Ted's gas station."

"What then? What did Gator say?" Stitch put both hands on the large steering wheel, trying to clear his mind of thoughts of cocksucking. It wasn't like him. "I need to get some pussy after this," he said even though he wasn't sure if that was what he actually wanted.

"We're gonna party after this so be sure to grab some nice piece of ass," said Captain, typing on his ancient phone. "They're gonna wait there with another truck, and you're gonna jump into the other one. Cox will face some shit we're moving tonight."

Stitch nodded. Captain shouldn't have said 'ass'. All Stitch wanted was a very particular piece of tattooed ass. Maybe he could actually fuck Zak again tonight. And tomorrow. And the day after. Twice a day preferably. "Yeah, good. So we'll hide this one at the station, right? I think there's a road into the forest this truck can turn into."

"Just do your thing as long as Cox doesn't catch up on us before we get to the station," said Captain as they got back into the highway. They were close to their goal, and Stitch could already taste money on his palate.

They drove into the beat-up station, and stopped right next to one of the identical trucks their moving company owned. One of the guys was at the back of it, already holding the registration plate and making a run for the other one as soon as Stitch parked.

Captain slid out of the car and ran to the other truck. "Get this baby into the bath, guys!" he yelled as he reached the replacement and kissed its white door.

Stitch nodded at them and went straight for the gas station, where a single attendant watched them with his jaw open. This guy would need a talking to. Behind his back, the new driver was parking their valuable cargo in the car wash, but Stitch was already running over to close the attendant's mouth.

"What are you..." uttered the gangly boy, who couldn't be even twenty.

"Hey boy, how would you feel about a new Playstation?" Stitch asked, as soon as he covered the guy with his own shade. They would talk differently if he didn't comply quick.

"A what? Why?" The guy crossed his thin arms on his chest and frowned.

Stitch took a step closer and put an arm over his shoulders. "You see that truck?" He pointed to the one disappearing in the car wash. "Well, you didn't. Are we clear? You play your part, and you get a brand-new Playstation. You don't, and you get into a lot of trouble. Clear enough?"

The guy let out a sharp breath. His eyes shone with greed of someone who could not possibly afford a brand-new console. "For real?"

Stitch inhaled deeply, happy that he wouldn't have to descend into violence. "For real. The new one, in the box, with all the shit that comes with it." The guys finished fixing the new registration plate just in time for officer Cox to appear on the horizon. "Deal?"

The attendant gave him a nod. "There was no truck. I must have seen a reflection in the window, sir."

Stitch grinned and strolled over to the truck full of furniture with his hands in his pockets. Captain smiled at him from the passenger seat the moment the police car drove into the station.

Cox stopped his car with a slight squeak of tires and rushed out, his eyes searching for Stitch. His handsome, smooth face tensed when their eyes met. "Were you the driver of this truck, or was it your friend?"

"Afternoon, officer," shouted Captain through the passenger's window, but Cox only waved at him.

"I'm the driver, Officer Cox." Stitch made sure for it to sound like 'cocks', just like he did when they were in high school. "What can I do for you today? We're in a bit of a hurry you see." He ran his fingers through his hair and pushed it back. Damn hairband disappeared somewhere, as usual. Cox's black uniform made him look as if he'd stepped out of a cop porno, all tight-fitting and showing off his figure. No donuts for officer Cox. Not that Stitch watched cop porn anyway.

"And why are you so eager to drive all around town without much purpose?" asked Cox, blinding Stitch with the reflection of sunlight off his badge. Stitch wondered whether it was done on purpose, or was Cox really that much of a freak to polish this thing during lunch break.

"Just some furniture for this family in Houma. They're missing their toasters and shit." Stitch grinned at him, watching the firm, square jaw tense up. *Go on, motherfucker, ask if you can see it.*

"May I see if you haven't broken anything? I would have done that sooner, but some young lady had car trouble a few miles from here," he said through his teeth. Stitch wouldn't want his cock between those lips, the guy had jaws like a gator.

"Of course, officer. Is that a thing now? Police providing escort for citizens' furniture?" he asked as they approached the back of the truck. He wouldn't dare try to steal a glance at Cox's ass, but he had done a few times in the past, and it looked nice and firm in those black trousers of the uniform. Sometimes, Stitch imagined Cox moaning under him when he was jerking off. The fantasy was quite elaborate as well. It included Cox in handcuffs and groaning stuff like: 'Oh fuck, I shouldn't be doing this'.

"Might be, we're intent on making their property even safer," said Cox, stopping in front of the truck. He gave Stitch an expectant look.

"Perfectly understandable." Stitch nodded with the most serious face he could pull off and jerked the backdoor open, revealing an inside full of furniture and boxes. There was even a huge, pink teddy bear wrapped in two plastic bags for protection.

Cox stared at it for a whole ten seconds before climbing up into the truck. Stitch was hardly keeping his grin in check when he looked at that tight ass and movements that did nothing to hide Cox's confusion. 1:0 for the Hounds of Valhalla.

"Right, I think you should get going if you want to deliver those on time," said Cox eventually and jumped off the truck without looking at Stitch.

"Thanks for checking up, officer. We wouldn't want our customers to feel unsure about our services." Stitch yawned and stretched.

Cox narrowed his eyes and nodded before making his way back to the police car. That had been close.

"Stitch, you coming? We have a transport to deliver!" shouted Captain, knocking on the front window of the truck.

Stitch nodded and jogged over to the driver's seat. As soon as he dropped his ass in place, he turned on the engine. "Wow. That deserves a cigarette." He said and pulled out a pack with his one free hand. "You should see that smug face of his turning into a puddle of sorrow."

"With that face, he shouldn't be a cop. How can you respect someone smooth like a baby's bum?" sneered Captain. He tapped the steering wheel in front of Stitch.

"Undercover underwear model?" Stitch snorted, unsure if he weren't taking the joke too far. He got Captain to light his cigarette and opened the window, feeling fifty pounds lighter without the stolen goods in the back.

"A fag's always gonna be a fag, even if he fucks women," said Captain, philosophically. He grinned at his phone and hid it in his pocket.

A queasy feeling swirled around in Stitch's stomach. The topic was getting him uncomfortable at best. "Suppose so," he muttered and took a deep inhale of cigarette smoke.

"Gator says they'll be picking Rat up from the station. He told us to come to the bar afterwards to celebrate." Captain shrugged. "I don't know what's with this little shit. It's as if he has no brain of his own."

"You were saying Gator has some new plans? I hope it's not more of this shit?" Stitch chewed on the filter of his cigarette.

Captain chuckled. "No way, he's planning to venture into something smaller and far more profitable."

Stitch glanced at Captain with a frown. "Oh, yeah? What's that? Isn't that just gonna bring us more heat?"

Captain shrugged. "I'm slowly getting too old to keep carrying those heavy appliances, but I would be glad to make people feel good by getting them what they want. It's not like Cox is going to try any harder than he is now."

That only confirmed what Stitch suspected. Drugs. He'd seen it coming for a while now, but had kind of hoped it wouldn't come to this. "Too old? What kind of talk is that? You're thirty and strong as an ox."

"Whatever, I'd rather spoil my old lady than worry about what we can afford." Captain leaned back in the seat and smiled at Stitch. "Don't tell me you're getting cold feet already?"

Stitch snorted. "Idiot. We'll see how it goes. Don't wanna see you end up in jail." He joked, but wasn't in the mood for laughter. The moment they move into this new 'venture', heat would rise, stakes would get higher, more people would want to put hands on their money. Trouble. That's what this idea was.

"Me neither, don't worry." Captain yawned, completely relaxing in his seat. "Anyway, party tonight. You'll have the opportunity to show off what you got to cover all traces of Crystal."

Stitch threw the butt of the cigarette out the window. "This Zak guy, he did a really good job. Decent guy as well."

"Yeah? Maybe let him know about tonight then? I might consider hiring him myself if I like the job he did on you."

Stitch couldn't help a smile rise up to his face and slowed down the truck before pulling out his cell phone. It was stupid, but he did want Captain's approval. He knew he'd never get it for what he'd done with Zak, but it would be nice for Captain to like Zak.

He chose the right number.

It took a total of three signals before Zak picked up, and the line resonated with his deep baritone. "Hi, Stitch."

Stitch had to hold back a groan. God, maybe calling Zak in public wasn't such a good idea. He felt like a schoolboy after the first taste of pussy. "Hi..."

"What's up? Is something wrong with the tattoo, or are you missing me?" murmured the sweet, velvety voice, trailing through the sensitive curves of Stitch's ear.

He was missing Zak. Every inch of his dick was missing Zak. "Um, yeah, I mean, we're having a party at Valhalla tonight, thought you might wanna come round?" His palm on the wheel got sweaty in a matter of seconds.

"Yeah, why not. When?"

Just inches to the side, Captain was messaging with his old lady, oblivious to what was going on with Stitch.

"Tonight. There's no set hour. Anytime in the evening and it'll last all night." Stitch wished he could add 'take condoms and lube'.

Zak laughed, and the melody of his voice was enough to make Stitch's dick stiffen a bit. "Sure, I'll be there."

He turned off the call before he could get any harder. Even talking to Zak got Stitch imagining all the filthy things they could be doing. It was as if the demons in Zak's ink were nesting under Stitch's skin.

Chapter 7

It was already late when Zak arrived at Valhalla. Judging from the sheer number of cars and bikes parked on the thinned grass around the bar, the place had to be packed. His eyes were drawn to the little lanterns of cigarettes burning in the darkness where a group of women were having a chat away from the noise. He double checked if he had a condom and a sachet of lube in his front jean pocket, and looked into the rearview mirror to make sure the ruffled hair he'd combed to one side of his head looked as good as when he left home. Ready to show himself to his new fuck buddy, he locked the car and made his way to the buzzing bar. Old school rock music was shaking the ground beneath Zak's feet, making him smile. He hadn't hoped there would be a place that played half-decent stuff in a place as small as Lake Valley.

It looked like he could be doing all right here after all, and he did need some time for the dust to settle before he would even consider moving back to his hometown. He might just as well have some fun while he was here. And so, his eyes went looking for Stitch's bulky form as soon as he entered the dark, somewhat stuffy bar.

Some gazes instantly clung to him, but he quickly found the man he was looking for, Stitch's blond ponytail making him stand out just as much as the perfect ass in a pair of beat-up jeans. What Stitch was doing though was another matter, and there was nothing pleasing about witnessing it. Stitch stood behind a girl playing an old school pinball machine. He looked massive next to her smaller frame as he ground into her ass every time she pulled on the levers in the machine.

Narrowing his eyes, Zak went straight for the bar, choosing to ignore Stitch. If he wanted to fuck around with girls—fine, but why would he invite Zak over to witness that? The earlier conversation was nothing more than a plea of a man starving for gay sex.

He climbed into the vacant stool by the bar and nodded at Joe, who waved at him from the pump of beer a few feet away. The counter was sticky beneath Zak's elbows, but he ignored it and glanced to the sides.

"Hey there!" Joe waved at him and came over. "What can I get you?" At one point, he had to yell over a roar of laughter at the pool table.

"Just a bottle of beer, thanks." Zak smiled and gestured to the crowds. "What's the occasion? Will there be live music later?"

"Nah, just the jukebox. I also DJ sometimes." Joe raised his chin and got Zak a bottle from the fridge. "The cops were after the club again and arrested one of our guys for no reason. So they had to let him out. You see that young guy over there? Rat." Joe pointed to a young guy sleeping in the corner with his head against the wall and an empty glass in his hand.

Zak smiled, wondering what the poor guy did to deserve a nickname like that. Rat still had a face covered in pimples. "Tough start. Why would he be arrested?" he asked, leaning over the counter. He took the first swig of the cold beer and smiled at the clear, slightly bitter taste.

"Probably had some weed on him." Joe shrugged. "Stitch said Rat's buying everyone a drink tonight, so your first beer is on him."

"He'll learn his lesson," chuckled Zak and used the curtain of his hair to glance toward the pinball machine again. Stitch wasn't humping the girl like an over-eager bunny anymore, but they were still talking, Stitch leaning against the wall like the alpha dog he was. Strands of hair fell on his face, making him look like a handsome rok 'n' roll Viking. Zak had no idea if Stitch actually swung both ways or what his deal was. It didn't really matter anyway.

"Exactly. It's no big deal, but it's nice to get a chance to show the cops the finger."

Zak grinned at him. He never had any bad experiences with the police, but when in Rome, do as the Romans do. Or just shut up altogether. "What do people around here do on their days off? Other than coming over here."

"Many of the guys own the company next door and work there. You know, the house removals. And then some of them use the workshop for all sorts of carpentry." Joe had a big wide smile as he spoke, pouring people's drinks in the meantime. "It's all locally owned, you know, we don't work for anyone else."

Zak sighed. So there was nothing to do other than hang out here and work. Maybe it was for the better. He would have a chance to recharge his batteries in peace.

"Are they selling the... wooden handiwork anywhere? Is there a store?" Maybe he could order something for his new studio.

"It's mostly commissioned work, but you can always come round to see the stuff that hasn't been picked up yet. Like, last month, they were making these custom-made BDSM benches. There was so much fun with those. And Stitch made a set of miniature table and chairs for his daughter's birthday."

Zak's face, which had relaxed into a smile at the mention of dungeon furniture, suddenly went slack. A daughter? That was the last thing he expected. He looked back at Stitch, squeezing and opening his fists. The guy looked like he didn't have a care in the world, pretending he was putting a glass of beer on a girl's rack. "I didn't know he had a kid."

"Oh, yeah. Four months after marriage if you know what I mean."

Zak sighed. "And now it's over. At least he has a kid out of it. How old is she?"

"Five or something like that. Cute kid, actually. It's a shame he got divorced, he and Crystal were a great couple. It's stupid, but I always kinda imagined, when I was younger, that they were this perfect couple. That I wanted something like they used to have." Joe looked like a stranded puppy when his gaze traveled to Stitch.

Zak blinked, surprised by the sentiment. "Happens. Anyone special in *your* life?" he asked, wanting to change the subject.

"Not yet, you? Came to get lucky tonight?" Joe grinned and looked over Zak's shoulder. Before Zak even turned around to follow Joe's gaze, he heard two female voices cutting through the noise.

"Hey there, Mr. Ink."

The smile tensed on his face but by the moment he turned around, he knew he had to look perfectly natural. "Hey there, ladies," he said, for a moment wondering if they might be twins. No, their facial features were different, but both had long, bright red hair, heavy makeup, and wore skimpy black dresses with some ink peeking out. They could be twin sisters of half the alternative scene.

"Are you up for fun, Mr. Ink?" One of them asked and ran her fingers down Zak's arm.

"Let me guess, you two are housemates," he said, grinning his way through the bizarre moment when he should have told them he wasn't interested but somehow couldn't make that push. His stomach twisted at the thought what the implications could be. In a place such as this, especially as a newcomer, he couldn't just ignore what anyone thought. It brought a whole new level of discomfort.

"I'm Vanessa." One of the girls held out her hand with a smile as the other gave a cat-like squint. "I love your ink. I heard you're a tattoo artist? It's your poster on the wall, isn't it?"

"Yes I am." He squeezed her hand, not for too long, to stay professional. "What do you want to know?"

Vanessa's full lips spread into a smile. "I want to know where you live." She took a swig of beer from the bottle in her hand. Her friend, obviously more shy, hid her mouth behind the bottle and gave Zak a little wink. He responded with a smile.

"If you guys want a consultation, you can see my portfolio online, and contact me so that we can arrange for a meeting. Is there any particular design you're interested in?"

"It's not the time for portfolios today," he heard the well-known raspy voice from the side. It tugged on Zak's nape, gripping the skin and sending a shiver down his spine. "I need a consultation on my new ink."

Vanessa moaned. "Go away, Stitch!"

Zak gave his savior a wide grin. "Didn't expect to see you here," he said, eager to dismiss the fake twins. He held out his hand and grabbed Stitch around the forearm, shaking his hand. He noticed that twin number two turned halfway to the bar, apparently more sensitive to body language than her friend.

"Oh yeah?" Stitch held his hand for a bit too long, but backed off. "You seem to be having fun though."

"Those girls here are interested in getting inked," he said as if he hadn't noticed the flirting. "You three know each other?" he asked, keeping up Stitch's gaze, intense in the dark room.

"Sure we do. Go on, Vanessa, stalk my new friend another time." Stitch smiled and patted her ass. She pouted, but eventually waved at Zak with just her fingers and left along with her friend.

Zak leaned in to whisper, "Thanks." He breathed in the already familiar scent of Stitch's cologne, complemented with a note of liquor.

"You think I did it for you?" Stitch gave him a crooked smile and pulled on his arm to lead Zak away from the bar. "I just need my ink tended to."

"Do you? You seemed to be tending to it very well by the pinball machine," said Zak, slipping off the stool and following Stitch anyway.

"It was just a bit of fun." Stitch shrugged and led him through a backdoor, behind which the music was instantly dulled down. The corridor was dim and dusty, with only a few old band posters on the walls.

Zak bit his lip, his skin burning up where Stitch's big hand was touching him. "Is this still the bar?"

"Nope. It's the clubhouse. We have a few guest rooms and a place to lounge around." Stitch took his hand away, but not before he stroked Zak with his thumb. "Guys from the club can stay around here sometimes if they need to."

Zak exhaled, looking down into Stitch's hazel eyes. "So, we're not alone here," he guessed, looking at the posters of bikes and naked women, which had been clearly torn out of some magazine in the 90s.

Stitch pushed on a door and all of a sudden grabbed the front of Zak's top. With a force that had Zak stumbling forward, Stitch pulled him into the dark room. The door closed, and the same moment Zak heard a click of the lock, he was against the wall, with Stitch's lips on his and Stitch's firm, broad body squishing him flat. "Now we are."

There was a somewhat stale scent to the room, but Zak held onto Stitch's arms anyway and opened up for him, sucking on his wild, restless tongue as it fucked his mouth with an urgency unmatched by any of Zak's previous partners. He groaned and slid his hands down Stitch's back, massaging the tight muscle.

"All I could think of all day was how much I wanna be inside you," Stitch rasped into Zak's lips between one kiss and another, his breath as hot as rum-infused. Zak barely had time to think before Stitch grabbed his thighs and pulled them up. He lost ground and had to grab onto Stitch's neck when the guy held him up against the wall, grinding his hips into Zak.

"Ohh, fuck," whispered Zak, shuddering against Stitch as this big, butch guy simply raised him off his feet like a puppet. Stitch's words stung right into the center of Zak's chest, knocking air out of him and pulling invisible strings that made him open his thighs wider, relax his ass in preparation for that thick, juicy cock. In an ideal world, Zak would have Stitch tear the back of his jeans and fuck him into the floor, crushing him with his weight in a way that was completely primal. The mere thought of it made Zak's stomach shudder in anticipation.

"What do you want? You want my dick inside, don't you?" Stitch whispered in the darkness, his cock already hard in his jeans. "Pumping my come deep into your hot ass." Stitch groaned and thrust with his hips. He licked the side of Zak's face in a languid move, all the way from the jaw to the ear.

Stitch was raw, and rough as a sex-starved caveman. His declarations made Zak's toes curl as he squeezed his thighs around those powerful hips. Zak sucked on the rum-flavored lips, already getting drunk on their taste. His head spun, light as an empty eggshell, with all the blood in Zak's body migrating south. He'd love to be fucked bare by a hunk like that, in an ideal world without STDs. But he could still fantasize about it.

"Uh-huh, I want you to push my legs up and stick that dick in me," he whispered, suddenly biting into the tender flesh of Stitch's lip.

"You're my choice of poison." Stitch held him tightly as he turned away from the wall, carrying Zak somewhere in the dark room. A tiny bit of light from a dusty window made the edges of furniture blur, but it was no surprise when the world became horizontal, and Zak's back met a mattress. He didn't have to see Stitch to know he was unbuckling his belt, the metallic clang went straight to Zak's cock. "Gonna kill me, but I can't stop," muttered Stitch.

Zak shuddered on the mattress and fumbled with his pocket to get out the two packets. He was so hot he felt like shedding everything, including his own skin, and feel Stitch even closer, accept his almost bloodthirsty passion. This was a twenty-something, possibly gay man who suddenly got a chance to have sex with a guy, no wonder he couldn't help himself. But there was something strange in the sheer intensity of Stitch that made Zak both uncertain and hornier than a mating bull. "Kill you?" he uttered, pushing down his jeans for more freedom. "I'm not that dangerous."

The shape of Stitch's body mingled with the darkness, as if he were a biker demon, ready to possess Zak with those big hands that were now kneading his chest, and a dick that was probably already ready to fuck like a devil. Zak half-imagined Stitch growing horns and his dick getting nubs and ridges all over.

"You are if you keep being this hot," Stitch whispered, and the longer they were in the room, the more Zak's eyes were adjusting to the darkness. Still, he couldn't keep up with Stitch's hands. Pulling up his top, sliding to his ass, and squeezing it hard. His knee pushed Zak's legs apart, and all they had for a soundtrack were their shallow breaths, exchanged between trembling lips, sweet enough to send Zak's head into a spin.

Zak pushed his fingers into Stitch's long, coarse hair and pulled him closer, eager to bite into his mouth, tearing out chunks of the juicy lips and tongue. Now that he'd lost his pants and underwear, he dug his heels into Stitch's ass and pulled him in. His ass was pulsing with need, as if there was a void within him that needed to be filled with hard warmth. He pushed the two packets into Stitch's hand, breathless. "Want you inside..."

"Fuck yes..." Stitch's hiss was accompanied by the condom wrapper crunching when he tore it open. Just seconds of fumbling later, a generous amount of lube drizzled down Zak's crack. "I'm gonna pound you into fucking oblivion," Stitch rasped, pushing the cockhead against Zak's anus and sliding it against the slippery, sensitive skin.

It trailed along Zak's crack like a snake, ready to bite into his flesh, and he clung to the strong frame on top of him, close to wheezing his excitement. He couldn't see much else than the contours of Stitch's hair and shoulders, like he was lying under some brute who would take whatever he wanted whether Zak liked it or not. But he did like it. He did want it, and raised his hips to brush them over the hard flesh. "Yeah...."

Stitch pushed a few times, spreading the lube all over, but his next thrust was stronger and got the cockhead right through the sphincter. "So fucking tight I wanna cream you already." Stitch panted over him, pushing Zak into the hard springs of the old mattress.

Zak gasped and bit the inner side of his lip, trembling with the searing pain that spread through his ass as it clamped around the invading cock in a vise-like grip. But he was too horny to complain and arched his hips off the mattress, stabbing himself further with the velvety steel between his legs. Without the aid of his eyes, his world narrowed down to the tactile sensations. The rough, old mattress below. Stitch's body, tense as a jaguar's attacking its prey, damp with sweat. Stitch's scent overcame Zak in violent waves, intensifying as Stitch started easing his thick cock back and forth through his clamped anus. The soft strands of his hair trailed up and down Zak's cheek in the same rhythm, surprisingly gentle and soothing.

The loud sniffing around Zak's neck only made the whole thing seem even more animalistic. "I could come from just smelling you," Stitch rasped just before pushing in up to the hilt, his balls hitting Zak's ass. Stitch lowered himself onto Zak, squeezing all air out of him and making him gasp. The hot flesh pulsed in Zak's ass, triggering sparks of excitement to rush up his cock, which was trapped between their sweaty bodies.

"You're such a caveman," whispered Zak against the throbbing lips, sweet and spicy with the taste of rum. The pain was subsiding to a burn that he knew would only feel better soon, and he pulled his legs up higher, resting his feet on Stitch's hips, completely opening himself up. "You're even gonna suck the marrow out of my bones."

"Hound of Valhalla after all." Stitch growled and a glint of teeth showed in the sparse light when he smiled. He pulled out slowly, only to stick his cock right back in, then started repeating the violent rhythm. "Suck the marrow, gnaw on your fingers, crush your flesh, and squeeze come out of it."

Zak bit back a moan, grabbed the tight, fleshy ass between his thighs, and forced his eyes open, gazing straight into the pitch-black darkness where Stitch's face was. His body was shaking as pain mixed with mind-numbing pleasure every time that thick, merciless cock brushed over his prostate again and again, pushing against it upon entry, and gently pulling when Stitch drew back. Each thrust was filling that painful void inside and pushing Zak to new heights.

Stitch grunted with every harsh move, but never stopped fucking Zak like there was no tomorrow. His ass was hot and tense under Zak's touch. "You like that? You like a good, hard fuck?" Stitch rasped, his hips moving in a motion so fast, he made the rusty springs in the mattress moan with them.

Zak let out a low growl, curling his toes when all of a sudden, the heat in his stomach started rapidly building up. His balls became tighter and tingly as his cock slapped against his stomach with each of Stitch's brutal thrusts. He was coming. He would be coming so hard. "Fuck me, yes, please do it like you mean it," Zak wheezed, pulling on Stitch's buttocks and sensing the warmth between. Grinning like a madman, he delved his fingers into the crevice and pushed his middle finger into the hot, dry hole. He hooked it into the flesh, pulling Stitch even deeper into his own body.

Not only did he get Stitch to moan and squeal, but Stitch completely lost balance and toppled over on top of Zak with his whole weight, his cock buried in Zak like it wanted to stay there forever. He came with a few punishing thrusts, his whole body shuddering. Each of Zak's senses felt heightened. The snaps and studs on Stitch's cut dug into his body through the clothing even as he trembled, pushed over the edge. He could sense Stitch's sweat and physically feel his orgasm with Stitch's anus clenching rhythmically over Zak's finger. He slipped it out as soon as Stitch relaxed, and gently massaged his buttock, kissing the sweaty face buried next to his own. The stubble caressed his tongue in return as he curled around Stitch, hugging him in the sweetest afterglow. Zak didn't even remember if they'd managed to stay silent, but it seemed irrelevant.

Stitch couldn't catch a proper breath, lying by Zak like a wounded animal, too hurt to get up, yet too alive to stop breathing. His body still trembled slightly, and he pulled out with the slowest of motions, so much in contrast to the way he fucked. The smell of come, woodchips, and leather was one Zak was sure he'd begin to associate with sex. He gasped when the cock slid out of him, leaving his abused hole empty, but Stitch's gentleness was enough to urge him on to reciprocate. He leaned up and kissed both of his partner's eyelids, hugging him tight.

Stitch held him close in return as they lay in darkness and silence, cooling off after the intense fucking. Only the faded sound of rock music from the bar seeped into the room like a reminder that the real world existed out of this fuck cave.

Zak cradled Stitch's head in his arm and kissed him gently, tasting his lips in peace now that they were both sated. He closed his eyes. This was one of the most amazing sexual experiences of his life, so primal, passionate, and intense. He was almost sorry they had to let go soon. "You made me so sore," he eventually chuckled.

"I— yeah, you weren't complaining," Stitch muttered and rolled over to his back, his breath slowly evening out.

"I know. I wanted it," whispered Zak, moving close to him and sliding his hand lower to play with the curly hair over Stitch's cock. The sweet burn between his asscheeks would make him walk funny tonight, but it was worth it.

Stitch went silent again, only his breath loud in the darkness as his chest moved up and down. "That... thing you did? Don't do it again."

"What thing? This?" Zak stretched and nuzzled Stitch's eyelid, wondering whether this level of tenderness with a man made Stitch uncomfortable.

"No. God." Stitch groaned and put his palm over his face. "The finger thing. You just... I'm not into this stuff, okay?" he muttered from under his palm.

Zak frowned. So there went his prospects at getting some. "Oh. I thought... you liked that. It made you come," he said, petting Stitch's abs.

Unfortunately, even when Stitch took the hand off his face, Zak couldn't see his expression very well. "I came because your ass milked me like it was hungry. It had nothing to do with *that*. I wasn't gonna make a fuss about it like some pussy, but... just don't."

Zak sighed and hugged Stitch closer, slightly disappointed by this development, but it wasn't like Stitch was the only guy around. "Yeah, sure."

"Good." Stitch pulled him in for a hug and kissed his chin. "Other than that, wow. I mean, *wow*."

Zak chuckled and combed his fingers through Stitch's hair, fighting the urge to close his eyes. He did *not* want to be caught here. "Yeah, you're a good fuck."

Stitch gave him one more kiss before rolling out of bed. By the sound of it, he was pulling up his pants. "So, can I come over tomorrow?"

"I suppose, just let me know because I might have a customer over," he said, slowly walking over to where he'd shed his pants. Eager to get decent, he pulled out a handkerchief and cleaned himself up.

"I will. It will probably be in the evening, after work. I'll call." There was a sound of a clattering belt buckle, and Stitch came closer. "You are the hottest thing that's walking this Earth," he said and planted a kiss on Zak's lips, making him breathless. Stitch was disarming him with the contrast between his usual rough demeanor and moments like this one.

Not knowing what to say, Zak laughed and gently punched Stitch's chest before pulling up his own pants.

Stitch sighed, his hands never away from Zak, they kept trailing between his shoulder and back. "You staying or going?"

Zak bit his lip and looked into Stitch's eyes, which were now turned toward the light. "I think it's better if your friends don't see me walking like I have just dismounted a horse after a day-long ride." He brushed his fingers over the metal buckle over Stitch's crotch, hard enough for Stitch to notice.

Stitch chuckled, slid his hands to Zak's ass and squeezed it. "At least it was a fun ride."

Zak put his arms around Stitch's neck and kissed him, rolling his hips into the waiting hands. The residual electricity on his skin was ready to spike.

"I'll check if the coast is clear," Stitch said and pulled away. When he opened the door, the tiny room got illuminated by the dim light from the corridor, trailing down his gorgeous body. Zak smiled and followed the ray up Stitch's back with his fingers. If there was a gay bar around here, he'd suggest going out for a drink, but that wasn't an option.

Stitch looked back at him, his hair in a mess. "Let's go." He opened the door wider, and Zak walked into the corridor with a satisfied smile. He made a move back toward the bar when Stitch held his shoulder.

"Through the back," Stitch said and nudged him to go down the corridor, following close behind. The walls were adorned with posters and cutouts, but also had framed photos of bikers.

"Why, you want to show me something?" asked Zak with a wide grin.

"Nope, just might be safer for no one to see you." Stitch patted Zak's ass again, and it felt like a gesture of appreciation. They passed an open door to a kitchen, which was cleaner than Zak would have expected from a bunch of rough guys. The small, windowless space was tidy, even if a little beat up.

"Why?"

"You said it yourself, you're walking funny." Stitch laughed. For a guy who complained even about getting fingered, he was awfully comfortable making fun of someone else's ass. So typical.

"True." Zak sighed and walked right up to the door at the end of the corridor, which he supposed was the exit. "Isn't your cock sore?"

"It's the pleasant kind of pain." Stitch grinned at him like a maniac and opened the door for him with the courtesy of a prince.

"So, where's my carriage?" asked Zak, stepping out and stretching his body. He was pleasantly tired. Now all he wanted was a long bath and his bed.

Stitch exited behind him into a dingy back lot with a yellow streetlight and a few beat-up cars. "You want me to take you home?"

Zak looked back at him, surprised. "I... don't want to leave my car all the way here."

"Yeah, makes sense. I'll take you for a ride sometime though." Stitch led him along the empty back lot with a smile.

Zak chuckled and pulled on a belt loop of his jeans. "Yeah, when you aren't drunk."

"Makes sense. My boy likes safety." Stitch snorted and winked at him.

Zak frowned. "I'm not a boy," he said, matter-of-factly.

"Just sayin'." Stitch shrugged.

Zak pushed his thumb under Stitch's shirt and pulled it over the warm skin. "I respect that you don't want certain things, but I also have stuff that I don't like. I'm telling you this so that you know."

Stitch groaned. "Okay, okay, so 'boy' is off limits. Such a pain in the ass."

"Well, it's a pain in my ass that I'm not getting any," said Zak, looking at him with a slight frown.

Stitch went silent and pulled away like Zak burned him, but his gaze was fixed on something farther behind Zak's back. "The fuck is he doing here? Does he not have a wife or something?" he snarled and looked to some car in a dark part of the street.

Zak looked back and narrowed his eyes when he noticed a cleanly shaven man in a dark shirt staring right at them. He raised his hand and waved with a slight smile from inside his car. "And who is that?"

"A proper pain in *my* ass, that's who that is. Officer Cox. That man needs to get a life." Stitch raised his hand and showed the man his middle finger. "You bored, Cox?" he yelled at the officer.

The man leaned over the steering wheel of his red Chevy and shook his head with a small smile. Zak exhaled and looked down to Stitch's chest, only to spot...

"Stitch, you have come on your cut."

"Fuck. Not like he's gonna see it from over there," Stitch whispered. His face darkened even as his expression remained like carved in stone "I'm gonna be going. Let me know when you're home."

Zak grinned and slapped his back. "It's just a short drive. I'll make it there safe. Later," he said and stepped down from the porch, making his way toward the wild parking.

Stitch nodded and turned around, returning to the clubhouse without another word.

As Zak walked along toward his car, moving with the steady rhythm coming from the bar, Officer Cox watched him intently. Choosing to ignore it for the time being, Zak tried to walk as straight as possible, despite the burn in his ass. That had been a passionate quickie if he ever had one.

"Hey there." Officer Cox got out of his car.

Zak stopped in his tracks and turned around, taking a quick glance to where he had been standing with Stitch just moments ago. Why was the police interested in Stitch of all people? Was it just because of his membership in the club? "Good evening."

"Haven't seen you around here before," the officer said and leaned against his car. He wasn't wearing a uniform, but his smart, dark clothes were in stark contrast to what people at Valhalla wore. He was quite handsome, in a regular citizen sort of way, like someone your parents would like you to be with. If they agreed with you being gay in the first place.

Zak pushed his hands down his pockets and shrugged. "I only moved here recently."

"No club colors?" Cox crooked his head to the side.

"I don't even own a bike." Zak spread his hands and let them fall to his sides. "Why?"

"I like to keep an eye on what's going on in my town. You're Stitch's friend?"

"I only got to know him a few days ago. I'm a tattoo artist, so I hope to get to know the citizens as well as you, officer," said Zak with a small smile. What was this about? He couldn't ask him directly.

Cox laughed. "Ah, yeah, that makes sense. The one aspect of the Hounds that I actually like. Though most of these thugs have ugly tattoos. They could use someone like you. You're going to have a good market here Mr....?"

"Richardson." Zak frowned, not sure how to react to his new fuck buddy being called a thug. "Yeah, I hope I will find a market here."

"Can I see your arms?" Cox asked with that same smile and kept looking into Zak's eyes. Zak held the eye contact, and then it hit him. Cox wasn't keeping him here in hope to get some intel, the guy was *flirting* with him. He couldn't help but snort. What were the odds?

"Sure." He made an inviting move with his head and exhaled, watching the man's shapely body as he walked across the road to join Zak.

"That is some nice work. I'm Peter." Cox held out his hand. "I always thought of getting one, but it wouldn't be a good idea in my line of work."

Zak shook his hand and slowly moved his thumb over the sensitive place at the side of Cox's wrist. He was watching every twitch on that square, clean-cut face. "I guess that depends on where you have it. There are places on your body that your colleagues won't see, am I not right?"

When Peter's smile widened, Zak knew he'd hit the right spot. Tall, all-American Officer Cox could turn out to be the other side of the coin Zak needed. "Might be true. Maybe you should show me the best place to have one?"

Zak raised his brows and smiled. Maybe he would get some ass after all?

Chapter 8

A tiresome day deserved a good ending, and it was exactly what Stitch was planning to get. A happy ending. When he met Zak two months ago, he was a twenty-seven year old gay virgin. Now? Under the pretense of getting new tattoos and helping Zak with DIY, he was getting a piece of prime male ass twice, sometimes three times a week. He'd do it every fucking day, morning and evening if it wasn't for having to keep things quiet. After that crazy fuck in the clubhouse, he knew he overdid it. Clubhouse was off limits.

Zak turned out not to just be a good fuck either, it was nice to spend time with him, chilling in the garden, or watching stupid reality shows. Zak was addicted to watching travel shows, and was always drawing with one of them playing in the background. They gave him the right space of mind to do new designs, apparently.

Zak's house was like a safe haven, a place where they could be together in peace. Once, they fucked in the paint on the newspaper-covered floor. At another time, Stitch fucked Zak in the shower, and they toppled over. Stitch limped for a whole week. That other time, he did Zak doggy style so hard Zak had carpet burns on his knees and hands. It was a fuckfest like no other. Zak had the best ass, the best lips, the prettiest ink on his skin, and the sexiest voice. Staying for the night every now and then became a habit Stitch wasn't giving up any time soon. Even Versay accepted him as part of the pack. Zak told him the dog's name was actually 'Versailles', after a famous French palace, but they both decided 'Versay' sounded much better. He held the beast when Zak chose to give it a makeover. The pedigree poodle now had a mohawk running along his whole back, and the name Versay stuck.

Stitch made sure no one followed him to Zak's, that their relationship was kept clean and secret. As a result, Stitch became a more satisfied individual in general. He was taking out the trash, doing his own laundry, and taking Holly to school every other week. Perfect fucking ex-husband. Okay, so he did argue about Crystal seeing Milton in his house, but in the end, they did come to an agreement, and Milton got his visiting days. Stitch generously offered to be out of the house on those nights, which perfectly coincided with him needing a cover for staying at Zak's. It was also more convenient than staying at Captain's, since he had an old lady and all.

Stitch had no idea how long this honeymoon period would last, but it could last all his life for all he cared. Once, Zak even made him pancakes. Fucking *pancakes.* He knew he had arrived the moment he saw those. They had blueberries, cream, and the works. Stitch had eaten seven of those, and then burnt all the calories by fucking Zak twice in one night.

Spending so much time with Zak, he started enjoying his little quirks, like the silly habit of always checking all the locks and windows before going to bed, or the way he liked his coffee with fresh lemon juice instead of milk or sugar. On the days when Stitch stayed the night, they would eat something while watching television, play some videogames, fuck like rabbits. It felt oddly normal, and Stitch grew to love the smell of Ms. Abbot's sheets, the tacky decor, hell, even the occasional bit of gardening Zak made him do after he decided to save some money by growing a small vegetable garden. Unfortunately, Zak's business meant that he was spending more and more time with customers, but at least he would always let Stitch know. And even when Zak was working on their home nights, he had no problem letting Stitch wait for him in the living room.

Being post-divorce was the perfect excuse to avoid getting together with any girls, so Stitch was safe on that side as well. All he needed was to keep club business under the radar, and he was set. With Gator pushing for more runs, it wasn't easy, but Stitch stayed in line with club orders and in effect had more cash to help out Crystal when needed, buy shit for Zak, or even for his personal carpentry projects.

He had just finished work for the day and texted Zak that he would be at his place in half an hour. Stitch waved at the guys already heading for the bar and hopped on his bike, eager to see his... that was another problem. What should he call Zak? Lover? Boyfriend? Old lord? Even thinking the last one made Stitch cringe. He was halfway to Zak's house when his cell phone started buzzing against his skin. Being only minutes away, he chose not to pick it up and drove straight to Zak's place. It was still very early, which meant they could finish a chair they were making together. He was doing most of the job, but it was fun to be a teacher nonetheless.

He smiled, remembering all the lessons he got from Zak. What angles were good during the fucking, that Zak liked to be held down because it excited him how strong Stitch was. One time, they spent an hour just touching. Zak held Stitch's hands and moved them all over his body, made him suck on his pierced nipples. It was sweet torture, but made them both so excited that they came within two minutes after actually getting down to business.

With that thought, Stitch parked in front of Zak's house and checked his phone as he walked up the porch. It was just a missed call so he knocked on the door, like a good citizen.

Versay ran up to the door and jumped on it, barking with glee. Zak came soon after and smiled at Stitch through the small round window.

"Hey, didn't expect you today," he said, showing him in.

"Yeah, I was supposed to have a job to finish, but it got postponed, so I'm all yours." Stitch grinned at him and walked right in, petting Versay on the way. He especially wore the leather pants laced at the front because he'd noticed Zak's hungry stare when he saw Stitch in them the other day. And the stare was back, trailing down Stitch's crotch like it was already unlacing the front. But then Zak looked up and gave a low sigh.

"I'm happy to see you, but I already have plans for tonight. I'm leaving now."

Stitch closed the door and never stopped grinning. "Too bad. Your plans are about to change." He wrapped his arms around Zak's waist, but the smile faltered on his face when Zak pulled on Stitch's fingers, untangling himself from his arms.

"No, I'm serious. Come on." Zak chuckled and pulled away. "You may stay with Versay if you want. I'll be back late."

Stitch frowned at him and spread his arms. "I'm not gonna fuck Versay. The fuck? I came here just for you."

Zak patted him on the shoulder, wiggling his eyebrows. "I don't know, there should be some red lingerie in my aunt's drawers. Maybe it could improve the mood so that you two can get to know each other better."

Stitch slapped his hand. "This isn't funny at all. Why won't you stay?"

"Because I'm meeting a friend back at home." Zak moved to the door, as if he didn't care about Stitch's opinion at all. "So, you're staying? Because I need to lock the house otherwise."

"No, I'm not staying! I'm going with you. Who's the friend?" A red light started bleeping in Stitch's brain, screaming "danger, danger!". All he could think of was how he'd found out Crystal was cheating on him. And with a guy called Milton at that.

Zak frowned, opening the door. One movement of his hand made Versay sit, even though he was wiggling his tail like a mad hound. "Whoa, what's up with that attitude? And of course you're not going with me. I haven't seen him in three months."

"I just wanna know who it is. What's the big deal?" Stitch was getting more agitated by the second. Why did Zak think this was okay?

Zak frowned, turning in the doorframe. His eyebrows rose on his forehead. "Wait. Are you jealous?"

Stitch swallowed, shifting his weight from one foot to the other. "It could be anyone." Stitch wasn't gonna answer stupid questions. Of course he was jealous, Zak was his to spend time with. They had a thing going on. If Zak were a woman, Stitch would have a claim on him and no other guy would dare approach him unless he wanted to go on a date with Stitch's knuckles. But with things as they were, Zak was fair game for anyone.

Zak shook his head with a chuckle and pinched the base of his nose. "It's a friend. If you want to go somewhere else, now's the time because I need to go, yeah?" He stepped on to the porch.

"Why don't you tell me who the friend is? I have the right to know where you're going," Stitch rasped, clenching his hands into fists not to have his fingers tremble with anger. Why was this being thrown at him now? He'd had his hopes up for a fun evening.

Zak rolled his eyes. "No, you don't have the 'right' to know, but if you must, his name's Travis." He gestured for Stitch to leave the house.

"Did this *Travis* fuck you?" Stitch rasped and pulled him back into the house. Zak was *not* going on a date with some fucking Travis.

"Hey!" Zak slapped his hand and rushed out of the house. "What the fuck is up with you?"

With him? Stitch followed Zak, shaking with a barely contained promise of violence. "Simple question. Did you, or did you not sleep with Travis?"

Zak backed away even farther, his eyes narrowed. "I did. So?"

This was all the red cloth the bull in Stitch needed. "So you're not going! I don't allow it," he growled and grabbed Zak's arm. Why the fuck would Zak prefer to go see an ex-lover than spend the evening with him?

Zak stared at where Stitch held onto him, his face flushing. "Fuck off, you can't tell me who I can see."

Stitch let go of him when he saw a neighbor's face in the window of the house next door. "This is how it's gonna be?" He lowered his voice.

Zak shook his head and pulled the door shut, locking it with a flick of the key. His shoulders were all tense. "Go home, Stitch. I don't want to see your face tonight."

"Oh, so you can tell *me* what to do, huh?" Stitch sneered at him. He was *not* letting this go.

"You're freaking crazy, you know that?" growled Zak and rushed to his car. He jumped right in and started the engine never looking back to Stitch.

Stitch screamed out into the sky and kicked the wooden railing on the porch so hard he broke one of the posts with a loud creak. How dare Zak disrespect him like that? Stitch watched the car drive away, the purple flames on its sides almost glowing as if Zak was using them for speed. With a snarl, he walked over to his bike. This was crazy? Stitch would show him crazy.

Chapter 9

Zak groaned, enjoying the feeling of the machine prickling his skin as Travis added more shading to the new tattoo on Zak's neck. The constant, somewhat numb pain was just what he needed after the fight with Stitch. He couldn't believe this guy. Sure, they did have minor arguments, and he'd noticed that Stitch had been coming over more and more, something he didn't mind and in fact enjoyed, but at the end of the day, they were still fuck buddies. There was nothing that would give Stitch the right to control who Zak was seeing, or what his plans were. What did Zak miss? They'd been having such a good time for the last two months, with Stitch staying over at least twice a week. They had been doing various projects around the house and walking Versay together, he taught Stitch how to cook dried pasta (it was pathetic that a grown man didn't know how to do it in the first place), and they were generally having lots of fun.

He groaned, remembering how good it had been just the day before, when they had sex on the sofa in front of the television, with him on his stomach and Stitch gently grinding his cock inside as he clung to Zak with his whole body. It got them both insanely hot before they came. Rough boy was doing his homework.

"How are you finding your new place? I didn't think you'd actually move out of New Orleans. You loved it here." Travis smiled at him as he worked on the ink. Zak had barely recognized him through the beard he'd decided to grow. He didn't like beards.

"It's different, your neighbors actually take interest in your life, which isn't a good thing, but at the same time, it's much more peaceful. I'm enjoying myself so far, but I don't think I could stay there in the long run."

"Let me guess. You're running out of guys to hook up with?" Travis laughed and shook his head.

Zak chuckled, yielding to the cool touch as Travis moved the machine over Zak's nape. "I'm not really looking. That guy I told you about earlier, he's super hot. I'm not bored with him yet."

"Oh, yeah? How come?"

Zak sighed, remembering Stitch's lips on his, so soft in contrast to the stubble. "I don't know, he's just... sexy, and very passionate. He's this sort of butch guy who suddenly gets his hands on a man for the first time. It's like he's insatiable, and I guess I like to teach him new stuff," he muttered, stroking the leather of the tattooing chair. It wasn't nearly as soft as the skin on Stitch's sides. "And besides, he's fun to be around."

"Oh! You got yourself a virgin? Did he last more than thirty seconds?" Travis's hands were as steady as ever, but he grinned from behind his black beard.

"He's not a virgin. He's bisexual, and yes, he can last much longer than thirty seconds." Zak chuckled, wondering how long it would take for Stitch to apologize. His earlier behavior was not on.

There was some commotion in the reception room of the tattoo parlor, and Zak's hairs bristled when he heard Stitch's voice.

"Do I look like I care?"

"Oh, fuck..." Zak uttered, clamping his fingers on the edge of the chair. "It's him. It's his voice." His heart started racing with anger. There was just no way Stitch's presence here could be accidental.

"Is he picking you up or something?" Travis asked. "Lois, tell him it's gonna be another half an hour," he yelled to the other room, oblivious to who he was dealing with.

"No, he's not. I told him I had plans for tonight," growled Zak, "What a crazy piece of shit."

"Sir, you can't..." They heard Lois say, but by the sound of heavy steps against the floor, Stitch ignored her. Seconds later, the bulky body in leather leaned against the doorframe.

Travis looked up with raised eyebrows. "Well, hello there..."

From his position, Zak was looking straight into the lacing at the front of Stitch's pants. He'd recognize that groin area anywhere by this point. Heat coursed throughout his body, so intense that Zak half expected his eardrums to burst with anger. "What the hell are you doing here?"

"Just thought I'd check out what's so important. Nice place you got here, Travis." Stitch said and walked around Zak in slow steps.

"I— Thanks," Travis uttered. "Do you want to get a tattoo as well?"

"No, he doesn't. He's a controlling piece of shit who doesn't know the meaning of the word 'privacy'," growled Zak, increasingly agitated. Every footstep sounded like that of a lion rounding up his prey.

Travis was completely silent as his gaze followed Stitch around the room.

"I just wanted to know where you are." Stitch scooted in front of Zak's face. He spoke casually, but his face had none of that crooked smile he so often gave Zak.

Zak snorted through gritted teeth. "What are you? The fucking NSA?"

"I like to know where my stuff is. I'm an orderly guy like that," Stitch said through clenched teeth, and Travis breathed in loudly through his nose, pulling away his hands.

Zak blinked and with the tattoo machine off his skin, he rose to a sitting position. His whole body turned into wood. "*Your stuff?* Did you just call me that?"

Stitch stood up in front of him, imposing like a fucking baobab. "I think we need to have a chat. Travis?" He looked over Zak's shoulder. "You've got half an hour to finish up."

Zak shook his head, gritting his teeth. "We are *not* having a chat. Fuck off."

"Oh, we sure are having one." Stitch said and turned around without another word. He disappeared behind the door, leaving Zak gawping at the empty space.

"That's it," he growled, hitting the chair. "Forget what I said, I'm breaking this thing up. He's not right in the head."

Travis swallowed. "Zak, I don't want any problems in my shop. He looks like he wants to wreck something. What did you get yourself into?'

Zak narrowed his eyes. "He's not doing anything to your shop. Just look at him, acting like a big baby that can't get the toy it wants." He shook his head and rolled back to his stomach.

"These guys don't fuck around. You know that. You must have inked at least a few." Travis went back to tattooing, but kept looking back to the door. "Not to mention he's most probably in a closet so deep he's, like, in Narnia."

"You got that right. But he's all talk. Seriously, he helped me trim my dog's fur and plant strawberries in the garden. And he likes cartoons." Zak sighed, lying still to be done with it. "I guess I can't stay tonight after all."

"I was looking forward to a night out... but to be honest, you better go and sort your shit out with him. He didn't seem 'all talk' to me."

Zak growled and stretched over the chair. "I'll let you know."

*

Twenty minutes later, Zak said his goodbyes to Travis and walked out of the shop, going straight for his car. He knew he'd find Stitch somewhere on the way, waiting for him like a jealous dog. Stitch wasn't to be seen anywhere in the street, but the moment Zak started the engine, the familiar black bike roared behind him, and he didn't need to look into the rearview mirror to know who was following him.

Zak shook his head and turned back to show him the finger. He couldn't believe this... thing they had would be ending in such circumstances. Stitch was an ass, how could Zak have missed this amidst all the hot fun they had been having. He drove straight for Lake Valley, eager to just be done with this shit. How dare Stitch intimidate his friends, or talk to him as if he were his slave or some shit like that? What was going on in that dumb head?

The menace on the bike was never out of sight, and Zak didn't know if he should be happy or annoyed when on an empty road in the middle of nowhere Stitch started driving past him. At least that was what Zak thought until Stitch kicked his door.

Zak blinked, looking at him, only to glance back at the road. What the fuck was up with him? Zak started furiously turning the handle to lower the window. "Get lost!"

"Pull over!" Stitch yelled back at him, baring his teeth like a mad dog.

Zak rolled his eyes. "I'm going home."

"Pull. The fuck. Over!" Stitch's eyes weren't visible from under his shades, but Zak knew him enough to imagine just how much fire they were throwing his way.

Zak gritted his teeth and knocked his forehead on the steering wheel so hard the horn went off. They might as well talk here if that would send Stitch away from his tail. He slowed down the car and pulled over to the grassy side of the road, into the shadow of the trees. Stitch stopped right in front of him, and as much as Zak was annoyed with him, it was hard not to notice how good his ass looked in those leather pants. Then again, it was an ass Zak had no access to, so it only pissed him off more.

Stitch took off his helmet and made his way to Zak just as he shut the door of his car and leaned against it with a frown that he hoped would give Stitch the message. He was so angry his fists kept clenching on their own.

Stitch walked up to him and pushed his chest. "The fuck was that, huh? Why you giving me so much attitude? Am I not good to you?" he hissed at Zak.

Zak growled but crossed his arms on his chest, choosing not to push back. "Get your hands off me."

"Or what?" Stitch looked into his eyes with a sneer.

"Or nothing. I'm through with you anyway." Zak shook his head. He couldn't believe this guy. Who gave him the right to act all bossy all of a sudden?

Stitch's eyes went wide, and he actually took a step back. "With me? You are through with me? The fuck is this supposed to mean? You wanna go back and fuck Travis or something?"

Zak rolled his eyes. "I don't want to fuck Travis, and I didn't want to in the first place. That's not the point. The point is, that you threatened my friends, manhandled me, fucking *spied* on me, and now you demand something from *me*? You're not right in the head!" he yelled, pointing his finger at Stitch's chest. His jaw was aching from how tense it was.

"What are you, a fucking flower? I'm gonna do what I need to do. You can't just fucking disrespect me!" Stitch's face got red from rage.

Zak let out a snort. "If you want respect, then you should be respectful in the first place. I'll not accept you trying to control what I do. What did even give you that idea?"

"It's not control. It's... surveillance. You can't be with me and just go off to another city without letting me know!" Stitch walked to the other side of the empty road, breathing in deeply.

"What world do you live in?" Zak raised his hands, almost ready to yank his hair out of frustration. "I will fucking go wherever I want. It's not like I was leaving for a week."

"That's it, I can't take this bullshit. I'm not fucking air. You need to think of me when you make plans!"

"Unless you drop this attitude, don't come over to my house again. It's fucking creepy," growled Zak, looking straight into Stitch's brown eyes. As angry as he was, he knew he would miss him around. But there was no way around it.

"Fuck you then." Stitch emphasized it by showing Zak the finger. "You either ride on the bitch seat, or you can find yourself a different guy. A fucking preschool teacher for all I care." He stormed off to his bike, reminding Zak of the snarling dog on his club patch.

Zak's eyes opened wider as he watched Stitch jump on his ride. Zak scratched his head, staring at Stitch's back. Did this guy actually think what they had was something more than fun? What a bizarre development. Not that it mattered because a controlling, aggressive type was the last person Zak would want to be with.

All he got from Stitch was a swirl of smoke left by his bike shooting off like a rocket.

*

Zak came back home to a wrecked porch railing and a broken window. He cursed beneath his breath and walked up to the door, unlocking it without much haste. Versay barked from somewhere in the house. The pest didn't even greet him at the door, that was how much everyone wanted to see him today. He supposed now that Stitch wouldn't be coming over anymore, his life would get much less exciting.

He dropped the keys on the cupboard and walked in, his gaze searching for the dog, but he stopped mid-stride when he noticed an odd, darker pattern on the wood. It wasn't immediately recognizable, but when he moved his gaze all the way to the broken window, and the shards of glass scattered around a large rock, it all became clear.

"Versay?" he yelled, following the trail all the way into the kitchen where all his worries were confirmed. The dog was curled up in his basket and whimpering. The poor thing was shivering all over and when Zak kneeled next to him, he noticed all the little shards of glass in his paws. Stitch was so gonna pay for the vet. And for the window. And for the fucking porch railing.

Chapter 10

"Fuck off, Milton," Stitch said without even turning around from the fridge to look at Crystal's not-so-new boyfriend. Since breaking up with Zak, everything seemed to go to shit. Not to mention the guilt he felt over Versay getting hurt on the glass. He hadn't meant for that to happen, he had just been so angry. He got treated worse than a dog, and for what? For trying to know what Zak was up to. Big deal. It looked like homo relationships worked differently, and Stitch was shit at them. To make matters worse, he was spending more time at home, and Milton was making him crazy with everything, from his tendency to leave the toothpaste on the sink, to his choice of tea. Fucking herbal. Milton was like a fucking rusty nail that sat in Stitch's ass and never let him relax.

The only good thing that came out of this situation was that Stitch was spending a bit more time with Holly, but even that was shrinking now that the stakes at the club were getting higher. Just today, he was rushing for a meeting at the clubhouse because Gator wanted to talk about some new opportunity for the Hounds. Which in real-talk meant most probably muling drugs.

"I would just like to get to the refrigerator," Milton said in that ridiculously polite tone of his.

"Well, I'm choosing a snack, so you need to fucking wait," Stitch snarled, looking at the empty side of the fridge.

"But, I would like to point out, it isn't your kitchen time."

Stitch turned around and looked into the guy's eyes with heat rising in his body. "It's my fucking house, Milton, so I will do what the fuck I want!"

Milton's gray eyes narrowed, but he stepped back, crossing his arms over the Superman symbol on his T-shirt. Stitch had no idea what Crystal saw in this guy. He wasn't completely ugly, and not too skinny, but ditching a prime example of man such as himself for... Milton? He couldn't get his head around it.

"What's going on in here again?" hissed Crystal, rushing into the kitchen with her red hair wild and still wet from the shower.

"It's not his time," said Milton matter-of-factly.

"Crys, this is ridiculous." Stitch grabbed a sandwich from the fridge, to get this over with.

"That's not yours, Stitch!" Crystal raised her voice and walked up to him. He raised his hand up so she'd have to jump if she wanted to take the sandwich from him.

She pressed her lips together tightly and stepped back, with a flush across her cheeks. "Can't you buy your own food?"

Stitch opened his lips wide and pressed the whole sandwich into his mouth at once. He pushed Milton on his way out and went straight for the door. He was late anyway and couldn't speak with his mouth so full.

"You're such an ass!" Crystal yelled at him, but didn't follow. Like she had the right to nag him after having woken him up with loud sex sounds yesterday.

The moment he got on his bike, the world became clearer. The bike didn't have a gender.

*

Captain took a big swig of his beer and leaned over the table with a wide smile. "Just think about it. The cash we get now is nothing. Sure, it's decent money for you, could allow you to keep a woman, but think about Holly. What life can you give her now?" He spread his hands, bushy eyebrows gathering over his nose. "If we go with Gator's plan, you can send her to a private school, maybe even save some money on a college fund." He stabbed Stitch with his index finger. "Your daughter won't have to work at the gas station. She could be a doctor and treat your gunshot wounds," he finished with a smile.

Stitch groaned. "Yeah, or visit me in jail. I'll do it, you know I'm loyal to my brothers. But I want it to be done well. If we do this wrong, the Hounds are dead. There should be a better plan to it. If I take a parcel to Baton Rouge, the guys over there are gonna notice the Hounds are expanding."

Captain scowled. "You know Gator's a brainiac. He has a fucking accounting degree, I trust his judgement completely." He patted his fat hand on the table with a wide grin shining in the middle of the black bush of his beard. "Hell, maybe I could earn enough to retire in fucking Florida."

"Yeah, I can see you in fuckin' Disneyland." Stitch shook his head. "We'll just have to keep each other's backs and see how it goes in a month. I'm sick of all the shit in my life. I don't even care anymore."

"What's up between you and Crystal? For some time it seemed to be going well. What's up?" Captain drained his beer and gestured to Joe, who immediately ignored the civilian patron he was talking to and got a new glass.

"It's the living together. It's shit, you know. But if I move out I'll see less of my kid. And then I see this Milton guy. If I took care of him, she'd know it's me. I can't be stirring up more shit with her. At the moment she's fine with shared custody, but you know these things are always against us if they end up in court."

"I know man! As a guy, and as a biker, you'd have zero chance." Captain bit his lip and shook his head. "But if being there is making your relationship worse, it might push her to try to take the kid away from you. That's what worries me."

"Maybe more money will help. We'll see. But I'll try to keep my head clear at home." Stitch shrugged. He couldn't even drink, because he was picking up Holly from kindergarten later today. "Anyway, Zak's been around? I saw someone with a new tattoo from him."

"Yeah, I got one, too. He's much better than Troy," said Captain with a sly grin, wordlessly accepting the new beer. "I'd show it to you, but this one's for Melissa only."

Stitch shook his head, imagining Zak's face when he tattooed Captain's cock, or ass, or something. "I haven't seen him here though." Two weeks. Two fucking weeks without Zak were taking their toll on him. He missed having his hands on that lean, mean body. He'd even make pasta for Zak. *If Zak weren't such an ass that is.*

"You must be missing him because he does come over, at least two times last week. I thought you were staying at his on Milton's visiting nights." Captain shrugged. "Is he too busy now or something?"

Stitch groaned. So the sonofabitch *was* coming over. Just avoiding him. "Yeah, yeah. I don't wanna hear Milton's name. Even hearing it fucking pisses me off." He kicked the bar counter in a useless attempt to blow off some steam. He wanted to break things, smash a chair to pieces, but it wouldn't really help him anyway.

"Calm down, brother." Captain's hand on his forearm did nothing to soothe Stitch, but he squeezed his teeth tighter. "If bad comes to worse, you could take the guest room at mine."

"Thanks. I'll go for a ride, clear my head." Stitch got off the barstool and gave him a wave. He'd really thought he and Zak could be something stable, something to last. No such luck in the fag world apparently.

He walked out of the bar and waved at a group of girls he knew, on his way to the bike. He needed to keep up appearances. He mounted his bike and just squeezed it between his thighs as he gently petted the front. It was high time to polish his baby again. He started the engine and pulled into the road, exhaling when the air pushed back his hair.

He liked to drive around town, see what was happening, watch and be watched. It helped him think as well. But when he drove by the police station, he had to do a double take. He turned around at the end of the street and drove right back to check if his eyes didn't deceive him.

On the steps to the station was Zak. Tall, with the strange hair he was easy to spot. But next to him, with his face relaxed into a carefree laugh was no one other than Officer Cox. And just in the moment when Stitch looked back, Zak was busy fondling police arm.

"The fuck is this?" he whispered to himself and drove into the parking lot in front of the station in one smooth move. He was finding out what was going on, and he was doing it *now*.

Zak's eyes narrowed, and even Cox looked back with a frown before taking Zak's attention again. What the fuck was up with that? Once Stitch got closer, he noticed that Zak was actually drawing on Cox's arm with a pen.

"Hey, Zak. Hello, officer," Stitch said, already climbing the stairs, bristled up like a rabid dog.

"Hi," said Zak but didn't look up, busy creating little swirls on the pale skin.

"Can I help you, Larsen?" asked Cox with a lazy smile. His dumb self-confidence was only causing Stitch's anger to overflow.

"Yeah, I was just worried about my friend Zak, officer. Wondering what business he could have here." Stitch stopped two steps below them. His blood was at a boiling point.

Zak sighed. "It's all right, Stitch. Officer Cox wants a sleeve."

"Still in the planning phase." Cox laughed.

"Oh, yeah? Maybe Officer Cox should join the Hounds after he gets inked? Wanna prospect, Cox?" Stitch curled his fingers into fists, remembering how that smirking face had looked covered in pimples back in high school.

Zak stepped back and mouthed something, but Cox just shrugged. "What does than entail?"

"Oh, you know, cleaning the shitter, guarding my bike. Sounds good, Cox?" He was not stepping back from this. What the fuck? Was Zak friends with this motherfucker now?

"And what else? Polishing your cock?" asked Cox with a face of stone.

Zak groaned. "Guys, that's very funny, but let's break it up, okay?"

Stitch ignored him and pushed Cox's chest. "Oh yeah? You want that? You a fag, Cox?" he hissed into his face, his body burning with adrenaline. Just the idea that this guy could be fucking Zak had Stitch completely uncaring whether this was a police station or the fucking FBI headquarters. He would smash this guy's face, consequences be damned.

Cox grabbed his hand, and before Stitch knew it, a metal ring was around his wrist. He frowned and pulled his hand away, but he was like a wild animal caught in a trap. The other handcuff clattered around the steel railing at the side of the stairs, and Stitch felt blood drain from his face. Zak stared at him, wide-eyed from where he stood next to Cox, who had a shit-eating grin on his face. "You've attacked a police officer, Larsen." He pointed to the camera over the station door. "We have it all on tape."

"Really? That's your fucking agenda, pussy?" Stitch reached out with his other hand to smack Cox, but the fucker stepped away.

"Whoa! You're a very aggressive individual, Larsen. I think I need to call my fellow officers to make sure you don't hurt anyone. Are you drunk? Are you on drugs? We'll need to check that."

Stitch growled at him in aggravation and pulled the cuffs so hard the railing rattled.

"Stitch, stop," hissed Zak even as he looked to Cox, spreading his arms. "Come on, it was just a quarrel."

Cox sighed, his face getting more serious, but the glint of pleasure was unmistakable in his eyes. "Well I can't let this go if it's been filmed in front of the station. I'll get someone to take him in," he said and rushed up the stairs and inside. The moment he disappeared behind the door, Zak moved to face Stitch, his face contorted into a mask of rage.

"What the fuck, Stitch? Attacking an armed policeman like that?"

"He pissed me off," Stitch hissed. "Fuck, Zak, come close, from my right." He breathed faster, trying to calm down. The situation was bad enough, and he couldn't allow for it to get any worse if he wanted to still be seeing Holly.

Zak's brows lowered, but he eventually did as Stitch asked. "That's not an excuse. Lots of people piss me off, and I don't do this kind of shit."

"I've got a gun in the inner pocket of my cut. Take it, please, Zak, do this for me," he whispered, getting frantic. "Away from the camera." He turned around to have the camera on his back. Zak drew in a sharp breath, going ghastly gray. His eyes widened, but his hand was underneath Stitch's leather vest before he managed to urge him on again.

He pulled out the gun and put it in his messenger bag the moment Stitch heard the approaching stampede of steps. He knew he wouldn't be having fun tonight, but at least he got the iron off himself. "Zak... Sorry."

Zak's Adam's apple bobbed, and he stepped away, making way for Cox and Mahogahan, one of the other officers.

"Has Zak talked some sense into you?" asked Cox, stopping right out of Stitch's range. "If you behave, you'll be out tomorrow, Hound."

Stitch pouted, already seeing a few more officers looking out through the windows and laughing their asses off as if he were some sad clown in a circus arena. He wanted to spit at Cox, but managed to stop himself from stepping into even deeper shit.

"Stitch, you are one dumb fuck," laughed Mahogahan as he approached him with his arms spread wide.

Zak shook his head. "Isn't that enough? Just take him in if you must," he growled, and Stitch noticed how he kept his hand on top of his bag.

Cox nodded at Zak, removed the handcuff from the railing, and pulled Stitch along into the station. "See you, Zak," he said. "I'll call you. Drive safe."

Stitch barely stopped himself from head-butting Cox.

Chapter 11

It was late in the evening when Stitch was about to get out. Thanks to Zak's intervention, at least he didn't have to spend the night in a cell. Zak also made sure to let Cox know what he thought of the way Cox provoked Stitch for no reason, and after a bit of pseudo-flirting, Cox agreed to let Stitch out early. The fucker had actually been prepared to cuff Stitch before the shove. The gun was still burning a hole in Zak's bag (and his brain for that matter). Stitch was carrying a concealed gun, and based on some of the things Cox had already told Zak, he wasn't supposed to possess one either. What was Stitch involved in that he felt the need to carry a firearm on him? And what was up with that jealous fit in front of the station? He needed to control himself better, especially when having something to hide.

Zak took another sip from the can of Coke he was holding and checked the time for the fifth time in the last ten minutes. When he looked up, the familiar, broad-shouldered figure was standing at the top of the stairs. Stitch had his hands in his pockets, and his eyes locked with Zak's as he slowly made his way toward him. The look he was giving Zak was so intense, Zak had to avert his eyes, feeling a bit awkward.

"Hey," Stitch said when he walked up to Zak who shook his head and sent the can flying into the nearest dumpster.

"I heard they towed away your bike," he said, squeezing his hands into fists. "Thought I'd take you home."

"Thanks," Stitch muttered. "Crystal got so pissed she said she wouldn't come to get me. I only told her because she had to go pick up Holly instead of me. Fucking Cox."

Zak sighed and pinched the base of his nose. In the last two weeks, he had been doing his best not to bump into Stitch, he even went to Valhalla only on nights that he knew Stitch would spend with his daughter. And within those two weeks, Stitch somehow started looking even more delicious than he used to. His good-bye words from a few hours back still rang in Zak's ears. "Let's go. We'll talk on the way."

Stitch nodded and walked over to Zak's car. He had this confidence to his moves even now, as he just came out of arrest and barely managed to get a gun off him. "I didn't want to call the guys about it."

"I thought so." Zak moved his hand over the cool exterior of his car and unlocked it. Maybe now that the dust had settled, Stitch had more perspective on what had happened? Zak didn't want to keep avoiding him while living in the same small town. "Why did you stop by?" he asked as soon as he settled in the driver's seat.

Stitch dropped his ass next to him and groaned. "I don't know. I just saw you there with him... I know it's stupid. Is he a fag?"

Zak patted the steering wheel, pouting. Cox's sexual orientation was the last thing he wanted to discuss here. "How is that relevant?"

"'Cause if he is then you were fucking flirting. If he's not, he needs to mind people's personal space." Stitch sat lower in the seat, throwing Zak these hungry looks that made his skin break out in goose bumps.

He gave a shuddery breath. "Well, what if we were flirting? I don't get you, we haven't even seen one another for two weeks," he muttered in resignation.

"I just want to know, intel is important. If Cox is into cocks, I need to know. Why is this such a big deal? I wasn't spying on you or nothing." Stitch took a deep breath and grabbed Zak's bag like it was his.

Zak counted to three and started the car, slowly driving out of the small parking lot. He couldn't help but think about just how much Cox was into cocks. "I don't kiss and tell. I'm not gonna tell anyone about you, and I'm not gonna tell you about anyone else."

Stitch fished out his gun and put it back inside his vest. "Do you even... I mean... do you miss me?"

Zak swallowed, squeezing the steering wheel as he took a turn to the right. His heart skipped a beat, and the whole right side of his body started burning up with the electricity between them. "I... What's with the gun?" he asked, deciding to change the subject halfway through the sentence.

Stitch sighed. "It's just for security. Sorry I got you involved. I saw his fucking face, and I couldn't hold back."

"But you shouldn't have it, should you? You guys own a club and a workshop. Why would you need this?" Zak exhaled, driving slowly not to reach Stitch's house too soon.

"You never know what's gonna pop up. Some guys see a bike and try to pick a fight."

"Stitch, why is Cox after you? What the fuck is going on? I need to know this," uttered Zak, getting increasingly nervous. Stitch was a good guy, deep down, and Zak didn't want him to get into serious trouble.

"You don't. Cox is a pain in *my* ass. And not the good kind." All of a sudden, Stitch's fingers were on Zak's thigh, burning through the denim and sending thousands of ants up his back.

"I thought you don't like any kind of pain in the ass," Zak whispered, trying not to pant too much.

"Don't go there, it's not cute." Stitch never took his fingers away. "Cox has nothing on me, that's why he's so annoyed. I think I commit crimes against his fashion sense."

That comment was so unexpected, it went right through Zak's barriers, and he laughed out loud. "Yeah, I bet. Jerk."

"Jerk? You guys seemed to be awfully close. He really wants a sleeve? What the fuck?" A little smile bloomed on Stitch's lips. "That guy should get a butterfly on his hip."

Zak chuckled. "Yeah right. Just ignore him. You know he has the upper hand."

"Fuck his upper hand if I have Zak's leg." Stitch smirked, now stroking him with an open palm.

Zak bit his lip, staring straight into the road, lit only by the headlamps of his car. He couldn't help but react to the touch. "You're just holding it now," he muttered.

"I suppose I have to be satisfied with holding if I can't own," he said in that quiet, raspy voice that made Zak want to hop into bed.

Zak took a shuddery breath and for a moment thought his vision was shaking, at least until he realized it was his hands trembling on the steering wheel. He squeezed it immediately and cleared his throat. What could he possibly say to that?

"People can't be owned," he whispered in the end, much quieter than he'd have liked.

"Can I at least rent you?"

Zak swallowed, slowly pulling into Stitch's street. He was trying to calm his breathing, but it was hard with Stitch's big, warm hand trailing ever closer to his crotch, triggering little explosions along its way.

"How badly do you want me?"

Stitch pulled out his keys from his pocket and clicked for the garage to open. "I can't afford you, so I guess I will have to steal you."

"Nah, I'm cheap, you don't have to steal," muttered Zak, slowly driving into the garage, which was cluttered by tools and all kinds of trash that he didn't find interesting at all. He exhaled and stopped the car, pulling out the key. It felt like driving into the dragon's lair. Even more so when Stitch pressed on the button again and the garage door started closing. The lair had a drawbridge and it was being pulled up.

"You're priceless to me," Stitch said quietly, his eyes shining and aware.

Zak stared at him, his lungs emptying so much they started burning. With his throat tight, he turned to Stitch, overwhelmed by the intensity in those deep brown eyes. Stitch wasn't lying. It was the raw truth presented on a platter along with a still-beating heart. Zak never expected to hear anything like this, from anyone, and as much as he liked to listen to reason, the confession sent his mind into chaos. "I'm gonna kill you if you're just trying to get into my pants by saying stuff like that."

Stitch smirked and leaned over to kiss Zak's lips. It was the slightest brush of mouths, but it sent a powerful charge all the way to Zak's feet. "I'll die a happy man," he said and left the car. Zak watched him move in the darkness, marvelling at those wide shoulders and tall body. Bright light made him blink, but it made Stitch look even more tempting.

Zak exhaled and slid his hand lower, grabbing his cock through the thin denim. He refused to look away from Stitch, imagining his thick, bulky form hovering over himself, big hands holding his hips in place, coarse hair tickling his skin.

Stitch grabbed a blanket off one of the shelves and shook off the dust. He walked over to the front of the car and in one move rolled the blanket out over the hood. It felt like an invitation to the wedding bed. Stitch looked at Zak through the front window and stroked the blanket with a crooked smile.

Zak smirked, leaned forward, and slowly brushed his fingers over the glass. Biting his lip, he pulled down the zip at the front of his vest, making sure not to show too much skin yet.

Stitch gestured for Zak to come over, that sexy smirk still in place. The pull was irresistible, and Zak found himself opening the car. He approached Stitch in slow, calculated steps, sliding his hands along the deck of the car. As tacky as that sounded even in his own mind, his body was ready. He couldn't deny himself Stitch. After two weeks, the jealous fit was just a fading memory, paling with every step Zak took. What was real was the man in front of him, a man smelling of leather, wood chips, and testosterone. A man in a pair of well fitting jeans, with a bulge just below his skull-shaped belt buckle, and a tight black T-shirt under the leather vest.

Stitch enclosed him in his hot, strong arms, making him groan. Zak buried his hands in the soft leather at his back, pulled his fingers over the patches, and opened his mouth, tasting the salty sheen off Stitch's neck. The taste made him shudder and fall deeper into the hard chest.

"You don't want me to freeze my ass off on that hood?"

"Or your dick." Stitch lapped at Zak's lips before abruptly turning Zak in his arms. He pushed Zak onto the hood without too much force and hugged Zak's back, slowly grinding into his ass. That bulge was riding Zak's buttocks good and slow, massaging the outermost part of Zak's buttocks as if preparing him for the ride, slowly easing him into the rhythm. He rolled his hips and arched his back, so that not only Stitch's erection but also the hard buckle bit into his flesh.

A knee pushed Zak's thighs apart, sending a jolt of excitement to Zak's balls. He could feel the chill of metal through the blanket, but it was nice to have that bit of insulation. "I missed this so bad," Stitch whispered into his ear, tickling his skin. Stitch's fingertips slid to the front of Zak's pants and pulled open the zipper.

Zak's cock twitched in his pants against Stitch's hand, and he started panting for air, but what he got was the scent of oil and leather, skin-meltingly sweet and spicy. He spread his legs, waiting for those rough, thick fingertips to slip inside and take him in hand. But there was something he wanted even more, even though Zak found it so hard to utter a coherent sound. "Can I suck you first?"

"Baby, can you ever." Stitch pulled back, and Zak slid to the concrete ground with knees so soft he wouldn't be able to stand if he wanted to. He was faced with those thick, veiny forearms dusted by golden hairs, but his gaze already slid lower, to the big hands opening the skull belt buckle. He leaned forward with a low gasp, holding onto the belt loops of Stitch's jeans and pressing his nose to the bulging zip. It was all leather and musk, so very Stitch that his own dick almost jumped out of his pants. He shuddered, gently biting around the denim-encased flesh and looked up, straight into the hungry eyes shining from a flushed handsome face.

"Oh, Zak... Show me how bad you want it." Stitch rasped and left the package to be unwrapped. He slid his hands into Zak's hair with a firm grip that made all the hairs on Zak's nape bristle.

Zak groaned and dug his fingers into Stitch's hips, sliding his tongue beneath the fold of fabric at the front. He lapped up and down the zipper and pulled the slider down with his teeth, releasing more of Stitch's scent right into Zak's nostrils. "You have no idea how much I want it," he whispered, fumbling with the top button only to force himself to lean back. "Give it to me."

Stitch pulled down his jeans and briefs. His cock popped out, already half-hard, thick and bulging. "Come to me." Stitch pulled Zak's head closer, forcing his lips to the tip of his dick. They'd done this so many times, yet after two weeks apart it felt completely new.

Zak opened up, swallowing half of the cock in one go and cradling the heavy, hairy sack in his hand like the most precious thing he ever held. He groaned and hollowed his cheeks, savoring the pulsing meat that at this moment became the center of his world. He couldn't care less about anything outside of the garage, hungry for every inch of cock that opened his throat, and pushed its way deeper, led in by Zak's tongue, all the way past his gag reflex. He shuddered, breathing in the scent of Stitch's pubes only to draw back for air. His eyes were watering, but he smiled around the cock, and then swallowed it again, arching against Stitch's thighs.

"So good... Yeah? Get it ready," Stitch rasped, his hands cupping Zak's head like it was the thinnest porcelain. It still rang in his head how Stitch called him priceless. Right now, Zak didn't even care if it was an act or not. It felt like it was true, and that was what he chose to believe.

Slowly he pulled back and kissed the wide cockhead while slowly jerking the spit-covered length. He pulled out the condom and packet of lube, raising them in his hand for Stitch to grab. "You feel so good inside me," Zak whispered, very slowly getting to his feet. "I want it again."

Stitch's eyes darkened, and he licked his lips, pushing Zak right back onto the hood. "Spread 'em," he ordered and pulled down Zak's pants in a rush like that of an immoral knight storming a convent. His cock was already rubbing against Zak's naked skin, all hot and pulsing.

Zak shuddered, spreading his feet as wide as he could with his trousers still on. He leaned down over the hood and looked back over his arm, pulling on one of his nipple rings. Each tug fuelled his lust, sparking heat all over and making his asshole burn. Stitch looked so grand with his gaze glued to Zak's ass, his chest expanding under the T-shirt. He gripped onto Zak's hips with one hand, holding the lube and rubber in the other.

"Man, I'd love to cream your ass," he said between one deep breath and another. His cockhead was slowly moving up and down Zak's crack, licking the sensitive flesh. It made Zak's stomach pulsate, and he gasped, twisting his head back. He wanted this. He wanted Stitch's load in his ass, he wanted this cock completely bare, enveloped in the sheath of his own body, but he couldn't let that happen with Stitch sleeping around with random girls. That was the only thing that kept him from nodding.

"No..."

Stitch let out a deep breath, but put the condom on like the good boy that he wasn't. He poured some lube between Zak's asscheeks and slid his fingers in there to tease the sensitive skin around the anus. Stitch leaned down and kissed Zak's arm. "One day, I'll do it. I'll come deep inside of you so hard, you'll fall in love. It's gonna be like Cupid's arrow."

Zak let out a high-pitched moan, squeezing his fingers over his nipple, and pushed his ass into the warm, coarse hand. The vision painted before him was both obscene and beautiful, and this time, he nodded. "Yeah, and then you'll break my heart, you bastard..."

Stitch laughed into his shoulder and pushed two fingers in at once, but with the generous amount of lube, it was only a slight discomfort numbed down by his own dick throbbing in excitement. Not to mention his heart beating fast as never before. "I would never do that. I would care for you and keep your heart safe," Stitch whispered.

Zak whimpered, straightening his elbows. He leaned back and hooked his hands over Stitch's shoulders. That warm T-shirt, the flaps of the cut were touching his back all over. "You can hold me now," he whispered, turning his face to find Stitch's lips and the stubble he was becoming positively mad about.

Stitch's lips were right there, waiting for his kisses and giving them back oh-so-eagerly. He stretched Zak's hole as they ground against each other and when he pulled out his fingers, his cockhead was right there to replace them. Zak couldn't wait to have it inside. "I'll take what I can get and snatch more when you least expect it." Stitch licked Zak's lips, and his slippery dick pushed in, forcing its way through the sphincter.

"Oh, fuck... oh, God," uttered Zak as the wave of steel hard heat slid into him in one long, languid move. He held on to Stitch for dear life with his hands, with his mouth, with his ass. His hunger was growing ever stronger, and he pushed his hips back until Stitch's balls slapped his ass. He didn't want this to end. He wanted Stitch holding him so bad.

For the longest moment, Stitch just hugged him, with his cock buried deep. He left kisses all over Zak's arm, but then started making slow circles with his hips, pushing Zak back on the hood of the car.

Zak refused to let him go, and they collapsed on the hood with a loud thump. He grabbed Stitch's hair, pulling him closer. Their bodies fit together so well, hard and slim against one a bit softer, bulkier. Zak couldn't remember a cock ever feeling so good in him. It was as if his body had been waiting to accept it for the last two weeks.

They began a slow, but intense movement against one another. Stitch held him close, and knew exactly how to start teasing Zak's prostate. He was a quick learner, and in the two months they had spent together, he went out of his way to learn about giving Zak pleasure. Maybe he didn't suck cock or give up his own ass, but he was set on hearing Zak moan and seeing him writhe in excitement. With time his moves became more abrupt, and his hands slid under Zak's vest, to pinch his nipples. It made Zak's balls draw closer to his body.

He arched into Stitch, brushing his own cock over the blanket. His mind was overloading, clouded and exploding with colorful sparks every time Stitch pushed into him, heavy, fragrant with fresh sweat. Back to their previous relationship or not, Stitch was Zak's best sexual partner ever. So passionate and intense that even the tackiest things sounded sincere on his lips. He was caring, in his own way, always eager to be there when Zak needed him. What was there not to like? And that cock? It was pushing Zak right into orgasm.

"Don't touch yourself," Stitch muttered with another thrust. "I'll fuck you so hard you'll come just thanks to my cock. I love getting you off." It was the sweetest confession, but combined with the fucking that reached Zak so deep and so hard, it sounded like a promise, and Stitch was delivering.

Zak groaned, sprawled on top of the hood, with those powerful hips slapping against him like a machine. A warm, gentle tongue sliding over Zak's ear did it for him. He came with a growl he could only describe as animalistic, thrashing under his partner as waves of heat first took him to the peak, and then sent him crashing into pleasant calm. It was like diving in a deep, warm ocean, with Stitch still penetrating him like a piston.

"Best... fucking... ass!" Stitch growled, coming soon after, right into Zak's tender ass. Zak loved how it felt to squeeze around that hot rod inside him. Stitch grabbed his hips so hard it hurt, but by now, Zak couldn't care less. It was glorious.

"Pump it in, baby," whispered Zak, reaching back to caress Stitch's hip. He smiled, imagining that they were doing it bare. He hardly remembered how that felt.

"Oh, fuck." Stitch pushed in one more time. "I could come again right now."

Zak gasped into the blanket, keeping his body still. His hole felt a bit numb and tender, but it just made him smile with satisfaction. "That good?"

"Yes, I don't know how I lived without it," Stitch whispered, planting kisses on Zak's neck.

Zak swallowed hard, relaxing into the hood. He didn't want to rush Stitch, it felt far too good to be under him. "You got really good at this," he eventually whispered.

"I want to make you never want to leave from under me." Stitch gave him one more kiss before finally pushing himself up. Stitch had no idea he had already reached his goal, but Zak was a reasonable man, and he wouldn't make teenage-worthy promises or declarations. Life didn't work that way in his world.

Instead, he reached back with his hand without yet looking up. He was heavy with lazy, sweet exhaustion.

"What's this?" Stitch chuckled and pulled on his fingers.

"Nothing. Just wanted to touch you," muttered Zak, slowly turning his head and sprawling his cheek on the blanket to look back. He took a deep breath when Stitch pulled out his cock, leaving him boneless.

"You can touch me whenever you want." Stitch smiled at him with his eyelids lowered. He was the picture of satisfaction.

Zak snorted and pulled on Stitch's hand, getting to his feet. He didn't want to think about the bad blood left over from the spying. Or the broken window. "That's handy."

Stitch got rid of the condom and stroked Zak's ass with a lazy grin.

Zak sighed, looking at the large hand on his asscheek. "You know how to make a man feel special."

"Are we good?" Stitch slid his fingers between Zak's slippery buttocks. Heat rushed to Zak's head, and he leaned on Stitch, breathing in the warm scent of his skin as the gentle fingers rubbed his tender entrance. Just what he needed after that rough ending.

"I still don't have a porch railing, and the window replacement was expensive," muttered Zak, holding on to him.

Standing so close, he could hear Stitch swallow. "Sorry," he muttered. "Is Versay all right? I didn't mean to hurt him."

Zak exhaled, sliding his hand under the cut. "I think he misses you a bit. You know, you have more patience for rolling around on the floor."

Stitch nodded and embraced Zak with his beefy arms. "I know, sometimes I just lose it. Sorry."

"If you want us to be good, you can't spy on me, or trash my stuff." Zak rested his head on Stitch's shoulder and looked at the blanket, which was still wet from his come.

Stitch hugged him so tight he almost picked him up. "I won't. I'll be a good boy." He kissed Zak's ear.

Zak couldn't help but smile. "Yeah, right. Trouble–that's what you are."

"It's like a dog's name." Stitch snorted and started pulling up his pants.

Zak leaned his ass on the hood behind him, and whistled, suppressing the wide smile that threatened to stop him. It was true, Stitch was like a possessive dog.

"I'm a Hound, not a dog." Stitch glared at him as he buckled up his pants.

Chapter 12

"But Daddy, Mr. Parrot needs a home as well," Holly made the saddest eyes at Stitch as they sat on the carpet in her room. Stitch had already created a whole wall-based doll house for his daughter for her last birthday, but it looked like it only made her appetite grow. Crystal shouldn't have gotten her that parrot plushie.

"Can't he sit there, with the bears?" He walked up to the shelf and tapped his fingers on it.

She shook her blonde curls with a pout. "No, he has too many colors. Bears don't like that."

It looked like he was making a bird cage in the foreseeable future. "So what color would go with the parrot's feathers?"

Holly's blue eyes lit up and she jumped in place, twisting the front of her bike-print T-shirt. "Gold and silver! He's got expensive taste."

Stitch laughed out loud and stroked her hair. "His wish is my command."

Holly laughed and rushed to hug his leg with a wide smile. "Daddy?"

"What's up, sweetie?" He poked her nose.

She reached her arms up and jumped in place, a well-known sign she wanted to be picked up. Stitch fulfilled the request without complaint and hugged her close. She smelled of the bubblegum deodorant he got her last week. "You can't go on my bike yet, you know that?"

"I know, but I wanted to ask about something else," she said, pulling on a strand of his hair.

"Go on." Stitch held her up higher, so she could reach his ear.

Her thick fingers curled around his ear, and she whispered, "When will I have a second mommy?"

Stitch stiffened and hugged her tight. "Why would you want another mommy, Greedy Holly?" he asked, trying to turn it into a joke, even though the question stabbed him right in the chest.

Holly groaned. "Because second daddy's not much fun, and with a new mommy, me and the two mommies could have beauty days, and watch *My Little Pony*, and bake cupcakes..."

"You don't wanna watch ponies with me?" He rocked her slightly in his arms. Stitch knew more about *My Little Pony* than he would ever agree to admit.

Holly frowned. "Yeah. Can I paint your face?"

"Not today, I'm going out soon. But we can do it on Saturday, yeah?" Stitch kissed her forehead and put her down. "Be good."

Holly groaned, but nodded and hugged Mr. Parrot. "Are you going to work?"

"Yeah, gotta have money to buy that gold and silver for the expensive tastes of your parrot." Stitch pulled on one of her curls before walking to the door.

"Bye, Daddy!" shouted Holly before returning to her toys.

Stitch waved at her and walked down the corridor, ready to go downstairs, but stopped at Crystal's door when he heard sniffing from the inside. With the background of Holly talking in character voices from her bedroom, it didn't feel right.

He knocked on Crystal's door, since he knew Milton wasn't in today. With the fridge recently moved out of the kitchen, maybe he could sneak something out.

All sound stopped, and only after several seconds, she invited him in. She'd kept the master bedroom, but with Stitch moved to the former guest room, she'd made it into a larger, more elaborate version of the one she had as a teenager. That is, before Stitch got her pregnant at seventeen. With velvety drapes, leopard print upholstery, and a large dressing table with a well lit mirror, the room was a boudoir on a budget.

Crystal was sitting cross-legged on her king-sized bed, with a box of tissues by her side, and a book in her hand, even though it was too dark to read. Her wavy hair was tied into a messy bun on top of her head, but she looked natural and pretty in the black capri pants and a wide-necked white T-shirt.

"Does Holly want me?" she asked, her voice raspy.

"No, she's fine." Stitch leaned against the door frame, uneasy about entering her space. "I was just... I'm going out soon, and I kinda... Are you all right?"

Crystal exhaled, and her Adam's apple bobbed ever so slightly. "Why would you ask?"

"Come on, Crys, your eyes are as red as your hair." He shifted his weight, worried he'd done something wrong again, and it was his fault somehow that she was upset.

Crystal looked at the book, and suddenly knocked it off to the comforter. "It's nothing, really. We're still working some things out with Milton. It's harder when you're older, you know."

"Yeah, I suppose. Is he being an ass or something?"

"It's just… about boundaries in a relationship. I'm used to doing things differently than he is." Crystal took a deep long breath and started twisting the flesh on her forearm.

"What do you mean? What kind of boundaries? You know you can tell me if he's doing something off? I'd take care of it." With a nice set of signets on his knuckles. As much as Crystal knew exactly how to piss him off, she was the mother of his child, and Stitch didn't want to see her hurt any more than she was by their marriage. She was family. No fucking Milton was allowed to hurt his family.

She stared at him, unblinking, but eventually leaned forward and shrugged. "He has this side job, photographing alternative girls for a website. Some of those photos are nude, and I'm just…" She bit her lip, staring into space, "I don't know, jealous. We had a fight about it earlier today."

Stitch looked at his own feet, trying not to think too much about how he'd found out Crystal was cheating on him. "Yeah, I suppose you don't want the person you love to do shit like that," he mumbled.

Crystal flinched, pulled out a new tissue, and put it against her face. "I'm sorry. It wasn't working between us, but I should have broken up with you first."

"I wish it had worked out, you know, for Holly's sake." Stitch sighed and rubbed his forehead. It felt strange to actually have a conversation with Crystal that didn't involve throwing plates.

Crystal sighed. "Well, it's too late now, isn't it? I still want to make this family work. I know you love Holly more than anything," she said, raising her eyes at him.

"Yeah. I won't bail on you and Holly. If Milton gives you more shit, let me know, yeah?" He ran his fingers through his hair.

Crystal smiled and looked away again. "You're a good guy, Stitch."

"You remember that next time I steal your burgers." He couldn't help a smile.

Crystal chuckled and slowly got up from the bed. "If you pay for your part of the groceries, I can just cook more, and some of it will be yours. Does that sound all right?"

"Babe, that sounds amazing." Stitch exhaled with a wider smile. Were they actually coming to an agreement after so many months of constant fighting?

Crystal stepped closer and slid her arms around him, resting her red head against his chest. It felt oddly familiar, and on the other hand, it was not. She was tiny, nothing like Zak's tall, firm body, but it felt good to hold her in his arms after so many months.

She slid out of them all too soon. "Get 'em, Tiger," she said with a smile and gently kicked the side of his calf. The roar of engines downstairs was loud through the open window.

"I'm counting on those burgers." He gave her butt a sneaky pat and rushed downstairs. The nice afternoon with Holly and the prospective of being friends with Crystal again were a nice touch before setting foot in shit deeper than ever before.

When he opened the door, Captain and Gator were already waiting outside.

"Yo, you ready?" asked Gator, leaning forward on his bike, without even a trace of worry on his face.

"Yep, let's do this." Stitch nodded and walked over to the garage where he stashed the two pounds of coke he was responsible for. All three of them had one of those packets, but they were making the trip to their contact together for increased security. If this worked out, each one of them would be making five thousand, so the stakes were high.

Gator had orchestrated all this, and he seemed so proud of it, he'd be smoking a cigar if he weren't driving. "Boys, we have a long way ahead of us, we can't let Smoke wait," he said and made his engine roar.

Captain grinned at Stitch from behind his goggles. "Apparently, we'll need gas masks not to get lung cancer."

"I'll manage." Stitch shook his head and zipped up his jacket with the drugs tucked under his T-shirt in two sealed plastic bags. "Let's make this quick."

He jumped on his bike, and soon they left town, sliding farther and farther away, chasing the setting sun. Gator skipped the highways, and so they drove through small towns and townships, past beat-up buildings, and some that had been abandoned long ago. The plastic became sweaty against Stitch's skin, and burned him with each breath. It almost felt as if he were smuggling the drugs inside of his own body.

He liked the roar of the engine, not having to talk to anyone, having his thoughts enclosed inside his helmet. Sometimes, just going out for a ride helped Stitch clean his mind, but today, his brain was only getting more clouded by the mile. They needed this money, his family needed it, but if he ended up in prison or dead, he wouldn't get to see his kid grow up. He knew Gator was hungry for more, to give their club a higher profile. Stitch would be lying to himself if he thought he didn't know how this venture would develop. They would get more of the guys to mule, get bolder with the amounts they were taking. That would bring need for more guns and more guys. The expansion Gator wanted. Stitch, on the other hand, was fine just hustling with TVs and iPads like they'd always had. It was a tough nut to crack.

After about an hour on the road, Gator pulled into the small parking lot by a beat-up diner. The place was so low profile it had two unrepaired holes in the asphalt right at the front, and it allowed Stitch to believe there weren't any cameras inside. With only three cars parked in the lot, it seemed like a good transfer point.

Gator stretched as soon as he was off the bike. He radiated confidence. "You ready?"

Captain and Stitch got off as well and left their bikes close by, so they could see them. "Yeah. Is he in yet?" Stitch asked as they made their way up the wooden stairs. Because the ground was so damp in this area, the diner was mounted on short wooden pillars, so they walked up to the porch and entered, led by Gator, who moved like a king entering his stable. Stitch closed the procession and glanced around as soon as he went through the door. It was a sad place, with tables that had chipped edges and smudges of dirt on the floor. The upbeat pop music didn't fit in with the ghastly, hospital-like light coming from behind the counter.

It soon became clear where they needed to go as they noticed a table in the middle of the room clouded by smoke, with a hairy older man drinking coffee and eating cheesy fries. Stitch had to stop himself from sneering at that meal, but his attention went elsewhere when he noticed two guys who looked like they'd stepped out of fashion ad , sitting in the corner and chatting over pie. It was ridiculous how strange they looked in a dump like this, across the room from the Lord of Lung Cancer. Stitch almost bumped into Captain.

To say that they were not 'from here' would be an understatement. Stitch hadn't seen a guy with skin so smooth other than on TV. And if that wasn't enough, one had the shiniest Kim Kardashian hair, while the other wore his in a sort of modern pompadour. He wanted to ignore them, but Gator nudged him with an elbow. "Get rid of the outsiders," he ordered. Captain, the sly motherfucker, rushed to the front already, leaving Stitch to deal with the very-not-locals.

Stitch exhaled and slowly made his way to the table. He couldn't hear the conversation itself, but the constant chuckling made it clear they were having fun. The guy who faced the room, buff and dressed in a T-shirt that showed off every asset of his upper body, blinked but smiled when his eyes met Stitch's.

"You guys finished? The diner's gonna be used for private... use now," Stitch said and leaned against the side of the booth. The second guy looked up, and only now did Stitch see a detail he hadn't spotted from afar. The freakishly handsome, chiseled face was marred by a twisted scar trailing across the man's nose and cheek.

"This booth's in private use," he said in a deep baritone, leaning back. The white shirt he was wearing expanded over his chest, showcasing naked skin below his collarbones where the garment was unbuttoned.

Stitch frowned. Was this guy actually challenging him? Did he have a death wish? The one with short hair snorted and calmly had another piece of pie.

"You can take this pie to go. I think you better leave." Stitch pulled out his wallet and put five bucks on their table.

The one with the scar and long hair showed Stitch the place across the table from him, his olive-skinned, veiny arm jerking with the motion. "Sit down."

Stitch looked over his shoulder, feeling like in a surreal movie. Like one of those European arty-farty projects. Gator gestured at him with a frown, while Captain spoke to Smoke, not even noticing what was going on over here. Why did Stitch get the shit job of dealing with civilians?

"Why would I do that?" Stitch groaned, watching in amazement how the buff guy slapped Scar's forearm with a laugh.

"Come on, Dom, don't mess with him." It sounded as carefree as a butterfly on some field in Montana.

"I don't mess with people." Dom grinned and looked up at Stitch. "I eat them."

His friend started chuckling, and Stitch had the loudest freak-alert ringing in his head. The fuck was this? "Is this your next meal then?" he pointed at the laughing guy, who only got louder. Stitch didn't want to get into a stupid discussion, he really didn't, but these two civilians were asking for it.

Dom smiled at him and pulled his friend closer. He pressed a kiss to his temple without ever breaking eye contact with Stitch. It was like having an ice pill stuffed down Stitch's throat. Stitch couldn't believe his eyes. Those men really weren't from here, which was also quite obvious from their Italian accents. What was he supposed to do? Aggression would only attract more attention.

"You bet. I've never tasted meat so tender and sweet," said Dom and showed Stitch the seat again. Was this an invitation for a threesome or something? The pack of cocaine was now so sweaty it felt like it was swimming in Stitch's T-shirt. He slowly sat down and pushed the pie toward Dom.

"Better eat the fucking cake and have your dessert at home," he hissed, feeling increasingly intimidated by the way the guy who got the kiss looked at his partner. So openly affectionate it left Stitch powerless. Could he ever sit with Zak in a diner like this? Eating pie from the same plate? If Gator and Captain got a scent of this, it could end bloody for those poor, clueless tourists.

"Relax, my beautiful American friend," said Dom, pushing the plate with the last piece of pie to his partner. "Your colleagues are still in the kitchen."

"What 'colleagues'?" Stitch lowered his voice, looking to the kitchen door and the single waitress far away at the other end of the diner. He chose to ignore the 'beautiful' comment. "You guys better leave if you don't want to get your heads bashed in." He made sure to make it sound more like a warning than a threat.

Dom leaned forward and sighed, a small gesture he made with his hand enough to pull Stitch lower, to listen to the silent words. "I'll tell you something because if I weren't practically married, I'd fuck the likes of you any day. You, your friends, and I aren't the only armed people in this establishment."

Heat exploded all over Stitch's body for a whole array of reasons. No guy ever dared talk to him like that. His buttocks clenched on their own accord, but his brain desperately tried to pull itself out of the murky waters of homophobic inadequacy. Guns. He needed to focus on guns. The short haired hunk just smiled as he swallowed the last piece of pie. He didn't seem at all bothered by talk of armed men. Stitch didn't like the idea of Italian strangers with guns in a diner they were doing fucking drug deals in. He didn't like it at all. But even more men in the kitchen? He could smell trouble from a mile away, and it didn't smell half as good as the cologne of the guy sitting next to him.

"How many?" he whispered back, looking to the kitchen door. He needed to get them all out.

Dom sighed and gestured for his friend to get out from behind the table. "Your friends already passed whatever it was they had on them to Mr. Cloud there. My guess is that the six people in the kitchen are waiting for all three of you to be in one place." He grinned, but unlike so far, his hazel eyes remained cold. "See, I'm keeping your precious head safe by just talking to you."

Stitch slowly nodded, ignoring the gay aspect of the situation in favor of staying alive. When the other guy got up, the table creaking against the floor in the quiet diner sounded like an elephant in a glass store. Stitch grabbed his cell phone, to text Captain. Fuck.

Stitch froze when Dom put his finger against his chest, only to frown. The freak factor became all the worse when Dom spoke, and this time he sounded like the most local of locals, Louisiana born and bred, as if he'd pressed some switch inside his head.

"Listen, you never met us. In fact, you've never met a true Italian in your life. If any word about us bleeds out of your mouth, I will find you, I will choke you with your own cock and slit the throats of every single person you love. Understood?"

Stitch swallowed. He could lash out, punch the guy, pull out his own gun, but all those ideas seemed futile. It wasn't just the raw confidence the guy exuded, Stitch had confidence too. Maybe if they weren't dealing drugs in the middle of nowhere, Stitch would take it as a bluff, but right now, he knew they were in way over their heads, and he wasn't taking a risk on assuming these guys were just messing with him. As if the situation weren't surreal enough, the other guy, who clearly must have heard every word his partner said, looked away and stretched with a yawn, looking like some goddamn fashion ad, all tall and handsome. That was a trophy boyfriend right there if Stitch had ever seen one.

Stitch nodded slowly.

Dom snorted and eased back into the Italian accent as if it were the easiest thing in the world. "Calm down that heart. You need nerves of steel to deal in this business," he said and casually walked over to the door. Not ever looking back, he let his partner go through first and stepped out. The metal door slammed shut with a ghastly creak.

Stitch was glued to the seat, but he knew he needed to act fast. Gator had been acting with all the confidence in the world, but it turned out he knew shit, they had no idea who they were dealing with. He got up even though he wanted to sit in this booth forever. His fingers never texted as fast as they did now.

'When I come over, duck under the table. Just do it.'

He walked in slow motion, every step weighing at his feet as if they already had rocks tied to them so they'd drown quicker in the swamp.

Captain raised his eyes to Stitch. To any outsider, he wouldn't seem nervous, but Stitch recognized the slight frown, Captain's upper cheek pushing on the eye patch and creating a fold. He was tense as a string next to Gator and Smoke who were enjoying a conversation so smiley it looked almost like flirting.

Stitch approached their booth, aware of every sound in the diner. The steps of the waitress by the counter, the insects making noise outside of the window, and finally, the creak of the kitchen door. The moment Stitch heard the latter, he yelled to Gator and Captain.

"Duck!"

Stitch threw himself under the table in the booth opposite to them to avoid the onslaught of bullets raining through the air. The waitress screamed, a thud of a dozen boots resonated on the floor, Smoke gurgled, five bullet holes dripping with blood on his chest. Stitch watched life leave his body like the last puff of smoke he would ever exhale.

The seats exploded with sponge, marked with the chaotic pattern of bullet holes. The noise took Stitch's senses into overload. He curled up on the floor of the booth and frantically fumbled with the gun under his cut. Across the aisle he saw Captain and Gator, who had already pulled out their guns, but the moment they dared to fire, the kitchen men switched to assault rifles.

"Drop your guns!" came as another cascade of bullets burned out. Stitch tried to breathe as quietly as possible, but it still came out as a rasp when he met Captian's gaze under the counter. They were sitting ducks.

Captain swallowed and looked to Gator, whose mouth was open, all teeth bared. He looked like a cornered pit bull, still wondering whether he'd turn the attacker into a bloody pulp or die trying. Stitch's blood turned cold when their president shuffled closer to the aisle, moving the gun as if wanting to shoot, but Captain reacted immediately. He grabbed Gator's wrist and hissed into his ear, back arching under the table, which was now covered in fresh biowaste, straight from Smoke's head.

Stitch shook his head, slowly putting his gun on the floor. "We're putting them down," he yelled to the attackers, taking lack of bullets in answer as a promise of survival. If the Italian wasn't lying, there were six men, all armed, now in an advantageous position. With guns that were much more efficient than their handguns. He would not die because Gator couldn't hold his gun in his pants.

"Shove all your guns our way, don't think of doing anything stupid, and you might leave here alive," yelled a young, somewhat raspy voice.

Stitch watched Captain put his gun down like a mirror image of himself and finally, Gator did the same. All three of them sent the guns sliding down the aisle. "There, man, we don't want any more dead!" Stitch yelled with blood pumping in his ears. The smell of blood was getting him nauseated, but he knew he had to keep his cool if he wanted to survive this.

There was a clattering noise, which Stitch guessed was someone picking up the firearms, and after a moment's wait, the same voice told them to slowly get up, with their hands over their heads.

Gator spat to the floor but slowly pulled himself up, holding onto the seat and the table. He let go of the latter very quickly and shook the blood-stained hand, sending a piece of red mush to the floor. His scowl was so deep Stitch's stomach twisted. The whole club was likely to be lost within those deep, bloodied folds. If they got out of this alive, Gator's need for vengeance would have the force an alligator's jaws have on a human leg.

They slowly got up, and Stitch was surprised by how steady his knees were. Nerves of steel. That was what he needed. The handsome Italian would be proud.

He exhaled but kept his face cool when he gazed down the aisle, at the six bikers standing there like smiling statues.

The oldest, a silver haired man with a thick moustache, grinned and pulled up his shades, showing off his smiling eyes. "Little fish cruising the territory of the sharks. It's kind of amusing, isn't it, guys?"

His men all nodded in agreement, relaxed as if they had no single care in the world. From the corner of his eyes, Stitch could see Captain's profile. He made no sound, standing with his arms up as they had been told.

Stitch looked around to assess the situation. They were surrounded. When one of the men turned around to reach for Smoke's duffel bag full of coke, it all became clear. The patch on his cut said 'Coffin Nails, Louisiana' with a demonic hand sticking out of a coffin pictured between the two patches. They were so deep in the shit that Stitch wanted to scream in frustration.

"And they are...?" asked the boss, who could only be the Nails's prez, Ripper. The guy who snatched the coke replied with their MC name, and the Nails burst out laughing.

"What kind of shit is this? Petty crime not enough for you anymore?" snorted Ripper and shook his head. "Who's your prez?"

Stitch and Captain glanced at one another, the air between them burning with tension, but Gator stepped forward. Streaks of sweat on his bald head made him look as if he had just put his skull under the shower.

Ripper poked his forehead with the gun he was holding and laughed again, like a kid being told a poo joke. "And you thought this was a good idea? Stepping into our fucking territory?"

Stitch's hands were sweaty, and his heart raced against his will to stay calm. It was a lot easier to deal with the likes of Officer Cox. These guys weren't fucking around. They were *the* MC in Louisiana no matter how much Gator strived to change that.

"Ripper? There's only four packs here," said the guy who took Smoke's duffel bag.

Ripper poked Gator's head with the barrel of the gun. "We all know there should be two more."

Gator's nostrils flared, and he opened his mouth, almost choking on the words. "Stitch, give them the fucking stuff."

One of the men in front of them, a muscular redhead with a wild beard, stepped closer and reached out his hands with a smile. "Or shall I self-serve?"

Stitch unzipped his jacket and pulled his T-shirt out of his pants to reach the packages. He passed them over to the guy with no expression whatsoever. This was ten thousand dollars leaving his hands. He thought he'd earn five on this run, and here he was, losing ten and possibly his life. *Fuck. Fucking fuck.*

He didn't even know what hit him when Redbeard slammed his knee into his crotch. He saw stars and toppled forward, sinking to his knees with a gasp he could not stop. His vision dimmed at the edges as he looked at the red stains on the floor, and he braced himself, knowing only his cool could get him out of here alive. He had a little daughter waiting back at home for him, one whom he'd promised a bike ride once she was old enough. He couldn't have his brain join Smoke's all over the place. The next punch hit him straight in the face and sent him back to the floor, spread eagle. From the sound of it, Captain and Gator were getting a pounding as well.

"See that fucker on the seat? That's what we do with people who don't honor agreements with us," growled Ripper.

To Stitch, his voice sounded like an echo, resonating through his skull.

"I think it's only fair you pups hand over the cash and tell your friends never to step foot on our turf."

Stitch got a kick in the ribs, but his balls were still his main concern as he curled up on the floor.

His head shot up when Ripper commanded his men to hold Gator in place, and he paled at the sound of a zipper opening. The sound of spraying liquid and Gator's growl made it all too clear what was happening, and Stitch put his forehead back on the floor, pretending he didn't see their president getting pissed on. But he was close enough for the stench of urine to get to him. His body was one big aching mess, and every single bruise he'd hopefully wake up with next morning was like a fucking message from God.

He stole a glance at Captain whose lips were a bloody mess, not to mention the teeth he was baring like a rabid dog. Stitch clenched his sweaty fists, wishing he could send his brass knuckles into each grinning face.

The zip went up again, and Stitch felt the thick, ridged sole of a boot press on the back of his head. "This is the one time we let you off, so be good pups and fuck off out of the business that's too big for your paws, huh?"

Gator gasped but didn't try to put up a fight with all six guns pointed straight at them. They would have no chance. Stitch groaned, but only gave a short nod. Even if they were to plan retaliation, this wasn't the time for it. Fortunately, Captain did the same.

"Just so your buddies don't think you gave in easily, we'll make it easier for you." The red bearded guy laughed and grabbed a bottle of ketchup off the counter and pressed a steady stream over Stitch's head and face. "See, you gave such a fight, you're covered in blood all over." Two guys grabbed Stitch's arms and forced him to turn around. He didn't feel it through the leather, but by the sound of it, the ketchup drizzled all over his cut.

Once they were done with him, a sudden kick to his ass pushed him right back on the floor. He didn't dare get to his feet. They all stayed silent, listening to the heavy footsteps farther and farther away, and just as Stitch got his hopes up, with the creak of the entrance door, another series of bullets from a machine gun forced his body to almost melt into the floor.

He covered his head with his hands, but then the noise was gone and seconds later they heard the roar of bikes cutting through the mind-numbing silence. Stitch had always thought of himself as a tough guy and a hothead, but this? The Nails had fucking ambushed them like children.

Gator got up with the speed of an alligator attacking its prey and kicked something with a loud scream. "Fuck!"

Neither Stitch nor Captain said a thing. They both stood up slowly, and all Stitch wanted was to hop on his bike and head home. The staff would have called the police. They could hear the waitress crying behind the counter. Stitch didn't even want to see her face, so he kicked the counter with a growl. "I bet you know the drill, bitch. You didn't see any faces."

"Y-yes," she uttered with another sob.

Stitch gave Smoke's body one more glance before walking away. He was both relieved and disappointed to see that the Coffin Nails hadn't even bothered to topple their bikes. Apparently, they weren't enough of a challenge to humiliate them any further. None of them said a thing, and within two minutes, they were on their way back, racing toward Lake Valley with just their headlights as guides.

It was the MC equivalent of the walk of shame. Stitch didn't even put on his helmet, disgusted with the thought of cleaning out the ketchup afterward. They'd lost ten grand each, as well as their dignity. They were criminal cock-ups, like from a fucking Disney movie. Like villains from *Home Alone*.

They stopped at an empty car park at the outskirts of Lake Valley, to discuss what to tell the rest of the guys and what the course of action would be, but it was a short chat. None of them wanted to go into detail, too humiliated by the night's events. Stitch's ribs hurt, and he didn't even want to start thinking about how he would fork ten grand for the club. The debt would surely push him even deeper into shit because he had been responsible for that fucking parcel.

Gator's fury was also as clear as the piss that had hit his skull. All he had to say was talk of revenge, getting more men, more guns, and a plan to take down every last piece of shit that fucked with them. Stitch only nodded in silence. There was only one place where he wanted to drown his sorrow tonight, and it wasn't in a bottle. He needed to climb into Zak's warm bed and hug him close so he could forget all of this, even if just for a few hours.

Chapter 13

Stitch felt as if he were twenty again, climbing into Crystal's bedroom in the middle of the night. Only this time, all he wanted was to slip into bed without too much fuss and fall asleep next to his lover. Last week they'd straightened up their relationship and had made a promising new start, so he hoped Zak wouldn't feel spied on with Stitch showing up in the middle of the night. He left the cell phone he used for him at home so he wouldn't be able to call anyway. He just needed to feel close to something real.

Zak probably wasn't sleeping yet. There was a small light on in his bedroom, with loud rock 'n' roll music thumping through the glass. The climb up the drainpipe was slow, with all the aches in Stitch's body screaming when he pushed himself farther, but he didn't want to wait at the door. All he wanted was to just be greeted at the small balcony, taken to bed, maybe take a warm bath together.

He groaned as he forced himself to pull himself up all the way and exhaled, holding on to the railing. Two more moves were enough to put him on the balcony itself, and he leaned against the wall, looking at the thick curtain. It wasn't drawn over the whole length of the window, and Stitch slowly limped to the ray of light coming out into the night like an invitation. He knew he'd promised not to spy on Zak again, but all he wanted was to look at Zak, all immersed in a book, with Versay at his side. He was surprised there wasn't any barking yet, but then again Versay was useless as a guard dog.

With caution, Stitch gently leaned forward so that just a part of his face would push out from behind the curtain. His heart stopped, only to rush to its full speed when Stitch took in what was going on inside. Taken aback, he stumbled, watching Zak's long, patterned body stretch over one that was smooth, much meatier. On the bed he and Stitch had fucked so many times, Zak was twisting the other man's arm back, grinding his hips into his bare ass.

Stitch lost it. That promise not to break any more windows? Fuck that promise if Zak couldn't keep his. Stitch slammed his elbow into the glass and easily smashed the old window into pieces. He pushed his hand through and opened the balcony door for himself. The anger and hurt flooding him was only spiked by all the rage he hadn't been able to unleash earlier tonight. When the door wouldn't budge, he pushed on the door frame and cracked the old wood with a howl that came deep from his hurt pride.

He emerged from the folds of the curtain only to see Zak's wide eyes looking straight at him. Rushing off the bed and to a neat pile of clothes was Officer Cox, naked as the day he was born.

"You have got to be fucking kidding me!" Stitch's own voice sounded to him as if it came from someone else's throat, raspy and higher pitched than normal. "You motherfucker, you fucking slut!" He leaped at Zak like a doberman let off the leash in front of the butcher's and slapped his face before grabbing his neck. It fit in his hand like it was made to be crushed in it. Zak gasped for air, grabbing Stitch's forearm with both hands. He opened his mouth, but Cox was already in the background, holding up a gun.

"Larsen, let him go, now!" he said in this raw, commanding tone Stitch hated.

Stitch tightened his grip on that cheating, cocksucking throat. "I only wish I got to you first," he hissed at Cox, not at all happy with seeing him naked. He wanted to squeeze every last one of Cox's muscles through a meat grinder and make a burger.

The unmistakable click of the safety was a bit of a cold shower, even with Zak's wide, reddened eyes looking straight at him, as if he wanted to pull out his soul.

"Let him go, Larsen. I am arresting you for forced entry and assault," growled Cox, but Zak pulled away one of his hands off Stitch's wrist and raised it, as if gesturing for Cox to stop.

"You stay here one more second, and you're gonna have to arrest me for murder," Stitch lowered his voice, looking between Zak and Cox, but pulled his hand away, panting as if air just weren't coming to his lungs. What kind of pathetic chump was he to be cheated on by Crystal and now by Zak? And with Cox of all people? Zak knew very well Stitch hated Cox. The bastard had arrested Stitch just last week for fuck's sake, and Zak had called him a jerk back then.

Zak swallowed hard, his chest moving in a quick, nervous rhythm, but he didn't move an inch. "Peter, I think you should go," he eventually said, without ever looking away from Stitch.

"No, no way!" Cox raised the gun again. "I am not leaving you alone with this criminal. I am arresting him."

"He did nothing wrong," muttered Zak slowly, very clearly. "It's a game we play. He must have stumbled and crushed the window."

Stitch kneeled on the bed, unable to speak. This had to be the most humiliating day of his life. Not to mention his reaction most probably told Cox a lot more than Stitch wished to disclose.

"Why are you protecting him?" Cox hissed, but pulled the safety on again. Stitch found some satisfaction in the fact that his hands weren't all that steady.

"He's a friend." Zak exhaled and leaned forward, brushing his fingers over Stitch's hair. "Jesus, that window could have cut your hands open," he whispered, but there was a slight tremor in his voice.

Cox took a step closer. "Your friend is covered in blood. Where the fuck were you, Larsen, huh?"

Stitch wanted to scrub that frown off his face with a grater. He slapped Zak's hand away and ran his fingers through his own sticky hair. "It's ketchup," he uttered through gritted teeth and extended his fingers to Cox. "You wanna suck my fingers for a taste? Or are you here to suck something else?"

"Peter, go. I need to patch him up." Zak held onto Stitch's hand. "I'm asking you to leave my home." He sniffed, massaging the wrist slowly.

Cox stepped back but lowered the gun. "Don't be stupid. Look at him."

Stitch bared his teeth at Cox. Zak's touch wasn't helping at all. What he wanted was to bite Zak's fingers off like the rabid dog Cox always claimed he was.

"He's telling you to go," he groaned at Cox.

Zak dragged his fingers down his tired face and shook his head. "Go. Just put your fucking clothes on and leave."

Cox stood there, motionless, staring at Stitch for a moment too long before grabbing his briefs. "If I don't hear from you by tomorrow, I'm gonna break into this house, and we can have our own fucking *game*."

Stitch eyed him as he put his clothes on at the speed of lightning. If it wasn't for the fact that Cox was a police officer, Stitch would smash his handsome face into the wall. Was there something Zak liked better in that pompous fuck? A clean shave? Shorter hair? He pulled his hand out of Zak's grip, and as soon as he was free, Zak rushed for the closet and pulled out an oversized black T-shirt, which he put on, covering his naked chest and upper thighs. He said nothing and stayed in place, watching the shards of glass on the floor until Cox shut the door behind him without another word. His footsteps were loud on the staircase, but neither Stitch nor Zak spoke before they heard the door slam downstairs.

"Are we not back together?" Stitch rasped, unable to look up at Zak. He clenched his fists on his thighs. "Cox? Fucking *Cox*?"

There was a very long pause, but when the music died down and Zak spoke, his voice was every bit as hoarse as Stitch's. "You thought... we're an item?"

Stitch slowly dragged himself off the bed, unable to comprehend what he was hearing. How was this even a question? They had sex, ate together, went for dog walks, and Stitch even made him a fucking cupboard. What did this guy think they were? He looked up at Zak, haunted by the memory of how he'd first seen Crystal kiss Milton at the shopping mall. This was worse. Crystal was a question of pride, of possession. Zak? Zak had just put all the shards from that fucking window into his heart.

"You've been fucking him all this time?"

Zak scowled and crossed his arms on his chest, his posture tense. "Just a few times. He's a bottom," he uttered.

"That's it? That what you need?" Stitch whispered, afraid his voice would tremble if he spoke up. He'd done everything he could to learn what Zak liked. He'd even started considering sucking him off despite the anxiety he felt at the thought. But no, it wasn't enough. Once again, he couldn't satisfy his partner.

Zak gasped and bumped his head against the closet. "I don't understand. You fuck girls, why would me fucking another guy from time to time be so different. Is it because he's got a dick?"

Stitch suppressed the urge to once more wrap his hands around that slim throat. "What is wrong with you? I don't fuck girls! I flirt with them, I can't avoid it in the club, but I don't fuck them! Why the fuck would I do that?"

Zak made an abrupt turn and stared at him with a frown. "What? But you... hump them, and go to the back with them." He raised his hand and let it drop again.

Stitch sneered, fighting back the itching under his eyelids. "I don't fuck girls," Stitch repeated. "Are you blind? I'm a fucking fag. I've always been. I couldn't even fuck my wife properly. Why do you think she divorced me? This is some bullshit!" He kicked the broken window and cracked the wood with his boot.

Zak let out a long breath, his mouth pressing into a thin like. "Why didn't you say anything? You never said you were gay. How could I know that?" he asked in a small voice. "I thought... that we were just buddies."

Stitch walked up to him and cupped Zak's face, digging his thumbs into his warm cheeks. "I don't like to talk about this kind of shit. There is no other option for me. Either you're in, or you're not. We're not 'buddies' and we never were. We're not friends, we're not mates. I see you as a... lover. Someone to get close to, someone I can be myself with. If you need to *arrange* to be exclusive, then it looks like this dog was barking up the wrong tree."

Zak opened and closed his mouth, his shining blue eyes looking straight into Stitch's soul. "I've never been with anyone like this."

Stitch couldn't help himself and stroked Zak's cheeks with his thumbs. His heart was cut open, bleeding, and he didn't know what to do with it. He'd never actually admitted he was gay to anyone, until now. Deep down he'd always known it, but saying it out loud made it that much more real.

"It's about time to decide if you want to. I don't do half-assed."

Zak gasped and leaned forward, his eyelids dropping into that sexy, half-lidded look. "Being your *lover*?"

"Your *only* lover. I'm not gonna date a slut. Next time I catch you doing shit like this, it won't be pretty." Stitch whispered and slid his fingers to Zak's jaw. He could feel the tender flesh shift beneath his touch, and Zak snorted.

"If I weren't a slut, you wouldn't have me, remember?"

Stitch took a deep breath, unable to organize his thoughts. "I like you being... enthusiastic. I just can't share you, yeah?"

Zak smiled and gently stroked Stitch's hands with his fingertips. "And do you think... you sucking me off and bottoming will arrive on the table eventually? I love what we do, but..." He shrugged and looked down at their feet. "I'm a guy too, you know."

Stitch's stomach clenched, and he curled his toes in his boots. "I want to be everything to you," he said before he could give it proper thought. It was the truth though. That much he knew. No matter the heat his body had radiated before, now it got covered with cold sweat. His mind rushed back to when Zak fingered him. It was his mind that was against it, not his body. Probably.

Zak gasped, and his grip tightened on Stitch's wrists. It was dead quiet, with just their breathing echoing under the high ceiling. "I'd like that. I can promise it'll be good."

Stitch didn't know what to say. It was all too much. Maybe if it stayed a secret between them, it wouldn't be all that bad? He was twenty-seven, if he wasn't gonna do it now, then when? Instead of trying to choke out an answer, Stitch did what he came here for and pulled Zak into an embrace. He was so out of his depth, but Zak's arms pulling him close against the safety of his shoulder were exactly what he needed. No one ever held him like that.

"Stitch?" whispered Zak against his ear as he stared at the wooden door of the closet. "Who did this to you?"

Stitch swallowed a hitched breath and gripped Zak's T-shirt. "I had a bad night. All I wanted was to come home to you."

Zak blinked rapidly and pulled Stitch close again. "It's gonna be okay. I'll give you a bath, patch you up, does that sound good?" he whispered, petting the back of Stitch's head. It was such a sweet gesture, full of familiarity. So different from the way Stitch's friends acted toward him.

Stitch nodded and gently kissed Zak's ear, enjoying the tenderness no one else could give him. With Zak he could relax, not be so tough all the time. "I'd like that."

Zak's hands slowly trailed down his sides, and he entwined his fingers with Stitch, pulling him toward the bathroom. The house was silent, peaceful. Zak led him without putting on the light, and nothing was as soothing as the familiar sound of wood creaking beneath their feet. Zak's hand was soft and smooth, and held him so gently as if he were afraid to hurt Stitch. It was only in the bathroom that the small flower-shaped lights brightened up the darkness, revealing the familiar pink tiles, artificial flowers in a vase, and a large corner tub.

Stitch threw his stained cut to the floor, and followed it with his jacket. He was too ashamed of his failure to look in the mirror and face himself. Still, he had to ask what lay so heavy on his chest. "Do you like Cox? You meet up with him?"

Zak pinched the bridge of his nose, pulling on the piercing. "I just told him to leave."

"And you won't see him again?" Sitch knew Zak seemed to have already agreed to that, but it was like an itch he couldn't scratch. He pulled off his T-shirt and sneered at the bruise covering half his side.

Zak's eyes went wide, and he brushed his fingers over the surface of the bluish flesh. "Did your friends do that to you?"

"No. We had a scuffle with someone else. Answer me." Stitch ran his fingers along Zak's forearm.

Zak sighed and leaned down, pressing a kiss to Stitch's shoulder. "I promise not to see him," he whispered. His hand reached down and unzipped Stitch's pants but it was a practical gesture, not meant to arouse.

"Thank you." Stitch took a deep breath, trying to focus on the now, not on the humiliating past or the violent future to come. "I'm sorry I look like shit."

Zak shrugged and pulled off his own T-shirt. "I just hope you don't need any stitches."

"Nah, I don't think I'm cut anywhere." Except his bleeding pride. Stitch pushed his pants and briefs down before leaning in for a kiss, still smeared with blood and ketchup, with pieces of Smoke's brain possibly tangled into his hair, sweaty. But Zak just opened his arms and gave him the sweetest smooch, brushing the back of his hand down Stitch's chest.

"What about the hands?"

Stitch looked down at his hand, only remembering the cuts now. With all the things going on, the bleeding had gotten numbed out by his brain. He sneered at the numerous cuts on his fist and the blood dripping to the tiles. Fortunately none of them were all that deep.

Zak leaned over the huge tub, started the water, and climbed in as soon as he got rid of his boxers. Instead of settling down in the tub itself, he sat down in the inbuilt seat and looked up at Stitch, who climbed into the tub, groaning when he twisted his body in a painful way, but Zak's fingers were there to comfort him.

"Relax," whispered the deep, familiar voice straight into Stitch's ear. Warm, tattooed arms slid around his neck until he had Zak's chin resting on his shoulder. The warm water was pulling the exhaustion out of his body, letting him relax into his lover. Just like he had planned to, yet in different circumstances. He took a deep breath and closed his eyes, thinking of the one good thing that came out of this night. He set things straight with Zak, and Zak agreed to be his and his only.

Zak reached out, grabbed the showerhead, and very soon, hot droplets cascaded down Stitch's face and back. He put his arms on Zak's spread thighs and settled between them with his eyes closed. All he focused on was the now, the hot skin under his fingertips and the care his lover offered him.

"Do you want to tell me what happened?" asked Zak, slowly untangling Stitch's hair in the stream of water.

"I just want you to be here for me." The last thing Stitch wanted was to involve Zak in club matters. "I lost a lot of cash today."

Zak sighed, and the stream of water was replaced by a cold dollop of herby shampoo squeezed straight onto the top of Stitch's head. "You weren't gambling?"

"No." Stitch gently picked at the hairs under Zak's knee.

"Good." Zak started slowly massaging the shampoo into Stitch's hair, his fingertips sliding over the scalp, warming it up, rubbing Stitch's nape, the sensitive skin behind the ears. "Do you need money?"

Stitch shook his head. "No, I'll sort out my shit. It's just so fucking annoying. Thank you." He let his head fall back so he could look up at this angel in a demon's body.

Zak smiled, his face relaxing into a blissful expression as he leaned down and kissed Stitch's mouth. "You can tell me if you need anything, since now you're mine and all that."

A silly smile exploded on Stitch's lips as they kissed. "I thought you can't own people."

"You can't own them, this isn't ownership. You want to be mine, told me so yourself," muttered Zak into his lips.

Stitch raised his arms and cupped Zak's head. "But do you want to be mine?"

Zak's mouth stretched against his. "You know I do, you greedy pup."

Stitch grinned and lapped at Zak's face. "Woof."

Chapter 14

Stitch had no idea how much time they'd spent in the bathroom, but it was as if all his worries went down the drain along with the dirty water. Zak massaged his whole body with soap, and while he had done that before, it felt different this time, much more intimate, gentler. Like having all the pain and humiliation of the day washed off him with the blood and dirt. Even after Zak was done washing himself, they lay together in the cooling water, exchanging chaste kisses, which Stitch knew were just the silence before the storm.

Stitch still wasn't sure how it would play out, but there was no denying that his imagination suggested all sorts of images of how it would be to bottom for Zak. 'Bottom', the nice gay word for 'getting fucked'. None of his friends would call taking it up the ass 'bottoming', but to Zak it seemed to come naturally. With the window broken, and sheets stained with the stench of Cox, Zak walked over to the bedroom to get the necessary supplies. He led Stitch to a room on the other side of the house, much smaller and less pink than the master bedroom. It had cream-colored walls and housed a queen-sized bed, covered with yellow bedding with a pink flower print. It was so unlike Zak it hurt, but having dated women for such a long time, Stitch wasn't bothered by it.

Zak left the lube and condoms next to the bedside lamp, and walked over to the window to close the curtains. Even taking a glance at the lube had Stitch hitching a breath. It was like a promise that he'd be the bitch tonight. He swallowed and wrapped his hands at the back of his head, unable to relieve the tension. The stress that Zak had untangled in the bath now crept back into Stitch's stomach in a completely new form.

He hoped this change in bed arrangements wouldn't muddle things between them. One thing he was sure of—he was not gonna chicken out.

Zak turned around to face Stitch, unusually quiet. His naked body was dark and mysterious in the sparse light of the bedside lamp. He circled the bed in slow, languid moves, reminding Stitch of the demon cat Zak had tattooed on his chest. With his wet hair down and falling into his face, he looked like a nightmare. A hot one, like a nightmare and a wet dream all at once. Stitch licked his lips, trying to comprehend that he was about to freely give something guys in the club mocked as the worst humiliation one could get in prison. Did this make Stitch a 'virgin'? The thought made him uneasy.

Zak's hands on him felt different this time. Still warm, still gentle, but somehow they seemed like a threat to who Stitch was. Zak pulled back the duvet and climbed on the mattress first, smiling at Stitch in invitation. "You okay?"

"Yeah." It turned out more raspy than he wished it would. Stitch slid next to Zak, really feeling like a virgin bride, all scrubbed and in the fresh bedding. Was he supposed to be just passive now? Wait for Zak's move? It wasn't what Zak did when he bottomed, but Stitch couldn't just spread his legs for a guy. He couldn't.

The moment Stitch settled on the bed, Zak slid his arm under his nape and pulled him close, cradling him in the warm embrace of his inked arms. "What are you thinking about?" he whispered, moving his hand down Stitch's side. It pulled on his ribs, sliding lower and lower, all the way to Stitch's hip. In return, Stitch stroked Zak's arm, out of his depth and gasping for air.

"I think..." He looked into Zak's eyes, clear and blue even in the sparse light. "I think I wanna do it bare." If he was gonna do it, he wasn't gonna half-ass it. He wanted to go all the way, to let Zak in. Stitch's body felt hot and cold at the same time, like there was a constant power struggle in him between running for the hills and giving in.

Zak blinked and gently pulled on his hair, staring straight into Stitch's eyes as they lay in the clean, somewhat stiff sheets. His breath quickened, and Stitch would swear Zak's pupils dilated, consuming the blue of his irises. "Okay," he eventually said and stroked his fingers through Stitch's wet hair. He leaned closer, and his hand slid from Stitch's hip, stroking the line where his thighs met.

Stitch really needed to get a grip on himself and stop tensing up or this would end up more painful than it needed to be. He swallowed and forced his muscles to move, parting his thighs. It felt like jarring open the jaws of a dead alligator. Stitch pulled closer and kissed Zak's neck. Maybe focusing on Zak's body would help him relax? His hands explored Zak's side and back, learning each muscle by heart. Since he could remember, he was drawn to the masculine shape, and Zak was just like he liked it: toned but not too buff, tall, taller even than Stitch, with large palms and long fingers.

The warm digits were now teasing the inner side of his thighs, fingertips massaging the flesh while the knuckles dug into Stitch's other thigh. Smooth lips trailed all over Stitch's shoulders and neck, pressing tiny, sensuous kisses to his tense skin. It was pleasant, and he could imagine he'd be mad with lust if it weren't for the fact that he knew how this night would end for him. This knowledge was always in the background, ready to kick him in the balls.

Zak bit into Stitch's ear. "I've never met a guy as hot as you."

Stitch chuckled and wrapped his arms around Zak's chest. "Tell me more." He rubbed his cheek against Zak's, feeling as if the soft mattress was swallowing him into a whole new world where he hadn't lost ten grand and where he and Zak could fuck without fear.

Zak drew in a sharp breath against his cheek, triggering explosions of sensation all the way down Stitch's back. "You're so incredibly intense. When you look at me, I know I can trust you. This never happened before," he whispered, and his hand rapidly climbed higher between Stitch's thighs, pressing against Stitch's balls.

Stitch groaned in pleasure. That he knew, so he leaned into the touch. His own fingers slid down Zak's back, exploring every ridge of his lover's spine. He also had never felt so obsessed with anyone. The sex with girls was incomparable. It was nice to be touched, but the softness of their skin, the breasts, the pussies... it didn't do it for Stitch like Zak's body, his ass, even the cock he would willingly let in tonight.

Zak pulled him closer, opening up Stitch's lips with his tongue and kissing him so deep that Stitch shook with the sensation. Those long fingers squeezed around his scrotum only to trail higher, stroking the length of Stitch's cock in the same lazy but confident way he already knew so well. Letting his hands trail to Zak's ass was like a well-known, but exciting routine. Stitch loved those inked buttocks so much, he would pay to have a photo of those framed and put on his ceiling so they could be the first thing he saw when he woke up.

His only slightly stiffened cock was now waking to life as Zak stroked it.

The small balls of Zak's piercing teased Stitch's lip even as he was withdrawing to look Stitch in the eyes. "You know what I want to do today? Slide into the hottest ass I have ever seen." He leaned down, nuzzling Stitch's ear. "I will cream you with all I've got. You have no idea how long I have been thinking about this," he uttered in this hot, raspy voice, squeezing Stitch's cock tight.

Stitch could hardly breathe, but only held on tighter to Zak's ass. So maybe the no condom thing wasn't playing out the way he imagined it, with him on top, but the idea of having their sweaty bodies together, and come spurting freely, got his balls to tighten. Feeling Zak's cock, hot and throbbing against his thigh, was getting Stitch more into the mood. A sense of pride and vanity did push to the surface when he heard such good things about himself. That it was him who was the prize. He was sure his nerves would ease after they did it for the first time. He was a fucking Hound, there was no way he would be scared like a Catholic school girl on the night she gets her cherry popped.

And as if responding to his thoughts, Zak flipped Stitch to his back and slid between his thighs, grinding their hips together as he rushed forward, nipping on Stitch's wide-open lips. "And you know what that means, baby?" whispered Zak, grunting with each push of his cock against Stitch's balls. His hand squeezed over Stitch's nape, gently pulling on it. "I'm gonna let you do me too, all bare and sweaty. You'd like that, huh? Empty your balls down my tight asshole?"

Stitch's lips parted, and he opened his eyes. The idea went straight from his brain to the tip of his cock. He arched against Zak and groaned, spreading his legs for a better fit. "Oh, fuck yes," he hissed and bit on Zak's bottom lip. "You'll be dripping with my spunk."

Zak grinned at him and made a circle with his hips, bringing their cocks together. The metal of his nipple piercings kept brushing over Stitch's skin like cold fire. "Fuck the rules, yeah?" he whispered, descending down Stitch's chest. He was trailing wet, openmouthed kisses all over the hypersensitive skin, closer and closer to Stitch's cock.

Wasn't that the way of the outlaw after all? Why the fuck should Stitch be constrained by rules? Wasn't lack of them what he loved about the biker lifestyle in the first place? Some arrangements made sense: don't rat, have your brothers' back, don't mess with another guy's bike, but cocksucking, ass-fucking? Why the fuck would anyone in the MC care whom he fucked? Because someone believed it's disgusting? Hell, he thought Freddy puking all over the pool table was disgusting, and no one kicked *him* out.

"Fuck the rules." Stitch bit his lip, looking down and already awaiting those skilled lips.

Zak, shameless as he was, grinned at him from between Stitch's legs and descended on his hard cock like a hungry panther. The raw need on that handsome face made Stitch's cock bob over his stomach, which in turn got Zak to open his eyes wider. "He needs some love," he whispered, sucking on the base of the cock.

"Oh, yes... he does," Stitch groaned and arched up his hips. He was proud that after three months of intense fucking, he wasn't coming within two minutes of sucking anymore. They could extend their sessions and explore. But this time, he just wanted to lie back and feel that sweet, warm mouth opening up to him, the spongy surface of the tongue arching beneath his shaft as it slid farther into Zak's throat. A moment of pure bliss turned even better when Zak pulled back, holding Stitch's dick up and sucking on the head, flicking his tongue over the sensitive flesh just beneath the cockhead. Even the long fingers sliding over the skin of Stitch's ass couldn't distract him.

"That feels so good, Zak." Stitch relaxed into the touch as more blood pumped down his body, getting his dick rock hard in that delicious mouth. He loved how the lip piercing ran along the sensitive skin on his penis, giving Zak's blow jobs that edge.

Zak hummed around his cock, vibrating like the bike, but his finger slowly moved in between Stitch's buttocks, pushing the flesh apart as it went for its goal.

"Wait," Stitch grabbed Zak's hair for lack of better idea what to do.

Zak groaned but pulled away, letting the cock slip out of his mouth with a loud slurp. "Hn?" he muttered, biting his reddened lip.

"I'll turn around, yeah?" Stitch just couldn't bear being watched, too afraid everything he was feeling would surface to his face like dead fish after a dynamite blast on the bayou.

Zak sighed and turned his face to kiss Stitch's thigh. "If that's what you want." He slowly pulled himself up and reached for one of the pillows, his hands never leaving Stitch's skin. "I will make it good for you, I promise."

"I just... don't know how it *should* feel, so I'll go with the flow." All Stitch knew was that when he fucked Zak, Zak whimpered, writhed, and sometimes came from just that. It had to be some kind of good. He turned around, never before feeling this self-conscious about showing his ass to a guy.

Zak was right next to him, pushing the thick pillow under Stitch's hips. He was breathing hard but behaved like a real gentleman, not rushing Stitch in any way. He leaned in, kissing him softly. "It's probably gonna hurt in the beginning, but I think you already know that," he whispered, putting an arm over Stitch's back.

Stitch took a deep breath and nodded, taking another pillow and hugging it to his chest, his back feeling scrutinized. Then again, he was proud to be a Hound of Valhalla and imagined the tattoo on his back would provide a nice view for Zak. Stitch's cock pulsed in a steady rhythm, trapped between his stomach and the soft pillow.

He felt the mattress shift behind him, and when Zak's hands gently pushed on his inner thighs, he spread them without a word. Zak's fingers trailed up and down his back, all the way to the back of Stitch's thighs, but eventually rested on his tense buttocks. The silence in the room was complete until Zak made a low, shuddery rasp. "I'm so fucking horny right now."

Stitch flexed his back muscles in an attempt to look more impressive. His thighs were getting sweaty, but he still said, "I'm ready. Go on." He was actually looking forward to feel Zak's firm body on his back, the nipple rings teasing his skin, but what came next was the wet softness of Zak's tongue sliding all the way along his crack and then back. His body was in a strange place between relaxation and sudden tension as his stomach burned with numb need.

Stitch opened his eyes wider and looked over his shoulder, even though Zak's face was buried between his asscheeks. "Y-you sure?" he uttered, but it was just a courtesy question. All the nerves down between his buttocks yearned for more attention from that hot, slippery muscle. He parted his thighs more. He never expected this to feel so... good, but his hole was opening up to the soft invasion.

Zak moaned, digging his fingers into Stitch's flesh as he lapped along the crack, paying special attention to the asshole. It was such an overwhelming feeling that Stitch's thighs started trembling. "You taste like a real man. So fucking good," whispered Zak.

Stitch didn't even think about it when he raised his ass slightly, loving the touch, so firm and gentle at the same time. And the compliment? Only making him feel more comfortable. He let the pillow swallow his face and moaned as his dick was back to a steady pulsing again.

Zak's breath was bathing him in warmth, and Stitch's pulse rose even more when Zak trailed his tongue lower and gently nipped on the taint. His hands were roaming his buttocks and thighs, gently massaging the flesh and holding Stitch's ass apart for the licking, kissing, even sucking of the sensitive skin right next to his anus.

It was head-meltingly good, and only got better when the hot muscle probed his hole. Best of all, Stitch didn't feel like a bitch, or even a girl. He arched his back, as masculine as ever, groaning to be pleasured. In a way, it did remind him of getting a blow job, with less control than he had on top. The realization only made him ponder sucking Zak off. Taking control of his dick like that and teasing him to orgasm.

"Oh, God," he muttered when Zak's tongue screwed his ass like it was the best thing since the invention of a deep-fried Mars bar.

"Yeah, you like it when I eat you out?" mumbled Zak into Stitch's hole, lapping and sucking all over it before going into him in earnest. His tongue stabbed right inside, all the way in like Stitch imagined Zak's cock would later. The idea didn't seem all that threatening anymore. Zak was groaning in pleasure, grabbing onto Stitch's buttocks.

"It's good, yeah," Stitch muttered into the pillow, enjoying being the center of Zak's attention and being taken care of.

Zak laughed, a hoarse, pleasant sound, and started slowly, methodically thrusting his tongue all the way up Stitch's ass. It was such a strange sensation, being fucked this way, both dominated and dominant, with a man's face between his buttocks. It wasn't long before there was a fingertip rubbing the flesh right next to the invading tongue, trying to sneak in. It was the sweetest torture Stitch could ever imagine. He stirred his hips, unable to keep still. His cock, trapped in the heat under his belly, yearned to get into a rhythm of rubbing on something. Not to mention his anus started pulsing in the strangest way. Stitch was not about to pull away, but on the other hand he was torn about asking for more. What kind of guy would he be if he asked for it?

Fortunately, he didn't have to, as the fingertip slipped into the vacated hole. Stitch shuddered when the knuckle of Zak's hand touched his ass and the finger gently wiggled inside. "Wow," uttered Zak. "You feel amazing."

A moan forced itself out of Stitch's lips as he gripped the pillow, trying to keep himself in check. It felt so... weird, but didn't hurt, thanks to all that tongue work. He wouldn't have done this three months ago, but now? Stitch was lost and he would give anything to his man.

Zak's warm hand trailed up Stitch's back, steadying him for the slow but deep thrusting he was doing with a single finger. The moves were becoming more and more bold as Stitch's hole relaxed even further.

Stitch was starting to sense a strange pressure deep inside that he couldn't pinpoint. His body was giving in as Zak accelerated the thrusts, slapping his hand against Stitch's ass over and over again.

There was a shame to feeling this good about the fingering, but with just them in the room, it was getting easier to forget it with each jolt of pure, fresh squeezed lust to his balls. Stitch grunted into his new beloved, the flowery pillow. He hugged it and didn't even notice when he started moving his hips against the other one. A deep heat gathered in Stitch's chest, and a little voice in his head kept urging him to ask for more, telling him that it would be good to feel Zak sliding his cock inside, all bare and ready to spurt come inside of him.

But he didn't have to ask. There was pressure at his relaxed hole, and slowly, very slowly Zak screwed in two fingers. He kissed Stitch's spine, petting him with the other hand. He was taking it slow for Stitch's sake, spreading him with those two fingers, moving them in and out faster and harder as Stitch's tolerance grew. Then, with a sudden change of angle, Stitch saw fireworks exploding beneath his eyelids as intense pleasure spread all around his stomach and pulled on his balls.

"Oh fuck!" He scrambled to his knees, overwhelmed by the touch. This had to be the prostate Zak was so eagerly on about. It all made a lot of sense now. Stitch's breath trembled, and he really wanted to be done with the fingers. He wasn't some flower that had to be pampered for ages. The fingers were fucking him in earnest now, Zak's fist slamming against his butt like he imagined his balls would once they'd get on with the real thing.

He let out a low groan when Zak's hand slid all the way up to his nape and pulled his head up by the hair. Stitch's whole body was a minefield, where every single touch could end up with an explosion of sensation so intense it made his cock drip. The pangs of pain in his ribs only messed with his mind and made the pleasure more intense in comparison.

Stitch let Zak pull his hair with no complaint, and even pulled up to his elbows, open to his lover like to no one ever before. It was like getting his soul pulled out for inspection. He couldn't help but tense his ass on the fingers every now and then when the pressure was too much.

The third finger stung a bit, but it was nothing he couldn't handle, especially with Zak whispering into his ear about how he loved Stitch's muscular body. He was moving the digits in Stitch's anus in a gentle circular motion, spreading him farther in preparation for the main dish.

Stitch's whole body trembled, unable to comprehend all the sensations it had to process. The strangest thing was, he didn't feel like this feminized him at all. With a guy like Zak next to him, Stitch felt as masculine as ever even when he was about to take a cock up the ass. He didn't even bother to muffle his moans and grunts, too lost in the moment.

"You ready for me now?" whispered Zak, pushing his fingers in deep as he bit into Stitch's shoulder blade. Only now that he leaned closer did Stitch notice him trembling slightly.

"Yes," was all Stitch managed to breathlessly choke out. He was getting exactly what he came for here tonight. He was getting lost in Zak and letting go of the outside world, connected to his lover only. With Zak he didn't have to pretend. He fell back down, with his ass up high and his cheek on the fresh pillow. There was the sharp sound of plastic, and soon after, the fingers were gone, but he wasn't empty for long with a blunt cockhead pressing at his entrance slowly, gently. Zak gasped behind him and pressed one of his hands into the small of Stitch's back. He was radiating heat so intense it almost burned.

"Oh, fuck... bear down on me, baby."

Stitch swallowed, suddenly unsure if he could actually take all that cock. There was lots of lube though, it should be fine. His breathing got completely erratic with a sudden panic that ambushed him when he least expected it. Zak's hand on him felt good, but everything else was a blur, and Stitch was sure it would be until he found out what being fucked felt like.

"Stitch? You okay?" Zak's hair brushed over his spine as his lover leaned down to kiss his skin. And that cock was still there, waiting for the green light.

"Yeah, I just... It's all a bit much," he said between one deep breath and another. The hot cockhead at his sensitive anus had him excited even if just for the reason that it was Zak's dick between Stitch's buttocks.

"Sure," uttered Zak, and his rock hard cock slid all the way down the taint, just to trail its way up Stitch's crack. It only reminded Stitch of how good the rimming had felt.

"I didn't say you should stop."

Zak drew in a sharp breath. "You know I'm all ready for you," he whispered with one more kiss, but his cock was back at the starting line, ready to breach. A bit more lube poured between Stitch's buttocks, and then Zak pushed in with one strong thrust, holding on to Stitch's hip. The world shrank down to the sharp but short-lasting ache in his ass. Stitch didn't even know when, but he gripped on the sheet so hard his knuckles went white. No matter how he stirred his hips, Zak's cock was now there, with the pulsing shaft stretching Stitch's sphincter. Breath caught in his throat. It was all too much, even though it wasn't at the same time, because there would never be too much of Zak for Stitch.

Zak shuddered on top of him, and with a rapid move, his warm hand was against Stitch's ass. "Oh, God, you're so tight, baby. So tight," he rasped, burying his face and still wet hair against Stitch's spine. His breath was caressing Stitch, soothing him even as the pulsing pain continued making him stiffen up against the intrusion.

Stitch's body was torn where his mind was already set. He could hardly breathe, even with the neverending, fervent kisses constantly showering his back. He imagined he'd be embarrassed to hear words like this from a man, but he only felt appreciated, excited, and ready to be free of society's constraints. His lover was clearly turned on like a dog in heat, his own dick throbbed and dripped with precome, and both their bodies were on fire. Stitch let go of his inhibitions and slowly circled his hips against Zak's. Even with his ass hurting slightly, it was nothing like what he'd experienced earlier tonight.

Zak groaned, rolling his head over Stitch's back. His mouth was there, sucking, biting, pulling on the skin as he pushed his cock farther in, shivering. His hand was all the way up on Stitch's nape, but it wasn't a gesture of dominance, it felt as if Zak was protecting him, calming him down with this simple gesture. His hips were making tiny, shallow moves, but even that was straining, the thick meat making Stitch's tight flesh burn. But the more they ground into one another, the more pain seemed to disperse, replaced with wonderful friction, generating a heat that enveloped Stitch's whole groin, stomach, legs, chest.

"You good?" whispered Zak, sliding his free arm around Stitch.

"You're so hot and amazing," Stitch said, surprised by how his voice trembled. Having Zak's dick inside, pushing and throbbing, was so intense he barely managed to speak at all. He never thought it would be so freeing to do this. His knees were too strained, so he slowly slid back to the covers with Zak on his back. His thighs shook with the effort, but his pride wouldn't let him just collapse. When he lay on his stomach, his ass only clenched on Zak's cock harder. All the emotions rolling over Stitch's body were simply too much. He had to close his eyes to stop the stinging underneath his eyelids. Only it didn't work.

The room was silent, coming alive only with the sounds they were making. Tiny groans, gasps, the occasional moan, skin slapping on skin, the scratching of Zak's fingers over Stitch's back, the crisp bedsheets rustling, the gentle creaking of the bed somewhere in the background. It was so pure and wonderful, just what he needed to feel safe and cherished, with nothing distracting Zak from him. That strong wonderful body was trembling every time Zak pushed his cock in, every time he pulled out. He was being slow and gentle, but still stopped from time to time, clearly giving himself a moment to calm down. No one had ever wanted Stitch that much. And with that cock making Stitch feel so incredibly good, warm and soft inside, it was getting harder and harder to control himself.

Stitch was open to each of Zak's moves, his own cock stiff as steel and twitching each time Zak's cock brushed against Stitch's prostate. It was bliss. Stitch pulled one of his arms back to stroke Zak's ass, the skin so hot and tense under his fingertips. He was overwhelmed by just how at ease he felt with this man. A deep sob was building up in Stitch's chest, and he couldn't push it back. It surfaced with all the other memories. The divorce, the arguments with Crystal, messing up at cooking, Zak cheating, Smoke's body mauled with bullets, losing all the drug money, the impotence of not being able to fight back. He could let all that go with the man he loved.

He dug his fingers into Zak's skin and let go for the first time in years, without even trying to muffle his sob.

Zak stilled over him before quickly pulling him into a close hug. His mouth was right next to Stitch's ear as he spread his body over Stitch's back all the way, with his cock lodged deep inside. "What is it? Do you want me to stop?" he asked, breathless.

"No, please, be close to me," Stitch whispered, feeling the wetness under his eyelids. He lived in a culture where being tough was the only currency. He didn't even cry when he was alone. Being able to let it out made him just as relieved as having the amazing hot body on top of him. Made him remember he was still human, not a man whose muscles were made out of violence and bones out of fury.

Zak's hand slid under Stitch's jaw and turned his head to the side, just in time to meet his lover's hungry, fervent lips. In comparison to the primal rhythm of a cock pushing into Stitch's ass, the kiss was surprisingly gentle, and he couldn't bring himself to break it despite the pain in his back and neck.

Zak growled into his mouth like the animal he was, his hips slamming against Stitch faster. Harder. Stitch knew Zak was going to come soon, so he moved with him, rubbing his own dick against the pillow and only stimulating the thrusts. The thought that Zak was bare and would be coming inside of him had his cock eager to join the orgasm bandwagon. Stitch was close, so close. He moaned, kissed, bit, uncaring if Zak saw him crying or not.

Within seconds, Zak's mouth fell off his with a sharp gasp, his cock slammed into Stitch with two powerful stabs only to remain there, buried to the hilt as Zak's body became a burning hot statue. His cock was pulsing with a well-known rhythm, spilling right into Stitch's willing hole, filling him up, creaming him, and yet Stitch felt as masculine as ever. He wasn't 'serving' another man, they were doing this together. With the pillow not being a good enough lover after all, Stitch made the effort of lifting Zak slightly and reaching to his own cock for a quick jerk off. His ribs hurt, but nothing could distract him from the thought of sweat, come, and hot, firm muscle. Stitch was more aware of his body than ever, but his body wasn't his anymore, it was connected to Zak's. He came with the lowest of grunts, with his ass clenching over the hot meat still throbbing in him. His balls pulled up when he stained the pillow with more spunk than he imagined to have.

Stitch panted, his whole body trembling with in the aftermath of the visceral orgasm. It felt as if it wasn't even his. As if he were reliving the orgasm he felt inside of himself just moments ago.

Zak whimpered, brushing his fingers over Stitch's sides. His breathing was coming in sharp pants, even more so when he slowly moved, his cock slipping out of the hole with a sloppy sound. "Oh, fuck," he whispered, moving the back of his hand over Stitch's ass as if it was something delicate and pristine.

Stitch lay in the stained sheets, out of breath and pumped out. "That was... wow. You're so fucking good."

Zak's exhale turned into a breathless laugh. He pushed on Stitch's arm and rolled him onto his back. With his face flushed red and a big smile on his face, he looked like the happiest man alive. "You have no idea how hard it was for me not to come right away. You're so fucking hot you make me turn into a teenager," whispered Zak, landing in the covers next to Stitch. He immediately rolled closer and pulled him against his chest. The movement made sperm drip out of Stitch.

Stitch hugged Zak close and smiled back. "Did the teen-Zak wet himself over fucking a big, bad biker?" He kissed Zak's sweaty forehead. Just a few hours ago, Stitch wouldn't even consider bottoming, and now it felt like the best idea on the planet. He felt so light he could fly.

Zak grinned, pulling Stitch into the safety of his tattooed chest. He rested one hand on Stitch's hip and nuzzled his cheek. "Can't you tell? I think you're pretty hydrated, Mr. Biker."

"You liked it bare?" Stitch took a deep breath and fit his face into Zak's neck. He watched the inked chest expand and listened to the quick, healthy heartbeat.

"It was... amazing," whispered Zak, seeking Stitch's fingers with his hand. "Never done this bare before, and you... agreeing to this, letting me come inside you. I just... don't know what to say without making it seem cheaper than it was, you know."

Stitch squeezed Zak's hand and delighted in a slow kiss. "My inhibitions were bullshit. Now I know. I had the shittiest day and you made it better. Thank you."

Zak pushed his fingers into Stitch's hair and looked into his eyes. His were this beautiful, deep blue that Stitch could look into all the time. It was different to lie in Zak's arms for a change, him being a bit sore in a way that Zak sometimes mentioned but Stitch could never understand. It really was pleasant, hot, tender. A remainder of being so close with another man, closer than he ever imagined.

"I'm here to serve," chuckled Zak, but his face became more serious when he leaned in for another kiss. "You are an amazing man. Nobody's anything like you."

"I love you," Stitch whispered and kissed Zak's lip piercing. Everything about his man was perfect.

Zak stared at him, his eyes going wide, still glossy from the sex.

Stitch shook his head with a smile. "You don't have to say it back. I just want you to know."

Zak took a shuddery breath and blinked, leaning in for a deep, sensual kiss that took Stitch over the moon with its raw need. But good things come to an end, and Zak pulled away, keeping their foreheads together. "You make me feel all those things, you stupid man," he grunted, gently punching Stitch's chest.

Stitch wrapped his arms around Zak's waist and kept kissing those glorious lips. He knew tonight, he'd sleep like a baby.

Chapter 15

Stitch looked around the bathroom for his cut. He was sure he'd left it here the night before with the rest of his clothes, but it was nowhere to be found.

"Hey, Zak?" he yelled from the shower as he toweled himself off. "You seen my cut?"

The door opened, and when he looked back through the wet plexiglass, he stared straight into Zak's smiling face. "Yeah, it's all ready for you downstairs," said Zak, slipping into the steamy bathroom in just his narrow jeans. Stitch flinched at the sight of the bruises on Zak's neck, but tried to erase the memory of the fight from his mind no matter how persistently the ugly marks stared at him in accusation.

Stitch paused for a moment, remembering the ketchup-stained patches. Zak was the sweetest thing ever. Stitch had already thought he wouldn't be able to wear his cut when it was so desecrated. He got out of the stall and started putting on the rest of his clothes. He was worried he'd feel awkward with Zak after yesterday, but there was no shyness at all. Stitch closed the distance between them and gave Zak a kiss.

The soft mouth stretched into a smile, and Zak put his arms around him, uncaring that he'd get wet. He'd been out of bed when Stitch woke up, but the smell of frying bacon had been like a soothing blanket on his shoulders. Stitch fell asleep again and let his lover wake him up with the breakfast of the gods, which they ate cuddling, without a trace of awkwardness or tension.

"Will you be ready to go soon?" asked Zak, gently petting the small of Stitch's back.

"Yeah, I gotta go. We're gonna have a club meeting later." Stitch gave him one more kiss and pulled away to put on the rest of his clothes. His skin tingled when Zak brushed his hand over Stitch's buttock and walked out. The dynamics of their relationship felt different now, but not bad at all, so since he couldn't pinpoint it, he stopped trying. Anyway, they wouldn't be doing the same thing tonight. Or maybe even for a few days, because his ass felt tender as a prime cut of beef.

He combed his fingers through his hair and walked out, ready to face the world. He didn't care if no one knew, but he was stronger today than he was the day before.

As he walked down the stairs, Zak was sitting on the floor with Versay between his legs and a cup of his ridiculous coffee—black with lemon pieces. The dog immediately rushed up the stairs to meet Stitch, his tail wagging like a windscreen wiper during heavy rainfall. The poor thing didn't know who hurt his paw.

"Hey, boy." Stitch bowed to stroke his head, but groaned when pain reminded him about the aching ribs. "Have a good day, yeah?" He smiled at Zak, who already pulled himself up and walked over to a chair where he'd left Stitch's cut. In the bright daylight Stitch could see without a doubt that the patches had been thoroughly cleaned.

"Will you be in tonight?" asked Zak, grabbing the cut. He held it up for Stitch to slip into. It was the sweetest gesture Stitch never wanted to part with. He let Zak put it on him, and it felt like his armor for the day.

"I will."

"All right, I'll get some Chinese for us, yeah?" Zak put his arms around Stitch's neck and kissed him again, pliant and sweet as candy.

"Sounds good to me." Stitch extended the good-byes as much as he could, not wanting to leave yet, but it was time, so in the end he said one more 'bye' to Versay and left the house.

It was only when he approached his bike up close when he noticed the front tire was flat. And the back tire. "The hell?" He scooted next to the bike and ran his fingers along the punctured rubber. He knew exactly who did this to his mount. "Motherfucker!" he screamed out.

"Stitch?" shouted Zak from the door. "What is it?"

"Cox slit my fucking tires!" Stitch put his arms up in frustration. He wanted to strangle the fucker, but there was no one to take his anger out on.

The door slid shut. "You want me to give you a lift? I'm going to town anyway," said Zak after a moment of poignant silence as he rushed down the stairs.

"Fucker doesn't know who he's messing with," Stitch snarled, circling the bike to check for other damage, but there was none, fortunately. This was *war*.

"Don't do anything reckless," muttered Zak as he joined Stitch by the motorcycle. In the bright sunlight, it looked ready to hit the road, even though, sadly, it wouldn't.

"You don't mess with another man's bike, Zak. He should damn well know this. And he's the cop here!" Stitch took a deep breath. He couldn't deal with this now. "Give me a lift, yeah?"

"Right, you can mess with his tires when the time comes," said Zak and walked up to the beautiful car, which said much more about Zak than the house he lived in.

Stitch took a deep breath that only hurt his ribs more, but followed. The fact that Cox now knew about his sexuality had been in the back of Stitch's mind since yesterday but only now it dawned on him with full force. He joined Zak in the car, and immediately, the slim fingers wrapped around his hand.

"Do you want me to pick up new tires for you?"

Stitch squeezed back harder than he intended to. It was so fucking strange to have an ass so well fucked that he still felt it today. How was Zak coping with being fucked like this on a daily basis? "No, I'll call Captain from home. We'll take it to the garage."

"Sure." Zak sighed and let go of Stitch to move the car back. "Will it be ready tonight? You can call me if you need a lift, yeah?" he said with a small smile. His hands looked so fucking good on the steering wheel. Stitch bet they'd look even better if they were tattooed like the rest of Zak.

Stitch nodded. "I'll see how it all goes." He took a deep breath to calm down. "I've got my phone at home."

Zak frowned. "No, it was in your pocket. Did you leave it in the bathroom?"

Stitch pursed his lips as they started driving down the street. "I have a *special* phone for you," he muttered.

"Do you?" Zak grinned and took a turn on the empty road. "Zak the dirty secret, huh?"

Stitch looked away and rubbed his forehead. "Sorry, it has to be like this."

Zak exhaled and put his hand on Stitch's again. "I know. You wouldn't want any of those dirty messages to accidentally end up at your friend's phone, yeah?"

"God, no. I just can't help myself when I think of you. All I wanna do is fuck all day."

Zak pushed his sunglasses down to his nose and laughed out loud. "Always the romantic. You can write a poem about my ass. Do it, I dare you."

"You can be such an asshole." Stitch groaned and pulled down the window, feeling too hot.

Zak grinned and patted his back. "Just joking. I know you're serious."

"Yeah, yeah. Just drive." Stitch shook his head, but let his fingers trail Zak's knuckles.

"At least you have a lot to think about now," said Zak, and they accelerated, turning into a wider street. Stitch couldn't help a smirk. That he did.

It only took ten minutes to reach Stitch's home.

Zak parked in front of it, and they didn't waste more time. It was about time to part and start thinking about business. Ten grand that Stitch had to come up with. He followed the car with his gaze as long as it was in sight, and opened the door, then entering the quiet corridor. When he got to his room though, something was off. The floor seemed to creak louder and the house was dead silent, even though Crystal's car was in the garage.

When he walked into his room, he tripped over a whole pile of bags and suitcases. "The fuck?" he uttered looking around the stripped-down space. Even his bedding was ripped off the mattress and stuffed into a black trash bag. "Crystal?" he yelled out.

Her voice echoed back with so much disdain and he didn't even know what he'd done to deserve it. "Come to the *family* room, you piece of shit!"

He sneered and curled his hands into fists. What now? What else was life about to throw at him? Stitch stomped down the stairs and to the living room. Was this Milton's idea? Filling her head with bullshit again?

"What the fuck is wrong *again*?" he asked, but stopped mid-stride when he saw her sitting by the table with his other cell phone placed in the empty space like an insult. His mind went blank, and all blood drained from his face.

Crystal looked at him, her hair wild as if frizzed from all the anger in her eyes. "My mom's phone's not working, and she's leaving for the weekend, so I thought you wouldn't mind her borrowing this old piece of junk," she said and shoved the phone away. It slid across the table and stopped an inch away from the edge

"You gave it to your mom?" he wanted to say, but managed to only whisper. All his muscles froze, making it hard to even breathe.

Crystal snorted, and the dragon tattooed on her hand seemed to move as she flexed her muscles. "Thank God, no. I had enough sense in me to check if you didn't have any fucking porn on there." She took a deep, long breath, which made her breasts move up and down in the neckline. "You're a fucking deviant."

This couldn't be happening. He didn't need this shit on his plate right now. "Who told you that you can touch my stuff?" he hissed and walked up to the table on wobbly legs that felt like marshmallows. The soreness in his ass was now a stark reminder of just how 'deviant' he was. His heart was beating faster than a machine gun, and all he could think of was just how badly he was fucked. And not in a good way.

Crystal rose from the chair and pushed him back, following the shove with a hard slap to his face. "You sick fuck! How long have you been fucking guys behind my back, huh? You got me pregnant so that I'd be your excuse?"

Stitch swallowed and took a step back. "I... It wasn't like that!" His stomach shrank to the size of a bullet.

"Stop bullshitting me!" Crystal's voice turned into a scream. She kicked the chair to the floor, breathing hard and fast. "You made me feel so bad about myself when you didn't want to sleep with me, or when you couldn't get it up, and now it turns out it was all because you want a 'juicy ass'? It's been the best years of my life, and now I'm divorced and stuck with a kid!"

Shame bled onto Stitch's face with burning heat. He remembered those moments all too well. He was such a failure. "I never wanted to make you feel bad." He raised his voice as well. "I always cared for you, Crys. I wanted to make it work. You were a cool babe, so I went for it. You weren't just an excuse." He tried to touch her shoulder but only got another slap.

"Don't you dare!" hissed Crystal, her big eyes turning away with a deep shine. "I thought you were different than all the others in the club, but turns out you're just a faggot! You won't deceive me any longer. Holly doesn't deserve a father like you."

"Don't call me that!" Stitch snarled at her and spread his arms. "I always tried my best. I earn for this family, care for the both of you." How much was he supposed to take?

Crystal's face was a mask of anger. "I don't want to see your face ever again. And fuck off from Holly, or I'll let everyone know who you really are."

Stitch grabbed her wrist and shook her small frame, feeling guilty about it before he even stopped. "Don't you dare tell anyone. You have no right to keep me away from Holly."

Crystal stared at his hand around her wrist but then lashed out at him like a pit bull protecting her cub. "I'm her *mother*, and it's my duty to protect her from cocksuckers like you!" The unexpected stab of pain spread all over Stitch's groin, making his knees softer than cream cheese as she kicked him in the nuts. "Leave, or everyone's gonna know!"

Stitch bowed down in pain but managed to hold in a yelp through sheer willpower. He did not deserve this. "You crazy bitch!" he hissed and backed off slowly. He was so completely screwed. The last thing he wanted was to have even a suspicion like this float around the club. But the worst thing was that by her knowing, it all became as real as the lost drug money. He *was* a fag. With Zak everything became blurred, and Stitch loved that cocoon of safety they shared. No one outside of it needed to know Stitch liked cock, but it was too late now. Cox yesterday, and now Crystal. It felt like shit. He didn't want to be defined by who turned him on. He was a Hound of Valhalla, a father, a lover, an outlaw. Not a *fag*.

"Take your things and fuck off," growled Crystal, and with one last push to Stitch's chest, she stormed out, leaving him in the empty family room to a whirlwind of thoughts.

Chapter 16

Zak parked his car by a toy store in the town center and looked at his phone, slowly turning it in his hand as he leaned back in the seat. It was a quiet day, with people walking by going about their everyday business, but to him it seemed so surreal. He had a boyfriend. Monogamy had seeped into his life so unexpectedly he hadn't even noticed, and when the time came, he just went for it without question. It was different with Stitch. Unlike any other guy Zak had ever been with, Stitch really was dedicated to him. Being with him didn't feel just like having fun together, Stitch gave him 100 percent of his attention, and was always willing to help when it was needed. From the very beginning, his eyes had been so intense. And the things he was saying from time to time, they would sound corny on anyone else's lips, but coming from him they were sincere and moving.

Zak bit his lip and messaged Cox to meet him in a nearby coffee shop, one Zak believed neither Stitch nor any of his friends would visit on a club day. He needed to stop the conflict between Stitch and Cox before it was too late. The reply came as quick as it always did, and Zak slowly slid out of the car and walked down the street to the café itself. It was a pleasant, rustic shop called Granny's, owned by three old women who had been friends forever. Upon entry, he made some small talk with Marge, one of the Grannies, but he couldn't even remember what he talked to her about the moment he sat down in the farthest corner of the café, with a piece of cheesecake and a big cup of tea.

He deserved the extra carbs after yesterday's workout. He'd never expected Stitch to ever be willing to put out, he'd never expected them to become as close as they did, but last night made him feel like a real man. He'd topped many times before, but it was the first time it meant something more than just having sex and feeling good. He felt responsible for Stitch, and at times it seemed like one wrong move could shatter Stitch's thin-lined confidence. And he couldn't let that happen. With that big, strong body opening up to him, not just for sex with a hot guy but to *him* alone, it'd been harder to control his body than ever, but he'd managed. For Stitch. He wouldn't have forgiven himself if he couldn't give Stitch amazing sex in return for his trust.

He was so lost in thought, he hadn't even noticed Cox walking up to his table. "Hey, Zak." Cox sat opposite to him in the booth and leaned over the table, his arms looking as hunky as ever.

Zak froze with the fork at his mouth. "Hi," he muttered with his mouth full. He'd been thinking all morning how to talk to Cox about last night, and whatever was between them, but now his head was empty as a balloon.

"You wanted to chat?" Cox smiled at one of the waitresses when she brought him coffee. "Because I do."

"Yeah, I think we need to talk," said Zak with resignation, pushing away the remaining part of the cake. He decided to start with the unpleasantries. "Why did you puncture Stitch's tires?"

"What? Someone slit his tires?" Cox asked so innocently that Zak would actually believe him if he didn't know better. "A dangerous lifestyle leads to things like that, I suppose."

Zak forced a smile to his lips and looked straight into Cox's eyes, shocked by the blatant lie. "Don't try to bullshit me. It's not gonna stand."

"You should worry about the bruises on your neck, not the slit tires." Cox pointed to Zak's neck, and his voice had real concern in it.

Zak kept up a straight face, but the tender spots on his neck suddenly became hot. He hadn't fully registered it at the time, with adrenaline rushing through his veins as he looked into Stitch's eyes, but his new boyfriend had actually choked him the night before. Though as unpleasant as that thought was, he'd never believe that Stitch could seriously harm him. The moment he saw the intense hurt in those dark eyes, it was a stab in the stomach, and he knew he deserved every single bruise.

"I'm fine. Don't change the subject."

"Zak, I don't think you know who you're dealing with here. I thought you were just friends. Larsen is a criminal. He broke into your house yesterday, and we both know it was no game." Cox shook his head and sipped his coffee.

"I know very well who I'm dealing with, thank you for your concern," said Zak, patting his cup. The flash of dried blood and dark bruises all over Stitch's body went through his mind. What had Stitch been doing before he came to his house the night before? That question kept popping into Zak's mind over and over. "He *is* my friend, and I don't like the idea of his tires being slashed in front of my house."

"Let's just agree we all got overheated yesterday. I'm sorry, but you have to admit our meeting ended abruptly to say the least, huh?" Cox raised his eyebrows.

"Yes, that's why I'm meeting you now." Zak pressed his thumbs together, watching the handsome officer. "Why are you actually after Stitch?"

"The Hounds of Valhalla are an organised crime group. They steal all sorts of goods and pass them on, own illegal weapons, and God knows what else. They're growing bolder, but we don't have enough evidence. Half of that club has already been to prison. Larsen is no different. Though now I know that he is very different," he ended on a thoughtful note and looked out the window.

Zak clenched his fist and shrugged even though his nerves went alert at that information. "How do you know if there's no evidence. Why was Stitch in prison?"

"Assault. He broke the man's ribs and jaw. Zak, he is no teddy biker. You've seen yourself how aggressive he can be. And there's no evidence for another charge, but the guys who have actually been to prison, they didn't work alone. They claim they did, but it's never the case. The Hounds are like a pack of rabid dogs."

Zak wanted to tell Cox that Stitch worked at the workshop, but he knew how stupid that would sound, so he just shrugged. "We're still buddies."

Cox sighed. "He is trouble, Zak. I don't want you to get hurt, or entangled in their shady business. I know you're a nice guy under all that ink, but a lot of people don't and it could make you a target if you hang around the Hounds too much. But still, Larsen being gay is quite a revelation." He rubbed his angular chin.

"Is he?" asked Zak with a face of stone, even though he was burning with tension.

Cox looked up at him with a frown. "Come on, Zak. He didn't attack you just for being with me. He looked like a jealous pit bull."

"People he's not sleeping with shouldn't talk or know about who he is sleeping with," Zak said, looking Cox straight in the eyes.

"He was the one breaking into your bedroom. Anyway, it's a catch-22. I can't use it as leverage, 'cause he would out me."

Zak snorted. Yeah, right, as if Cox would risk the same consequences as Stitch. "I'm just saying that it's good policy not to out anyone."

"It's a good policy not to sleep with violent men."

"He's not violent to me, I already told you." Zak took a big gulp of the tea. He was starting to feel uneasy about this whole conversation.

"You know what? I can see you're into all of that biker shit. I just want you to know that if something does happen, you can come to me, and I'll help you out. I'm on your side here, yeah?" The worst thing was Cox did sound as earnest as they came.

Zak gave him a small smile. "Thanks, I will," was all he could give at this point before hiding behind the mug. Stitch had told him that he'd killed a man and burned down his house, but at the time Zak was convinced it was just to threaten him. As much as he believed Stitch to be a good guy at heart, Cox's words made doubt push its roots into him.

"You wanna meet up next week? Preferably when we can actually be alone? I was kinda left hanging yesterday." Cox laughed and had that twinkle in his smiling eyes.

Zak gave a mental sigh. That was the part he was really queasy about. "Don't take this the wrong way because I think you're a great guy, but I don't think we should be doing this anymore."

Cox's smile stiffened and he shook his head. "I knew it. He's threatening you, isn't he? It's 'cause he hates my guts."

Zak wanted to howl. "God, no. Of course not. It's my decision," he said, as serious as he could. "I'm not some girl beaten into submission by her abusive boyfriend."

"Let's just leave it at that. I won't lie, it sucks for me because I think you're really hot. I'll be around if you change your mind," Cox said and got up without further ado.

Zak couldn't help but look up at that wide chest and tight waistline, even though Stitch was hotter. "See you around."

Cox winked at him. "Your next coffee's on me," he said and walked off, giving Zak a view of that tight ass in the uniform.

Zak leaned back in the chair and hugged the tea to his chest. He hoped that was the last unpleasant meeting of the day.

*

Zak did his shopping, bought dinner, met two customers for out-of-studio consultations, and eventually made his way home after the string of activities that took the whole day. He should still have plenty of time before Stitch came back from his organized crime group meeting. He gritted his teeth, hoping that asked directly, his new boyfriend wouldn't lie. But when he parked his car, he saw no one other than Stitch sitting on his porch. His bike was parked a few meters away, and only the light from a cigarette illuminated Stitch's face in the darkness.

Zak sighed and got out of the car smiling. Thug or not, Stich was enough to lighten his mood. "What is it, Trouble? Maybe I should give you the key already?" He laughed, feeling a slight warmth at the idea. "Did you guys finish your meeting early?" he asked, opening the trunk to retrieve his groceries.

"Crystal found out. She found my other phone." Stitch didn't even look up at him, curled up in his leather jacket, and looking like a stray dog on that porch.

Zak put down the plastic bag he'd just picked up and rushed to Stitch's side. "Oh, no." He scooted down in front of him, unsure what to do, and how to comfort him. "What can I do, baby? Do you want to come inside?"

Stitch hid his face behind his big palm. "She threw me out of the house. I didn't want to break into yours," he said quietly. "I want you to take me in, but only if you want to."

Zak's first reaction was to lean in and hug him, but with neighbors around he couldn't do that so he just put his hand on Stitch's thigh and squeezed it gently. He couldn't bear to watch him like this. "You know I will take you in. Didn't I just propose to give you the keys?"

"It's different though. I'd be here all the time. You could get tired of me." Stitch threw out the cigarette butt and looked up at Zak with tired eyes.

Zak slowly sat down next to him and discreetly slipped his hand under the cut to touch Stitch's back. He could at least hug him this way. "Why would I? We're together, aren't we?" he whispered, suddenly tempted to just lean in and kiss him.

"Yeah. I wanna make this work. Crystal gave me so much shit today, you know?" Stitch took a deep breath and rubbed his eyes.

"You know what? Let's take the frozen stuff into the freezer, and we can talk, because five more minutes, and I will be kissing you in public, okay?" muttered Zak, swallowing as he looked into Stitch's eyes. His heart was trembling in his chest like a little caged bird.

Stitch bit his lips and nodded before getting up. Without a word, he went over to the trunk of Zak's car and took the bags. Zak hurried to collect all the remaining items and let them inside.

He went straight for the pantry where his aunt had put an industrial freezer, and tossed every bag that contained something frozen inside before turning to Stitch. The guy looked so out of energy that Versay started whimpering around him when he didn't get the usual Stitch-attention. He looked lost in the living room, even though he spent so much time here.

Zak shut the freezer and started slowly approaching his boyfriend. Stitch was such a big man, with hands that could break necks, but he now seemed vulnerable enough to shatter at a careless touch. "Stitch?" he whispered, brushing his fingers down his arm.

Stitch turned around and hugged him close. "She told me I can't see Holly. That I'm a bad father." He squeezed Zak and put his head on his arm. It was just as heavy as Zak's heart when he pulled Stitch tighter against him with a low sigh.

How had it come to this? Stitch had to be devastated. He wasn't one of the men who let their wives handle all kid-related stuff, he enjoyed playing with his daughter. "I'm so sorry. If only I could help you, you know I would," he whispered, pressing his mouth to Stitch's hair.

"Will you go with me, help me get all my stuff? I didn't want to just assume you'd want to live with me." Stitch gently kissed Zak's neck. "She said I'm disgusting, but I tried to be something else than I am, and I can't do it."

Zak pressed closer to him and slid his hands to the sides of Stitch's face, making their eyes meet. "You are *not* disgusting. You are a real man. You are beautiful. Don't ever forget that," he whispered, holding onto Stitch's jaw.

Stitch chuckled, trying to look away. "Me? 'Beautiful'? Like in that Christina Aguilera song?"

Zak groaned, hitting his forehead against Stitch's. "No, not like that. Just beautiful. I look at you, and the first thing I think of is how handsome you are."

Those words did force a smile to Stitch's face. "Is my cock 'beautiful' too?" he teased, tracing his fingers over Zak's back. Stitch always knew how to turn him into butter.

Zak snorted and nuzzled Stitch's nose, suddenly calmer now that he'd squeezed a smile out of his lover. "Of course. I munched it down the moment we were alone, don't you remember anymore?"

"Yeah, you were really hungry for it." Stitch bowed to give him a kiss, but even though his words sounded dirty, his lips were nothing but sweet and tender.

Zak took a sharp breath and stepped forward so that they were chest to chest. He inhaled Stitch's warm breath, gently suckling on his lip. "I am always hungry for you."

"Let's get my stuff and have that over with, huh?" Stitch slid his hands to Zak's buttocks and gave them a firm squeeze.

Zak curled his toes and nodded, slowly withdrawing. If they had to go, they needed to do it now. "At your service."

*

They drove out as soon as they'd put all the food into place and out of Versay's reach. Zak was tense all the way to Stitch's former home, but he was putting up a brave face for his sake. They would get this shit done. Zak parked the car with the trunk facing the door and gave Stitch an encouraging smile as he was entering. The lights were on in the living room and Zak found himself wondering what Stitch's former house looked like. It was nice from the outside. Old, but clearly cared for.

Stitch came out with his first round of bags, but Zak could already hear a high-pitched female voice following him all the way to the door.

"Don't forget anything, because I want none of your shit here!"

Zak moved closer to the porch. "Maybe I should just go in with you? We'll be quicker this way," he said, wishing he could screw his ears shut.

Stitch stuck the bags in the trunk and nodded. "Yeah, let's just do it and leave." He went back in quickly. "I got it the first time, for fuck's sake! Shut your mouth and let me pack!" he yelled.

Zak rolled his eyes and rushed in behind him, stealing brief glances at the rooms on both sides of the corridor. It was a simple home, but just as well maintained as the outer walls. With Stitch's inclination to handiwork, he imagined why that was.

But as he turned into one of the rooms on Stitch's heel, the female voice got louder and he almost walked into a petite redhead with tattoos all over her arms and neckline. Her eyes widened, and she stepped back.

"Is this him?" she shouted, waving her hand in front of Zak's chest. "I can't believe you would bring your man-tart here!"

Stitch ran back down the stairs making half the house tremble. "Give it a rest, Crystal. Zak just came here to help me take my stuff!"

Zak blinked, staring at her. "I'm Zak, you must have confused me with someone else," he said, raising his eyebrows.

"Oh, yeah?" She sneered at him and cocked her head to the side, her hands firmly resting on her hips. "You think I'm stupid, Zak? Or should I call you the way Stitch put you in his cell phone? 'Sexy tattoo Zak'."

"Shut up, Crystal!" Stitch yelled at her and came between them, only to get punched in the arm with her tiny fist.

"I am not the reason for your divorce, so I don't see why you're trying to insult me," said Zak, trying to keep his cool. If he was to help

Stitch start seeing his daughter again, he needed to make Crystal see him in a positive light.

But things took an instant turn downhill when Holly started crying upstairs.

"See what you did?" Stitch hissed at Crystal, who clenched her fists.

"Me? I'm not the one breaking up the family because I'm a deviant!"

Zak squeezed his teeth tightly. "Weren't you the one who cheated on *him*? He and I only met on the day of your divorce," he uttered, bumping his fist against the wall.

Her eyes went wide. "Who the fuck are you to lecture me on my marriage?" She turned to Stitch. "So now you tell your new boy-toy everything? Watching too much *Gossip Girl* since you turned gay?" she hissed so much venom Zak could hardly believe how it fit into her little body.

"Don't call him that! And he's right that it was you who cheated—" Stitch started, but Crystal interrupted him.

"And I'm glad I did because otherwise I'd be stuck with a monk of a husband forever!"

"You have a crying child upstairs. We'll just gather his things and go, all right?" Zak decided to ignore the boy-toy comment. She was the one to talk, only about two thirds of his height. He looked to Stitch for directions.

"Exactly!" Stitch said through gritted teeth and pointed Zak to the stairs. "I'll take care of Holly if you need a breather," he said to Crystal as they started walking toward the stairs.

Crystal pulled his sleeve. "Don't you dare go to her. I'll go."

Zak ignored the commotion, nearing the high-pitched sobbing. This was such a disaster. At least he knew where to go, as Stitch's room was the only one that had an open door. He gathered two large boxes and started carefully climbing down the stairs.

He heard some more screaming, door slamming, something breaking, cries of a little girl. It sounded like the worst fight ever, but at least he wasn't involved in it anymore. He was happy to see though that as mean as Crystal was, and as horrible the verbal fighting got, Stitch never hit her back. Cox knew shit.

Zak was calmly walking up and down the stairs, filling up first the trunk, and then the back seat, while the fight was still going on. As much as he sympathized with Crystal, he couldn't help but detest her behavior. Stitch had been faithful to her all this time, he didn't seek out guys to hook up with. He didn't deserve half of the stuff she was throwing his way.

Seeing that he was done taking out Stitch's things, he decided to break the two bulldogs apart and followed the barking all the way into a tidy kitchen.

He frowned at the sight of shattered cups, and a broken bag of flour on the floor. At least the little girl wasn't crying upstairs anymore, but who knew, maybe her throat got too sore?

"Why the fuck would you do that?" Stitch hissed at her, but looked to Zak when he came in.

Zak sighed and stuffed his hands down his pockets. "Done," he said, looking between them with a frown. He didn't want to ask about the mess.

Crystal panted like a hungry bear. "Go, Stitch. Fuck his 'juicy ass' for all I care. There, free as a bird!"

Zak dragged his hand down his face, wishing this were over already.

"Fuck you! Don't come crying to me when Milton acts like a cunt again!" Stitch gesticulated wildly, all red on the face, but at least he instantly rushed to Zak. They were making their way toward the exit when Zak heard a thud. He turned around to see that Stitch got hit on the head with the bag of flour and had the white powder all over himself. He didn't lash out though, just showed Crystal the finger and tagged along.

Zak was happy the upholstery of his car was made of leather. It would make mopping up that flour so much easier, but he was even happier when he pulled out of Crystal's yard and drove home. The silence in the car was almost tangible.

"What a mess," Zak uttered in the end, glancing at Stitch.

"I'm sorry I dragged you into it. I didn't know she'd go crazy again," Stitch groaned and bumped his head against the window. "Thanks for the help. I'd be stuck there forever without you."

Zak snorted. "Yeah, I know." He stared at the road, pondering whether to have the talk now that Stitch couldn't leave, or wait. He decided on the former. "I spoke with Cox today."

The car went silent like a coffin on wheels. Stitch scowled. "The fuck did he want?" he muttered in the end.

Zak shrugged. "I told him slicing your tires was a dick move, and that I won't be seeing him anymore," he said, looking straight ahead while his heart picked up its pace so much he felt it pulse in his throat.

Stitch took a deep breath and wrapped his arms around his chest. "Good."

Zak bit his lip and tapped his fingers against the steering wheel. "Is your club involved in criminal activities?"

"Huh? What did that shithead tell you?"

Zak groaned. "That you were in prison for assault, and that you and your friends are handling stolen goods and illegal weapons." He bit his lip and shook his head. "You were so beaten up last night. Tell me what's going on."

Stitch ran his fingers through his hair. "Why do you want to know?"

Zak slapped the steering wheel, his arms getting rigid. "Oh, fuck. You *are* a criminal..."

"That's not fair. We just don't always do things by the book." The look on Stitch's face told Zak that his new cohabitant was dying to be home.

"We're a couple, you're moving in with me. Don't you think I should know what's going on in your life?" He shook his head in helplessness. He should have known this from the start, before he got so fond of Stitch.

"I take care of my stuff. You won't get involved, so don't worry." Stitch's fingers climbed to Zak's thigh.

"Stitch, stop fucking trying to distract me, and tell me the truth," growled Zak. "Is that all true?" He asked, boiling up inside like a sealed pot on high heat.

"So I was to prison, yeah. Jeez. You don't tell me everything about your past. What made you come to Lake Valley, for example. You don't know anyone here. Why didn't you sell the house?" He never stopped tapping his fingers on Zak's leg though.

Zak swallowed, feeling his stomach squeeze. "I'll tell you if you tell me if you're still involved in some shit."

Stitch was silent for a while, his frown deepening. "I am involved in shit, okay?"

"I know that much already." Zak shook his head, increasingly nervous. "What is it exactly? Drugs? Guns? Human trafficking?" he uttered in distaste.

"You make it sound like I'm some mafia boss. It's low profile stuff. We take stuff places, sell it on. And no, it's *not* human trafficking." Stitch pulled his fingers away.

Zak sighed, stiffening his elbows. "I just... don't want you to be hurt or end up in jail. At this point, whatever happens to you will hit me too."

"I'm trying to keep it contained." Stitch pondered on something for a while, but when he spoke again it was in a quieter and steady voice. "I told you that I lost a lot of cash yesterday. What happened was a real shock to the system. I don't think shit like that is for me. But I need to get the money back before I can try and work out something new."

Zak exhaled and before he knew it, his hand was on Stitch's, squeezing it tight. That was a good sign, Stitch wanted change. "How much? Is it like, a million? Hundred thousand?" he uttered, hoping Stitch wouldn't put himself into an even bigger risk.

"Ten grand," Stitch muttered and didn't look Zak's way but squeezed his hand back.

Zak relaxed, taking a turn toward his home. That was all right. It was a large sum of money but manageable. "Okay. Thanks for telling me."

"But it's not your responsibility, yeah?" Stitch looked like he was doing a silent prayer when he saw Zak's house.

"It's not, as long as you don't do anything reckless to get that money back," whispered Zak as he parked the car.

"So what's your story?" Stitch nudged Zak's side before getting out.

Zak sighed and rested his forehead against the steering wheel before leaving the car. He gestured for Stitch to follow him home. There was nothing in those boxes that couldn't wait in the vehicle.

"I'm not trying to sell the house because the economy's terrible for that now."

"But you left your old home." Stitch put an arm over Zak's shoulders as soon as they walked into the house.

Versay rushed from his bed in the kitchen and circled them with a wide smile, accepting the gentle petting.

Zak shrugged, not sure whether he was ready to talk about it. Even to him, the situation was silly. "I was betrayed by someone I trusted, and I guess I just took the opportunity to leave."

"What do you mean by 'betrayed'?" Stitch pulled Zak along to the living room and they cuddled up on the couch.

Zak sighed and sat cross-legged, leaning into Stitch. He chewed on his bottom lip and held on to Stitch's hand, which made him feel warm and safe. "I was the co-owner of a tattoo studio. The other guy, my partner, had started it but he wasn't doing well. I guess he isn't that good of an artist either, but I talked to him, and he promised me fifty percent if I could help him make the studio work, even though on paper I only got thirty. He wanted to keep control of the business, and I got that because he didn't know me yet." Zak inhaled some air, playing with the numerous signets on Stitch's thick, strong fingers. "He kept his word and we were splitting the money fifty-fifty. At this point, he was the closest thing I ever had to a boyfriend, so I trusted him," he said with a shake of his head. Now that he thought about it, it seemed like such a bad idea. All of them, actually, from dating your co-worker to not pressing on the changes in the contract.

"I can see how this story goes," Stitch said, but there was no mocking in his tone, just compassion, and he kissed Zak's temple. The gesture was so tender Zak actually had to wait for his voice to return to normal before he could speak further.

"Yeah, at some point he got greedy and told me that there is no reason for me to get that much money, that he was the one who created the studio. And you know, I helped him hire all the artists he now has, to make the studio known. I worked so hard for it." He shrugged, his face turning into a scowl. "I couldn't stay there. Neither with the studio, nor in his bed, you know." Slowly, he turned his head to look at Stitch.

"So you thought to make it on your own here in Lake Valley?" Stitch stroked Zak's hair, embracing him with his wide arms. Zak immediately turned around to face him, curling his legs against Stitch's side.

"I thought I could get some rest from all this bullshit and work from home at the same time, but now... I don't know," he whispered, slowly resting his head on the wide chest. Even now Stitch smelled of wood chips.

"No? You seem to be settling in well." Stitch gave him a kiss.

Zak sighed and picked on Stitch's cut with a small smile. "Yeah, I didn't think I'd stay this long. It's all on you."

"Yeah? I'm anchoring you here?" Stitch nuzzled his neck. "I hope you stay so, you know, I have a place to live." He nipped on Zak's bruised skin.

Zak snorted. "Men, always using me." He didn't really mean that, but his dark humor got the best of him.

"You love to be used by me." Stitch murmured into Zak's collarbone.

Zak closed his thighs and pushed his fingers into Stitch's mane, getting flour all over his hands. "I know, you make me so helpless when you kiss me."

"I'll remember that for the future, thanks." Stitch chuckled. His stubble scraped Zak's skin as he let his lips explore.

Never breaking the close contact, Zak climbed into Stitch's lap, straddled him, and let his head fall back, accepting the sweet kisses all over the skin.

"You'll stay with me here, won't you?" Stitch murmured and slid his hands to Zak's ass. It was so good that Zak's balls tightened at the contact, and he pushed his body closer to Stitch.

"Yeah."

Stitch pulled up Zak's hand to his lips and kissed its knuckles. Without a word, he took off one of his signets and slid the heavy thing on Zak's thumb.

Zak stared at it, hardly breathing, his mind still frozen on the moment when Stitch's lips touched the back of his hand in a gesture that spoke of devotion. The metal on his finger was still warm from its former host. Zak exhaled, looking at the hammer adorning the ring, his heart already rushing, pulling him deeper into Stitch's body, but he resisted and looked at his lover instead.

Stitch pointed to the little runes around the heavy signet. "It's Mjölnir. And the runes around are for protection. My granddad gave it to me."

Zak bit his lip, his mind going astray just as his pulse quickened even more. "I... but it's important to you."

"You're important to me," Stitch said with a smile, sliding his fingers under Zak's T-shirt. Their rough skin was the sweetest kind of touch Zak could imagine, and he hugged Stitch closer, brushing the ring over his lover's jaw over and over again. He wasn't sure what it all meant so he abruptly kissed Stitch's mouth, robbing them both of breath.

"I... why the ring?" he whispered, closing his eyes.

Stitch grinned into Zak's lips. "My name is Thor. And I gave you my hammer. Does that sound dirty?"

Zak laughed out loud. "Super dirty. Is that a sign that you're the only one allowed to hammer me, or something?" He brushed his hand over Stitch's face and kissed him again, slowly calming down even though the warm metal seemed to burn his finger. "And you never even told me what your name is, you jerk."

"I just told you. Thor. Blame my Norwegian parents. And yes, I am the only one allowed to hammer you." Stitch started a languid move of his hips under Zak while looking into his eyes.

Zak let out a laugh. Even the sensuous grinding between his legs couldn't distract him from what he had just heard. "You're serious? Oh, my God, you're actually called Thor?" He felt so light he could fly up to the ceiling, still clinging to Stitch with his thighs.

"Don't you dare call me that though. It's embarrassing, especially after the movie. Being a tall blond doesn't help either."

"No? You don't want to hammer me in a Viking costume?" chuckled Zak, making a languid move with his hips. His eyes were completely taken by the handsome face in front of him.

Stitch frowned, but Zak could feel his dick stiffening under Zak's ass. "I knew I shouldn't have told you."

"No, you totally should have," whispered Zak, rocking in his lap. "Didn't you just put a ring on my finger?" he asked, looking deep into Stitch's eyes. He had no idea what was going on in that Nordic head. The last thing he wanted to do was make false assumptions.

"I did. I like it, so I put a ring on it. Dibs." Stitch had that silly smile on his face as he paraphrased the Beyoncé song.

Zak gave a dry laugh as he put his arms around Stitch and hugged him close. This was insane. Things were getting far too complicated, far too soon, and with a man who was a known criminal and ex-convict at that. But that didn't change how natural it felt to be in his arms, and how easy it was for Zak to commit to monogamy after all the years of carefree sex. He was getting old. Old and corny.

"And now that it's legit, I *am* gonna hammer you," Stitch's grin widened and in one abrupt move, he arched his hips and threw Zak over to his back while still holding on to his legs. "All night. And then the night after... and after..." He lapped at Zak's neck.

Every single nerve in Zak's body stood alert, as if waiting for Stitch's command. Zak moaned, feeling a rush of heat to his face, and rapidly pulled on the sides of Stitch's cut. The moment his lover's weight collapsed on top of him, he knew there wasn't anything he wanted more.

Chapter 17

It had been over five months since Zak moved to Lake Valley, two since Stitch moved in with him, and it had passed like spring break. They were oddly good together, and Zak hadn't even thought of kissing another man since then. His new boyfriend kept him busy and satisfied, even though he still had doubts about giving head. Zak suggested it once, but Stitch approached his dick like it was a porcupine. Then again, the last thing Zak wanted was to force him into it, so he fucked Stitch's tight ass instead. That man had such a gorgeous, muscled butt. Zak could play with it for hours.

They were spending so much time together too. Zak was hanging out with Stitch's friends at Valhalla, and already kind of liked most of them, even though they could be homophobic jerks at times. Since the situation with Crystal, they deleted all messages and made sure no one got their hands on their cell phones either. She at least didn't try to hurt any of them physically, which couldn't be guaranteed if any of the Hounds got their hands on the correspondence between Stitch and Zak. It was NC-17 to say the least.

Stitch on the other hand helped Zak around the house a lot. They painted a new room, and Stitch made an amazing table for Zak's studio space. He even made a carving in the counter, of one of the demons Zak had tattooed on his body.

In a surge of goodwill, Stitch even let Zak teach him some basic cooking, which ended up with a somewhat burnt but heartwarming breakfast in bed one Sunday. Unfortunately, Stitch was a useless case when it came to cooking, and Zak ended up planning their fridge contents and preparing food a lot more.

Despite him being such a sweet, caring guy, Zak couldn't help but worry whenever he went out to be with his club buddies. Stitch never explicitly told Zak what they were dealing with, and Zak didn't want to pressure him since Stitch had already declared he wanted out of the illegal business, but it was hard not to know where Stitch was late at night. Especially when Zak had jobs to do and needed to stay professional and focused.

The worst time of all was when Stitch told Zak he'd be out for the weekend to do a job in another state, but when Zak noticed Stitch's gun was gone and tried to call him, all he got was a dead line. He couldn't sleep at night, sick with worry, only to find Stitch sleeping on the couch next Monday. Of course, Stitch wouldn't tell him where he'd been and why he got Zak worried sick. Another time, he came home with an incision that Zak ended up stitching up, and even more bruising than usual. It hurt Zak to even look at his lover injured, and not knowing the cause was killing him. It provoked a few arguments, which dispersed eventually without solving the problem. Usually through Stitch's sneaky seduction techniques.

And there were the nights when Stitch simply went out with the guys and when Zak drove by the bar, none of the motorbikes were there. He wanted to confront Stitch about it, but seeing him come back home, looking like an empty-eyed puppet, made Zak ignore his own insecurities and get down to making Stitch feel better. And on top of that was the matter of Holly. Despite their initial assumptions, after two months, Crystal still wouldn't budge and stood firm by her decision not to let Stitch see his daughter. He was only allowed to occasionally deliver some treats and small toys for her but never play with her. The most he got was half an hour, and those days were actually worse than having him *not* see her. Stitch wouldn't even want cheering up. He just drove off for a ride for a few hours. He was so obviously upset that it also made Zak push away any issues he wanted to confront Stitch over.

And then there was Cox and a few of his cop buddies, sniffing around the Hounds of Valhalla. The worst thing was that Zak was increasingly aware that the cops actually had good reason to investigate, but any attempts to get Stitch talking ended with them not speaking for hours.

On top of that, Zak found himself back in the closet, and while he understood that Stitch couldn't be open about his sexuality in his circles, the secrecy and necessity to tell lies whenever someone tried to flirt with him or asked about him not having a girlfriend were slowly choking Zak. It was like a noose around his neck, always ready to tighten, and the longer it lasted, the more suspicious looks he was getting, and the more uncomfortable he became.

He thought a weekend trip to New Orleans where he and Stitch could hold hands in public, dance in a club or even have a beer as a couple, could relieve the tension, but the idea was instantly shot down. Zak believed part of it had to be about Stitch not really being comfortable with his sexuality, not just the danger of being spotted. To Stitch's credit, he had toned down his flirting with the girls when Zak told him how much he hated seeing him humping or kissing someone else, but that didn't change much about Zak's situation. He hadn't even noticed when he'd crawled all the way behind the thickest coat in the closet, and he was ashamed of it.

Zak's day had been slow. He did a small tattoo on a girl's wrist in the early afternoon, had a long walk with Versay, and spent the rest of the day making designs and drawing in front of the television. Stitch was supposed to be back late at night so Zak wasn't rushing to do much but he smiled when he heard the doorbell ring. Sometimes, Stitch had this quirk of ringing just so Zak would greet him at the door, even though he already had his own key.

Zak threw down his sketchbook and rushed to the door with a wide smile. He was happy to be dressed properly, with his hair down. But it wasn't Stitch who smiled at him when he opened the door.

Cox gave him a curt nod. "Hi Zak, is Larsen in?" he asked, but it was the sight of the other cop next to him that made Zak's eyes go wide. The guy had a massive police dog with him. Versay was already trying to push through Zak's legs to run out and greet the buff German shepherd, but Zak pulled the door shut behind him, leaving the furry pest in despite its whining.

"No, why? Is something wrong, officer?" he asked as carefree as he could, even though his stomach became a tangled web of thorns. What was going on? Were they suspecting Stitch of dealing drugs?

"We need to speak to him. He agreed to talk and then disappeared. Would you know where he is?" said the other policeman in a rich baritone.

Zak shrugged, hoping he was good enough of an actor to give a believable performance. Not to mention that he was hoping the dog wasn't about to smell his weed-scented fingers. "Sorry, no idea. You could come by later."

"Thank you, we will. Could you give us a call when he's in?" Cox asked in a deadpan voice. He probably knew what the answer would be.

"Why are you looking for him?" Zak asked back, hoping they'd forget to repeat the question.

"I'm afraid we can't disclose that," said the other officer, and Zak wished the guy weren't here, because he was sure Cox would actually give him some insight into Stitch's wrongdoings.

He straightened up and leaned back against the door. "Well, if you can't tell me anything then I don't see a reason to spy on him," he said with a straight face. "The government already has too much surveillance power over its citizens," he said to make his stance seem more legit.

Cox, who actually knew him well enough to recognize the bluff, raised his eyebrows. "Er... We'll be on our way, Zak."

"Sure, it's been nice to meet you," said Zak with a wide smile and popped open the door, pushing in through the crack to prevent Versay from socializing with the wrong crowd. At least the beast was happy to see *him*. He patted the dog's side, squeezed the elongated, fluffy mohawk, and walked all the way to the kitchen. He got himself a glass of milk and returned to the sofa, where he'd left his phone. He needed to see Stitch ASAP.

But before he could make the call, he heard the backdoor slam, and Versay ran toward the rattling in the kitchen. He dropped the phone and rushed to the noise. "Stitch, is that you?" Zak hissed, walking in with his heart in his throat.

In the kitchen, Stitch was just about done stuffing some bag into the breadbox, and opened the cupboard under the sink to fit in a piece of machinery that made Zak think of the post-apocalyptic shooter game he once played.

"Hey," Stitch huffed, barely catching a breath.

Zak raised his hands, air going through his windpipe at an agonizing speed. "What the fuck is that?"

Stitch finally looked back at him, trying to push the concoction of shotgun and gas canister under the sink. "It's... It's a flamethrower," he finished flatly after a moment of hesitation. Zak knew that voice all too well. It was Stitch trying to come up with a lie and not being able to on the spot.

"No," he said through gritted teeth, "I won't have shit like this in my house. What's in the breadbox?"

"It's just for the night," Stitch assured him and shut the cupboard, ignoring the other question.

Zak walked past him and opened the lid of the breadbox, and it seemed that all blood was draining south from his head. There was a large, mean-looking gun next to fresh sliced bread.

"Be careful!" Stitch rushed up to him and closed the breadbox. He stood between it and Zak as if he wanted to protect the firearm. "It's all fine."

Zak shook his head, clawing his fingers in the air. "No, it's not! I just had cops asking about you. They had a giant fucking dog with them!"

"Fuck. Are they gone?" Stitch asked as if it was all normal. It was dawning on Zak that he sure as hell was an accomplice. "They have no business with this shit, flamethrowers are legal."

Zak pinched the base of his nose, trying his best to contain his anger. "Get this shit out of my house. I mean it. You promised me you won't get me involved, remember?"

Stitch did a double-take. "I need to wrap stuff up, I can't just ignore what's happening. And... this is *our* house."

Zak groaned. "On paper, it's mine, which means if they find some illegal shit in here, it's gonna be on me, do you understand that?" He stepped closer to Stitch and poked him in the chest. "I've been patient enough with you disappearing and coming home fucking wounded, don't you think?"

"Cox got a permit to search the club. This needs to stay here till tomorrow. Day after tops." Stitch inhaled deeply, his eyes dark.

"No." Zak crossed his arms on his chest. "I don't care where it goes, but you're not keeping it here."

"Baby, you need to help me out here. This stuff needs to be kept somewhere safe. No one will get a warrant to search your house." Stitch cupped Zak's face and looked into his eyes.

Zak trembled with anger and pushed him away. "Don't you 'baby' me. I don't want this shit in my house, end of story. You will *not* get me involved in this!"

Stitch gritted his teeth, his blond hair in a tangled mess. "So forget you ever saw it."

"I will, once you get it out of the house. Don't make me repeat myself," growled Zak, kicking the cupboard. "And why would you even need a flamethrower, huh? You want to burn down another house?"

Stitch's frown deepened. "What the fuck is wrong with you today? I just need a bit of leeway for us to finish business with the Nails. It's not gonna affect you. I can't bail on my brothers, Zak."

That was it. Zak pushed past him and reached for the breadbox, but Stitch grabbed his hand in an iron grip.

"The fuck are you doing? Don't touch it!"

Zak saw red and pushed him away with his whole body weight. He grasped the breadbox and threw it out the open window. A dull snap outside made him freeze, subconsciously expecting pain, but nothing hurt. He was all right. "Fuck..."

"Are you mental?" Stitch yelled at him and slapped him hard right in the forehead. He ran out the backdoor, probably to get the gun.

Zak stepped back, blinking at the thudding in his skull, and looked up, shocked that Stitch would actually hit him. He'd done it once, when he discovered him in bed with Cox, but that had been different. "You piece of shit..." he muttered, staring at the open door.

"What?" Stitch hissed at him like a snarling dog and picked up the breadbox with care.

"You fucking hit me! The hell!" Zak ducked for the flamethrower but stopped with his hand over it when a vision of his kitchen going up in flames flashed through his mind like a bullet train.

Stitch rushed back into the kitchen, slamming the door behind him and gently put the gun on the counter. "You threw my fucking gun out!"

"Because you wouldn't listen. Take this out. I fucking mean it, Stitch." Zak swallowed and shook his head. "I can't believe you hit me."

"I can't believe you're being such a cunt about this shit when I need some help." Stitch watched Zak's every move, all tense and ready to bite.

Zak narrowed his eyes even as his fists curled by his sides. "*I* am a cunt?"

"At the moment? Yes." Stitch looked out the window, but then right back to Zak.

"Fuck you." Zak bit the inner side of his cheek, doing his best not to lash out.

"Are you done?" Stitch asked with that voice that meant business.

Zak could hardly believe the bastard wasn't budging. "I'm telling you, you can't keep this here. This is the last time I'm telling you this," he said after counting to ten in his mind. This was getting ridiculous.

"Oh, yeah? What are you gonna do?" Stitch spread his arms. "Throw it out when I'm sleeping?" A smirk so mean-spirited curled up his lips that Zak actually took a step back. This was weird. Zak swallowed hard, unsure what to do.

"I could ask Cox to check my fucking kitchen sink because I know shit about plumbing," he uttered in the end, challenging Stitch with a deep frown. It didn't sound as loud and threatening as he'd like to. And he would never actually do that, but he wanted to give the fucker a taste of his own medicine.

It must have put the message across, because Stitch grabbed the gun off the counter with a stern face, put the safety on, and pushed it into the inner side of his hoodie. "Why don't you fuck him while you're at it, huh?"

Zak sighed, squeezing and opening his fists. "You know I'm not gonna sleep with him again. All I want is for you to honor our agreement about not bringing this kind of shit home. It's still the same deal as two months ago."

"And I usually don't! I told you there's a shitload of heat on us today. But you have to throw a hissy fit about it like a little bitch. You call fucking Cox if you want, I'm out of here." Stitch walked over to the sink and pulled out the scary-looking flamethrower.

"You ungrateful son of a bitch," muttered Zak through a deep breath he was taking. He was so deflated that all he wanted was to take a nap with Versay.

"You have no idea what I have to deal with, and you won't even support me with a little thing like this!" Stitch covered the flamethrower with a large black bag.

Zak shook his head. "You don't *have to* do anything. You just won't stop."

"This shit doesn't just stop overnight. I've made a commitment." Stitch put the bag over his back and poked Zak's temple like he wanted to perforate the skin and give Zak an impromptu lobotomy. "Have a think about that. Commitment. You help out your man when he needs it."

Zak pushed Stitch's hand away with more force than he had intended. He didn't want to deal with this anymore. He felt... used and hurt by Stitch's demanding behavior, by the pressure he was trying to apply to him, by the manipulative sweet-talking. He just wanted Stitch to leave him alone. "Come back when you want to apologize."

Stitch just gave him the most brooding look and walked out the backdoor without a good-bye. He didn't even turn around.

Zak stared at the floor in front of him, unable to put into words what he was feeling. Slowly, he walked back to the door and locked it both with the key and sliding bolt.

"Versay, you want a treat?" he asked the empty kitchen, resting his hands on the counter, but the dog ignored him, so he slid to the chair like dead weight. He couldn't believe what had just happened.

A flamethrower? In his house? He couldn't believe how vicious Stitch had been when he didn't get what he wanted. Even remembering those angry eyes was making Zak's stomach throb. What had he got himself into?

The empty, quiet house gave no answer whatsoever.

Chapter 18

The scorching heat and all-consuming flames were exactly what Stitch needed to somehow burn the anger charring inside of him. As he walked along with the flamethrower, leaving the field of marijuana to become ashes and coal, peace came back to him, even if slowly. He couldn't wrap his mind around Zak not wanting to help him, but it was the threat of police, especially Cox, that threw Stitch over the fence of annoyance into a sea of berserk. The betrayal was so deep Stitch didn't want to see Zak's face for a while.

"Burn it all the fuck down!" he heard Gator yelling from behind. The words were followed by a mad cackle. Stitch didn't need to be advised on that. Burning something to the ground was exactly what he felt like doing tonight.

"Burn, motherfucker," Stitch muttered to himself through the white mask as he threw another portion of liquid fire on the plants.

The lights were dancing over the walls of the large warehouse in the middle of nowhere. It was such a beautiful carnage, smelling sweet, of pot and gasoline, and Stitch couldn't take his eyes off the flames that were already making his skin burn like after a whole day of sunbathing without any protection. Blood was soaring in his veins, coursing under the skin only to return back to his innards, cleansed by the fire. It was such an exhilarating moment that he stopped to smell and sense the destruction that he brought upon this place. It was only when Captain pulled on his arm that he realized the smoke was getting too thick. The warehouse would soon be no more, and they needed to be far away from here once someone noticed the bright glow and alarmed the emergency services.

Stitch backed away, almost sorry to leave the flames on their own. It wasn't just the three of them extending their greetings to the Coffin Nails anymore. Joe and two more prospects had got patched in just last month, as Gator wanted to expand, so they would have more manpower if the Nails retaliated. Stitch couldn't help a smirk when he saw the youngest prospect, Rat (called so for his ugly-ass front teeth and skinny figure) watching him in awe and hypnotized by the fire.

"Let's go." Stitch grabbed the guy by the collar and pulled him along to the adjoining room. There was only one guy here tonight with the club having a party at their clubhouse in the nearby town. Stitch walked out of the greenhouse just in time to see blood spraying a beat-up fridge when Gator slit open the Nail's throat with Captain's hunting knife. The guy gurgled, shaking in Captain's grasp as Gator held his head up by the hair, letting him drain as the air started to burn with heat. It wasn't the blood that made Stitch freeze but the crooked, pleased smile on Captain's face as he looked at the nameless rival.

With the flamethrower still on him, Stitch had reason to be close to the exit, but if he were honest, he'd rather be out. This wasn't what he'd signed up for. They were supposed to burn the place down and send a warning to the Coffin Nails. With the bloodthirsty Hounds killing the only person who could have delivered that message, the whole idea behind tonight's plan went to shit. Sure, they were supposed to beat up the guy, but this? Stitch's body went ice cold even with the hot sweat dripping from his skin when he saw both Captain and Gator open their zippers and piss on the bloody mess of a body. He couldn't help a sneer and looked away, only to find Rat just as enchanted with the view as the boy was with watching the field burn. Something snapped in Stitch, and he pushed Rat out through the door.

"I said 'let's go'," he snarled and used it as an excuse to leave himself. He never considered his sensibilities to be fragile, but what he'd seen in there was sick. Fucking gross.

The fresh air outside didn't do much to relieve his tight nerves, but he made his way to the bike, hoping the others would follow suit. He'd had enough of this shit, and already couldn't wait for a chance to forget about this with the help of a generous amount of liquor. His eyes went for the package at the back of his bike, containing a serious stash of the ready-to-sell product. At least he could get back a good chunk of the money he'd lost. The sooner he did that, the sooner he'd be out of the illegal shit. He wasn't a murderer. So, he wasn't on the right side of the law, but when he'd got into stealing shit with Captain as a teenager, they'd never considered killing someone for it. This was truly messed up.

The other five patched members were already by their bikes, chatting and watching the flames.

Gator raised his hands in a gesture of triumph as he left the warehouse alongside Captain. Loud roars tore through the silence, and they all mounted their machines as the warehouse started going ablaze in earnest, like a closed pot with boiling food inside.

"Ready for some well-earned clubhouse action, boys?"

Captain laughed as he put on his helmet. "I don't think there's enough pussy in Lake Valley to satisfy me tonight!"

Stitch was the first one to start his engine, wanting to get the fuck off this property. There was only one person he wanted to celebrate with right now, but he doubted that person would come to their party. It was worth trying to invite him anyway. Maybe having a drink together would clear the atmosphere.

He hit the road as soon as Gator and Captain drove past him.

*

You knew it was a closed, MC friends-only party when Captain was eating out a girl on the pool table. The music was so loud Stitch's eardrums were close to bursting, and he was drunk enough not to care what was passing through his mouth anymore. Past this point, all liquor was just a bit... spicy on his tongue.

As he turned his head away from his best friend, the girl, and some guy who joined the fun and squeezed the girl's tit in passing, Stitch looked straight into Rat's face. The boy's wide brown eyes were riveted on the pool table, as if it were a vision of the future he hoped for. Stitch scowled, somehow drawn into thinking of sucking dick. He couldn't pinpoint why he had such a problem with it. Zak's cock was this glorious thing he fantasized about, yet the idea of actually being *that* guy, the guy who sucks a man off, made him panic. All the preconceptions of who that would make him had Stitch so queasy that he couldn't do it. But wouldn't it be a bit like Captain eating out that busty blonde? *He* wasn't ashamed to go down on her. Why was Stitch so uncomfortable about having a cock in his mouth then? With enough alcohol pumping in his veins, he might just go for another attempt tonight. That was if Zak actually showed up, which was a fifty-fifty kind of thing with the way things had gone down the day before.

"Good work out there!" Gator pulled Stitch so close to his chest that he almost spilled his drink. The prez's head was red as an egg dipped in cherry sauce, and his eyes shone with the liquor. On his shoulder was a red-nailed hand, which Stitch established was just a part of a beautiful girl with a face painted on without much care for the actual shape of her lips. Just like Gator liked them.

"Doin' my best," Stitch muttered and patted Gator's back. "We got so much weed we can get a good thing going with it." He tried not to slur, but it wasn't going all that well. His tongue seemed to thicken in his mouth even further when his eyes were drawn to a familiar figure at the door. Zak was dressed in a pair of tight leather pants and a long tank top, which showcased the broad shoulders Stitch loved so much. It was like suddenly getting hit in the back, as he slid off the barstool, drawn to Zak, who was busy talking to Joe.

Stitch smiled at Gator but went right next to Zak and leaned his elbows on the sticky counter. "Vodka for my friend here, Joe!" he said and tried not to stare at that leather-clad ass. If they were alone, he would squeeze it like he was making juice.

Zak's blue eyes moved to him in a slow, languid move. He bit on the piercing in his lower lip, sending all kinds of sensations down to Stitch's groin with the view alone. "Hey. What's up?"

"Good party, right?" Stitch said as if they hadn't been living together like a newlywed couple for the last two months. Spending a night in the clubhouse yesterday had given Stitch some perspective on how much he liked sleeping with Zak next to him, ready to cuddle in the mornings, and always eager to chat over breakfast. The best Stitch could do tonight was get one of the female hangerons to make him a sandwich in exchange for flirting that he didn't initiate.

"Pretty wild," agreed Zak, gazing to the pool table of all places. "Is he gonna fuck her here?"

"Might do. You probably don't wanna watch, do you?" Stitch asked, standing closer, but the loud heavy metal music drowned their words anyway so he wasn't all that afraid of lack of privacy.

Zak crooked his head but with eyes as bright as his, the dilation of his pupils was visible even in the dimmed bar. He didn't move by an inch, letting Stitch get closer. "I've seen straights do it. I had very open-minded friends, you know."

"I don't know. Tell me." Stitch moved his head to the rhythm of the music.

"What about?" asked Zak, accepting the vodka shot Joe put in front of him. He downed it in one go. He didn't even blink.

Stitch wanted to kiss him so bad his lips itched. "About your friends, fucking in front of you."

Zak slowly turned toward him, leaning his ass on the bar stool. "They did it in the bed I was trying to sleep in. Can you imagine?" he asked with a wide smile, but his eyes were searching for something in Stitch's face.

Stitch laughed out loud and had some more beer. "Oh, God, Captain did that to me."

"He could have at least invited you to join the party." Zak brushed his fingers through his hair, never stopping to look at Stitch.

Stitch shook his head. "The girl was trying to grope me all the time. Thanks, but no thanks."

Zak smiled, lowering his gaze as he played with the shot glass, swirling his fingertip over its inner edge. "Why did you call me to come here all of a sudden?"

Stitch licked his lips. "I was kinda... I thought it would be more fun with you around."

Zak's brows twitched, and he leaned back, widening the distance between them. "And?"

"And I thought I could suck you off," he leaned toward Zak. It rolled off his tongue on its own accord.

Zak's plump mouth dropped open as he stared at Stitch without a word. It took him a total of about fifteen seconds to choke out, "Is that an apology?"

Stitch cocked his head to the side. It wasn't, but it could be if Zak wanted it to. "I suppose."

Zak exhaled, biting his lower lip again. Did he even know how sexy it was with those metal balls sliding against his flesh? "Okay," he whispered, but Stitch could read it on his mouth, even with the commotion all around.

Stitch's smile widened, and he nodded to the back of the bar. He wanted to slide his arm over Zak's waist, but he knew he couldn't so he just gestured for Zak to go first. He would not deny himself the sight of that glorious ass, even though it was halfway covered by the tank top. The black leather accentuated the well-formed calves and toned thighs, slightly reflecting the green light Joe switched on behind the bar. Stitch loved how Zak's walk tended to gently sway. Not in an effeminate way, it was just very relaxed and sensuous. And it led him, hypnotized, all the way to the door to the clubhouse.

Stitch took one more look at the wild party they left behind and wondered if he would still be a part of it if he backed out of the illegal business side of things. He needed to have a proper chat with Captain about it, but his thoughts dispersed when Zak reached the 'Private' sign and looked back at him with a small, teasing smile.

"Go on. Third door on the right." Stitch smirked, ready for a good fuck. What a day. Burning shit down, drinking hard, and now a night with his lover.

Zak pushed open the door and walked down the hallway, past an open door, past a room full of girly giggling. Stitch didn't look inside though, his eyes drawn to Zak's ass and back like a moth to the flame. He stopped breathing the moment Zak entered his temporary lodgings without even bothering to put on the light. Stitch did though. He wanted to see every last inch of skin. He locked the door and grabbed Zak's ass without a second of hesitation.

"Those pants are so goddamn hot."

"Yeah, you like them?" whispered Zak against Stitch's lips, teasing him with the warm breath and soft skin. It was a torture that had Zak holding onto Stitch's dick without actually touching it.

"It's like they hug your ass," Stitch murmured. He slid a finger between Zak's thighs and stroked Zak's balls through the leather. Amazing.

"They hug my cock as well." Zak gasped and gently spread his legs, pushing his hands under Stitch's cut.

"You know what else is gonna hug your cock?" Stitch murmured and embraced Zak while leading him to the bed.

Zak's mouth spread into a vicious grin. "Thor?"

"Nn, don't call me that." Stitch moaned, pushing Zak down to the bed. "My tongue will hug you tight." Even saying that had Stitch's blood pulsing faster.

Zak uttered a low moan and kicked off one boot while fumbling with the top button of his pants. They were so tight that his stiffening cock was clearly outlined beneath the leather. "That's so hot."

Stitch wasn't one to hesitate once he made up his mind, so he got to his knees, hot and panting already. It felt so weird to be kneeling in front of a man, but he wouldn't chicken out. His hands went straight for the buttons on Zak's pants, but Zak pulled him up by the hair and opened Stitch's mouth with his tongue. He pressed Stitch's hand against his erection and blew hot air from his lungs straight into Stitch's, making him high with breathlessness.

Stitch put his hands on the bed next to Zak's hips and only now realized how much he missed kissing him. One day was enough to make it feel like it was a month of separation.

Zak gasped into Stitch's mouth and proceeded to unbutton his pants completely, writhing already. His nipples were probably all hard by now. To be completely honest with himself, Stitch didn't think getting back together would be so easy. He expected Zak giving him a hard time, being a pain in the ass for a few days.

Stitch's finger's traced the sides of Zak's ass as he waited for the prize to be revealed. It sprang free in front of his face the moment Zak pushed his pants past his buttocks, hard and dark with the blood that must have left Zak's head the moment Stitch declared his readiness to suck.

"Oh, fuck, you're so hot, baby," whispered Zak, dropping to the mattress, which was neatly covered by an old plaid blanket.

"Remember that as I fail at this," Stitch laughed nervously, but wasn't about to be shy about the blow job and bowed to give the cockhead a long lick. The skin was salty and smooth. His heart trembled in his chest like, but fuck, if he could burn down a field of illegal weed, he could suck a cock.

Zak bit his lip and stroked Stitch's back, gently massaging it through the fabric. His eyes were dark with a haze of lust as he watched Stitch with a half smile. "Come on, you can't fail at blow jobs. As long as you don't bite it off, I'm gonna be over the moon."

That was the encouragement Stitch needed. He breathed in through his nose, trying to fight away the thoughts of being submissive to a man. At least with anal, there was the excuse of getting off on it as well, but this felt like servicing, or at least that was the logic his friends would suggest. He sucked on the tip, hoping his head would clear thanks to alcohol. It was smooth, and the slight saltiness penetrated Stitch's mouth as he opened up to the new sensations. A soft sigh from above told him he was doing well, and soon, there were fingers tangling into his hair, gently petting his scalp.

Stitch lowered his head over the dick, which was definitely thicker than a banana. For a moment, he pondered whether he should deepthroat, but decided trying wasn't worth the embarrassment of gagging and failing at it. He was so focused on Zak's dick that only now he realized his own was stiffening quickly. Just looking up at Zak's darkened face was getting him horny. Their eyes met, and Zak slowly pulled up his tank top, revealing more skin for Stitch's viewing pleasure. His bright smile was like a balm on Stitch's tense nerves as he explored the tip, moving his tongue around the head.

"Take it in your hand," whispered Zak, curling his fingers around Stitch's ear.

Stitch slipped his fingers over the base of Zak's cock. That he knew about. It throbbed so familiarly he groaned into the hard flesh. His eyes were glued to that nicely toned torso, all inked and amazing. He slid his other palm up that firm body and to the piercing in one of Zak's nipples.

Zak's eyelids fluttered, and he gasped at the gentle tug on the metal hoop. "Yeah... do that." He slowly thrust up, pushing slightly deeper into Stitch's mouth, over his palate but not deep enough to make him choke.

Sucking on the hot flesh came naturally, Stitch just imagined what he would have liked. He gave Zak's pubic piercing a teasing pull and breathed in deeply when he felt the cock in his mouth throb faster. He looked down at the snake tattooed all over the penis, and it made his throat pulse with lust when he imagined Zak getting it done, all spread out over the tattooing chair with his legs wide open.

He slowly relaxed, breathing in his lover's smell, which never seemed as intense as between his thighs while tasting his cock. The muscles shifted under the inked skin, making tiny movements each time Stitch moved his lips over the head while jerking off and squeezing the lower part of the penis with his fingers.

He gave the corona a teasing lick and started bobbing his head on the shaft with vigor, just so he could see more of that lust on Zak's face. He wanted to have Zak moaning and panting by whatever means.

"Slowly," whispered Zak, moving his thumbs over Stitch's cheek, his stomach shivering. He made a slight move, as if checking whether Stitch would be willing to take physical instruction. As long as it wouldn't mean a cock down his throat, Stitch let the hands guide him to what excited Zak. He supposed that just like they had different preferences when topping or bottoming, Zak could want to be sucked in a particular way, and it turned out he did. He wanted Stitch to focus on the head, gently sucking and lapping all over it like it was the sweetest lollipop. He liked to get his balls pulled and squeezed, and with the instruction, Stitch quickly got into the rhythm.

Now that he wasn't as worried about his incompetence, he could freely savor the sensations coming from the warm, masculine thighs squeezing around his head and shoulders. There was the distinctive sweet and salty flavor to the precome, which he tasted as Zak became even more excited, arching and stirring on the bed. He didn't stop petting Stitch, and even when his hands became stiffer and more tense toward the end, Stitch never sensed any attempts at dominating him. Which was a relief 'cause it was the last thing he was into.

When Zak whispered that he was about to come, in a voice so soaked with desire Stitch could bathe in it, Stitch pulled away and started jerking Zak off, with his lips on the throbbing vein on the underside of the cock. It drummed against his lips as if welcoming what was to come, and very soon Zak started gasping, his chest moving faster. With a powerful pulsing, the cock spurted several white streaks all over Zak's chest and stomach. He closed his eyes, twisting his nipples hard.

There. Stitch was officially a cocksucker. He was breathless as he watched the personification of his deepest desires in front of him. It was as if Zak was made for him and when he was ready to walk into Stitch's life, he came to Lake Valley to be picked like a ripe apple.

His muscles relaxed, one leg falling off Stitch's shoulder as he opened one eye and peeked at Stitch with a small smile. "You need a hand?"

"Fuck yes," Stitch groaned and couldn't pull his pants down faster if he tried. He got off the floor and instantly slipped to the best bedding he knew—Zak.

Zak chuckled and pulled him in for a kiss, letting his thighs fall to the sides to accommodate Stitch with more ease. "So good," he whispered, but breath died on his lips in the same moment as a thick, sharp onslaught of noise seared right through Stitch's brain, making him freeze. Zak's eyes went wide, his whole body tensing under Stitch, and Zak's hands squeezed around Stitch's biceps like vices.

Stitch's mind processed the sounds so reluctantly it felt as though his thought process was in slow motion. Gun shots. A lot of them. Possibly assault rifles. Taking into account that their club didn't own any, this wasn't good at all. He rolled off Zak, but panic stiffened his muscles into stone when he heard someone whacking at his door.

"Stitch, get your fucking ass out here!" he heard Captain shout, but instead of another whack that would give them a few more seconds to at least try to get decent, Captain busted the door, bursting inside like a wrecking ball.

He opened his mouth, stepping back when his gaze wandered past Stitch to a very naked Zak, who was still lying on the bed with his pants down at his ankles. In the dead silence, broken only by female screams from the bar and Stitch's own frantic heartbeat, it took Captain several seconds to speak again. "Nails just said 'hello' while you were getting your cock dipped in shit," he growled and left the room, giving them both a look so bloodthirsty it made Stitch want to crawl under the bed.

"Fuck, fuck, fuck, fuck," he uttered, pulling up his pants with trembling fingers. This was bad. So bad. So bad. A thousand cockroaches crawled all over his skin, and he couldn't shake them off. Not to mention there wasn't even time for it. He needed to go see what the damage was. "Stay here," he choked out.

Zak was already frantically pulling up the tight leather pants, his chest still stained with come. "But what if someone needs help. They stopped shooting," he uttered, but it was hard to miss that he'd gone pale as a sheet.

Stitch took a deep breath that did nothing to calm his nerves. He needed to talk to Captain, explain. "Okay, but if anything happens, you don't question what I tell you to do, understood?"

Zak nodded and quickly slipped on the tank top. He reached out and grabbed onto Stitch's belt loop, looking at him like a deer in the headlights. All Stitch wanted was to take Zak on the back of his bike and drive away to another state. Or country. In Europe preferably. The last thing he needed was the Hounds finding out he was a fag.

"I'll take care of it," he said to Zak and gave his arm a quick pat. He kept his cool only for Zak's sake.

Zak bit his lip and nodded, crossing his arms on his chest. "Let's go?" he asked in a quiet but steady voice.

The yelling and crying wasn't helping to keep the situation in check, but Stitch nodded and rushed out of the room. He ran through the corridor and into the bar, hit by the stench of blood and gunpowder the moment he opened the door.

It was carnage. With dust still in the air, all he could see were stiff figures wandering around like they couldn't believe what had just happened. Others were still crouching by the walls, under the knocked-over tables. Gator stood in the middle of the bar, holding onto a limp arm as he spewed obscenities and orders to everyone around him.

Stitch stepped into the scene of the massacre and it felt like being late to a party in hell. He looked over to Zak, but it was too late to put hands over his eyes.

"Stitch! It was a drive-by, they're gone, so let's take care of this first," Gator yelled at him over the other shouts. Someone was on the phone, someone else wouldn't stop crying, a girl sat shaking on a table with a huge shard of glass in her arm. Stitch didn't know where to even start helping.

A sharp cry tore through the room, and Stitch's eyes went to the bar, where a girl stumbled back and fell over, her gaze wide open in horror as she looked to the floor. Zak rushed over to her side, coughing as he entered the cloud of dust. Stitch followed, even though he felt Captain's gaze on his back, as if it was already painting 'FAG' on Stitch's forehead with a Sharpie. But that became so much less important when Stitch looked behind the bar at two dead bodies. But they weren't just 'bodies', they were people, two dead men. Rat and Joe, their bodies still warm in a puddle of dark blood, mouths open in a silent cry for help.

Stitch scooted down the moment he saw one of Rat's fingers still tremble, all red from the wounds on his stomach. When the movement stilled, Stitch knew it was just false hope he'd tried to cling to just like Rat had done to his life.

"Is he dead?" shrieked a girl, and Stitch could hear Zak trying to calm her down, but all noise clashed and mingled in Stitch's head. His friends were dead. Their bar was ruined. There were sirens approaching fast, and at the back of his mind there was hope that they had nothing illegal on the premises.

"Can't you shut her up? We have enough trouble without all that whining!" growled Captain somewhere from across the room.

"Zak, take the girls out." Stitch saw Captain sneer at him, and it hurt like it was him getting a shard of glass slice his chest.

Zak looked up at him, and for a horrible moment, Stitch realized his lover was looking at the dead bodies on the floor. But Zak shook off the stiffness and helped the crying woman get up. "Everybody out," he shouted, his voice a bit flat. "Help is on the way!"

Stitch ran his fingers through his hair and walked between the broken furniture. In the far corner, hidden under a table, he saw a man sitting with his back turned to the room. His shoulders were shaking and Stitch could swear he heard a sob, so he left the guy, unsure what he could possibly do for him. He helped the girl with the shard in her arm instead, picking her up into a careful embrace. "It's gonna be all right, an ambulance is coming."

Stitch didn't even know if it was good or bad that he didn't feel all that much. The stench got him nauseated, seeing a seventeen-year-old boy and all his dreams dead hit Stitch in the gut, but most of all, he felt numb. As if he were sinking into a swamp, the alligators approaching him with their sharp teeth and big jaws. But he could do nothing to escape so he didn't even fear them anymore.

Chapter 19

Zak dropped to a chair that was randomly standing in the parking lot by the entrance to the clubhouse. He felt boneless and burnt out. He'd never seen a dead person before, and the sight of empty eyes, blood covering hands that had earlier put a fucking vodka shot in front of him, was just too much. He rested his elbows on his knees and hid his face in his palms, which still carried the smell of crushed wood and gunpowder. His car was close by, but he wouldn't drive it tonight. The windows had been smashed, and there were two bullet holes in one of the doors. He shuddered at the thought that they could have been made with intent of injury. Three people had died. One random girl and two of Stitch's friends, but many more were wounded after a surprise raid from what he understood was a rival gang.

What had Stitch gotten himself into? This could not continue. *He could not continue* constantly worrying about Stitch getting hurt. An ambulance was still there, providing care to those lightly wounded, but Stitch was still inside with his homophobic buddy who had walked in on them like their life was some bad TV drama. How would that develop? Maybe if the guy chose to talk, Stitch would end up leaving the club and all its dirty deeds? It would probably hurt Stitch, and he'd be brooding, but Zak figured it would be good for both of them in the long run.

"I told you this man was trouble," he heard a calm and quiet voice from the side, and Officer Cox scooted next to Zak's chair.

Zak snorted and pulled himself up to sit properly. Like this conversation was something he wanted or needed now. "Of course he is," he said with a shrug. "But it wasn't him who did all this."

"I know, but you wouldn't be in danger if it wasn't for whatever you have going with him. Come on, Zak, I'm not the enemy here." The worst thing was that Cox's concerned expression really was as sincere as a fucking golden retriever begging for food at the table.

Zak pinched the piercing at the bridge of his nose. "Look, I appreciate your concern, I really do, but I wasn't in danger. I was at the back, and he never includes me in anything they do within the club. Whoever did this was plain crazy. Who does that?"

"Criminals, Zak. I would bet my right hand this attack wasn't unprovoked. This time, you might not have been in danger, but what about the next time? This is only going to get worse. You deserve something better."

Zak curled his toes in his boots and looked straight into Cox's eyes. That was true, so very true. He was still feeling shaken with the knowledge that had they stayed by the bar, they would have been sitting between the firearms and the now-dead. And if those men got inside, they wouldn't have treated him as a club-affiliated woman, for them he would be as much of an enemy as Stitch and his friends. But he couldn't help his nerves spiking at Cox stating that Stitch was bad for him.

"And what is that?"

"A boyfriend who won't end up in prison or dead. Someone you can build an honest life with." Cox didn't dare touch Zak in public, but it was clear the sparks between their bodies were there.

Zak snorted and hardly contained a shake of his head. Was Cox really pulling the boyfriend card here? They'd only fucked a few times, and didn't really have much to talk about. "I've been having honest boyfriends for the last ten years," he said, brushing his fingers over the heavy signet on his thumb. He was sometimes getting the impression that it burned with the power of Stitch's passion for him.

A heavy hand slid to Zak's shoulder. "We're done here," Stitch said in that tone that always made Zak want to spread his thighs. He looked back and gave him the best smile he could muster, which wasn't all that great. The only regret he had was that he couldn't hold him.

Cox straightened up like a proud turkey and crossed his arms on his chest. "Really, Larsen? Haven't you caused enough damage?"

Stitch's lips were a thin line, and he didn't even bother answering. He wore a black hoodie under his cut and leather gloves. "I'm taking you home," he said to Zak and passed him a helmet, yet Zak was sure those words were partially for Cox's ears.

He got to his feet, a bit lightheaded, and struggled to stop himself from grabbing Stitch's hand. "See you around. Hope you can find those guys," he said to Cox before walking off. Home sounded good. They would be safe at home.

Captain watched their every step toward Stitch's bike as he stood by the door, smoking and talking to another police officer. The gaze was so menacing it gave Zak shivers. There was a promise of something sinister in those eyes, but he wouldn't let himself think about it too much. The ground under his feet seemed a far better place to look at. Or the patches on the broad back of his man, even if they did bring them so much trouble and arguments. Stitch got on the bike without a word, looking back at Zak with an unreadable expression.

Zak put on the helmet and climbed into the bitch seat, grabbing its back like a good straight boy. This wasn't how they'd ridden a few times down empty roads, with him clinging to Stitch's back, taking a quick fuck break somewhere in the woods. All he wanted was to get going, and it looked like Stitch had the same idea.

With a roar of the engine, they sped forward as if shot from a ballista. Well over the speed limit, but with three dead bodies and a shooting, no one would bother to stop them for speeding. Wind hit Zak's naked arms, but soon enough they were out of sight, on an empty road, leaving all the bloodshed behind them, and Zak could slide his hands around Stitch's waist.

A flood of relief washed through him as soon as he could squeeze his arms around that thick torso and bury his face in the leather of the cut. His heart was racing against his ribs as the bike went, way, way past the speed limit, and he closed his eyes, digging his fingers into Stitch's chest. There was only darkness around them, the only lights in the windows of the houses by the road.

With his hand on Stitch's chest, Zak could feel every heartbeat drumming fast. It only made Zak hug Stitch tighter. Sitting at the back of the bike wasn't all that bad when he could trust Stitch to get him home safely. The speed gave Zak an adrenaline rush, but he felt as safe as ever. At a hundred miles an hour, no one could disturb them, it was only him and Stitch. The feeling it evoked made Zak want to never leave the bike and ride on forever.

*

When they arrived at Zak's, the whole neighborhood was dead silent. No one seemed to know what had happened just a few miles away, and Zak hugged Stitch hard as soon as he was back on his own two feet. His mouth spilled what he had been thinking for the last two hours, continuously grinding it through his brain along with the horrific images of Stitch lying dead instead of Joe. "We could have been there."

"I know, sweetheart." Stitch pulled him close and cupped his head with his big, leather-clad hand. Zak breathed in Stitch's scent and followed it, his mouth finding those familiar lips by heart, and he grabbed the sides of Stitch's cut, pulling them even tighter together. He needed to be close *now*, not in a few minutes, or once they reached the door. It was a desire so basic and profound that he couldn't care less if anyone recognized them at this point.

The hiss he got in return was full of the same need for connection, better than words. Stitch's arms around Zak's waist were so solid and firm that within the embrace it felt like nothing could hurt him. His lover's hot tongue explored Zak's lips in an eagerness only comparable to their first kisses.

Zak pulled him toward the house without breaking the embrace. They were stumbling over uneven ground but neither wanted to part from the other's warmth. Zak pushed the gate shut with his boot, and only blind luck saved them from falling down on the stairs to the porch. His skin was on fire, and the need in his chest could only be filled with more closeness, more of Stitch.

They got into the house to a greeting from Versay, but Zak quickly let the dog out so they wouldn't be interrupted. Stitch grabbed him from behind and pulled him to the living room, walking backward and kissing Zak's neck. His grip was so tight it left Zak breathless. They could stumble over one of Versay's toys or the coffee table, and he could then end up with a broken neck, but at this point he didn't care, entrusting everything to Stitch. He clung to him, kissing his mouth with abandon, as if this were the last time he could ever touch him, and the mere thought of it made him tremble with fright.

Stitch pulled Zak to the couch in the darkness that was only sparsely illuminated by the light seeping in from outside. "Whatever happens, I won't let you get hurt," he whispered and pulled off Zak's top. His eyes had an intensity to them that would make Zak believe in anything Stitch said. Zak nodded and pushed on Stitch's cut, spreading his legs to pull him close. His throat was slowly choking up.

"I don't want you hurt either."

Stitch parted Zak's lips with another greedy kiss, at the same time trying to pull Zak's pants down. The tumble of hands and kisses ended in them falling to the floor from the narrow couch. At least it wasn't far.

"My shoes," uttered Zak, trying to quickly push them off without parting from Stitch, but his lover grunted in protest.

"I don't care about your shoes." Stitch was already rubbing against Zak with his groin. Before Zak could protest, try to get naked, do things properly, even if on the floor, Stitch flipped him over to his stomach and pulled Zak's pants down to his thighs.

Zak's face met with the dusty carpet, but with Stitch's fully clothed form covering him like the sweetest, thickest blanket, he couldn't care less. All he could hear was Stitch's panting and the sound of his zipper being pulled down. It was as if that zipper moved all the way down his spine and into his crack, opening him up for Stitch.

With a deep shudder, Zak curled his spine and raised his ass to brush against rough denim and a very hot, very hard cock. "Oh, God," he uttered, clawing his fingers into the carpet. His stomach was like a firepit, and he needed something to stir the burn.

Stitch bit on his nape instead of an answer and fumbled with something for just one second. Lube dripped between Zak's buttocks, and Stitch's cock was right there to follow that dribble, already aligning with Zak's anus. The heat, Stitch's weight, the dusty smell combined with Stitch's cologne and the scent of leather sent Zak's senses into overload. He tried to push his knees wider apart, but it was no use with the tight pants holding them together.

He moaned, tilting his hips and pressing his ass against that big, wonderful cock. He needed it now. Now. "Stitch..."

"What is it?" Stitch rasped, climbing on top of Zak like a wild beast and already pushing in with his cockhead. As much as Zak wanted to believe he was ready, there was a stinging burn from the push, which was immediately cooled down with a long lick at Zak's neck.

Zak opened his mouth, but no sound came as he stiffened, feeling the hard shaft push its way into him like a merciless machine. Yet that was what he was waiting for, and he moaned Stitch's name again, shuddering with the shock of intermingling pain and pleasure. He was burning up from the tips of his toes all the way to his head, and with Stitch's heavy, strong body on top of him, he was more helpless against raw emotion than ever.

"I need to melt into you," Stitch whispered into Zak's skin, his cock so hot inside, like it was a piece of Zak's body. It fit in him so perfectly, even with the burn. Stitch didn't stay still though. He put his hands on the floor to hold his weight and pulled out halfway only to slam back in.

Zak yelped and grabbed onto Stitch's wrists, digging his fingertips into the hot flesh. He was already breathless, but all he wanted was more warmth, so he pulled on his lover's hands. "No, I want you on me," he uttered as pain turned into a pleasant friction.

Stitch murmured something and bit into Zak's neck, distracting him from the intensity of the fuck. Stitch's hips moved back and forth to the soundtrack of his grunts as he screwed Zak into the carpet. "You have me."

Zak stretched his body farther, arching his back to be even closer. Stitch's body was a warm cage shielding him from the world, from the gunmen from earlier on, even from his own fears as Stitch pinned Zak down with his cock. Waves of sensation washed through Zak just as rapidly as the storm spreading in his chest, fueled by each thrust, each grunt above him. "*You* have *me*," he uttered, squeezing his eyes shut. He couldn't even comprehend the depth of what he was feeling at this moment. All the horrible things he'd seen tonight, all the hurtful things in the past, it was all nothing in comparison.

Just a few thrusts later, Stitch came, biting Zak's neck even harder than before, like he wanted to eat him alive. His hot come filled Zak as Stitch made the most teasing circles with his hips. It felt like having Stitch plant his seed deep inside, dirty, erotic, and emotional all at the same time. His thick arms slid under Zak's body and Stitch hugged him tightly, still panting and burning Zak with his desire.

"Don't pull out," uttered Zak, pulling his thighs together to trap the cock inside him, still pulsing, still very much alive even if softening. He grasped Stitch's hand, turned his head to the side, and rested his cheek on the carpet, looking up at his lover. Even with the burning need still tugging at his cock, he wanted to stay like this for a little longer, safe and cared for in Stitch's arms.

"Can't say no to that." Stitch kissed Zak's aching neck. "You're my natural high. I needed it after tonight."

"Me too." Zak reached back and smiled when he touched the longish hair. His breathing was slowly getting back to normal, but he raised his hips to reach his cock even if just barely. He was pulsing all over and needed the release that built up in his balls. "I needed my caveman..."

Stitch pushed himself up on his elbows so Zak had less to carry, but the slippery feeling on his ass was only going to get him closer to orgasm. "Your Thor." Stitch bowed and kissed Zak's back.

Zak whined, arching for more as he started jerking off at a furious speed. It only became more urgent when he noticed Stitch's cock slowly shrinking, withdrawing from his burning, slippery hole. His thoughts flooded with red and green shapes as he grunted, drunk on the closeness. Some of Stitch's seed dribbled out of Zak and down his balls, but it was when the head started slowly dislodging from his anus that he came with a sharp cry, curling up under the powerful body as all tension left him to the feeling of bliss. "You're mine..."

"I am." Stitch never stopped showering Zak's back with kisses and slowly fell to his side, pulling Zak along.

Zak turned in his arms and pushed his face into the soft hoodie, which was now warm as a radiator. He wanted to say something, but with his head completely empty, he just stayed silent, savoring his lover's scent and leftover energy. His ass was on fire, but he wouldn't complain and instead slowly unzipped Stitch's hoodie just enough to cuddle his face into the warm chest. The earthy scent of his lover was enough to set his mind at ease.

Stitch was the one to speak first, holding Zak close. "I'll tie up the loose ends and pull away from the club."

Zak looked up at him, his windpipe choking up a bit as their eyes met. And to think he was sure he'd have to somehow convince Stitch it would be the best solution. Him coming up with it himself wasn't what Zak had expected at all. Stitch seemed so close with the club members. Could he really go through with this? This situation must have shocked Stitch, and Zak wasn't surprised because if he were the intended victim, he'd be scared shitless. "I... wanted to suggest that."

"It's just not gonna happen overnight. I wanna stay in the workshop and be around the club, but this shit was too much." He stroked Zak's head. "The club's changed. It's not what it used to be."

Zak exhaled, pulled himself up, and slid his arms around Stitch's neck, drawing him in for a slow, gentle kiss. Just touching Stitch was making him feel so alive, and the fire was back in his chest. "Will they allow that?"

"I'm gonna have to try. Today wasn't random, Zak. We're into deeper shit now, and I can't have you in danger."

Zak's heart stopped before sprinting into a furious gallop. Stitch was committing to Zak more than he had imagined if he was willing to break up the most stable relationship he'd ever had. "I'll be fine..."

"No, you won't. Especially now that I don't even know yet what Captain will do." Stitch tightened his hug around Zak. For all Zak was concerned, he could stay for the night in this embrace on the floor. "I'm not such a good guy, Zak."

A sharp laugh tore out of Zak's throat, and he shook his head. "Yeah, I know. You're a criminal with a flamethrower. What did you burn this time?" he whispered.

Stitch closed his eyes. "I burned their drug field. As retaliation over them stealing our money... and drugs, beating us up. Gator killed one of their men. It's a mess. That's why they attacked tonight."

Zak sighed but stroked Stitch's face not to discourage him from sharing. This was much worse than he had assumed. Gator, the silly bald president of the club? A murderer? Zak had a hard time getting his head around that. "Maybe it's better if we just move? Or did they see your face?"

"Lake Valley is my home, Zak. I'll sort it out. They don't know who exactly burned down their field, but they know it was probably us three who had the biggest grudge against them. I got a lot of weed from their warehouse, so it will cover most of my debt to the club. The guys who died tonight? Rat became a prospect two weeks ago, and Joe only patched in last month. Not to mention the girl, she was just a hangeron. I can't stand that it could have been you, or that you even had to see it." Stitch opened his eyes and cupped Zak's face. "I never really killed that guy whose house I burnt down, the one who stabbed me. I beat him up, but I couldn't finish him. Actually... I didn't want to, you know. That's not what I want my life to be."

Zak felt his whole body melt into Stitch, and he nuzzled his cheek with a smile. "I know. You wouldn't have done that. I knew you just said that to scare me."

Stitch groaned. "Do I really seem like such a teddy bear?"

Zak shook his head, playing with the dry, long hair. "No, but you're not a murderer either." He smiled and brushed his fingers over the middle of Stitch's chest. "You have a soft center."

"Maybe because I'm a fag." Stitch frowned but stroked Zak's face. There it was again, the language Zak wanted to roll his eyes at.

"No, you're a masculine gay badass. Killing people is hardly the norm, you know. I wouldn't have fucked you if I believed that you killed that man." Zak swallowed hard and cupped the side of Stitch's face, moving his thumb over the ever-present stubble.

Those words finally brought a hint of a smile to Stitch's face, and he turned slightly to kiss Zak's finger. "'Gay badass', I like that. I can't be here until I sort things out though. I can't have someone come round here someday and attack you. I *would* kill that sonofabitch and go to prison forever. And that you don't want, right?"

Zak chuckled and hugged him hard, pressing a kiss to the side of Stitch's neck. "You think that's gonna last long? A week?" he whispered, already feeling strange at the idea of not sleeping with Stitch for several days in a row.

"I don't know, baby. It's gonna get ugly before it can get pretty." Stitch slipped his palm over Zak's and entwined their fingers.

Zak bit his lip, raising his head to look at him. "So... where will we meet up?"

"We probably won't for a while." Stitch pulled on Zak's lip piercing with his teeth. "But I'll try to call and let you know how things are going."

Zak stiffened and pulled on the folds of Stitch's hoodie. "Come on, we're in the same town. Won't you miss me?" he asked, not sure what to make of this. Was he to wait and see whether Stitch got out of this mess alive?

"Are you kidding me? Of course I'll miss you. If it's not risky, we'll meet up. I need to pacify Captain first. I'm not looking forward to it."

"Isn't he your friend?" Zak sighed and pulled closer, pushing his arm under Stitch's head. "He'll come around. What do you think he'll say after tonight's 'performance'?"

Stitch petted the back of Zak's head. "Probably a lot. He's a friend of Straight Stitch. I don't think he'll appreciate the gay one much. But I don't think he'll out me. I really hope so."

Zak nodded and kissed the bridge of Stitch's nose. It was killing him that he could do nothing to help. "Will you let me know? If something's wrong, give me a shout or come over."

"I will if it's safe. Keep Versay fed, yeah?" Stitch gave him a small smile.

Zak shook his head, fighting the clenching feeling around his stomach. "Yeah, yeah, your favorite."

Stitch kissed Zak once more. "We better move to bed."

Zak nodded and slowly withdrew from his arms. He unzipped his boots and pushed them down so that he could remove the leather pants as well. He was increasingly agitated. "How long will you stay?"

"A few hours. I'll go in the morning." Stitch sat up and got some tissues from the table.

Zak accepted them and briefly cleaned himself up before taking hold of Stitch's warm hand and leading him away from the living room. They let Versay in and all three of them climbed the stairs. It was surreal how well they could move through the dark house, as if it had been their home for years. Darkness was safe, hiding them from the world, even if just for a brief few hours. Zak watched Stitch climb into bed first, naked, and he joined in, sliding under the thin sheet to feel the warmth of his lover's body again. He didn't want to fall asleep before Stitch needed to go, watching the line of fine hairs on his body in the weak moonlight, playing with his coarse mane as worries toppled over him like cold waves. But after they fucked again, he gave up and let Stitch's scent lull him to sleep.

Stitch was gone when Zak woke up the next morning.

Chapter 20

Leaving Zak's house in the morning was the hardest thing Stitch had done in a while, so to save himself the good-byes, he slipped out without waking Zak up. He took a shower and packed a bag of essentials. He didn't bother with the rest of his stuff, since he was planning to come back soon. Soon. It was a vague term for the time being, but Stitch kept it in his heart nevertheless.

In the morning, he also dared to check his phone, where Captain's text message stabbed his eyes.

'Meet me at Granny's at 9'

Captain didn't even want to talk to him at the clubhouse. The police could still be there, but it also meant Captain wanted to talk one on one. Stitch had no idea if it was a good sign or not, but ten to nine, he parked in front of Granny's.

Captain's bike was already there, so Stitch didn't hesitate and walked in, smiling at one of the owners, who greeted him with a wide smile and presented the cake of the day. He hadn't had any breakfast yet, so it might be a good idea to get his stomach full while he could. He didn't even want to look for Captain, who was probably hidden away in the deeper corner of the cafe. He ordered his food by the counter and took it himself, spending a bit of time chatting to Maggie. If he were honest with himself, he would admit that he was avoiding having to talk to Captain, but he couldn't stay at the counter forever. He took his food and turned around to face his friend. This wouldn't be a pleasant morning.

Captain sat, as predicted, in the shadowy corner in the second room of the cafe, with a large black coffee in front of him. His single eye trailed up and met Stitch's gaze like an ice pick ready to strike.

"Ahoy," Stitch tried at a joke, but only got a scowl in return as he sat down with two pieces of cheesecake. Captain's face became even more stern.

"What is this? A fag breakfast?"

Stitch was so taken aback by this notion that he had to re-evaluate his cake. It didn't look very gay to him. "I don't know," he groaned. "I'm just fucking hungry, jeez."

"Should have taken a proper breakfast, not one that's suitable for a divorced wife crying over the paperwork," growled Captain, squeezing his hands over the cup. It wasn't a good start of the conversation.

"Okay, okay, I get it, you're pissed. I'll have some toast if that makes you feel better." Stitch tapped his fingers on the table as Maggie got him his coffee.

They waited until she went off with the jug, and only then Captain leaned forward, drilling his gaze into Stitch, as if he expected to extract the elixir of truth from him with the look alone. "Since when?"

Cold sweat already beaded on Stitch's back, and the cakes looked more appetizing than ever. "A while," he muttered.

Captain sucked in some air and shook his head. "Fuck. I should have noticed how much of a freak he was. Weak, no interest in women whatsoever. It should have been fucking obvious."

It struck a nerve that Stitch found hard to keep in check. "But it wasn't, 'cause he's not obvious at it." And Zak wasn't 'weak', just not used to fighting. Like any normal person.

"And what, you just went for it? What can he do that's so much better than what you can do with a girl?" Before Stitch could even answer, Captain waved his hand in the air with a sneer. "Don't tell me. I'm gonna fucking puke."

Stitch grumbled as a waitress brought him a full breakfast with eggs, bacon and toast. He waited till she left to speak. "It's just blow jobs," he lied, hoping that would go down better than anything else. He got used to feeling so liberated with Zak that having to deal with actually talking to someone about it was surprisingly uncomfortable. Looked like he wasn't so liberated after all, and joking about being a 'fag' became all too real. He didn't worry all that much about what Zak thought of him bottoming, because Zak was doing it himself. Zak was gay, he got it. But Captain? Crystal? What would his daughter think if she ever found out? All those questions were falling on his head brick by brick. He was finding out that he himself wasn't feeling all that good about being gay anymore, now that 'being gay' didn't just equate to having mind-blowing sex with Zak.

"There are plenty of girls who'd love to swallow your dick, so what the fuck's wrong with you? How did he pull you into this?" Captain leaned in, his brows lowering over his eyes. "Is this fucker blackmailing you?"

"No." Stitch looked up at Captain, with his eyes going wider. "He's a friend. It's not like we do it all the time or anything. He's got those tats and that lip ring—" He figured it was about time to shut up, so he stuffed his mouth with bacon.

"So get a fucking chick with tattoos and piercings. What the fuck's your problem? You're handsome enough," growled Captain. He had some more coffee, watching Stitch's plate rather than his face. "Who else is he fucking in town?"

"I don't know. We don't talk about shit like that," Stitch mumbled with his mouth full. As much as he hated Cox's guts, outing him could provoke Cox to out Stitch in return. Fucking catch-22.

Captain shook his head. "He needs to go."

"What do you mean?" Stitch hunched over his food. Even with a half-truth of 'just blow jobs', or that Zak was the only guy Stitch was attracted to, Captain was already on the edge of doing something stupid. This wasn't some Kumbaya coming out, this was about survival.

"He leaves town. That's it," muttered Captain, tapping his fingers on the table.

Cold sweat was back on Stitch's skin. "Come on, give the guy a break. I'll just tell him not to come over. It's not like he's a Hound."

Captain sneered. "He might not be a Hound but he bit one's balls off apparently."

Stitch filled his mouth again, but barely had enough appetite left to chew. Was he really all that gay now? He didn't notice any particular change in himself other than being satisfied like never before in his life. "My balls are firmly attached," he snapped at Captain.

Captain snorted. "We'll see about that. Gator's already planning to get back at the Nails. I hope your knees won't soften like a little girl's."

Stitch wanted to scream in frustration. This kind of shit was exactly why it was so hard to pull out. "My knees are firm, but aren't Rat and Joe dead enough? We really need more?"

"Are you chickening out?" uttered Captain with challenge in his eyes, and in the same moment, Stitch's phone buzzed against his hip.

He pulled it out and when he saw it was Crystal, he wasn't happy at all. Arguing with her was the last thing he needed today. "What?" he asked harshly when he picked up the call.

She sighed into the line, and when she spoke, her voice was worried. "Are you all right? I just heard what happened."

"Ah, yeah, yeah, I'm fine. It's just tense here." It was touching to hear that she cared enough after all that rotted between them.

Captain sighed, relaxing into his chair. He probably heard the female voice. Crystal always spoke loudly on the phone.

"Do you think you could come over? I was thinking maybe it could be good if we talked and you spent some time with Holly?"

"Yeah," he said before he could give it a second of thought. "Yeah, I'd love to see her." Stitch just hoped the 'talking' wouldn't develop into an argument, but he could take it if it was the price of getting to see Holly.

"Cool. We'll be home for the whole day, so come over whenever you have time, okay?"

"Yeah, thanks for calling, I really appreciate it. See you." He put the phone down only to get back to yet another uncomfortable conversation. "Can't we just leave the drugs? We're clearly still not big enough," he went back right where they finished before. "I'm not chickening out, I'm just being logical."

"You're being faggy." Captain shook his head and emptied his cup without looking at Stitch.

Stitch froze, using all the willpower he had not to slam Captain's face against the table. Enough was enough. "You're pissing me off. I'm gonna go see Crystal now, but I'll come by the club later on and deal with everything that needs to be done." He drank some coffee and got up, knocking the back of his chair against the empty table behind him. "You can eat the fucking gay cake if you want."

Captain leaned back in the chair and scrutinized him without even a trace of fear or shame. "I'm only keeping this secret because we've been friends so long, but that's your only chance with me."

Stitch bowed over the table, his chest heavy. He hadn't even noticed when Captain had become so different from him, when they started wanting different things. "Fine. I keep my dick in pussy, and you leave Zak alone, 'cause he's got nothing to do with this."

Captain's complete silence was hard to interpret.

"Good." Stitch snarled at him, even though this wasn't good at all. He turned around and walked off, tense like after a night of sleeping on the floor. He'd known yesterday that he would need to leave Zak for a while for safety reasons, but talking to Captain made him pessimistic about the future.

He mounted his bike and stormed to his former home. At least visiting Holly would maybe make him feel better, so he bought her a chocolate bar on the way. If she was to see him so rarely the memories should be good.

He was relieved not to see Milton's car in the driveway. The positives didn't end there. Crystal actually walked out to greet him. Not only that. When he got off the bike, she hugged him close, wrapping her arms around his waist like when they were still a couple.

"I was so scared when I found out about the shooting," she whispered into his chest. Her red lion mane tickled his neck, and when she looked up, eyes wide and sincere, he had a powerful sense of déjà vu. "You're not hurt?"

"Nah, I'm fine. Let's go inside, huh?" He gave her forehead a kiss that was so automatic he couldn't stop himself from doing it.

Crystal stiffened against him and pulled back with an unreadable expression. "I'm not jumping on that boat again," she muttered and turned on her heel to enter the house.

"I... That's not what I meant," Stitch mumbled and combed his hair back with his fingers. Why was life so frigging hard today?

"I know, it's just... weird." Crystal gave him a tight smile and moved toward the kitchen. The house felt so peaceful and familiar it was getting to Stitch immediately. "I heard three people died."

"Yeah, Joe, this new guy, Rat, and some girl. Penny was her name, I think." He sat in one of the chairs by the small kitchen table.

"Oh, my God..." Crystal slowly sat in the other chair, too shocked to offer him a glass of sweet tea from the pitcher on the table. "That's horrible. What have you guys gotten yourselves into this time?"

"Listen, Crystal, if you wanna lecture me, it's not the right time. I've got enough on my plate anyway." Stitch couldn't even look into her eyes, too beaten down by the earlier conversation with Captain.

His words seemed to have pulled her out of the stupor, and Stitch heard the familiar cling of ice cubes falling into the glass along with tea.

"What's going on?"

"Captain saw me with Zak," he whispered, accepting the tea like it was a peace offering. He didn't know who else to talk to about this.

Crystal leaned back in the seat with a deep sigh. "You really need to focus on what's important right now. Is that gay thing really worth your friends? Your daughter? Clearly, this situation you got yourself into isn't doing you any good."

Stitch wished he had actually eaten that cheesecake. He could use something sweet in his life. Tea had to do. "I know, I know..." He remembered how gorgeous Zak looked in the morning when Stitch had left him sleeping, curled under the sheet, with his hands next to his face. "I'm not like some typical gay guy or something..."

Crystal shook her head. "Do you need help? I know there are therapies for people like you."

Stitch licked his lips. Had he just been trapped in a safety cocoon with Zak for too long? He took it one day at a time and didn't really know what his life would look like in the future. How could he have been so stupid and believe that no one would find out about him fucking a guy? "I don't know..." He clenched his fingers on the cold glass.

Crystal's hand trailed across the table to grasp Stitch's fingers. "Look, I want you to be happy. If you agree to break up with that guy, I'll let you see Holly again. Wouldn't that be motivating?"

'Motivating'? Everything would be so much easier if he broke up with Zak. But it wouldn't make him happier. Why did he have to choose? This wasn't just about where he put his dick. Stitch had never felt such desperate love for anyone but Zak. But then there was Holly, and he wanted to be a part of her life so bad it hurt. He grew up with only his grandparents after his parents bailed on him and left, so having a family had always been high on his agenda. So much so that he didn't even feel bad about Crystal getting pregnant all those years ago. He was sure he could make it work. Was he a scumbag for wanting Zak more than to see his daughter?

"I could try," Stitch said as if he were on autopilot. The last six months felt like someone else's life, and that someone had it a lot better than Stitch did now. He wasn't going to see Zak for a while, so maybe he could at least see Holly a few times, see how it went. Maybe it was a bit like drugs, and after the initial withdrawal period, he would be clean from the dirty lust he had for Zak?

"You're a good guy, I know you are. Maybe I just wasn't the girl for you? There's no reason for you to just go with the flow like that. Girls need more work than guys, I suppose, but isn't it worth it to have a family?"

Stitch had some tea, but barely managed to swallow it. "If I had another girl, you wouldn't mind me seeing Holly?" Maybe he should give it try?

"No, of course not." Crystal sat up straight and smiled at him. "You need to make a life for yourself."

"And if I wanted a life with Zak, I wouldn't get to have Holly in it?" He kept avoiding her eyes, feeling like an abused dog, always ready for another kick.

Crystal pulled her hand away and looked at her lap. "Stitch, that's not how it works. You can't have a family with a dude, come on... You might think you're infatuated, but it'll pass. You know it will."

He nodded, knowing this was the end of it. The black hole in his chest grew ever stronger. "Can I go see her?" he mumbled.

Crystal stroked his hand again, gently moving her fingers over the knuckles. "Yeah, she's taking a nap in her room. But she slept enough, I think." She got up from the chair and looked at him with a frown. "You lost your signet."

Stitch had a whole bunch of them, but he knew exactly which one she meant. The one that actually had meaning to him, not like the random assortment of metal on his other fingers. "Yeah, I think I lost it." *Along with my heart.*

Crystal bit her lip. "Sorry. It was from your grandfather, wasn't it?"

"It was. Shit happens." He looked to the trash can, dying to change the subject. "What's up with that?" he pointed to the pile of broken dishes on top.

Crystal's mouth closed as if it was sealed, and she looked away, pulling a lock of hair behind her ear. "Just a misunderstanding."

"Fucking Milton. I told you he's an ass," Stitch groaned but made his way out of the kitchen, eager to see his daughter again. Crystal made no attempt to argue with him, so he rushed up the stairs, stopping only when he reached Holly's door. He took a few deep breaths and slowly pressed the door handle. The door opened with a quiet squeak, and he peeked inside. Holly was curled up in her pink bed covers, with the swan headrest Stitch had made himself spreading its wings over her like a guardian angel.

It was so fucking touching he wanted to cry. He came in quietly and pushed away the ballerina shoes from the carpet to sit by her bed. "Hey, sweetie." He stroked her blonde hair, and she opened her tiny mouth with a loud yawn, stretching on the bed.

"D-daddy?" she uttered, putting her fists against her eyes.

"Yeah, come give me a hug. I missed you. What have you been up to?" He couldn't help his throat constricting when he watched her little body climb from under the sheets and into his arms.

"You've been away so long. How was your trip?" she asked, pushing her tiny hands around his neck.

Stitch hugged her tight and closed his eyes. "It was amazing, but I had to come back to my Holly, right?"

She gave him a wide grin and pulled herself up, kissing his cheek. "What did you get me?"

Stitch laughed. "Always so greedy. Am I not enough?"

"Well, you have to say sorry for not telling me that you were going away," she said with a cute, childish pout.

"I'll make something nice for you, how about that?"

"I want a rocking My Little Pony." She climbed into his lap and tugged on his cut. "On a bike, and with a hound drawn on her butt."

Stitch scratched his chin. "That's... a challenge."

Chapter 21

It was the seventh day in a row when Zak tried to call Stitch with no success. Messages were left unanswered as well, and while Zak had several jobs throughout the week, even that wasn't enough to distract him from the growing fear for Stitch. His bike was in front of the club, but as soon as Zak got his car back, he started making rounds, hoping to catch a glimpse of his lover.

He found himself unable to sleep, with his head filled with images of Stitch beaten up, with knocked out teeth, or having his club tattoo burned away along with the skin, like in the television show they'd watched some time ago. Why else wouldn't Stitch let Zak know what was going on? For lack of a better option, he invited Versay into his bed. The beast preferred to lie on the floor and always climbed off the moment Zak slipped into a slumber, but at least it helped a bit.

The town was slowly getting back to normal after the shooting incident. Zak was sad that he couldn't attend the funerals, but he didn't want to interfere with Stitch's plans.

But after a week, the death-like silence was starting to sound like a hollow well, someplace that had swallowed his man and refused to give him up. It was a broken pencil that pushed Zak over the edge. He threw his sketchbook across the room, followed it with the pencil, and kicked the sofa with a low groan. Versay's furious barking was like an accusation, and Zak raised his hand, turning the signet on his thumb. If Stitch didn't come to him, he would go to Stitch.

The day was ridiculously sunny for October, and Zak was boiling in the car, but things like that wouldn't discourage him. He needed to know what the fuck was going on, even if he was uneasy about meeting Captain and the accusing stare of his one eye. When he got to the clubhouse, he could hardly believe his eyes.

Stitch was there in just his jeans, hammering nails into wooden boards covering the spaces where the windows used to be. He stood on a ladder, his wide shoulders and glorious back like a free show for a group of girls sitting by a table outside and sipping drinks. One of them, a tall, heavily tattooed brunette with piercings sprinkled over her face like raisins in a fruitcake, got up and took a glass over to Stitch.

Blood boiled in Zak's veins, and he pulled into the parking lot without slowing down much. The girl yelped in surprise and spilled some of the drink on her shirt. Zak was out of the car before she could even unglue the wet fabric from her small breasts. His whole body was at the same time freezing and hot like the hood of his car. He could hardly catch a full breath as he approached the ladder, his eyes focused on Stitch as if he were his lifeline. When had he become so dependent on this guy? Wasn't it always Stitch begging for Zak's attention like an underappreciated golden retriever?

Stitch turned around and gave a faint smile as he stopped the hammering. He looked so glorious Zak wanted to scream. The memories of seeing that club tattoo underneath himself as he fucked Stitch were so raw in Zak's mind, his whole body throbbed at the sight and his legs carried him closer on their own accord. The jeans Stitch had on today were quite loose, all worn and torn, showing one knee and a bit of skin on his thigh. Stitch wore them for the DIY jobs around Zak's house, and as much as Zak loved seeing Stitch in the tight leather pants, these were great for a tiny peek at the top of Stitch's ass when he bent over. That had to be what the women were out here for.

Zak stuffed his hands into his pockets and forced himself to make his breathing sound calm, even if it made his lungs hurt. "You skipped your tattoo appointment," he lied, staring into the tanned face.

Stitch licked his lips like he did when he was about to lie. "Yeah, I kinda—"

"I don't think he needs that appointment anymore," Captain finished for him, walking out of the dark innards of the club like he was an emissary from hell.

Zak looked at him with fire burning deep in his chest. If only he could choke this bastard to death without any consequences... He bet Captain was the one behind Stitch's silence. "Nah, I'm pretty sure he does."

Captain approached Zak slowly with hands down his pockets. "I talked to him, and he doesn't want your ink anymore. Get it?"

Stitch wouldn't even look into Zak's eyes as he climbed down the ladder. It hurt much less to look into the hateful face of Captain, all tense and ready to sneer. Zak was surprised at how calm he was feeling.

"I don't think he needs a messenger."

Stitch passed Captain and slightly pushed Zak to the side and toward the club. "I'll talk to him, Cap. Go chat to Raven or something," he groaned.

The man didn't answer, but Zak didn't care much for him, too focused on the warm touch of Stitch's rough fingers. He looked at him even as they walked. "You've been here all this time?" he whispered.

"Yes." It was a barely audible mutter, and when they walked into the club, a dozen eyes watched them pass. It made Zak's skin crawl. He swallowed hard and rushed forward, leading the way into the corridor where Stitch had taken him a few times. His feet moved quickly, as if wanting to keep up with Zak's heart. He didn't know what to make of this. How could Stitch worry him so much?

The moment the door to Stitch's room shut, the silence became unbearable. And to make matters worse, Stitch actually backed off a few steps instead of following his usual voracious hunger for closeness.

Zak's teeth started slightly clattering, and he squeezed his jaw hard, his back hitting the wall. "What is this? What the fuck is going on?" he uttered, choking up at the back of his throat. His mind already knew, but he refused to believe it. He knew going into a relationship would end badly, he knew it!

"I have to take some time off, Zak." Stitch took a deep breath, which only emphasized just how ridiculously well chiseled his abs were. "There's all this shit with Captain, with the club, with Crystal. It's gonna take a while to sort out."

Zak laughed into his face, though to his own ears it sounded sad and desperate. "Time off? Are you fucking kidding me? Is that why you made me wait for a fucking message that you're all right?" Within a single second, Zak crossed the space between him and Stitch, and pushed him to the wall, breathing hard. His whole body was burning with the need to hit someone.

"I thought it'd be better if I stayed away. What if someone steals my phone and finds the texts, or sees you're someone I talk to all the time, and they track you down, huh?" Stitch didn't push back though.

"Oh, fuck you," growled Zak. He entwined his fingers over his nape and paced toward the other end of the small room, close to shaking in anger.

"Please don't be like that..." There it was. That puppy-eyed look that had no right to be there. Yet Stitch didn't move closer, as if Zak were some leper all of a sudden.

"Like what? Be like you and pretend that I don't love you?" Zak stepped back and kicked the single chair to the floor. Every part of his body was aching with tension. "What is this shit? Those girls? What the fuck, Stitch?"

Stitch frowned and hit his forehead against the wall. "It's stupid. Captain found this girl, Raven, and he keeps pushing me at her like she can replace you just because she's got tattoos and piercings. I'm playing along so he pisses off. He's changed so much I feel like I don't even know him anymore. I just need to make things right in the club and find a way for us to be together, but it's not easy."

Zak spread his arms in helplessness. "And how long it this shit going to take? You don't talk to me, you can't even fucking text me? Grow some balls!"

Stitch looked back at him with his face tense. "I'm sick of everyone trying to push me their way! You want balls, here's balls: I'll tell you when I'm ready. For now, we're done. I can't be split in half! If you can't wait, then that's it," he lashed out and punched the wall so hard his fist made a dent.

Zak stared at him, completely dumbfounded. So there it was. The truth about Stitch. His priorities, people who he considered more important than Zak. Maybe it was better to get the wake-up call sooner than later. He was already getting too comfortable in Lake Valley.

"Why did you do this to me? I was perfectly fine with my fun and relaxed sex life before I met you." Zak shook his head, pulling on the shirt over the black hole in his chest.

Stitch looked back into his eyes. "Me? I had none of these problems before I met you. I didn't ask for this to happen. I was a perfectly miserable closeted guy, and then you just walked in and... and..."

Zak raised his hand to shut him up. He'd just taken a figurative bullet to the chest, and he needed to get it out of his system. He walked over to Stitch, turning the signet on his thumb. It was a dead weight, squeezing over his pulsing finger like the jaws of a carnivorous bug. With each step, he was closer. First, close enough to sense Stitch's smell. Then, close enough to feel his warmth, and as they were almost nose to nose, he smiled, even though his insides felt like they were falling apart. "Then you've solved that problem. You won't be seeing me anymore. Enjoy Raven, or whatever her name is," he whispered and pushed the signet deep into Stitch's jean pocket.

Stitch watched him without a word, but it did give Zak a tiny glimpse of satisfaction to see his whites redden. "My problem will never be solved after I've been in that hot, tight body," he whispered, and his breath was so close it burned.

"That hot, tight body?" repeated Zak through his teeth, squeezing his right hand into a fist. "You even talk about me in third person now?"

"That's not what I'm trying to say." Stitch closed his eyes for a moment. "Why don't you *listen*?"

"You just dumped me." Zak laughed out loud and stepped back when his eyes started welling up. He was so done. If he needed a sign he was through with this town, this was it.

Stitch fished out the signet from his pocket and held it out to Zak. "Would you keep it?"

Zak stumbled backward as if the ring was a weapon and held onto the door handle, which he quickly pushed down, opening the door. He didn't need memories like this. Stitch didn't follow him out into the corridor, nor did he say another word. Without him by Zak's side, the corridor felt so alien and uninviting, Zak just wanted to leave.

Unsure whether the club door was open, he walked back to the bar and rushed straight for the door, not wanting to talk to anyone. Outside, he was blinded by sharp sunlight but found his way to the car, keeping his head low.

Captain sat by the table surrounded by girls, looking like a cock in a henhouse. He eyed Zak all the way to the car, but Zak chose to ignore it. He slipped his shades on and started the engine, pulling away without a word. The heavy metal that tore through the air the moment he switched on his MP3 player should suffice. He didn't want to go home yet. The sun was slowly setting, so there wouldn't be that many cars on local roads, and he could just go somewhere quiet to have a place to scream.

He pulled out of the club's parking lot and sped down the road, to be out of town as soon as humanly possible. The emptiness on the finger where he used to wear the signet still burned, so he forced his old car to go even faster, just so he could be as far away from the lying bastard as he could. Soon enough, Zak started passing little houses and neverending fields. It was getting dark when he finally stopped the car at the side of the road and got out, turning his face to the sun. It didn't burn anymore, leaving a pleasant warmth on his skin instead. Slowly, he made his way toward the trees by the road, all alone and with the hole in his chest still the size of the Grand Canyon. He swore into the creeping darkness and slapped his hand against one of the trunks.

He hadn't decided on what to do. Six months was a lot of time, and he'd started feeling homely in his new house. In the city, Versay wouldn't have as much space as he did now, and Zak didn't want to give him away. He had no idea what the best course of action was, and the chaos in his head did nothing to help.

All his senses stood to attention the moment he heard the roar of a motorcycle on the road. Did Stitch change his mind? Zak wouldn't accept it just like that, but if Stitch did his penance and said he'd leave the club, Zak supposed he could accept an apology. His heart leapt toward the still roaring engine, but his mind refused to just let him walk over to Stitch's feet like a beaten puppy. He turned around to face the sweet-scented bushes and leaned against the tree, listening.

The heavy steps of boots crushed the dried up weeds, but instead of Stitch's Nordic blond, what Zak saw was Captain's black bushy hair and beard emerging from behind a thick tree. Zak's first reflex was to step back, but he forced himself to stand his ground even though his insides froze, and his brain started looking for possible weapons around. Sadly, he was afraid breaking off a branch wouldn't do.

"Thought we needed to have a little chat," Captain said, clearly enjoying approaching Zak like a predator. They both knew who had the upper hand here, but Zak was intent on not showing any sign of weakness, as difficult that might be.

He shrugged with a deep sigh. "I don't think we do anymore."

Captain stood in front of him, all too close. "If I ever see you around the club again, you're as good as gator meat, get it?"

Zak knew what he should say, but anger got the best of him. He would not just piss his panties in front of the guy who took Stitch away from him. "Are you getting off on this?"

Instead of an answer, he got a fist to the face so fast, Zak barely comprehended why he ended up on the ground with his head still dizzy from the hit.

"Now I am." Captain took a step back and squinted at him. "I'm not gonna have some faggot degenerate my friend."

Zak swallowed the coppery taste in his mouth, his muscles stiffening as he checked his teeth. All were still in place. "Says the guy who eats out a girl in public," he muttered, slowly rising to his feet. This time, he'd be prepared.

"Better than having my ass fucked." Captain launched at Zak and even though Zak tried to kick him, the guy was like a bulldozer of muscle next to him, pushing Zak to the ground, hit by hit.

Zak's head was a mixture of panic and resignation. He managed to deliver a few punches, but it didn't seem to slow the fucker down. "No one wants to fuck your ugly ass," he growled through clenched teeth as he shielded his skull from the punishing blows. He was caught on the edges of a tornado, tossed around without a way out. His mind turned to autopilot, searching for an opening to Captain's groin, but it just wouldn't come.

Captain managed to kick Zak's shin and send him to the dirt again before taking a step back. He spat at Zak with an ugly gurgle. "Keep your fag ass away from Stitch."

Zak flinched, curling into a ball in the wet dirt. He watched Captain through the slit between his half-closed eyelids, ready to move to avoid a kick in the back. His whole body was screaming with dull pain, dizzy from the powerful blows to the head, and he sealed his mouth shut, wishing only that this menace would turn around and leave.

And he did. Without another word, Captain walked off, leaving Zak to swallow his own blood along with his pride. This day just couldn't get any worse. Slowly, he wiped his face with his arm and turned to his stomach with a low groan. It was exhausting enough with his muscles tense as strings, but the sudden roar of a motorbike engine spiked something deep in Zak's stomach, and he lurched forward, vomiting on the dirt. He heaved over the puddle and rolled to the side, looking into the treetops looming over him. He didn't even notice when he started shaking.

"Fuck..." he uttered, spitting blood as he pulled himself up by a tree that he used as support. Each of his joints twitched, as if every punch he got had been precisely aimed to turn him into a ball of pain. His eyelids were burning, he didn't know whether because of shame or loss, but he hugged the trunk, digging his fingers into the bark as if it were the patches on Stitch's cut. A low, breathless sob left his lips, and he opened his eyes, blinking away the haze of moisture before slowly making his way forward. It felt like he was moving like a penguin but with each step, his body got more used to the sting. When he finally dropped into the seat of his car, the safety of the known upholstery, of the familiar smell, made the situation dawn on him even more.

He started the car gently, afraid the rattle would get him hurting even more, but when nothing changed, he sped up, wishing to be home as fast as possible. Driving out to think in the countryside when a mad biker hated your guts wasn't such a good idea. Maybe even staying in Lake Valley wasn't such a good idea. With every mile closer to town, he drove faster. What if that motherfucker came to his house and poisoned Versay or something?

"Nonono," whispered Zak, pushing the pedal even lower as he drove down the empty road. Each pulse in his temples was like a strobe light exploding in his head. It was making him dizzy again, but he was too close to home to stop in the middle of the road, so he sped up even more, focusing on the fluorescent markings on the road.

An ear-piercing signal of a police vehicle dug into his skull, and he saw the car in his rearview mirror, like a piranha approaching him when he was already deep in water, bleeding and unable to swim away. Could nothing go his way today?

Gritting his teeth, he slowly pulled to the side of the road and put his hands on the steering wheel. He regretted obeying the protocol the moment he saw his fingers trembling, but the policeman was already approaching in the bright lights of his car.

And of course, it was no one other but Cox. Was he the only fucking cop in this town? Zak groaned when Cox knocked on the car window. He pulled down the glass, trying to keep his face in the shadow. He just wanted to be home.

"Hey," he muttered.

Cox bowed down to his window. "Hey, Zak. You hurrying somewhere?"

"Sorry, my mind drifted away," he said, wondering if Captain had castrated his tongue as there were no clever remarks coming Cox's way.

Cox frowned, taking a better look at Zak. "Did Larsen do this to you?"

Oh, for God's sake. Zak turned his head toward Cox, knowing there was no point to hide his injuries now that they have been spotted. "What? Why would he do that? Of course not."

"Maybe because he's been out of your house for the past week?" Cox held out his hand to hold Zak's chin for inspection.

"That's because we broke up," said Zak, pulling away from the touch. "Listen, I'm fine. Let's not talk about him."

"No, let's talk about him. I can't believe this motherfucker would do this to you. You need to get that photographed and signed off by a doctor, and press charges. Come with me to the station." Cox was breathing hard and watching Zak with a manic expression.

"No." Zak drew in a sharp breath, surprised by the outburst. "It wasn't him. Can I get my speeding ticket and go home?"

"You're going to let that scumbag walk all over you like this? You know what?" Cox pulled out his booklet for tickets, but never even opened it. "I am done watching him assault and torment a nice guy like you. I don't care if he outs me in retaliation. I am going to put his gay ass in prison, and you can thank me later." Cox's fingers squeezed on the booklet so hard that Zak heard a crack in the finger joints. With a harsh bang to the roof of the car, Cox walked off back to his car.

Zak blinked and leaned out despite the painful pull in his back. "Are you sick in the head? I fucking told you it wasn't him!"

Cox got into his car and slowed down as he passed Zak. "I'll deal with this, Zak," he said with a serious expression and didn't wait for an answer before speeding up.

Zak stared at the lights of the police car disappearing in the darkness, a hot urgency burning in his chest. He reached out to the passenger seat where he'd put his cell phone and fumbled with it to find Stitch's number, which he fortunately hadn't deleted yet. "Pick up, you dumb fuck," he hissed when the wait lasted more than three signals.

Chapter 22

Stitch sat on the bed in his room, feeling as empty as never before. He kept putting on Zak's ring (as he now thought of it), but it only reminded him of Zak being gone from his life. The Hounds were out in Houma to party with another club they were becoming allies with thanks to having the Coffin Nails as a mutual enemy. Stitch chose not to go though, knowing it would be shit. He was in a bad mood and on top of that Captain would probably keep pushing Raven at him. There was nothing wrong with the girl, she was a cool rocker chick, but she wasn't Zak. And it wasn't just about dick or no dick either. With Zak, the whole world disappeared as they fucked each other into oblivion, then just lay there as if they were one body, until they had enough energy to come again.

Stitch looked at his phone where he had three missed calls. The last thing he wanted now was to have people trying to talk him into going to a party full of booze and tits. Something that used to be his element now felt as alien as never before. As if Zak had changed something in his DNA. He wanted Zak back so bad it hurt, but he couldn't do it just now, when an explosion of violence was threatening to tear the town apart. So if Zak couldn't wait, then this was it. Stitch could already imagine Zak finding some cool guy to start a life with and gritted his teeth so hard it began to give him a headache.

Stitch was such a waste of space. A problem for Crystal, a selfish father, he couldn't make it work with Zak, nor could he blindly follow the club's increasingly violent rulings and plans. He put on his cut and pulled out the gun hidden in it. The barrel was shiny and black, the heaviness so certain in his hands. Maybe there was something he could do right? He dug his fingertips into the hard steel when he heard a harsh rapping at the club backdoor. It was as if someone was beating on the wood with both fists.

"Oh, for fuck's sake." He got up and went out into the corridor. "Shut the fuck up!" he yelled before opening the backdoor with a kick.

Cox stepped back, his hand trailing dangerously close to his gun. He was the last person Stitch expected to see.

"Someone has a violent streak today," growled Cox.

"The fuck you want, Cox? If it's 'cock' then you're not getting it from me." He sneered at the cop, the image of Cox in bed with Zak impossible to erase and now even more vivid than usual.

"It's not cock," said Cox with a smile that was dripping with poisoned honey. He made a move to enter.

"Go on," Stitch snarled at him and let him pass. All the weed had been taken to the party so he couldn't care less. "I suppose you don't have a warrant?" Stitch imagined pushing his thumbs into Cox's thick neck and holding them tight until he stopped breathing.

"I don't need one." Cox slowly walked over to the center of the lounge and crossed his arms on his chest. His eyes were dark and stabbed Stitch like invisible lasers. "You're such a sad excuse of a man, Larsen."

"You got something to say, Cox? Or are you just visiting for no reason?" Stitch frowned at him and clenched his hands into fists. He did not need to hear anything from this motherfucker.

"Yeah, I'm arresting you for assault." Cox sneered like a vicious dog. "That at least will finally keep your hands off Zak."

"Assault on who? Stay here longer, and it might be another assault on a police officer. Good stuff." Stitch put his hands in his pockets not to push Cox just yet. "You have no business with me or Zak."

Cox laughed, shaking his head. "You're unbelievable. What a piece of shit. You know what? I don't care if you out me anymore. I'll live, but if people find out about you where you're going, you're gonna be so *fucking* fucked." Cox stepped closer, showing his teeth like a rabid dog. He was rounding Stitch, readying himself to attack.

Stitch's body went cold, and he grabbed the front of Cox's uniform. "What did you say?" He didn't go through all of this shit with Captain to get outed and possibly killed by his former brothers. He was alienated enough already. "The fuck you want from me, huh?" He put all his effort into keeping his breathing normal despite the panic seeping into his brain.

They both turned to the door when it hit the wall, pushed from the outside. Zak stepped in with his eyes wide open, a thin layer of red smudged around his mouth, hair all messed up. He leaned his back against the wall with a low groan. "Told you it wasn't him," he uttered, but Cox was already back to the conversation he was having with Stitch.

"You're gonna cooperate. I want your gang of thugs behind bars!"

Stitch's eyes widened at the bruises on Zak's face. Did Cox dare touch Zak over this shit? "I'm not gonna rat on no one! You know very well it would get me dead!" he yelled at Cox and shook him so hard a few buttons popped off Cox's shirt.

"Oh, yeah?" Cox's breath was moist and hot on his face. "Then I'll make sure you'll be gang raped in jail so many times you'll call me, begging to rat out your own mother," he growled with his face tensed into a cross between a grin and scowl.

Stitch already felt like a rat, trapped, cornered, with no good way out. Every option was like a wall pushing him in, trying to crush him. Crystal, Zak, prison, the Hounds, Captain, his own sexuality at the center of it all. He wished he could just cut it out of his body like a tumor. Instead, there was one wall he could crush. A tumor to cut out.

He pulled out his gun and shot into Cox's chest. The impact sent Cox tumbling back, with his eyes wide open, so Stitch shot two more times just to make sure it sank in.

Cox's chest, visible through the half-open shirt changed color to bright red, while the rest of him became ghastly pale within a split second. With his eyes wide, he opened his mouth and pulled out his own gun. Zak's scream echoed in Stitch's head along with the single shot, but Cox already dropped his firearm to the floor and fell to his knees, only to drop face-first like a fallen tree. He was dead.

So much adrenaline rushed through Stitch's body that only now he put his palm against his arm, realizing the bullet had grazed its side. Blood dribbled down his skin, but he looked up at Zak, unsure what to do or say now. *Fuck. Fucking fuck.*

Zak was frozen by the door, his face a mask of shock. He was trembling slightly as he moved his eyes between Cox and Stitch. The room resonated his deep, hissing breaths. "You killed him."

Stitch looked to the body, and the dark stains on the floor. He'd never actually killed anyone before, but Cox had pushed him over the edge, threatened him. This was him or Cox. "He beat you up," Stitch uttered quieter than he intended to. His stomach was taking a tumble, but his mind was blank, still processing what had happened.

Zak shook his head. He pushed himself away from the wall as if he were glued to it and stumbled forward with stiff, careful movements. "Oh, God, Stitch... What did you do?"

"You heard him!" The icicles in his body were warming up and trickling fear and panic into Stitch's bloodstream. His hands shook, but he quickly put the safety on the gun. His breathing sped up. "What are you doing here, anyway?" he didn't want to raise his voice, but it was all too much. He had a cop's body cooling on the floor, a dead man's blood on his face.

Zak stopped halfway through the room and wordlessly nodded at Cox. If there was something Stitch didn't want Zak to see, that was it.

"What happened?" Stitch spread his arms, but then put his hands on his nape.

To make things worse, heavy steps resonated through the back corridor.

"Stitch! How many times am I supposed to call you? Get your ass ready for the par—" Captain yelled, but cut the sentence the moment he walked into the room. "What the fuck?"

Zak crossed his arms on his chest and looked to the cooling body, chewing on his lip like he wanted to bite through it. Captain quickly locked the door behind him, staring at the corpse as well.

"Is that Cox?"

"Yes, it's fucking Cox!" Stitch yelled at him, but when he noticed red stains on Captain's knuckles, a red light flashed in his brain. "Who's blood is that, huh?" He walked up to Captain, looking between his hands and Zak's messed-up face. He couldn't care less about the blood dripping from his arm. If they didn't get rid of Cox properly, he really would go to prison as a fucking cop-killer. This would be the end of his life. He wouldn't see Holly again. Zak would move on and forget him. No one in the criminal justice system would ever believe it was all an accident. He didn't want to pull the trigger. It just... happened.

Captain sneered and stomped toward Zak, as if he were trying to frighten a dog. "Seems it wasn't fucking enough for that fag."

Zak flinched, looking back. He actually moved closer to the body, hovering his hand over Cox's forlorn gun.

"I fucking quit him on your push, and told you not to touch him!" Stitch went straight for Captain, ready to pull him apart like he was slow-cooked beef. Enough was enough. "Told you to leave him alone! It's not his fault I'm like this!"

"Whatever. I don't want his dirty ass in my town. Neither do the others," growled Captain, pushing Stitch away. His dark hair was wild and unruly like some demonic villain's from a movie.

"Never touch him again!" Stitch screamed at him and punched Captain in the gut, even though he knew that would provoke an onslaught. He couldn't care less as they started hitting and kicking each other in an equal fight. The thought that Captain had beaten up Zak was the final straw.

Captain growled, twisting his body just enough to punch Stitch square in the jaw. Pain radiated through all of Stitch's head like a ray of heat. He could hear Zak's voice in the background, but he was completely taken by the need to twist Captain's balls off.

Anything could be used in the fight, knees, elbows, teeth. Stitch bit Cap's ear, almost tearing it off, but Captain elbowed his stomach and threw him to the coffee table. The rattle of broken glass accompanied his fall as he knocked over the old piece of furniture. Stitch kicked Captain's knee so hard, Cap screamed and threw himself on top of him. They rolled around in the broken glass like two pit bulls that had been trained for this fight all their lives.

"There's a fucking body out here!" It was a sobering hiss from Zak, but Captain only looked his way before headbutting Stitch so hard Stitch's brain felt like dripping out through his nose.

"Take care of it, pussyboy," he growled, spitting red to the side.

"Don't you dare call him that!" Stitch mumbled, still dizzy. He put his hand on Captain's face and dug his fingers into the skin, but as he noticed Zak's face above him, Captain got the upper hand again and pushed his thumbs under Stitch's ribs, making him groan.

"I don't care. Stitch, you killed a man, we need to do something about this!" Zak was close to wheezing. "Let's go before someone starts looking for him. The fucking police car is outside!"

That seemed to have sobered Captain because he pulled away, frowning at Zak. "Fucking hell."

Stitch rolled out from under Captain, pushing Cap to the glass. He was so done with this shit. The fact that he killed a man still hadn't seeped in, but looking back to Cox, lying there, facedown, made it feel real. "Right. Car," he mumbled and spat out blood.

Chapter 23

Zak settled in the passenger's seat, constantly eyeing Captain's shadowy face in the rearview mirror. They were waiting for Stitch, who was still fumbling with Cox's remains, which they had wrapped in several plastic bags to avoid any stains in Zak's trunk. Zak crossed his hands over his chest. They felt dry and tender after all the bleaching and scrubbing he had to do back in the clubhouse. He preferred that to getting rid of a car or cutting apart a warm body with a saw from Stitch's workshop. Zak couldn't bring himself to think of Stitch methodically cutting off arms, legs, the head, without feeling nauseated. Those hands, which he knew to be so gentle, weren't made for such an act.

The process of removing the puddle of blood from the club lounge had been painful, and he had to constantly tell himself it was not blood that he was soaking up with kitchen towels and washing off with a rough sponge, or he wouldn't have been able to go through with it. It took lots of disinfectants, but he managed to make the whole floor cleaner than it had probably been since being laid.

Stitch avoided Zak's gaze when he got back and sat in the driver's seat. He started the engine as calmly as an old lady. Zak couldn't help but glance at Stitch's hands, expecting to see red under his fingernails, but fortunately they were scrubbed clean.

Zak swallowed hard, turning his head to face him. Stitch was pale, with dark circles around his eyes, shoulders set as if fastened to a wooden frame. "Did you clean it all?"

Stitch nodded and drove toward the quickest route out of town, but Captain wouldn't keep his ugly mug shut.

"Of course he did. He's a fag, not an idiot."

Zak inhaled a gulp of air and leaned forward not to be too close to the bastard behind him. "Just shut up already."

"None of this would have happened if it wasn't for the homophobia in the club," Stitch snarled at Captain, keeping his eyes on the road. "If being out wasn't such a sin against humanity, I wouldn't have been so freaked out about Cox telling everyone."

Captain snorted in the back seat. "If we knew you're such a pussy, we wouldn't have patched you."

"You think this was always so obvious to me? You know shit."

"And you're not a pussy," added Zak, much to Captain's apparent amusement.

"Come on Stitch, now you have a personal protection poodle? What did you do to make him defend you so viciously? Suck his balls?"

"Shut the fuck up, Captain." Stitch frowned and turned into a smaller pathway leading to the forest and swamp. "I did whatever the fuck it is people do in relationships. I am sick of hearing this shit. You don't wanna know so stop asking!"

Zak had only just rested his back against the seat when Captain lunged forward, and his heavy, leather-clad arm rested against Zak's chest, keeping him in place like an over-the-shoulder restraint. Even without Captain, this ride had been far from enjoyable, and Zak was constantly reminding himself to keep his dinner down. He almost forgot to breathe, unconsciously imagining that arm pulling up to choke him.

"So it's a 'relationship' now, huh?" growled Captain. "You fucking bringing him flowers every Sunday?"

Stitch looked toward them, but didn't let Captain provoke him. "Yes, it's a fucking relationship, Jesus Christ! And no, I don't bring him flowers. I walk his dog, paint the house, and we fuck like there's no tomorrow. That enough for you, or do you wanna know exactly what we do? What the fuck do you want?"

Captain did exactly what Zak had feared. Within a split second, the muscular arm went up to press at his throat, but before he could as much as attempt to free himself, Captain pulled away as if it had been just a joke.

"Fuck," he uttered through his teeth. "This wouldn't have happened if it wasn't for this freak." A powerful kick shook Zak's seat, but he didn't even try to reason with the unreasonable.

"It's not his fault that I don't like pussy." Stitch briefly turned around and smacked Captain's leg. "I am done doing what others try to push me to do. Aren't we supposed to be fucking outlaws? Living life without rules? Who says I can't fuck a guy if I want to? Fuck that."

For a moment, Captain's face froze but only to explode with a snarl. "We're not bound by civilians, that doesn't mean we don't have fucking rules."

Zak swallowed, eyeing Stitch in silence. He didn't want to read too much into Stitch's words, especially not after seeing him kill a man. It hadn't been planned, and Cox's cruel words had been the trigger, but that didn't change anything about the contents of the trunk. He wanted to make a hole in the ground and scream into it until his voice would give out. If only he could bury all his worries and doubts this way. Cox didn't deserve this. He'd been a good guy, with dreams and hopes for the future that would never come.

Zak glanced through the window, watching the passing trees as they drove. He was too numb to despair yet, but logically, what was he doing? He was helping to get rid of a body. He never thought he would be *that* guy. He used to joke with some of his friends about being so close they would call one another if need arose to hide a body. But he wouldn't have done that for them. His eyes slowly turned to Stitch, who clasped his hands hard on the steering wheel, oddly pale in the face.

"They're *our* rules. Why don't we just change them?" Stitch turned into yet another small path and ventured deeper into the trees.

Captain leaned forward and grabbed both the front seats. "Because no real man wants to fraternize with a fag. Since you met him you even started lagging with club business. We need to expand. How can you not see that?"

"That has nothing to do with Zak. I'm pulling back because I don't want to get shot while dealing drugs. Is that so hard to understand?" Stitch scowled at Captain.

"Then buy a fucking Vespa," spat Captain and leaned back in the seat. He didn't open his mouth for the rest of the ride, and for once Zak was missing his voice. The silence made him think too much, and the more focused Zak was on the cramps in his stomach, the more he believed that he could smell decay, which didn't make any sense. After all, the body had to still be warm.

Stitch parked the car in the mud by the swamp. The eerie lighting from the car and the sounds of thousands of insects reminded Zak of an *X-Files* episode.

"Why? 'Cause I don't wanna mule drugs? I don't need more trouble in my life," Stitch hissed and got out of the car, slamming the door behind him.

"It's club business, and you're the only one who's got a problem with it. The vote passed, Stitch," growled Captain, exiting the car as well. He kicked Zak's door on his way to the water but Zak wouldn't give him the satisfaction and only moved outside more quickly, despite all the cramps in his body.

"It's bullshit," Stitch grumbled and went over to the trunk. "I don't even want to talk about this. Let's get this body to the gators."

Zak looked to his hands when Captain turned his smirking face toward him "I'll get some stones, yeah?" he muttered, stepping away the moment the trunk was opened.

"Thanks." Stitch sighed like an old man when he looked inside.

"I just don't get it," Captain continued opening his fugly mouth. "You were with Crystal for so many years, and it was fine."

Stitch snapped. "No, it wasn't fine! That's why we got divorced. You really are as dumb as a rock." He pulled on something that sounded like a plastic bag.

Zak looked away and switched on the flashlight in his phone, looking for stones or other heavy objects that could keep the body under the water. The situation was surreal. He had never done anything illegal. Okay, he'd done the petty stuff everyone does, but he never did anything that he actually considered 'criminal'. It all changed since he met Stitch. He had been turning a blind eye to the Hounds' activities, and now he was helping to feed the gators with a man he had slept with. A police officer. An overall decent man. Did it make him a bad person that he was willing to let Cox disappear without a trace because he didn't want Stitch to be taken away from him for something that was clearly the result of misjudgement? It hadn't been a cold-blooded murder, and Zak wanted to believe with all his heart that he was doing the right thing, even though most would disagree. But who could possibly benefit from Stitch doing time? If anything, putting him in jail would make his family miserable. And Zak would lose the only man who ever made him feel so intensely alive.

"Because it doesn't make sense!" Captain helped Stitch pick up the body parts with a grunt. "Why would you swap a life with Crystal for this dude? The blow jobs can't be that good."

They carried the body toward the shore. It was barely visible in the darkness, but Zak still noticed Stitch shake his head. "You don't know what you're talking about. When you fall in love, even a kiss is mind-blowing. You don't fuck other people, because there's only one person you want to be close to. When he fucks me, it's like I give him a part of my soul," his words became quieter. "I'm not looking for other guys, and I don't wanna do it with anyone else."

Zak turned around to face them, his heart tumbling all around his chest as if it wanted to break free and crawl to Stitch's feet. He wasn't a natural sap, but that was the most romantic thing anyone had ever said about him. Had Stitch reconsidered his decision to break up? Because Zak had already made up his mind, even if it meant being an accessory to manslaughter.

Captain dropped his side of the bag, and it fell down with a dull thud. "Did this fag make you his bitch?" he uttered, sounding genuinely surprised.

Stitch let go of the load as well. "You are not fucking listening, are you?"

"You're fucking delusional," growled Captain, kicking the carcass. "You need to be fucking locked up."

"Let's just get on with it. You can sit in the fucking car if you want. Zak, you got those rocks?"

"Yeah, give me a second." Zak breathed in the damp air and shut himself away from the conversation at the shore. He gathered a few stones and carried them back as quickly as humanly possible. He was happy that he kept the car keys on him because Captain walked back to the vehicle without another word.

The next half an hour was the longest thirty minutes of Zak's life. Whenever he tried to help, Stitch just told him to stay away, which Zak supposed was noble of him. Especially since killing people wasn't some routine thing for Stitch either. He had to be traumatized by having to cut a body into pieces. Zak knew he was, but at this moment, Cox's death was too surreal to sink in. It could be shock, but he felt cold inside, only focused on getting back into the safety of their home. An alligator peeking out of the water, with its eyes glistening in the light from the car, wasn't helping Zak's nerves. With every body part Stitch threw into the swamp, Zak's palms got more sweaty, his imagination leading him to scenes where the reptiles attacked Stitch, and it would be too late to save him. He'd seen enough blood tonight to last him a lifetime.

"I heard what you said," he eventually uttered into the silence, glancing at his lover. He wanted to hug him, but there was no way he'd do that with that one-eyed bastard watching.

Stitch didn't look back at him, dragging the last, and biggest, bag toward the swamp. Zak gagged at the thought of what was in there. "Yeah," he muttered.

Zak shuddered and hugged himself as a flash of cold went all the way through his body. "What changed your mind?"

"I never changed my mind." Stitch grunted as he threw the bag as far as he could into the black water.

Zak sighed, rushed toward him, and pulled him away from the shore. From the corner of his eye, he noticed the water getting rough in the moonlight as reptiles crept closer in the darkness, ready for some fresh meat. "Will you come back home with me?" he uttered, cold sweat sliding down his back.

Stitch took a deep breath and held onto Zak's hand. "If you'll have me," he whispered. "This was such a shit day, wasn't it?"

Zak squeezed his hand tightly with a shuddery sigh. A man who had trembled with pleasure in his bed turned into gator feed, and Zak was choosing to betray him. The death could still be discovered, they could still be charged with murder, but he was determined to keep himself in one piece. "I just want to kiss you so badly."

Stitch bowed down to him and gave the kiss Zak so deeply craved. His soft, warm lips were somehow making all the black thoughts flee into the depths of Zak's mind. "I can't please everyone." His voice was so weak it was getting lost in the sounds of splashing water and buzzing insects.

Zak pushed himself against Stitch and gasped as adrenaline shot into his brain. Stitch's scent was sharper than ever, spiked with all the stress and fear of the passing day. "I love you."

"I know, I love you too." Stitch kissed Zak's lips once more and stroked the side of his head. "Let's go home."

Zak held on to him. It was so hard to let go after all that had happened, but he finally untangled himself from the firm chest and faced the dark silhouette of the car with a small smile on his face. "How do you know?"

"You just helped me dump a body in the swamp so I wouldn't go to jail."

Zak swallowed, choking up, but he nodded and brushed his hand against Stitch's. He might regret his decisions in the future, he would mourn a man who didn't have to die, but at the moment, all he wanted was to bury himself in Stitch's arms and forget.

207 | K . A .   M e r i k a n

Chapter 24

On the way back, the car was silent as a funeral procession. At times, Stitch thought Captain had fallen asleep in the backseat, but as soon as they stopped by the clubhouse, he came to life and bolted out of the car, slamming the door behind him. A part of Stitch understood that tonight's confession was a hard pill to swallow, but it needed to be done. He hoped that in a year's time, they would look back at this dark time and overlook their differences.

Zak moved his left hand to Stitch's shoulder, reminding him that he wasn't alone in the ordeal. The silent gesture was all the comfort Stitch needed. The road seemed to go on forever in the darkness, with the pale smudge of the approaching dawn only grazing the horizon. Stitch tried to focus on the road, not the bloody memories of dealing with Cox's body. It had all gone so terribly wrong.

Stitch parked in the driveway, and when the engine of the car died, it seemed that all movement stilled. Zak leaned in and rested his head on Stitch's shoulder. It was so peaceful and quiet.

"I'm sorry for everything." Stitch stroked Zak's fingers, trying to ignore the smell of swamp in the car. This odor he would forever associate with a bloody cadaver sinking into the murky water.

Zak sighed and kissed his arm, leaning on Stitch harder than usual, as if he needed the support. "I know."

"I never wanted you to see me like this." Stitch couldn't force himself to move.

Zak stared at their entwined hands and stroked Stitch's with his thumb. "Like what?" he asked even though the answer was obvious. It was sweet of Zak to pretend it was all fine.

"Like a savage. Out of control. I hated his guts, but I never planned this." Stitch frowned, looking at the garage door.

Zak exhaled and slowly pulled Stitch by the collar so that their lips would meet. Sweet and chaste. "I know. I'm so sorry."

Stitch turned into the hug and put his head on Zak's shoulder. He wanted to stay like this forever. "I'm a bad person, but I can't say 'no' to you. Whatever happens, I'll try to make it work with you. Will you be my anchor?" Stitch sure as hell needed one after the darkness he'd experienced just before Cox barged into the club. His world seemed to be sinking away then. No way out, no one to keep him grounded through the storm.

Zak swallowed, squeezing Stitch's hand, with his own, which was burning hot and slightly damp. "You're not a bad person. You're just in a horrible situation, but we're gonna make it all work, yeah?"

"Crystal said she'd let me see Holly if I break up with you, but I just can't. I'm so weak when I see you."

Zak flinched, and his eyes widened. "Oh, God, I'm so sorry Stitch," he whispered, looking at his lover in the intimate semidarkness. "I'm sure this can be negotiated, she'll come around if she loves Holly as much as you do."

"I just can't go back to what it was anymore." Stitch wrapped his arms around Zak. "Even a week without you made everything seem worthless. You changed me, and I can't run from it."

Zak nodded and took a deep breath, looking at the dark house. "I never felt anything like this. Please, don't ever leave again," he whispered, curling up against Stitch.

"I won't. I'll leave the club altogether if that needs to happen. I don't want my Holly to grow up without a dad like I did. I want to be there for her." Stitch kissed Zak's jaw and pulled away. He was ready. Ready to take any and all responsibility for his choices. "Let's go home."

Zak smiled at him as he slowly made his way out of the car. Stitch would sell his pinky to see that smile every day.

"We both stink," Zak noted with a low laugh, but from the way his gaze trailed to the floor, it was clear where that thought led him to.

"Let's take a shower. Wash it all away, yeah?" Stitch kissed his temple and put his arm over Zak's shoulders as they walked up to the porch. Versay greeted them at the door and yelped, jumping on Stitch as if nothing had happened tonight. As if Stitch hadn't carved up a body into pieces.

Zak chuckled and blinked away the slight wetness in his eyes as he watched Versay jumping on Stitch as if they hadn't seen each other for years. That enthusiasm, all the needy whining, made Stitch smile for the first time in ages.

"Hey, Versay, I missed you, yeah, I did."

"Let him out. The poor guy is probably close to peeing his panties," said Zak from above them as soon as Stitch scooted down to hug the overexcited dog.

Stitch snorted and leaned over to kiss Zak's knee. He could just kneel at this man's feet forever, reveling in the soothing caress of Zak's fingers moving over his scalp.

The door opened, and Versay rushed outside with a yelp. Stitch didn't say a thing, listening to the clattering of paws outside and the sound of the lock. It was like coming home after months, not a week. All the exhaustion of the day was slowly leaving his body.

"I want to kiss you all over," Stitch said as he stood up and pulled Zak along toward the staircase.

"So gentle today," said Zak with a smile. He laid his head on Stitch's shoulder as they ascended the stairs hip to hip. It felt so right that Stitch ·didn't even have any words for it.

"I may fuck like a devil, but I'm not a brute by nature." Stitch kissed the side of Zak's head and stroked his back.

"Tell me something I don't know, Trouble." Zak chuckled, hugging him as if Cox were still alive. As if Stitch wasn't a killer.

"I fingered myself thinking of you," Stitch said with a crooked smile and started undressing as soon as they entered the bathroom. It was the truth, but he did say it just to mess with Zak. See what he would say. After all, Zak did ask for 'something he didn't know'.

Zak blinked with his lips parted. Mission accomplished. Zak was undoubtedly caught up in his own vision of what Stitch fingering himself looked like. Stitch was on the verge of passing Zak a towel to soak up the drool at the side of his lip. "Oh, fuck..."

"You've gone red like a virgin on her wedding night," Stitch snorted, taking off his cut and hoodie in a slow move intended for Zak's viewing pleasure.

Zak chuckled, lowering his head as he approached Stitch and gently brushed his fingers over the fresh bruises on his side. "Virgins? Do you even know any? In this town?"

"No, not adult ones." Stitch took in a deep breath that made his whole chest expand. Those slim fingers were so familiar and soothing.

Zak bit his lip when he had to raise his arms high to pull off his shirt. Even so many hours after the beating delivered by Captain, his body had to ache. The bruises peeking from between the tattoos on Zak's stomach were a reminder that Stitch hadn't been there to help him when it was needed. The attack itself was Stitch's fault and had set off a chain of events that led to a chopped up body in a swamp. "Anyway, that was super hot."

"You might see it one day if you stick around long enough." Stitch helped Zak undress without sparing him kisses and gentle caresses.

Zak let himself relax and rested against the wall. Despite talk of Stitch bottoming Zak seemed passive and ready to be the center of Stitch's attentions. "You know I will."

Stitch took off the rest of his clothes and stepped into the shower with Zak. "Tell me if anything hurts," he said before turning on the water. He leaned in for a deep, long kiss in the cool droplets and let his hands explore Zak's back and buttocks. It was like biting into a warm croissant after an exhausting, cold night.

"Can you even see anything wrong with me under all that ink?"

"No, you're as perfect as ever," Stitch whispered and slowly got down to his knees in the warming water. "Everywhere." He kissed the inside of Zak's thigh, which trembled against his lips.

Zak leaned back against the tiled wall. His body was gorgeous, slim but nicely toned, with broad shoulders and hips that were just right in comparison. The images on his skin came to life whenever he moved, drawing Stitch in. It was as if the ink on Zak's thighs and stomach was there just to showcase his crotch where the snake tat was waiting for Stitch, its fanged mouth ready for a deep, sloppy kiss.

Stitch licked the underside of Zak's cock, bringing it to life. Fuck the rules of who was allowed to do what. Stitch would suck that dick whenever he wanted. He looked all the way up his lover's body and at that handsome face, flushed and dripping with water, before letting his lips go higher, to the piercing at the base of Zak's penis. He loved this little piece of metal and how it contrasted with the soft skin. He pushed the tip of his tongue through the hoop, pulling on it gently. The head of Zak's cock slid over his neck as if the snake inked into the skin of this amazing dick wanted to smell Stitch where blood pulsed the strongest. Stitch sucked the piercing into his mouth and moved his hands up the lean thighs in front of him, following the steps of all the strange creatures climbing up Zak's legs to worship his cock.

He tried not to pull on the piercing too strongly, but he rubbed against the penis when he felt it twitch. Knowing that he was the source of Zak's excitement was arousing on its own. His fingers explored higher, up to Zak's ass, stopping in the curve where thighs ended and buttocks began. He smiled at the heat growing in Zak's cockhead and decided it was time to give it more attention.

Wet fingers pulled back his hair and held on to it, resting on top of Stitch's head, but there was nothing threatening about the gesture. Zak smiled at him and pulled on his pierced nipple with the other hand. The warm water was splashing their sides and at times forced Stitch to blink away the wetness, but it steamed up the shower stall, making them both warmer and more breathless.

Stitch began a massage of Zak's ass as he sucked more of the shaft in languid moves, caressing it with his tongue. Zak enjoyed a slow teasing and Stitch was ready to deliver just that. They weren't rushing for orgasm tonight. This would still definitely move to bed for a good, long fuck.

"You're so good," whispered Zak, brushing away moisture from Stitch's shoulder. The tiny droplets of water sliding down Stitch's skin were like the caress of a thousand fingers, arousing him even more as he sucked the now steel-hard dick into his mouth. It was smooth, warm, and pulsed on his tongue like it had a life of its own. Once Stitch got past his initial inhibitions, it became clear to him why people wanted to do this. It was like the most intense, most intimate of kisses.

Stitch already loved looking up at Zak's face when he sucked him. He could see the tensing, the blushing, the brow furrowing, all corresponding to how Stitch was caressing him. He moved one of his hands between Zak's thighs and brushed it over Zak's balls, slowly moving it back and forth.

Zak's thighs trembled, and he uttered a loud groan, tilting his hips toward Stitch, but as he moved his body, water started flowing down his chest more freely, streaming down his cock and splashing on Stitch's face. Stitch closed his eyes, which got him completely immersed in the world of cock. He focused on how it pulsed, how hot it was, what the smooth texture of the skin was. He tried to remember every vein he traced with his tongue.

"Oh, fuck, Stitch... Harder," whimpered Zak, who was slowly starting to thrust his hips back and forth, a clear sign he was close to coming.

Stitch pulled back and licked his lips. He wrapped his fingers tightly around the base of Zak's dick with a crooked grin. "You're not coming just yet, baby."

Zak groaned, his handsome face tensing, but he eventually nodded and pulled on Stitch's shoulder. "You're such a pest."

Stitch gave the tip of Zak's dick one more teasing lick before getting up. "Nope, I just want to feel your ass gripping my cock when you come."

Zak pulled close to him, sliding his beautiful body over his so they'd be cock against cock, thighs against thighs, Zak's nipple piercings brushing against Stitch's pecs. He kissed the side of Stitch's neck and rested his head on his shoulder, wet hair clinging to Stitch like tentacles. "Romantic."

Stitch snorted and hugged him close. "That's me." He kissed Zak's lips, shuddering at the taste of cock on their lips.

He was pulled into the warm stream of water, and soon he could smell the familiar scent of mint and bergamot when Zak started trailing his soaped fingers all the way across Stitch's skin. It was a ritual so familiar, it instantly made him feel even safer in Zak's hands. Zak was playing him like a well-known instrument, knowing where to press and where to pull for Stitch to play his part and join in.

As much as Stitch relaxed, his cock never softened all that much, always finding new excitement when it brushed against Zak's skin. By the time they were done, Stitch couldn't wait to just fall into bed and make love to his man. The day had been draining in every sense of the word. His emotions got taken on an unwanted roller coaster, he'd lost a friend, he'd killed a man, he'd broken up with Zak only to get back together, and had a fight on top of that. He needed the shreds that were left of him to be taken by Zak and put back together.

"Are you okay?" whispered Zak with a kiss to Stitch's cheek. His hand slid lower, between Stitch's pecs, across the tense stomach, all the way to his cock. Zak soaped it up, teasing the head as Stitch pulled him into a hug.

"Yeah, it's just been such a rough day, and I'm happy to be here with you. I never want to go through shit like today again." Stitch gladly arched his hips, but Zak's hand slid lower, massaging his sac in a move so sweet that it made Stitch's knees weaken.

Zak was there to soothe Stitch with a slow kiss on the mouth, pulling him even closer. "Me neither," he whispered, his voice blank.

Stitch didn't have any more promises in him, it was now about fulfilling the ones he'd already made. They kissed under the shower, melting into the warm tiles on the wall, but when their lips parted, it was time to go. Stitch turned off the water and pulled on Zak's hand to guide him out.

The warm fingers squeezed his hand hard, but Zak didn't make a sound nor protest when they walked out of the steamy room into the much cooler corridor without drying themselves up. This house had become their safe space, and it felt completely natural to walk around naked, all the way to the moon-lit bedroom.

"You hurtin' a lot?" Stitch stroked the side of Zak's body, marveling at the tattoos. He knew them all, yet he always found something new in there. A demon he hadn't noticed or a woman whose coat had disappeared, leaving her naked. Thrown in the crowd of other figures, she wasn't all that easy to spot.

Zak looked up at him with a small smile. "I'm gonna live but let's keep it simple tonight, yeah?" he asked, nuzzling Stitch's jaw as they automatically stepped closer by the bed.

"Whatever you need." Stitch sat down on the soft bedspread. He would do anything for Zak, and looking up at his gorgeous body, he couldn't stop himself from smiling.

Zak slid between his spread thighs and pulled him in, cradling his head against the inked stomach, with the stiff cock poking Stitch's neck again as if reminding him of its existence.

"Captain won't rat on you, right?"

"At this point, I don't know what he'll do. He'll keep Cox a secret, but I don't know about the rest." Stitch wrapped his arms around Zak's waist and listened to his heartbeat. It drummed slightly above where his ear was, firm and quick. Its rhythm was enough to spark a new energy in Stitch, making him feel more alive with each loud pulse.

"It'll be all right."

Stitch turned his face and kissed Zak's stomach above the navel. "I'll think about it tomorrow." He pulled Zak onto the bed, but not too harshly. He didn't want the bruises to hurt.

They rolled onto the mattress, and Zak pulled on Stitch's hair, opening his mouth for a kiss. His nipples hardened from the change in temperature, and Stitch felt them brush against his skin as soon as he leaned down.

The heat between them had their skin drying in no time. Stitch explored each part of Zak's body with his fingertips, but he made sure not to lean on Zak too much. He closed his eyes as the kiss deepened into a tongue lovemaking.

Stitch kept kneading Zak's thighs and was already imagining his dick in his lover's hot body, pumping that pulsing hole until he came. He loved going bareback, having his come ooze out of that tender ass and have his lover accept him so completely. He wouldn't say it, worried Zak would find it creepy, but sometimes he wished he could make babies with Zak. They'd have those perfect blue eyes, and Holly could have some siblings to play with.

Zak giggled as his warm hand rested over Stitch's cock, warm and inviting. In the semidarkness, touch, taste, and smell were enough for Stitch to savor him. "When you're with me like this, my skin feels like it's burning," came the soft whisper.

"Good. Remember, I'm the only one for you," Stitch uttered and reached out to the bedside cupboard for lube. He liked the neutral one, so he could focus on Zak's fresh smell.

Zak's warm breath ghosted over Stitch's spine. "I know."

Stitch kissed his ear, increasingly eager to get the lube where it belonged. He squeezed some out, remembering all the countless times they'd fucked. Fast, slow, rough, sweet, in the car, at the swamp, in the kitchen, in the garage, in the bath, in bed, on the floor. Each time was engraved in Stitch's muscle memory. Each time, Zak became more familiar and yet no two times were the same, with the deep yearning having Stitch constantly thinking about his lover. It was so different from anything he had ever felt for anyone, even for Crystal or some of the guys he was secretly crushing on. This time, he was choosing to follow his instincts, crawl deep into Zak's embrace and never let him go. He didn't owe anything to the people who'd call this love wrong, not when it felt so right, so fulfilling. Just looking at Zak smiling at him, drawing on the sofa, playing with Versay was enough to make him all warm and gooey inside.

"What are you thinking about?" uttered Zak with a small smile even as he slowly rolled over to his side.

"How much I want you to be my family." Stitch kissed Zak's shoulder and got some lube onto his fingers before sliding them between the warm buttocks. His cock was throbbing with urgency. It was nice to take your time with sex, but he was desperate to speed up.

Zak gasped and pulled up one knee. He leaned back into Stitch's chest and rested his head on Stitch's bicep with a low groan. "You, me, and the dog? The perfect gay family," he chuckled, kissing the inner side of Stitch's arm.

"I want it all. I want Holly in my life, and even Crystal. I want to make it work." Stitch trailed kisses along Zak's arm as he teased the anus with his slippery fingers, already excited by the heat of Zak's body. It would suck him in, tightening around him when he pulled out and opening up to swallow his cock when he pushed in.

Zak reached back with a moan, and his hand closed around Stitch's wrist, pressing Stitch's hand to his ass with a demanding gesture. He didn't have to suggest it twice. Stitch drilled in two fingers at once in a slow but firm circular motion. He already knew Zak would be ready for him in no time. Knowing a partner's body like this was a far cry from the first time they'd fucked, when he wasn't sure what to say, how to treat a guy, or what Zak liked. Bottoming also gave Stitch perspective on how it felt to be penetrated, and even though he topped more frequently than not, thanks to the experience he could better understand what his lover was feeling. It was both being vulnerable and empowered, the pleasure of being filled, entered by someone he felt so much for, and the sheer ecstasy of having his prostate nudged by a cock. There was nothing else like it, and when Zak's tight body opened up to his fingers, he groaned, sucking on his shoulder, driving the digits deep and scissoring them in the already relaxed hole. Zak loved being fucked so there usually wasn't much to overcome, but Stitch still enjoyed dipping his fingers inside and teasing the sensitive flesh wherever he could reach.

"You ready for me, Zak?" Stitch murmured into his skin, but already knew what the answer would be. He pulled out his fingers and pinched Zak's ass.

Zak's back arched, and for a moment Stitch believed it was the witch inked on the skin that moved but it was all an illusion. Zak buried his face in the soft inner side of Stitch's elbow and moaned, his ass brushing against Stitch's cock. "I need you to keep me close."

"I won't ever let you go." Stitch licked along Zak's skin, savoring the saltiness. He grabbed Zak's thigh in a firm grip and kept it lifted as he teased Zak's crack with his cockhead. On an impulse, he pushed in, breathing in Zak's smell as he sank deep into that welcoming hole. So fucking hot, slippery, and inviting.

Zak's groan echoed through the room. He arched against Stitch and pushed back his hips, impaling himself all the way and molding their bodies together. "We're in this together. No one's gonna take you away from me," he whispered, and it didn't matter whether he was talking about Crystal, the MC, or even the criminal justice system.

Stitch hugged Zak close, with his stomach against Zak's back, hand holding onto Zak's thigh. He pushed his dick in deep and started a rhythm of slapping noises. He already imagined leaving his come in Zak, marking him with his scent, as he bit on his warm ear. He needed Zak to feel him to the core.

They moved together, completely immersed in one another, Zak's breath burning Stitch's forearm, his ass tightening around him time and time again, as if Zak wanted to keep him deep inside, hug him both from the outside and from within. The shampoo smelled so good on Zak's skin, teasing Stitch into burying his nose in the damp mane as he drove his cock in a steady yet firm rhythm. Zak spat on his free hand and moved it down to touch himself with a low moan.

Stitch put his chin on Zak's arm and looked down at that beautiful cock, moving his hips at the same pace as Zak's hand. "Come first. I wanna watch," he panted, his body so hot he would probably need another shower.

Zak shuddered in his arms, squeezing the cock in his fist and clamping down on Stitch in the same moment. "My nipple," he whispered, rolling his head back to look at Stitch, his eyes glowing, lips dark and plump.

Stitch grinned down at the rings in Zak's nipples and let go of Zak's thigh to move his hand where it was clearly more needed. He pulled on the piercing and twisted it gently. "Come on, jerk off," he rasped.

Zak twitched against him and snapped his teeth toward Stitch with a manic expression. "Such a dirty mouth," he uttered breathlessly but his hand started moving faster, firmer, slapping against his balls.

"Such a dirty boy." Stitch chuckled and only fucked Zak harder, with sharp, fast jabs.

"Yes. I love your cock up my ass," growled Zak. He bit his lip, trembling ever so slightly as his eyes glazed over, and he came, thick ropes of come splattering on the duvet and Zak's hand. Stitch made sure not to blink, so he could watch the spectacle, but when the muscles in Zak's ass started clenching around his cock, he moaned, knowing it wouldn't take long for him to finish. He pinched Zak's nipple hard and slammed his cock in a few more times. He barely breathed when he came and pumped his come into Zak.

"So good," he rasped. "Take it all."

"Yes. I want it," whispered Zak. His fingers clenched around both of Stitch's wrists, keeping them close to his body. He leaned in and pressed quick, sensuous kisses to both, like they were the most precious things in the world.

Stitch didn't have any words left, so he just returned the kisses onto Zak's skin, wherever he could reach without moving too much. His muscles were goo.

"You're all mine," was the last thing he heard from Zak.

He'd never felt more like an outlaw than now.

Chapter 25

Zak touched the sand and looked up at the trembling surface of the water. It was so warm that he almost felt dry, with rays of sun caressing his skin. But he pushed himself away from the surface, and the rocks at the shore became more distant, like something belonging to a different world. His back hit the sand, and he rolled to his stomach to face Stitch. His lover sat cross-legged next to a large pink fish, which kept its eyes on something Stitch was writing in the sand.

Stitch smiled up at him, and Zak noticed it said 'Hounds of Valhalla' on the sand. "We should move to Mexico."

Zak smiled and moved forward on his hands and knees, pushing back the hair that kept floating into his face. He stopped when his hand grasped something strange instead of sand. It was a face, and his fingers were buried deep in the eyeless sockets, the heel of his palm resting in the open mouth. All of a sudden, Zak was out of air, his chest tightening as if something within it sucked in his lungs, as if there was a black hole in place of his heart. He tried to scream but no noise came, and the moment his mouth opened, bitter, salty water rushed down his throat like a fist. He yanked his fingers out of the face's eye sockets. It was Cox.

*

He was tossed around by a harsh wave, no, by a pair of strong arms. Holding on to the warm flesh in his arms, he screamed when a dull pain spread through his brain from a punch to its side. For a moment, he had no idea where he was, his eyes stinging, mind still clinging to the dream.

"You have got to be fucking kidding me." He heard a harsh male voice and suddenly met the floor, tumbling over it a few times. It was harder than he imagined, and he actually heard a sharp snap in his neck when he landed. But no, he could still move his head.

"Told you. Enough is enough," Captain said.

"What are you doing here? Get the fuck out!" Stitch.

Zak turned to his back and tried to get to his feet, but Captain launched himself at him like the embodiment of fury. One punch to the gut robbed him of breath, and his knees softened. He dropped to the floor against his will. "Leave," he choked out. "This is my house." The edges of his vision were darkening when he looked around, spotting six men in the all-too-familiar leather cuts. From the floor, they looked like demons who came all the way here from hell, ready to drag him and Stitch to the cellar and bury them alive.

"We're here to take what's ours, pussyboy." Gator said, smoking a cigarette by the window. "I wouldn't take you for a roses kind of guy." He grabbed the flowery curtain in his hand. "But then again I wouldn't take Stitch for a fag."

"He's got nothing to do with our business!" Stitch yelled at them, and Zak finally noticed Stitch had got pulled to the other side of the bed and was forced to kneel. One guy held his arms back and cuffed him, while another one had a knife to his neck. They were all people Zak knew, but at this moment, they seemed like a faceless mass, like ants sharing one goal: devour what stands in your way.

All thought left Zak's head, leaving behind chaos as his hands and legs suddenly burst with heat. He raised his palms, fighting for every word that left his mouth. "Leave him, please. You can have whatever you want," he whispered, choking up. His eyes stung, and he felt as if someone was trying to strangle him with a thick fist.

Captain snorted and smacked the back of Zak's head. Still, it was nothing like the beating Zak got yesterday, which only had him more nervous because it meant they weren't here to hurt him. They were here for Stitch.

"You touch him and I'm gonna k—" Stitch yelled, but got his mouth stuffed with a makeshift gag. Blood dripped down his neck and chest from where the knife dug in as he writhed.

"We'll leave today, I promise. You won't have to see us ever again," uttered Zak, afraid to make any sudden move with the blade against Stitch's skin. "I'll do anything you want. Let him go..." he whispered once again as his breath turned into a wheeze. This couldn't be happening.

Gator put out his cigarette on the windowsill. "Too late, cocksucker. I don't really care about you. I just don't want to see your face in the club ever again. Him," he pointed to Stitch, "we're gonna have to deal with. Fucking liar, rotting our club from the inside. No wonder you were such a pussy lately, Stitch. It all makes more sense now."

Stitch's nostrils flared with every deep breath he took. He was watching Zak with his eyes wide open and a face so red it seemed to contain most of the blood in his body. He was such a buff guy, but naked, kneeling on the floor with three men hovering over him, he looked as vulnerable as never before.

"What do you want to do?" whispered Zak. Maybe he could reason with Gator somehow, offer to give him the money the club lost on drugs. He slowly moved his way, completely focused on the bald head as if it were the Holy Grail.

"It's none of your business. My advice? Don't call the cops, and you'll get him back alive. Even if as damaged goods. Let's go," Gator waved his hands at his men, and one of them pulled Stitch up to his feet.

Zak's stomach tightened as if squeezed by a fist. He needed to come up with something. Instead, he was standing there like a scarecrow, unable to make a move to prevent the inevitable. He couldn't protect Stitch in his own house. "He has a little daughter, for God's sake. Don't hurt him!"

"Look, he's even got his dick tattooed," one of the guys, Tank, pointed to Zak with a child-like grin, but Captain pushed him out the door.

"Gator said 'go'!" The one-eyed villain pushed Tank out the door. The two men guarding Stitch followed.

Gator was the last one to linger and eyed Zak with a scowl. "Don't interfere with club business. He'll live. Probably."

Zak gritted his teeth, backing away into the wall. His skin was like a minefield, ready to explode with heat or frost as he looked into the dark eyes. He wanted to threaten Gator, promise him a painful death or police arresting all the club members, but he knew very well how that would end. He did not stand a chance with the Hounds. If he actually called the police, the club could retaliate by hurting Stitch more than they intended, they could reveal that Stitch killed Cox. Stitch could die, end up seriously hurt, or go to jail.

Zak slid down the wall into a tight squat and grasped onto his own hair in a mixture of fear, rage, and helplessness. He was so useless, unable to protect the one person he needed to have by his side.

Gator left without another word, leaving Zak in the pink, flower-patterned bedroom, with bedding that still smelled of Stitch. Zak gritted his teeth and slid to his ass. His chest tightened as he listened to the thumping sounds of heavy boots on the stairs. He was in limbo, his heart trying to push him up, make him go after them, fight, but that was exactly why he only held onto his hair tighter, curling into a ball. He couldn't go. It would only make matters worse. He needed to stay still like a little bitch and wait. It was only when the engines roared that all tension left his muscles, and he sobbed, letting the tears fall freely.

Chapter 26

Stitch watched the fire with a numbness in his head. There was terror to come, and all he could do was brace for it. The gravel underneath his knees dug into his naked skin, but it was the least of his problems. In the face of the bonfire, the kneeling was like a punishment in kindergarten. Blood rushed through Stitch's veins in a never-ending pumping, just like the flames in front of him.

It was ironic that the old scrap metal company out of town, the place where Stitch stole his first TV with Captain, where he stepped on a path that would lead him to the Hounds of Valhalla, would be the place where he got stripped of the privilege. Or was it a burden by now? The patched cut had never felt as heavy as it did yesterday when he was sawing through Cox's body like it was some roadkill. The vest stuck to him from all the sweat, yet he hadn't taken it off, it still defined him. After all the years of friendships, shared crimes and secrets, the club felt as much his family as Holly and Crystal. Not something that could be just discarded.

Even after the fight with Captain, he had deluded himself that he would be able to stick around, work on developing the carpentry workshop, maybe take on an apprentice. But now? If he survived whatever was coming, there wouldn't be a thread in his cut he could hold on to.

His and Zak's safe haven had been defiled, a fact that left him empty inside, as if everything he trusted in was to be stomped on and crushed. At least they didn't hurt Zak any further. He needed to keep strong and let them go through with whatever they considered necessary so he could return to his family in one piece.

Gator sat on an old cement block on the other side of the fire, smoking a cigarette with a thoughtful expression. Stitch kept silent, not even trying to defy all the homophobic slurs that had been thrown at him since they left Zak's house, ignoring the slaps and kicks. It would be over sooner this way. It seemed that everyone was waiting for Captain, who had walked off several minutes ago.

"So, are you a woman, or is he?" came from Jynx, one of the younger guys on the team, who had already launched two kicks at Stitch's kidneys when Gator wasn't looking.

"There is no pussy in our relationship," Stitch groaned through gritted teeth. He wished they wouldn't have left him naked, but complaining would only make this more humiliating.

"You're the pussy!" snapped Jynx. A powerful blow to Stitch's side tipped him over into the gravel. Stitch barely stopped himself from hissing in pain as the little, sharp stones dug into his flesh. It felt as if his thigh just got mauled

"'Relationship'? You're getting married next?" Gator bit on the cigarette in his mouth, his face tensing into the resemblance of the animal he was named after.

Stitch didn't react whatsoever to Jynx's attack. It looked like Stitch was fair game to anyone. Stitch looked up at Gator and squinted. He clenched his fists with all the pent up aggression he was stuck holding in. "I am an outlaw. I do whatever the fuck I want." He turned to Jynx and looked straight into the flat eyes that reflected the guy's latent stupidity. "If I want to, I get fucked up the ass."

The sudden silence lasted for a whole three seconds during which Jynx's face went from stunned to rabid. He kicked Stitch's ass with all he had, making him lose his breath. "Yeah? You want that? I can give you a fuckstick from that bonfire. Would you like that?"

"How old are you, you little fucktard?" Stitch looked back at him, trying to establish his position even if he was lying naked in the dirt. "You wanna touch my ass, is that it?"

Someone snorted in the background, giving Stitch a tiny glimmer of satisfaction. Stitch did hope his face wouldn't end up in the gravel though. The opposite happened. Gravel shot up to his face as Jynx kicked the ground, sending the little stones his way. By sheer luck Stitch managed to close his eyes in time, but the dust got into his nose, and he choked up, coughing.

"Give it a rest. Captain's coming," said Gator, and only now Stitch heard the roar of a motorcycle engine. He turned around, and his heart sunk at the sight of his own bike. It looked alien with Captain riding it. It felt like moto-rape or some shit.

Stitch remained silent, not wanting to give them the satisfaction of seeing his anguish, but that bike had to be here for a purpose, and that fact

223 | K . A .   M e r i k a n

was already making his gut clench. He remained on his side, watching Captain get off. Their eyes only met for a moment when Captain kicked the bike hard, and it toppled over into the gravel with a scream of damaged metal. Stitch couldn't believe they'd do something like this.

"Get the hook, Jynx." Captain pointed to the small crane used to hoist and move bigger objects, such as cars. Or motorbikes.

Stitch couldn't help a scowl despite the furious drumming of his heart. "Really? This is so low. Can't you just deal with *me*?" He acted confident, but his palms were sweaty like when he was going to jail for the first time.

"Don't you worry about that." Gator scowled and gestured for Tank to open him a beer. He got up, and when Stitch noticed a crowbar in his hand, his blood ran cold. Was it meant for him? Did they want to break his arms and legs, and leave scars for him to remember?

As soon as the crowbar hit the mirror on his bike, Stitch bit his cheek so hard he drew blood. *There will always be the next bike,* he told himself as he watched his precious vehicle, his partner of ten years, smashed to pieces by metal pipes and crowbars. He couldn't believe this was happening in front of his eyes. Such savagery only made him realize how much he didn't want to be a Hound anymore. The paint chipped when the metal dented, mirrors got dislocated and lay in pieces on the ground as the whole bike died in a puddle of its own gas.

Stitch couldn't believe they'd rather kill it than take it from him for their own use. Was this how much of a leper he'd become to them? There was nothing to salvage. Stitch didn't want to see his mount this way, but knowing his former friends were looking out for any weakness, he stared straight at it. Looked at each dent, each kick, and when his bike was pulled up with the crane only to be dropped to a pile of scrap metal, he never looked away, even though it was the ultimate crush to his dream of the free life with the Hounds.

"No one wants to ride a fag bike," growled Captain, his voice thick with satisfaction. He slowly approached Stitch, boots grinding over the gravel as he pulled out his hunting knife. It reflected the sunlight, stabbing Stitch right in the eyes. It was the same weapon that was used to kill the Nail.

The blade got Stitch to pay attention, and as much as he didn't want it, his breath hitched. What would this motherfucker do? His thoughts turned into a bright white whirlwind when Jynx and Tank suddenly grabbed Stitch's arms and pushed him down. The pain of having his genitals rub against stones made Stitch bite his lips.

He turned his head to the side just in time not to have his nose flattened on the gravel, but the dust got into his windpipe nevertheless.

Stitch coughed, not even trying to get away when he was so badly outnumbered. Each one of Captain's steps was like the thumping of an executioner's boots on the scaffold, and Stitch found it hard to breathe as soon as he understood that.

"No one wants a fag to carry our club tattoo either," growled Captain over him, the thick-soled boot digging into the dirt in front of Stitch's nose.

Stitch tried to deny the cold sweat on his back. Pretending he wasn't afraid was all he had left. There would be pain, and arguing or fighting back wouldn't help anymore. He bit into the inside of his lip and tried to take deep, slow breaths. He needed to find something to hold on to, but his scattered thoughts were hard to catch. One thing he was certain of—he wouldn't beg.

Captain kneeled by him, and the next moment, cold steel moved along Stitch's shoulder, startling him as if it was already digging into his skin. "You're gonna have some more stitches to match your name."

"Just get on with it," Stitch groaned, but could barely move his jaw, waiting for the incision. He'd been in many fights and knew what pain was, but it didn't mean he wanted to feel it. Not to mention lying there with gravel digging into his skin and looking like some bitch.

"So who'd you like to suck off in the club?" muttered Captain as he slowly moved the blade over the surface of Stitch's skin in a parody of a caress.

Stitch's face tensed so hard at the humiliation that he didn't even know anymore if he was scowling, or if his face was just a mask made out of wrinkles. He had never looked at his brothers this way, and it pissed Stitch off that Captain would suggest it. Sure, he could assess whether someone was his type or not, but mostly they weren't, and it would feel like incest to think of them that way.

"I'd have you suck mine, motherfucker. That what you want?" he spat, even though the goose bumps on his skin were giving away his fear. But when the blade dug into his skin, Stitch froze with his mouth wide open, desperately trying not to utter a sound at the barbaric, unforgiving cut that just wouldn't end. Captain was savoring it, taking his time as if the view of the splitting flesh, the cool blood Stitch could feel welling up, gave him pleasure. It was unbearably awful. Not at all like the pain of combat when adrenaline and anger were muffling the blow. This was long, painful, and calculated.

Stitch focused on not making a sound so bad that he lost contact with what anyone was saying. He heard Gator's voice, Jynx's laughter, other men making comments, but it blurred with the pain into an indistinguishable mass. Keeping silent cost him biting his lips bloody. He rubbed his sweaty forehead against the gravel as blood trickled down his sides. Captain was making long, parallel incisions, and methodically trailing the knife from one side of his back to the other.

The torture started all over again, when Captain decided he wasn't done yet and dug his knife in the other way, beginning to create a checkerboard made of gore on Stitch's back. Stitch tried to distract himself, go deeper into his own mind, all not to think that the man who had been his best friend since childhood would do this to him with so much pleasure. It was like when Captain once tortured a puppy, just to see how long it would take for it to die. But that wasn't what Stitch wanted to remember. He focused his mind on his daughter and that biker pony she wanted. She'd love it if Stitch could pull it off. And there was Zak, whose warm smile never failed to make Stitch all gooey inside, who was so sure of who he was and what he wanted to achieve in life that Stitch simply couldn't fail him.

Stitch needed to forget the blood burning his skin and seeping into the gravel, forget the knife and Captain's smile. His teeth clattered when he forgot to grit them. There was too much happening in his body for him to control it all. The muscles trembling with strain, the sweat dripping from his clenched fists, the heat throbbing in his face. It took him a moment to realize the blade wasn't ripping into his skin anymore, because the agony was so overwhelming it didn't just stop the moment the torture did. He realized he wasn't being pressed to the ground anymore, it was his own muscles that had given up, heavy and exhausted from the strain of withstanding pain. He didn't resist when someone roughly yanked up his head so he would stare into the fire, at the empty beer bottles standing around as if it were some kind of rave. He barely registered Gator, who stared at him from across the fire with something large in his hands. It took a moment for Stitch to register what it was. His cut, patches and all. With him for so many years. His identity.

"You're a bitch, not a hound," spat Gator and just like that, tossed the cut into the fire. "You're gonna wish you never met that fag if you wake up after this."

Stitch was half-conscious, but the sting of those words, the smell of burning leather, cut into his senses like Captain's hunting knife had cut into his back. His lips were dry and tasted of blood, but it didn't matter.

"I'll have no regrets," Stitch whispered. His body was one throbbing bundle of misery. He couldn't even hold up his head on his own, so when whoever held his hair let go of it, it fell back down like a lifeless weight of bone and flesh.

His face hitting the gravel was the last thing he remembered of the torment.

Chapter 27

Zak stared at the black and blue face in front of him. Stitch was lying facedown on a special bed, his battered back patched up, covered with some yellow goo and bandages, an IV bag constantly dripping fluid straight into his vein, as if to make up for all the blood he'd lost. As horrible as it was to see Stitch like this, the whites and greens of the hospital gave Zak some peace of mind. It was nothing like seeing Stitch pale under a layer of grime, tossed out of a car like a rag doll, straight into the dirt in front of Zak's house.

He'd spent the worst day of his life sitting by the window, clutching to Versay as soon as the dog returned from an unauthorized walk outside the fence. He couldn't eat, and as much as he wanted to drink himself numb, he couldn't allow himself to lose any awareness. He knew Stitch would come back hurt, and he needed to be there for him, but he still didn't expect his lover to watch him with glossy eyes and babble, coughing up blood from lips that looked like tenderized meat.

Zak didn't call for an ambulance. He managed to drag Stitch into his car and drove him to the hospital with unshed tears clouding his vision. He couldn't bear to look at Stitch brutalized like this. It was the flesh he had tasted and held so many times, it wasn't meant to be torn to shreds or bruised. And as much as he wanted to just hold Stitch, he needed to turn off his protective instincts and give him away into the care of medical personnel.

It was only then that hunger got to him, and the amount of chocolate he ate within half an hour gave him enough of a sugar rush to send a message to Stitch's ex-wife. With everything he'd heard of her from

Stitch, she was a prominent figure in his life, the mother of his kid, and despite all the bad blood, Stitch still seemed to love her in his own way.

All he got in answer was: 'I'll be there'.

Zak sat down, chomping on the chocolate. He felt relieved and lucky that no one actually gave him grief over staying with Stitch, since he wasn't family. He rested his head on the side of the bed and kept playing with Stitch's hair. Each single breath of his lover made him warm and shuddery with relief. He could have lost him to a gang of homophobic pigs.

Zak leaned in and kissed the scraped knuckles. He'd lick them, taste the metallic tang, but knowing it would have been creepy as hell, he just squeezed Stitch's fingers harder.

And there it was, Stitch squeezed back. It was a slight movement, but it still had tears spill down Zak's cheeks. A sob tore out of his throat, and he showered the hand with kisses, looking up into the puffy eyes, barely visible underneath all the bandages. His chest exploded with relief, and he almost threw himself all over Stitch, hugging him.

"Baby, I'm so sorry..."

But there was no answer, just that gentle touch still on his fingers. The door opened, and Crystal walked in, barely breathing, her face as red as her hair.

"Oh, God, I came as soon as I could. What happened?"

Zak looked up at her, his blood thickening with sudden panic. Their first meeting could hardly be considered civil, was he supposed to get up and greet her? Now that Stitch actually returned his touch?

"I... he got attacked," he muttered, never letting go of Stitch. His gaze scanned the room, and he was relieved to see there was another chair. She pulled it to Stitch's side, so close to Zak that it was almost touching his. The gesture had him so anxious he got goose bumps. What if she made a scene and tried to throw him out? Technically, she wasn't family anymore, but the staff could make them both leave in case of a loud argument.

"I can't believe they would do this to him," she said and ran her fingertips over Stitch's thigh.

"Yeah," muttered Zak, holding on to the large, meaty palm, somehow convinced that he'd lose Stitch if he let go.

"Listen, let's get this elephant out of the room." She looked to him with those big, attentive eyes, accentuated with a thick cat-eye line. "Is this shit for real?" She gestured in the general direction of Zak's and Stitch's hands.

She was one frisky, excitable woman, nothing like Zak. He wondered how Stitch and her had got along before she noticed she wasn't getting any orgasms out of her husband. Zak nodded with a slow sigh.

"We're together," he said, looking straight into her eyes, not exactly a challenge but close.

She pouted at him, and crossed her arms on her chest. "Okay, but are you gonna stay? Are you serious about this? Are you gonna be around five years down the road?"

Zak shook his head with a dark chuckle and leaned in to kiss Stitch's palm again. All this time, he hadn't wanted to commit yet there he had been yesterday, telling Stitch just how deeply he felt for him. His life has been turned upside down, but he had few regrets. He'd helped get rid of a body last night, and he did if for Stitch and himself, so that they could be together. If that made him a horrible person, then so be it. "He's mine. I don't want him to go anywhere."

There was a mumble from Stitch, and he half-opened one eye. "No one asked me..." he muttered.

Zak drew in a sharp breath and leaned in to look into his lover's face. "How badly does it hurt? Do you need some painkillers?" he whispered, gently petting the top of Stitch's head.

"I'm not Versay. And I think I'm on painkillers now." Stitch didn't open his eye wider, but his iris followed Zak's movements.

Zak's mouth stretched into a wide grin to match the warmth in his chest. "You are pretty much like Versay, Trouble. Don't kid yourself."

Crystal took a deep breath and cleared her throat, reminding them of her presence. "More importantly, what did you get yourself into, Stitch?"

"Just a misunderstanding..."

"'Misunderstanding'? Really?" She got up from the chair and Zak worried she was about to yell.

"Yeah, they did this over me being gay, but misunderstood that I don't give a fuck about their opinion." Stitch chuckled, but then winced in pain.

Zak bit his lip as anger bubbled up deep in his throat. If only they could safely get the police involved... With Captain having knowledge of what happened to Cox that was the last thing they could do. The fuckers would remain free, even though none of them deserved any happiness from life. No, they deserved painful deaths, being burned and having their nails ripped off. Zak sometimes wished he were more bloodthirsty than he was. "Fuckers..."

"It's not funny, Stitch." Crystal kneeled on the floor to have a better look into Stitch's face. "How much longer is this gonna drag? At this rate you're gonna end up six feet under next year."

Zak exhaled, looking away. They couldn't stay here if they wanted to be together, there was just no way this could happen. He looked at Stitch, swallowing hard as he waited for an answer.

"I won't retaliate," Stitch whispered and closed his eyes.

Crystal went silent.

"Thank fuck," whispered Zak, even though deep down he craved blood. He knew they didn't stand a chance. All they could do was to leave, that was the only option, and Stitch needed to see that.

"You're not gonna be a Hound anymore, babe?" Crystal stroked Stitch's arm so gently it seemed as though she barely touched him.

Zak blinked, staring at her without a word. He brushed his thumb over Stitch's hand, kneading it slowly.

Stitch's eyelid opened again. "I'm done. I don't want revenge. I just want to have a life. It would drag and never end. This is exactly what got so many people killed. I don't want to have anything to do with it anymore."

Crystal smiled at him. "You really did change."

Zak dropped to the chair, watching the silent exchange. He hoped at least the ordeal would soften Crystal's heart, and she would let Stitch see his daughter more frequently. Then again, how could this arrangement work with them being away from Lake Valley? Stitch spoke, as if consciously addressing some of Zak's concerns.

"I think Zak and I should leave Lake Valley, just in case. I'm sick of this place anyway. It's too full of memories." Stitch looked up at Zak and gave a groan of pain when he moved on the bed too much.

The gaze, still so cloudy from all the drugs and fatigue, made Zak's heart skip a beat, and he pulled closer, poking Crystal with his knee in the process. "Oh, God, I'm so happy to hear that. I will sell the house, and we can settle somewhere close enough for you to see Holly..." He opened and closed his mouth, suddenly realizing Stitch had told him their breakup was the price he was supposed to pay for the privilege. His eyes settled on Crystal.

She licked her lips. "If you are really so serious about this, Stitch, then maybe I could move as well. I've been having problems with Milton anyway," Crystal muttered as if it embarrassed her to admit that. "I still think it's weird, but... You don't deserve this, and Holly loves her daddy so much. And you owe me big time, so no dying, yeah?"

Those words squeezed a faint smile onto Stitch's battered lips. "I've never been happier, Crys." It sounded so surreal in his position, Zak wondered how high on morphine Stitch actually was.

He stared at them, surprised by how smooth it went. Like in a bad movie. Only after several seconds it occurred to him the move meant that they might be living with Crystal and Holly, at least for some time. He could accept that, even though he had never considered the possibility of living with a kid this young, but it wasn't what he was worried about. The presence of both Holly and Crystal meant they wouldn't be able to express their feelings as freely as they were used to. And as much as he loved Stitch, he didn't want to lose that part of their relationship.

"Zak? Come closer." Stitch asked, and Zak already felt something was off when he saw that stupid grin, even if it was weak.

"What is it, baby?" he asked, feeling the need to show Crystal just how close they were. Slowly, he leaned in and maneuvered his lips between the bandages to kiss Stitch's forehead.

Stitch reached up to the bedside table and fished out a signet from the pile lying neatly in a little bowl. "It's yours, remember?" His warm hand met Zak's and slowly pushed the signet with Mjölnir into his palm.

Zak sighed with a broad grin and kissed him again, and again, even if gently. He wanted to tell Stitch how this little piece of metal made him feel, but not with someone else watching. This was private, other things shouldn't be. "Is that Thor giving me his hammer?" he whispered instead, putting the signet on his thumb, which suddenly felt whole again, protected by the man who put it there.

Stitch's bruised and blue smile widened, and he moved his finger over the tattoo above Zak's collarbones, marking it with warmth. "I knew I shouldn't have talked to strangers."

The End

Thank you for purchasing *Road of No Return*.

If you enjoyed your time with our story, we would really appreciate it if you took a few minutes to leave a review on Amazon, Goodreads or your favorite platform. It is especially important for us as self-publishing authors, who don't have the backing of an established press. It makes the book more appealing to potential readers and helps others make an informed decision when considering a purchase.

Not to mention we simply love hearing from readers! :)

"Road of No Return" is the first in a series of outlaw biker books. The series is called Sex & Mayhem and will include both longer and shorter stories. Most will focus on gay relationships, but we do have a straight book planned in the series that will be published under our future M/F pen name. The books in the Sex & Mayhem series will generally be standalones, tied only loosely by cameos and mentions of clubs.

We already have plans for future books which include an amputee fetishist, a male prostitute, and a biker called 'Tooth Fairy' for his gruesome technique of ripping out people's teeth.

But if you loved "Road of No Return", make sure to let us know. There is a sequel idea floating around our heads, so with enough interest, that might just happen sooner than later.

Kat&Agnes AKA K.A. Merikan
kamerikan@gmail.com
http://kamerikan.com

NEWSLETTER

If you're interested in our upcoming releases, exclusive deals, extra content, freebies and the like, sign up for our newsletter.

http://kamerikan/newsletter
SIGN UP

We promise not to spam you, and when you sign up, you get any one of our books for 3.99$ or under for FREE. Win-Win!

About the author

K.A. Merikan is a joint project of Kat and Agnes Merikan, who jokingly claim to share one mind. They finish each other's sentences and simultaneously come up with the same ideas. Kat and Agnes enjoy writing various kinds of stories, from light-hearted romance to thrillers. They love creating characters that are not easy to classify as good or evil, and firmly believe that even some villains deserve their happy endings. It is easiest to find them in galleries, good restaurants and historical sites, always with a computer or notebook, because for Kat and Agnes, every day is writing day. Future plans include lots of travel and a villa on the coast of Italy or a flat in Paris where they could retire after yet another crazy venture, only to write more hot homoerotic stories.

Kat and Agnes started as popular authors of online serials written in their native language, but are now focused on reaching a wider readership by writing in English. As K.A. Merikan, they have published a number of books, which cross genres while always staying homoerotic.

More information about ongoing projects, works in progress and publishing at:

http:/KAMerikan.com

K.A. Merikan on Goodreads

Facebook

Twitter

GUNS N' BOYS

K.A. MERIKAN

BOOK ONE | PART ONE

Guns n' Boys
K.A. Merikan
— Love is sour like a Sicilian lemon. —

The Family is always right.
The Family doesn't forget.
The Family pays for blood in blood.

Domenico Acerbi grew up in the shade of Sicilian lemon trees ready to give his life for the Family. Ready to follow orders and exceed expectations. A proud man of honor.
When Seth, the younger son of the Don is kidnapped, it's Domenico who is sent to get him back. The man he finds though, is not the boy he knew all those years ago. Lazy, annoying, spoiled, and as hot as a Sicilian summer.

Seth Villani wants nothing to do with the mafia. Unfortunately, he doesn't get a say when the Family pulls him right back into its fold after his mother's death. Thrown into a den of serpents otherwise known as the Villani Family, Seth has to find a way to navigate in the maze of lies. But when Domenico Acerbi, the most vicious snake of them all, sinks his fangs into Seth, the venom changes into an aphrodisiac that courses through Seth's veins.

Domenico knows his life is about to change when he gets the order to train Seth up to the role of future Don. Seth isn't made for it. He isn't even made. But a man Domenico knows he would never have to fear might just be someone he's always needed.

If Seth is doomed to follow in his father's footsteps, he might as well enjoy himself—with the most intoxicating man he's ever met. Maybe he can even fool himself into believing that Domenico isn't a handsome sociopath who kills for a living.

POSSIBLE SPOILERS:

Themes: Enemies to lovers, mafia, homophobia, assassin, organized crime

Genre: Homoerotic love story / crime thriller

Erotic content: Explicit gay sex, coercion

WARNING: Adult content. If you are easily offended, this book is not for you.

'Guns n' Boys' is a gritty story of extreme violence, offensive language, abuse, and morally ambiguous protagonists. Behind the morbid facade, there is a splash of inappropriate dark humor, and a love story that will crawl under your skin.

Book 1 now available

Printed in Great Britain
by Amazon